SOVEREIGN BLOOD

HANNAH WHITTAKER
AND ROSE SERAPHINE

CONTENTS

1: Tainted Blood

Twenty-two years ago

As the day shining over the land of Aessatia came to an end, the Kingdom of Lucus began closing down its shops just before dusk to prepare for the sacred night ahead.

All was peaceful in the quaint kingdom, the ladies dressing up extra prettily while the lords wore their finest garb.

Those who lived in settlements outside Lucus' capital, Barness, would celebrate by singing hymns in the chapels and hosting parades while the more fortunate prepared for the grand ball, a formal dance held in the palace to commemorate the Day of Salvation. It was a holiday that not only the Lucian kingdom would celebrate, but also its neighbor, the elusive Astrian Empire, and the Folkvangrian Empire.

Inside Barness' palace, the demigods hailing from the three empires sat lined up along the table seating the honored guests: young Chasaka, the demigod of fire, adorned the far right side of the table while his father, the Lucian army general, sat to his right, sipping champagne. Occasionally, he would glance at his son, who hadn't yet touched a morsel of his food—which he found rather ungrateful of him.

Beside them were young Ruki and his mother, Elaine, the two demigods of water who hailed from Folkvangr. Ruki was never one for such formal events and stayed silent while his mother spoke to the nobles who approached to question the dignified general of Folkvangr's army.

Teira and her father, Tobias, the demigods of earth hailing from Lucus, were far too busy stuffing their faces with the leg of lamb and fresh garden vegetables to be doing any speaking.

Beside Lucus' king sat young Liland, the demigod of lightning, and his father, Asabüro, emperor of the Astrian Empire. They were far more reserved than any others at the ball that night, picking at their food and glancing around at the other guests.

Lastly, at the other end of the table sat young Sage and her father, Vincent, the two demigods of wind both hailing from Lucus. They, too, chatted happily with other Lucians who had attended the ball.

All of these honored guests were taking part in the night's festivities because it had been their ancestors who once saved the land of Aessatia from its demise.

"It's quite a shame that Chasaka's mother, and of course your late wife, couldn't join us for yet another year," King Taro told Asabüro as he sipped a glass of champagne.

"Unfortunately, the tragedies of death do take such luxuries from the living," Asabüro answered. His gaze focused itself upon the table for a brief moment before returning to the king. "Do excuse me, your highness, I'm going to get some air," he said before rising from his seat, making way for a balcony which jutted out from the side of the ballroom.

His son, Liland, watched as his father left the ballroom and also left the table to follow without response to the king.

"Father," the young man announced to make his presence known as he stood out of sight of his father, just behind him. "I'm confused as to why everyone seems so calm...you did warn his highness, did you not?"

"Yes, Liland," Asabüro answered. "I have, time and time again since you told me the details on the matter...but he simply won't listen."

"Surely you must try again!" Liland shouted. "You did ready the troops, right?"

"Of course. They're marching this way as we speak. The night is still young," answered his father.

Liland joined the emperor at the edge of the balcony and looked at his vacant expression with urgent eyes. "Still, there's no telling when their plan will unfold! If you won't try once more to warn the people of Lucus of their fate, that will entail the death of an entire kingdom!"

Asabüro straightened as he turned to his son and narrowed his eyes. "Calm yourself, Liland. I was going to go back inside once I was finished, but I can't think of a feasible way to convince the king to rally his troops with you pestering me!" Asabüro shot back. He sighed after that. "You aren't old enough to be concerning yourself with such matters, you're better off leaving that to me."

Liland appeared wounded by his father's words. "I'll go in and do it myself then," he growled before turning to go back inside.

Asabüro followed behind his son, eventually walking in front of him.

When they returned to the table of honored guests, Sage's mother was no longer there. This caught both Asabüro and Liland in a state of worry.

"Where has the eldest wind demigod gone?" Asabüro asked the king.

"Ah, she grew tired of the festivities and decided to go home," Taro answered.

Asabüro leaned a little closer to the king. "Sire, may I remind you of the conversation we had about a week prior to today?"

An exasperated sigh left the king's lips. "Don't be foolish," he said. "How dare you bring that up on a night as sacred as this?" He clenched his fist. "You dishonor your son's kind."

Liland couldn't believe the words he was hearing from the king and stepped up onto the table, grabbing his father's attention.

"Liland, come down from the—"

"Lords and ladies! Your attention please!" the young man shouted, his voice booming over the sound of idle chatter and music. "You're all in mortal danger! The demons from within the Darker Realm will soon be released upon this land! You must get to safety as soon as possible!" The ballroom fell completely silent, all eyes locked on the madman standing upon the king's table.

"Guards, seize him," Taro spoke out. The guards acted quickly and rushed toward the boy.

"Your highness, wait!" Asabüro shouted as his son fought against the men clothed in steel armor trying to pry him down from the table. "What he says is the truth, you must heed this warning or all of your people will be in danger. Folkvangr and the Astrian Empire have rallied their troops and are marching this way as we speak. If you refuse to help, it will be your negligence that will bring about the downfall of Lucus."

"This man is a liar!" Ruki's mother, Elaine, stood up and spoke out as she looked at Asabüro. "There were no troops dispatched from Folkvangr at all."

"Escort both of them out of the capital at once," Taro ordered his guards, who then grabbed Asabüro.

"Can we not have a night of silence?" Teira's father, Tobias, asked softly before his salmon-colored eyes locked with the man and his child slowly being dragged off, struggling to free themselves. Irises of stormy gold and soft pink locked with one another, both glaring into each other's souls.

"He and the other elders! Liars! Traitors!" Liland yelled. He wanted to strike them where they sat, but a glance toward the ceiling of the palace told him that wouldn't be an option without completely destroying it and the guests inside.

"How dare you speak such blasphemous words!" Taro spat back at him. "This man is a descendant of the gods! I would expect you to treat him with respect!" The king indicated to Tobias. "No matter, I said get them out of here!" he yelled at his guards, who were still struggling to seize the men.

Tobias gently eased the king back into his seat. "Pay him no mind sir, tonight is a night for us all to celebrate the coming of our ancestors. Would you care for any more champagne?" he asked.

Taro's eyes followed Asabüro until he and his son were carried away. A few seconds after they disappeared from sight, the question asked to him finally registered. "If you would provide, yes please," he said.

Hours dragged by without another word of Asabūro and Liland. The night was too sacred to worry much of what had happened, though there were few skeptics who decided to leave.

Not only did they disappear, but so had the elder demigods.

Regardless, the celebration carried on as it always had for the past few centuries, and the lords and ladies left with smiles on their faces and their minds in a stupor from all the drinking. The ballroom would clear before long, leaving it empty, yet filled with the mess left by the guests that the maids and butlers would clean up.

Feeling tired, the king decided to retire to his quarters for the night after giving orders to have the ballroom cleaned by sunrise. The halls were quiet; peaceful—and Taro was completely absentminded to the beauty of his palace as he trudged to his bedroom.

Suddenly, he heard the thundering of metal boots coming his way and was immediately awake. He turned to see one of his knights clad in bloodsoaked armor.

"Your highness! Demons have begun attacking the capital's defenses!" the knight reported.

By now the king had sobered a bit. This bit of information caused the man to grow physically shocked. "Demons haven't been seen since the time of our ancestors. Surely you jest." Though the man's words suggested a fib, the blood on his chain tunic was far more of a reality.

"I speak the truth, my king. What shall we do?" the blood-stained knight asked.

Such pressure hadn't been expected, but Taro knew he had to formulate a plan quickly. A pang of sudden guilt washed over him. Had the emperor been telling the truth the whole time? Were his people in danger as he had said?

Just as the king parted his lips to answer, another knight rushed in. "Sire, I've just received word from Seer Asanya of the Astral Clan. Demons are approaching at the forefront of the capital in overwhelming numbers. There have already been many casualties," he explained. Blood stained the blade he held in his right hand.

"Quarantine the children and young demigods to the Ice Sanctum and assemble our troops as quickly as possible," Taro finally spoke up. He couldn't allow any more lives to be lost because of his foolishness, but would there be enough time to rally all the troops together?

"Why has Rotos abandoned us...?" he muttered under his breath. The god of which he spoke was supposed to be guarding the tower which kept the awful beasts in Hell where they belonged, and now he was hearing that they had escaped, slipped past the divine being by some stroke of a miracle, at least for them. *But how?* he wondered. The elusive tower was tucked away deep within Carawe Forest, meant to misdirect all who would enter its depths. There were many defenses that should have kept the demons at bay. The king wondered where the fatal flaw in the tower's defenses lay.

The two knights rushed off to spread the word to their fellows. Some were too terrified or worried for their families to even consider taking on such a threat, but others were ready to lay their life on the line to protect them.

It took just twenty minutes for nearly the whole of Barness' troops to assemble in a large crowd in the palace courtyard. They murmured worriedly amongst themselves, some shaking in their greaves, knowing they might be the first to die. The fearful look on the king's face didn't help their feelings. At last he spoke out, silencing them.

"Men and women of Lucus," the king's voice boomed. "We come together on this night, not as blood, but as inhabitants of Aessatia with a drive to live. As some of you may be aware, demons have escaped from the tower within Carawe Forest. Outside these walls, there are already many others out there risking their lives to protect life as we know it. You're all expected to do the same."

The soldiers listened with fear masked by determination, all clad in armor, signifying the blood that would be shed.

"But worry not," King Taro continued, "our young and children too premature to fight have been safely evacuated to the ground floor of the Ice Sanctum. That said, they're counting on us to keep Barness safe." Taro paused. "It's been made apparent that our three elder demigods may have something to do with the incident. The emperor of the Astrian Empire told me that his son was approached by them, and I take the blame for not taking precautions earlier than now. I deeply apologize." He looked at the disappointment growing on his men's faces. "I realize that apologies won't win this fight, nor will they bring back the lives that have already been lost to the threat, but it's here right now, and if we don't act, more lives will be lost."

Metal gently clanged as swords and other weapons were grasped, and a glimmer of hope shone in the king's eyes. He knew he must have inspired some of them. "With all of that said, let us prevail!" The king ended his speech with an upraised fist and a cheer from the crowd as hope began to rise.

With that, the gathering was adjourned. Every person who had lined up charged toward the first district of the capital with one goal in their minds: push out the invading enemy. Upon reaching the capital's outer gate, they saw demons ripping apart the mechanisms inside the gate, jamming it from being closed. Men were killed in seconds. Most had never even seen a demon in the flesh, but the mere sight of them was enough to cause them to draw back and flee for their lives, only to be swept away by the immense speed the creatures possessed.

The battle seemed hopeless. Making it past the gate was a miracle, as there weren't nearly enough soldiers to outnumber the enemy. Not only that, but some demons were larger than others and caused more distraction for those who were still fighting, allowing for smaller demons to slip past and begin murdering the civilians who hadn't yet been able to evacuate.

To the relief of those still fighting, the soldiers from Folkvangr, which Asabūro had mentioned before, arrived to help them. Their numbers served as a slight advantage. Above them flew advanced ships; the Astrian Empire had also arrived to help them. They possessed technology unknown to man and that had seldom been seen by anyone. When the soldiers fighting below saw the behemoth contraptions, they cowered in fear of them, the distraction allowing some of them to be snatched up by ravenous demons. But it soon became apparent that the flying ships and new soldiers were helping, evident by the way they shot down the enemy scourge from above.

* * *

As the endless night crept along, the moon turned blood red and heavy rains fell from the sky, pelting soldiers and demons alike and soaking into the earth—diluting the blood that had spilled onto the battlefield.

Each demon had killed at least one soldier or civilian, and even the aerial advantage was beginning to fail since the winged demons were capable of taking down their ships. Even a man as skilled as Asabüro was growing weak from the fight. But he needed to reach the tower; he needed to know why this was happening. At the rate the battle was progressing, the demons would soon overtake Aessatia.

Liland had given up his fight far before him, a gash across his stomach and a skinned back preventing him from going on. He sat on the border of Carawe Forest leaning against a soaked tree, a demon's carcass beside him.

The emperor hailing from the Astral Clan had begun making his way to the tower which Rotos protected. It was a treacherous path, but one he had to take to get answers. He cradled his wounded shoulder as he stumbled up the tower's endless stairway, which was surprisingly empty. It seemed every creature which previously had been shackled to the flames of Hell had already left the forest, seeking more populated areas to feed. If he didn't find a way to drive back the demons into Hell, Aessatia would be forced to live with the horrid creatures until it met its doom.

When he reached the top, his eyes grew wide. The man wasn't sure what he was going to find once he was atop the structure, and he had really expected to die by now. But what he saw sent a wave of horror shooting through him.

The rift to the underworld had been ripped open, debris from the roof's pillars scattered about—and from that rift, something lethal emerged. Three heads rose up from its large, scaley shoulders, and hideous sounds left its maw as it attempted to squeeze through the rift. The proud body of the lightning god lay still a long way from that rift, covered in purple blood, the color which only ran through divine beings.

Three demigods stood before that creature, witnessing its release into the overworld, doing nothing to stop it. As Tobias, Vincent, and Elaine watched, the creature spread its massive plume-like wings after finally setting a steady foot atop the tower.

It was the hydra, the guardian of Hell, known to massacre all who tried to enter and exit. Now it was in the overworld. It let out an ear-piercing scream. Asabüro had to clamp his hands over his ears to nullify the sound if even a little. "Why are you doing this?" shouted the blond man. He could barely hear over the ringing in his ears.

But the hydra granted no quarter; it took to the skies to wreak havoc on the already perilous world, leaving the four of them behind.

Tobias stepped forward among them with a glare in his eyes. It took only one punch to send the emperor to the ground with a grunt. "You're a fool to have led your people against us, Asabüro," the man said as his body loomed over the other. "I would figure that after you wiped out those people upon the Silver River and stole away their magic that you would know a thing or two about what it means to strive for greatness. I chose your clan to aid us because we knew that you would deliver... but you betrayed us," he explained before kneeling down to grip the man's shirt, yanking him forward by the hem and rending it slightly. "To think that a clan that has already shed the blood of many would take Aessatia's side on this day. When a people commit such an ungodly act, and yet, they side with those they defy—how asinine, Asabüro. And now you've led each of them to death."

"It was your manipulation that led to that attack, and you know it." Breathing heavily, the emperor looked at the demigod with hazed eyes, rain soaking the both of them. "One m-moon..." stammered the emperor.

"What?" The demigod could barely hear him over the pelting rain.

"O-One moon...after the discovery...of two in the snow... betrayal shall be uncovered where o-once was hope and faith, t-tainted by heavenly blood...they will be the ones to break the cycle..." Asabüro finished, struggling to get it out. "Y—You and your followers will fail...the gods...will destroy you."

Another punch came flying across the man's face. But he hardly flinched from it. He knew that death was inevitable, and his muscles were too exhausted to tense up from the blow. "Shut up!" the dark-haired man shouted. "Look at you," he growled. "Shriveled into a whelp with blood spilling from its veins. Even with the powers you stole from those people, you're pathetic. Your clan will yet die out. And your son? He's as dead as all the rest of them—but he chose his fate when he rejected our offer. As did you." After muttering this, he grabbed ahold of the man's throat, but he didn't choke him. Instead, branches grew from his hands, piercing the man's neck and head, splattering Asabüro's blood onto both of them.

When the job was finished, the limp body was tossed aside and left to nothing. The brown-haired man turned to his fellow demigods and looked between the two of them. "Come, we shall return to the battle," he said.

With the hydra laying waste to most of the survivors, the tide of war had been turned in their favor.

* * *

Liland still sat, waiting for his wounds to heal enough to stop the creature scouring the skies. Once he had regained enough strength, the young man stood from his place beside the tree and set his sights upon the distant dragon burning down everything in its path.

The dark skies brightened as lightning began to heat them, and thunder boomed over the pouring rain. Liland drew in a deep breath as he prepared to strike down the fiend, focusing everything in his power onto the beast. "This war ends now..." he said.

A crack of thunder boomed in the night air, and as it did, a huge bolt of lightning struck down the beast. Liland watched it fall down toward the earth, a cloud of debris exploding from beneath its body, visible even from the distance at which the young man stood. But no sooner had he seen his efforts come to fruition did he fall to the ground once more.

The three eldest demigods watched grimly as their plan slowly fell apart before their eyes. Just as soon as the battle had all begun, it ended—over as easily as someone snapping their fingers. In reality, it wasn't as simple as that. Bodies still lay scattered about the land, indistinguishable from each other from the mutilation by the demons. The Astrian Empire had completely been annihilated and was no more. Lucus and Folkvangr were barely hanging on.

As the dust settled, it was eerily peaceful. Death and murder were far too chaotic, and even though its aftermath was saddening to see, it was a pleasure to finally breathe again. Even the clouds parted, allowing for the moon to cascade upon Aessatia.

Atop the tower through which the demons came into the world, a figure stood in the moonlight. His cloak mimicked the light of the celestial body above him, casting a menacing shadow down upon the three who had so forsaken the world. He stretched his hands toward their bodies, creating cold fractals of ice that engulfed them in thick casings of frost. Without the strength to resist, they succumbed to their frigid fate.

He stepped down from the fragmented wall of stone surrounding the roof of the tower and lifted his eyes, their frozen bodies following his gaze, rising into the air. "Your crimes against this world will never be forgiven by its inhabitants. As Cyero, the god of ice, I shall hang your heads for every eye remaining in Aessatia, so they may all know the faces of those who desecrated this land. Your bodies will be burned in the holy flames of Thosus and cast into the wasteland from which you ordered those demons to inflict calamity upon the peace of Aessatia. Now they will feast on your bones and dance in your ashes as they burn."

Cyero led the casings of ice down the tower and through the forest of blood and carcasses. He tried to stow his sadness as he left toward Barness. The survivors of the massacre had gathered in the square by dawn the next morning where Cyero ordered the three demigods' immediate hanging.

The survivors watched, somber yet relieved that their ordeal had at last come to an end. However, the apparent death of Taro was a blow that would leave Lucus wounded for years to come. Thus, the next of kin, his son, Zyair, was chosen to lead the kingdom. He had bravely led an army unit into battle and was left in despair after each had been slaughtered under his order.

Demigods became cursed instead of sacred under his rule, ensuring that Lucus would forever remember the dreaded night of the blood moon and rain.

* * *

Present day

The darkness brought about by night's presence slowly stole the light away from the dipping sun, as though it were slowly chasing it to swallow it whole. A gust of wind blew through the wastes of Tochfuyu, a land far north of the common region upon Aessatia—the place where no establishment dare settle.

But to its southwestern corner, a small igloo remained wherein two women sat around a fire, one with long red hair, whittling away at a thick branch with a sharp rock while the other tended to the fire, making sure it didn't go out or get too out of control.

"I'm almost finished," the redhead stated, causing the other with long blonde locks to look over.

"What are you doing anyway, Amaya?" she asked.

Amaya looked up at her friend in astonishment. "Isn't it obvious...? I was making a spear. The lake near us has begun to thaw...much like our home." Her umber eyes glanced briefly around their small home built from snow before returning to the branch. She then put down the rock and stood to a crouch. "Will you accompany me?" she asked, turning to her friend.

The young girl nodded her head, happy to go along with her.

The two set out for the nearby lake Amaya had mentioned, knapsack in hand. Once there, the pair quietly stole along the melted shoreline. There wasn't much to be caught, and soon they grew too cold and weary to continue fishing. At least Amaya had captured enough to last them a few meals.

After catching her last fish, she dropped the salmon beside her friend. "Put it in the knapsack. The sun is going down quickly; we will need to leave soon," she said.

At her request, the girl picked up the squirming, cold fish and placed it into the knapsack which had been strung across her back. She didn't like the idea of eating the poor living creature, but she had no other choice. "You don't seem very thrilled..." Her voice was grim as she then slung the bag over her back once more. With the arrival of spring, its heat was beginning to melt the snow that always covered Tochfuyu's lands. It was a strange occurrence, but it was melting the igloo they once called home, forcing them to relocate.

"I'm not, I'm sick of living in this place, Rose. It's been twelve years. Something has to give," Amaya answered before turning to head back toward their home.

"We will leave then," Rose said, causing her red-haired friend to whip around to face her once more.

"Are you mad? We will be killed if we leave! What about my uncle? He told us not to leave. And what about the guards hounding this place to make sure we don't?" she said, angrily motioning toward their home.

Rose's eyes shifted up toward her friend before refocusing on the distant, seemingly endless land before them. Wonder filled her mind as she tried desperately to remember what it looked like before the girl's uncle led them to Tochfuyu when they were young. They were only six years old at the time. It frustrated her that she could hardly remember what the world outside of their home looked like. "Who cares about him?" she snapped back once she had managed to return to reality. "This place is Hell. I want to get as far away from here as possible. It's killing us—wearing us down from the inside out. How do you know anyone would even recognize us once we leave? And we can run from the guards!" Rose pleaded.

These words were rather persuasive, especially due to the fact that Amaya wanted to leave as well. "Where will we go?" she asked.

"Wherever our feet take us," her friend answered.

"And if we're caught?"

"We run."

Amaya lowered her head and looked at the wet snow below her feet, deep in thought. It would be dangerous if the two of them were caught by someone from the kingdom. But their desperation to leave that land had been enough to push them past the threshold which kept them boarded up inside a prison with no bars. Lifting her head once more, Amaya craned it around in a couple of different directions, as though she were assessing their surroundings. "We will head south," she said before continuing their trek.

Rose was surprised she had been able to convince her friend to do something so risky, and yet part of her was starting to have second thoughts about mentioning it in the first place. Still, she kept quiet. She didn't want to voice her regrets.

Her heart pounded harder in her chest with each step, and heavy wings fluttered about her stomach; she and Amaya were finally going to escape.

The fire that once burned in their home had gone out, and the ceiling was beginning to dribble every so often, spilling water droplets onto their few belongings. Amaya started to gather what was left of their things.

"Are you sure about all of this?" Amaya asked her friend.

"Yes," she said, despite the worries in her mind. "I just feel like there must be more to life than this."

"And by *this*, you mean...?" Amaya trailed off, expecting Rose to finish her statement.

"Surviving," she said simply. "I don't want to live like animals. I want to live like humans."

Amaya was slightly appalled by this logic and cocked an eyebrow at her. "And you believe constantly running away would be more human than animal-like?" she asked.

"It's better than staying here; plus, we wouldn't be running away."

"Is that not what you said earlier?"

Rose gave a huff as her friend misunderstood her. "I meant that the path we walk will shape us into who we are and what we will do, no matter if we must run from anyone we come across. There are bound to be some who don't oppose us," she explained.

As they exited the melting igloo, Amaya replied, "I just hope this isn't a mistake."

It didn't take long for the two of them to reach a densely wooded area. They assumed that taking cover in there, with the help of the darkness, would help to keep them hidden should they run into any trouble. As they walked, Rose pressed close to Amaya as her eyes darted about the enigmatic trees, which left much to the imagination.

It was true, the young woman—even at her age of eighteen—was afraid of the dark. But she had her reasons, of course.

"Do we have to go through the forest?" Rose asked her friend quietly.

"It's the only way through, unless we plan on walking for days to go around. And it's also safer than walking out in the open," she added.

Amaya was quickly proven wrong by a distant rustling not caused by their own footsteps. Rose gasped quietly as her eyes began to dart faster, looking for the origin of the noises, which were starting to reach Amaya's earshot as well.

"It's only the fauna, right?" Rose whispered to her.

"No, it sounds too calculated to be anything wild...it must be human," Amaya replied.

The density of the trees around them made it hard to pinpoint the sound. It seemed like it was coming from every direction at once. So their pace slowed, making their footsteps quieter so that they could hear faint murmurs. Now they were certain; humans were around, and their noise was growing louder. Amaya glanced around before seeing a light emanating from some kind of lantern—and it was close.

"Damn it," Rose spat as her own eyes fell upon the flickering that grew ever-closer.

"Get in the trees," Amaya quickly whispered to her friend.

They both rushed to the nearest tree, scrambling to climb its plentiful branches. Amaya could feel small branches breaking beneath her feet as she ascended, hearing the sticks falling to the shallow snow below her and hoping the people couldn't.

She watched from the sturdiest branch she could get to while the men below her—who they could now tell were soldiers of some sort—walked ignorantly past their high vantage point.

Amaya looked across the thick expanse of trees to see if she could find her friend. She was well hidden in some foliage. If she hadn't been specifically looking for her, she wouldn't have seen the young woman at all.

And then came a loud "SNAP!" followed by Amaya shrieking before inevitably hitting the ground. Her heart continued to slam against her chest. She *knew* that this had captured the guards' attention. Right on cue, they rushed over after sharing a "What the Hell was that?" amongst one another.

They approached, one holding out his lantern while the other held out a halberd. "What are you doing so close to the edge of Tochfuyu?" one man asked the fallen woman. "And where is the other of you?" he added.

"I don't know what you mean, you must have me mistaken with someone else," Amaya sat up taller as she spoke defensively.

The man narrowed his eyes at her as she slowly rose to her feet while the other pointed his halberd at her. "What do you take me for, wretched beast? No one is foolish enough to come out here by themselves. Where is the other girl?" the knight growled.

The redhead clicked her tongue and shook her head. "Pointing a weapon at a person who hasn't done anything wrong?"

The man simply stared, staying silent as her question hung in the air. Without an answer, the young woman was getting impatient. She gripped onto the halberd past its blade and yanked it forward, avoiding stabbing herself, of course. "You would do well to leave this forest and go back to wherever it is you came."

"Unhand me! Well, don't just stand there. Seize her!" the man yelled at his comrades who then lunged forward to grab her. Rose watched from above, horror filling her gaze. On instinct, she jumped straight down from the branches, landing beside the incursion with a wooden dagger in hand.

"No, Rose, *run*!" Amaya shouted at her friend. She had to be mad to jump into this.

"I'm not going anywhere without you," the girl bit back.

A grin surfaced upon Amaya's lips. It was nice to know that of all those who opposed her in this world, at least one was faithful. She yanked her body from the guard's hold and pulled out the wood spear she had made earlier, pointing it at the man. Living in such an environment had honed both girls for battle, at least a little. "Stand down and let us through!" she snarled.

The guards all shared a look with one another. Both girls were sure they had them cornered at that point. But then the other two guards pulled out weapons of their own, one taking out a mace, and the other a hand-axe.

They had made it clear that they weren't going to back down, and so a vicious battle ensued between them. The redhead lunged forward to attack the one who held the halberd while Rose took the others.

Grunts and cries of pain went back and forth between the five battling people as they attacked one another with their weapons, steel and wood sinking into flesh and blood spilling out of wounds. But any further trifles were stopped as a distant roaring was heard. It sounded like the burly growling of a bear. They often roamed the forest, even with its frigid temperatures as the bears had adapted to the freezing climate. The clamor of their fight must have awoken it.

The three guards looked up from where they were standing before cowering away. They likely wouldn't be back after hearing the bear. It was cause for panic within the two young women, and Rose began hastily making her way toward the direction they were originally headed.

Before Amaya could start to run off into the distance to follow her friend, her foot crunched onto something that was unlike the snow. She looked down to see a piece of parchment paper. Amaya reached her hands down to pick up the object she had stepped on, brushing a layer of snow off of it. The ink was starting to bleed and the paper was folding from getting wet. It appeared to be a map of sorts.

"Amaya, what are you doing? We have to get out of here," Rose whispered to her friend before her eyes caught sight of the map. Now she knew what the delay had been about. "Come on, we can look at that later," she said before leading the way through the woods. She just hoped the direction they were headed wasn't any closer to the bear. After tucking the rolled parchment into her animal-fur cloak, Amaya followed her friend along through the trees.

The two walked on for only around two minutes more before being stopped again by the roar, this time louder.

Rose examined their surroundings while Amaya hadn't even given it a second thought. "I think it might be following us," Rose whispered softly, her breath wafting from her lips in the cold air.

"So, do you want it to catch up?" the other of the two asked as she continued onward.

Her blue eyes lingered behind her, squinting as she tried to make out some kind of shape with such low visibility. She began to peel them away to walk once more until she caught some movement in the brush behind her—a rather large amount of it. Her stomach dropped upon seeing the plants rustling, and she rushed toward her friend, shoving Amaya forward. "Run!" she yelled, pumping her legs as fast as they would carry her.

Before Amaya could even react to this statement, she fell to the ground, her hands burning as they scraped against the packed snow. "Agh, Rose!" Amaya yelled after her friend, who was already a good ways away. She rolled her eyes, knowing the other was simply paranoid. However, upon lifting her body to get up and look behind her, the girl's eyes gaped. The silhouette of a bear was beginning to emerge from the trees and walk toward her. "Rose! Wait!" she screamed as she began to panic, scrambling to get to her feet once more. Adrenaline rushing through her veins urged her to run faster, but her efforts were futile. The bear's paws pounded into the frozen snow beneath them, making a horrifying crunching sound, only serving to remind the young woman just how quickly the animal was approaching. She could hear its heavy huffing as it kept pace behind her. Amaya knew her small human legs were no match for the beast in pursuit of her life, and never before had she felt so helpless.

Even working so hard to pump her legs to escape, her body's best wasn't enough. She did, however, catch up to her friend.

But this didn't make the situation any better, it only meant a bigger meal for the bear. Fear kept them from stopping to try and hide somehow, knowing they would eventually be ensnared within the jaws of the beast, claws sinking into their flesh.

One hefty swing of its arm was all it took to send the girls barreling off their feet, their bodies scraping against the icy forest floor. The bear didn't waste any time looming over its prey to induce fear. It was a feral brute after all—and it was hungry. It lunged forward, jaws unhinged, its yellowed, blood-stained teeth sinking straight into Amaya's right arm. The force had been enough to break it, blood spurting from the wound, her screams echoing in the night, which only served to agitate the ferocious animal even more.

"Amaya!" screamed the blonde from beside her. Instinct pushed her to remove her wooden dagger from its sheath, springing toward the animal without hesitation or regard for her own safety. The blade dug into the bear's skin before she ripped it out to stab once more. Her aim was to slice open the bear's throat, but doing so with only a wooden knife would soon prove rather difficult.

The bear roared, immediately letting go of her friend. It reared back onto its hind legs, standing taller than a full-grown man. But this didn't make Rose back off, in fact, she only continued her pursuit, slashing at other parts of its body since its throat had become unreachable as it thrashed about, swinging its claws as the behemoth tried to strike the girl. Its musk and bad breath invaded her nostrils.

Amaya watched with wide, teary eyes as her friend tried to defend her against the beast. She wanted to help, but with her injury, she was basically useless, not to mention the fear coursing through her was paralyzing her. So she was forced to watch as Rose struggled to subdue the bear. It didn't take long for fatigue to set into Rose's body and for the cur to be able to knock her away. Its burly body lumbered toward her while she tried to recover from being slammed against the ground.

Things weren't boding well for Rose, her eyes focusing helplessly on the predator that stood on its hind legs to intimidate her. Its roar echoed through the forest before lunging its jaws toward her, aiming straight for the neck, which surely would have broken if it had the chance to clamp down. But the bite force never came down onto her. A series of growls and roars came from deep within the bear's chest. The wind had picked up just then and began to slice the bear each time it whipped past its body. Deep red blood stained the once-pristine ground as the creature was jerked around, soon unable to move and collapsing with a thud.

Rose couldn't say just what had happened then, it was astounding—but she wasn't keen on sticking around to find out. The girl stood up so she could be of more use to her ailing friend. "Come on, we need to go." Rose carefully helped Amaya to her feet, minding her injury.

"What—what was that?" Amaya stammered. Her chocolate eyes were glued to the dying beast while she was being led away from it.

Noticing her friend's fascination for the event that had taken place, she, too, had been looking at the creature for a few brief moments. "No clue, but we have to find somewhere nearby with medical personnel, your arm doesn't look so good," Rose answered. "Where was that map you found?"

Once the two were a considerable distance from their fallen predator, Amaya slid herself down against a tree, grunting a bit as she did. She pulled the parchment paper out of her cloak and showed it to her friend, who took to look for any nearby villages or at least a landmark. While she did this, Amaya examined the condition of her broken arm. She could see her Ulna barely escaping her skin just below her elbow. Around it, blood oozed from her flesh. The sight in itself was rather disturbing, not to mention it was coming from her own arm. She had to cover her mouth with her uninjured hand to calm her turning stomach.

"Bastard really bit me hard..." she muttered as her eyes averted from the wound.

"It was a bear, they're nothing to mess with, you know," Rose replied.

Her eyes scanned the map as she spoke to her friend. She could identify the Highspeak writing toward the northern part of the map which read "Tochfuyu." She knew that to be the icy prison in which they had spent the majority of their lives. It was colored in white chalk to further show it represented the tundra. Bordering the southern section of Tochfuyu was a deep green patch that Rose assumed to be the forest they were in. It was unnamed by the map. Though she couldn't peg exactly where in the forest the two currently stood. The only area for miles within their reach was a small establishment named "Dufmoore" by the map.

"Well, is there anywhere near here?" Amaya asked her, causing her to lose her focus. But she didn't need it anymore.

"We're going to a place called Dufmoore."

2: BEAST'S BLOOD

Nineteen years ago

Chasaka's deep-set, tired eyes watched outside the window of his bedroom, a place he often spent the majority of his time. The thick band of stars that spread across the sky seemed to be the only thing that calmed him nowadays, which is what his hues of ruby had their sights set upon. He would spend hours on end just doing this. It was lonely.

Humans were meant to be social animals, and yet Chasaka was silent, starved, and thirsty. His stomach growled, ravenous, his throat, dry. On the floor was a bowl of food and a wood cup of water; the food was cold and the water, room temperature. It was clear the redhead had no interest in the objects.

They had been brought in by his younger half-brother, Kye. He didn't understand how that boy still had the gall to approach him.

Chasaka's stare toward the outside world was more of a scowl. Anger nagged at the young man's face. He was always angry and seldom pulled a smile. It was like a flame burning deep inside of his core that would escape if he opened his mouth to speak.

Around him, the walls were torn to shreds as though what was being kept inside was a feral beast with no morals. Dents and holes damaged them, his knuckles, bloody. Any chance he got, he would diffuse that bomb inside of him, even if it meant striking his own brother.

That boy, his replacement—his branded reminder of all his failures as a human being—was so compassionate as if to draw him close only to hurt him. But all he knew was to burn and push away. He hated him. But there was none he hated more than the father who brought them into this world and the mother who had left him with that monster.

The woman had killed herself when Chasaka was only two years old, barely able to speak, yet that image of blood all over the floor was still thoroughly etched into his fragile mind. By his father's knowledge, it was his fault too. It made his stomach churn each time he thought his father might be right. She didn't want to be his mother anymore because, like his father, she thought he was a disgrace. Those powers of his were a curse even though they had been passed onto him by her.

Her intent that night had been to murder her own son, but she stopped and killed herself instead. Chasaka always took the blame for something in his father's eyes, including the death of his mother.

When his father had met another woman who gave birth to Kye, Chasaka was actually happy to have someone else around, someone he could make happy.

He wasn't always so angry and hateful. It wasn't until the day when those three demigods were hanged for treason and the murder of thousands. That's when he took the blame for being a part of that bloodline. That's when he stopped being the firstborn son. That's when his father told him he never should have been born, that Kye was the better son. That was when that monster started to beat him.

A hand was clasped around Chasaka's stomach, clutching a nasty bruise he had received not but a day before. The young man's body was littered with wounds similar to this, all ranging from nicks to slashes; bruises to broken bones.

The redhead's eyes peeled themselves away from the window when he heard the sound of his door sliding open. In the doorway was a shorter figure with hair reaching its lower back. Gentle eyes looked back at his glaring ones.

"Have you eaten yet?" the voice belonging to that shape asked him.

The washed-up and wounded animal didn't answer him. His mere presence made his blood boil. But Kye's condition? It wasn't all that far off from Chasaka's own. Those violent fits of anger he endured from his father were all unleashed onto Kye almost every single time.

The teen, who had only been two-and-a-half years younger than Chasaka, gave a sigh at seeing the untouched bowl and cup sitting on the floor just where he had left them. "I can get you something fresh. You really need to eat, Chasaka, it's been two days," his sibling told him with worry embedded within his tone. That sickened the older brother. This behavior was just something Chasaka himself would never display for his father, the man who beat and degraded him. Kye was more pathetic than he, and yet he still saw himself lower than him. That was what set him off.

"Stop wasting food when you know I won't eat it." His voice left like a snake bite against an arm, a sharp jab and the sting of venom as it ceased the coagulation of blood, leaving its victim to bleed out in pain. "Besides, **he'll** get pissed if I'm the one eating all the food," Chasaka added.

"**He** doesn't have to know," Kye replied as his suddenly-somber eyes glanced off to the side.

"You cretin. **He** always knows," the other redhead spat back. "Get out." Fire cracked from his tone, the cinders from that slowly-erupting bomb burning Kye as he spoke.

"Chasaka, I just want to help you," the young man pleaded hopelessly.

Just then a crash was heard in the bedroom. Though the older sibling was badly damaged by his father, he still had the agility of a cat. He was pinning his younger brother against the wall, glaring through his eyes as though they were a window to his soul.

Kye sat still, a tear slipping from his right eye as he was held against the wall. He knew what was to come and knew better not to fight it. To punch him? That was all his brother needed to feel at ease, to feel comfort—and for that, Kye would even subject himself to the same thing his brother was forced to sit through. The only difference was that Chasaka was strong enough to fight back, but he had lost his will a long time ago.

Kye could easily scream for his father's help, but that would only make things even worse for his brother. So he stayed silent, keeping his sobs at a minimum volume.

With each fist that split open his skin, Kye could feel a pinch of that pent up rage leave his brother. He could feel relief coming from him. It hurt so bad Kye's body shook, his stomach churned, more so after being kicked in the stomach.

But his twisted heroic efforts were for naught. Their father witnessed the ferocity thrown toward his perfect son by his tainted son. No, this was a monster. This was no son. This was a demon.

His father flung himself onto Chasaka, throwing him off the younger sibling. The sounds that followed were bone-chilling. Chasaka's screams always made Kye cry. He could hear his screams and pleas for mercy as his father unleashed his own wrath upon him, and Kye's mouth quivered for it all to stop. He was helpless to do anything at all, he could barely move.

"Your hands have no right to be on him! How many times do I have to teach you?" his father screamed at his older brother.

Kye could only sob, closing his eyes so he wouldn't have to see how those heart-wrenching screams were being produced.

The sounds of skin being stricken stopped, and Kye opened his blurry, tear-filled eyes to see the silhouette of his father's backside and Chasaka lying helplessly on the floor in front of him. They were both victims of a different predator, so similar—yet so polar. "Look at you...you aren't my son. You're a demon. I don't know what man my wife had to lie with, or how you could have ever been begotten, but—"

Chasaka shouted from the floor, tears falling. "I'm no bastard son! I'm your son. I have your blood in my veins, and believe me, I wish I didn't. But to know that my existence demeans you brings a smile to my face. You will rue the day you ever decided to lay a hand on me, to degrade a power far beyond your mortality!"

Hearing these words from Chasaka only reminded Kye of what his brother really wanted: to be accepted by his father. He just wanted to be his son, to be loved. But that possibility was so far out of reach, it was a shock he even spoke those words. He had forgotten that dream of earning back an ounce of respect from their father; smoldered them with the fire inside his veins.

"Listen to you, spewing worthless nothingness from your useless lips...you're nothing but a scourge," his father replied calmly.

Kye's wide eyes watched in horror as Chasaka was somehow able to stumble his way to his feet. He grabbed his father's throat and prepared to speak more but was shoved back against a wall, his hands bound by his father, bruised wrists squeezed with one burly hand while the other wrapped its way around his neck. "Don't you speak that way to me, Boy. Know your place, or so help me, I'll lynch you on a noose where you belong," he said.

"I belong on a black throne, ruling over your bones and bathing in your blood," he managed to choke out.

Kye couldn't sit by and watch this anymore. If asked, he couldn't say what made him strong enough to even stand up, let alone scream until his lungs grew hoarse. "Father, stop!"

Surprisingly, his father listened after a moment and glared his son in the eyes. "Yes, father, obey like the dog you are," Chasaka muttered under his breath. The blood in his veins blew open when he got those words out. "I'm going to kill you!" Chasaka threw himself onto his father. His strength and Chasaka's collided together as a scuffle with the redhead on top. His dead weight held down the man's stomach while his lanky hands grabbed his throat again, squeezing with all his might to collapse his windpipe.

The larger man below him writhed and bucked, kicking his legs like a child throwing a tantrum. Finally, he stabilized himself enough to grab at his son's own throat. "You're going to die," Chasaka sputtered, his jaw tight.

Slowly, he inched one of his hands over his father's mouth, eyes beginning to mist with tears.

"Chasaka, stop!" Kye screamed and rushed over to pry him away, but Chasaka was stuck there like glue.

Finally, he was able to pump flames into the man's mouth, keeping his promise to his father. The older man's organs cooked like meat over a fire, and the smoke that remained escaped through his nose and mouth. It was over within seconds.

Kye was in tears; he couldn't breathe and could barely see. He had no problem prying his brother away from the smoking man once it was clear that their father was dead. The two fought for dominance on the ground, grunts and the occasional sob leaving the mix of brawling siblings.

"Chasaka! Think of what you've done!" he yelled. His throat was raw from all the shouting.

The two brothers' muscles ached and begged for them to stop fighting, and eventually Chasaka was forced onto the floor by Kye, his left cheek pressed hard against it. They both took a few moments to regain their breath.

Past the tears in Chasaka's eyes, he could still manage a twisted smile of happiness—relief. But those red eyes held regret, strife, anger, pain, and most of all, sadness. His face held so many emotions that it was hard for Kye to believe that his brother wasn't insane. Or perhaps he just couldn't believe that he was.

"I've thought of it," the eldest said. "I've thought of it for so many days, Kye," he continued, his eyes focused on the wall in front of him as he still was overpowered by his younger half-sibling. "And it feels so good."

His visible eye flicked to meet Kye's cold stare. His own eyes had held many emotions too, ones so painful that his chest felt as though the life had been snuffed from inside, as though he were submerged beneath water, as though his lungs hadn't taken a breath in years. "I'm gonna make you regret holding me down like this," Chasaka growled through his teeth.

"Chasaka, why do you hate me?" Kye asked as he choked on his sobs. Rage ripped through the demigod, but he couldn't respond. "All I've ever done is care for you and help you. Why did you grow so cold?"

"You will pay," Chasaka replied. "Just as my every being reminds me of you..." he began.

Kye had let his guard down. A mistake he would regret forever. Chasaka had been able to overpower him after regaining some strength and held his face. He burned it. He burned while Kye screamed. His laughs combined with those screams. Those laughs came from Chasaka as he watched his brother's skin singe and turn to ash.

When he was finished, he shouted to be heard over Kye's screams of agony. "The scar I leave will remind you of me!"

* * *

Present day

Brown eyes watched through a mask as the waves of the ocean wiped back and forth upon the sand. The air smelled of salt, fish, and an acute scent of gull dung. It was a smell that Kye was fairly used to. He watched the foam of the sea slowly build up as he sat on top of a rock. He found himself sitting there rather often. Here, he would reminisce on the few memories he had of his beautiful niece and her best friend, Rose.

This, as it always had, would lead to the memories of his distant past, the ones shared with his late brother. Even in his death, the man who had induced many years of unrest and pain for him was still very prominent in his mind. The mask over his face only managed to hide part of those reminders.

He never saw death to be a fitting punishment for what Chasaka had done. He still left many to suffer in his wake, including those girls he left to carry his burden. They never deserved to be exiled, and yet Tochfuyu served to be their home for many years. It was a blessing in comparison to what the citizens had wanted; that being for them to be executed, of course.

The current king, Zyair, had been the one to make the decision. He and Kye had been friends since before he took the throne from his late father, Taro.

Kye had explained to the man that Rose and Amaya were only young and likely hadn't been corrupted as their parents had been. So having mercy on him, Zyair decided only to exile the two despite the countless of his subjects who had pleaded, "Kill them, end the bloodline of demigods." But even Zyair knew that killing them wouldn't end the cycle of reincarnation, even if the youngest didn't have children.

Kye never told the two what had happened to their parents, and who could blame him? How could he stand face to face with two six-year-old girls and tarnish their minds by telling them their parents had been murdered by order of the ice god, a deity who was meant to protect them. How could he tell them their kin wanted them to be cast out and abandoned? He couldn't.

It broke his heart to leave them to fend for themselves, they were so young, but even if Zyair was his friend, he was still a king, his king—a man whose orders he needed to respect.

Kye pushed a hand through his ever-growing hair as he thought of what had led him up to this point. As though it were yesterday, he still remembered the night of his brother's death and the death of the other three demigods. Closing his eyes, he could even picture it as if he were still there.

After their father's death, Chasaka left the kingdom to escape the charges of murder that would come with what he had done. But after that, the other three demigods, Teira, Sage, and Ruki, had vanished without a trace along with him. Kye hadn't seen him again until four years later when he returned with the others. Not only that, but his brother had returned with a child whom he had with Sage, while Ruki and Teira bore a child of their own, Rose.

Since their disappearance, a stigma developed involving the four of them; that they were corrupt and only existed upon the earth to taint the name of the gods and bring misfortune. After all, one of their strongest forms of protection had abandoned them.

But the four of them had gained the trust of each citizen of Barness—despite the crime Chasaka had committed, having claimed it was done in self-defense—far too quick. As fate had again intended, the four of them became an important part of the military, even if two of them were foreigners, proving their strength and loyalty to the nation. But Aessatia had been in an era of peace, so their forces were useless.

Months passed after their return, and still Kye hadn't even attempted to speak to his brother. He saw him often though. He was treated with more respect than he deserved, along with those who followed him.

For those four years of his disappearance, Kye grew to realize just how terrible a brother Chasaka had truly been, and instead of wanting to be his advocate, he feared him. Even if he had gained the trust of the whole kingdom, Kye could still see the darkness in his heart.

It wasn't until his curiosity to meet his niece got the best of him that he decided to approach his brother.

He seemed to be normal, happy even. Had it been love and that little girl who had made him find peace within himself? Was he truly back to normal?

It would quickly be made evident to Kye that this front was all but a mere trick—and he had regrettably fallen for it.

He, along with the other demigods and their daughters, had dinner one night to celebrate the unity of a family, the turning of a new page in their chapter of life. Later that same night, though, Kye made a rather alarming discovery. If asked, he didn't think he could recall how it happened, but fate found him in the study of his brother's home. There, he discovered numerous books talking about Lucian history. One in particular had been flipped open to one specific page about a demon called Waru and another called Tokiwa. It said how the two brought about Armageddon from within a place called the Tower of Twilight. Kye could swear he had only heard of such a place when the demons had attacked his home.

Other than that, the various texts and scrolls lying around his study were based around the gods. Perhaps his brother had become more involved in his bloodline. He was still convinced the man had matured since the days of his youth. But then he found texts which looked much older. They were of cults whose sole beliefs were on the destruction of gods and those affiliated with them, which by default would have included his own kind. This was enough to raise a few red flags in Kye's mind.

His brother wound up finding him snooping that night. Chasaka did nothing to speak in his own defense. But he would never forget his words that night: "I find their point of view interesting...without the gods, humans wouldn't be so reliant, now would they? It would be intriguing to see how humans might behave knowing no higher power exists above them. Would they be at peace? Would they still fight for power? It's all so...riveting."

Kye heard no such talk from his brother since that day. A year and a half had passed after that. His brother and his allies had shown no indication of being a threat. Still, the young man took caution with his actions. He found himself watching Chasaka any chance he got, even admitting himself into Barness' military to be just a bit closer to him at all times.

One night, the warrior had been patrolling the outside of the Ice Sanctum, the sacred hall of texts protected by the ice god who watched over their beloved kingdom capital; in fact, many of Aessatia's major villages and empires were built around these various sanctums and protected by the gods who inhabited them.

Kye looked up toward the beautiful sky full of stars. The atmosphere was relatively peaceful that night. He had heard the sound of metal clanking coming toward him, which caught his attention and caused him to peel his eyes away from the stars and to one of his fellow knights; the origin of the disturbance in the once-tranquil air. "Kye, one of our men has just been killed. We believe the wall has been breached. Come quickly," he said.

Not thinking twice, Kye nodded and grabbed his halberd into his hand, running with the other guard to their destination. There, they found one of the commanders giving orders to the others, who then dispersed to search the perimeter. Kye's orders had been to search one of the bridges connecting the palace's upper level with the rest of the network of pathways.

He patrolled the relative area for a mere few minutes before spotting three figures which happened to be heading into the relative direction of the Ice Sanctum. He was going to shout at them to stop, but he caught himself, knowing that it wouldn't accomplish anything. Instead, he decided to silently follow them. His suspicions had been correct. They had entered the Ice Sanctum right through the front door.

Kye waited a few moments before actually venturing inside. He had only ever been inside the sanctum once before, but had never seen the god which allegedly dwelled within. He was amazed to see the interior of the structure. Its architectural design surpassed even the palace. He supposed it made sense, given that a god lived there. He noticed that around the room, fractals of ice clung onto the walls and floors and some of the bookshelves had been knocked over, contents torn asunder. But this only caught the man's eye for merely a few seconds before his attention was brought toward the center of the room.

There in front of him, his brother stood looming over Cyero's body with Ruki and Teira standing beside him.

"Where is the location of the Tower of Twilight?" Chasaka's voice demanded.

There was the name of that place again. What was its relevance anyway?

The god looked fearful, a blade placed beside his head as he stared back into the demigod of fire's eyes. "You won't reach it. You can't," Cyero replied.

That blade was then held dangerously close to his neck. "I don't believe you're in any position to be telling me what I can and can't do," Chasaka sneered.

At this point, Kye silently took refuge behind a tall bookshelf, peeking out as he watched the events from behind it. "I refuse... to disclose...the information you seek..." the ice god answered.

"I suppose there is no harm in ending him prematurely," the man told the others as he raised the sword up over the god's chest.

Cyero had been about to open his mouth to speak before Kye ran out from behind the shelf. "Chasaka! Stop!" he screamed at his brother.

The man sighed in annoyance, his eyes flicking over to his younger half-sibling. "Kye..." he groaned.

"Well, this is a surprise," Ruki spoke up.

"The more the merrier," Teira said.

"Whatever it is the three of you have planned, I want no part of it at all! Step away!" Kye spat before pointing his halberd at them.

Chasaka stared back at his brother blankly before he began to let out a hearty chuckle as though he thought what Kye was saying was actually amusing. "Look at you, Kye...always the one to step in and play hero," he sneered, eyes narrowing at the man as the laughter drained out of him. "You can't prevent it this time...you won't. You're too afraid of me."

Kye balled his fists after hearing his brother speak, a frown contorting his features. "I'm not who I was six years ago, Chasaka," he growled at him. "I've changed." At that, he stepped forward, his halberd firmly grasped in his hand. "Now, step back."

Chasaka picked up his sword after seeing his brother in a challenging stance. Before the ice god could move, Ruki stepped into his place, pulling out his own weapon, a trident made of a bright silver alloy. "Don't move," the water demigod growled at him before stepping on his chest. "Tell us where the Tower of Twilight is!"

Kye started to sprint toward Chasaka, eyes blazing, halberd aimed. But before he could get less than five feet from his brother, he aimed his weapon upward and slew his halberd toward the atrium so it would break the stained decorative glass. Moonlight flitted in, illuminating the shards of broken glass as they rained down from above, showering those below it. Kye landed down on his side. Despite the wounds that now littered his body, he stood to his feet.

The three demigods were trying to recover from the minor injuries caused by the falling glass. That was when they heard Kye wailing as he called for the help of his fellows.

One by one, guards and even king Zyair himself had begun to flood the sanctum, each face astonished to see the sight before them.

"Chasaka—Kye, what is going on?" The king clearly had just been awoken from his rest and wasn't in any mood for whatever this was.

"His royal highness, Zyair, has come to witness the salvation of his people, how bittersweet..." Ruki sneered at them.

"I suppose there is no point in hiding it any longer...Zyair, we're in the midst of bringing salvation to all of humankind," Chasaka said.

Kye's eyes grew wide as he looked at his brother. Suddenly, he could recall those words from that day a year and a half ago. 'I find their point of view interesting...without the gods, humans wouldn't be so reliant, now would they? It would be intriguing to see how humans might behave knowing no higher power exists above them. Would they be at peace? Would they still fight for power? It's all so...riveting.'

"Your highness! He's a follower of Nature's Paragon!" he shouted.

Zyair looked at Kye as though he had gone mad. "What?"

"Don't look so shocked...The gods wish to oppress the human race as we know it. With their elimination, humans can finally thrive as the strongest beings," Teira said, encouraging others to join. But none of them seemed convinced. Zyair only stared, baffled, wondering how they could follow the beliefs of such a cult that would wish destruction upon even their own kind.

Cyero saw an opening and formed a shard of ice within his palm, attempting to strike Ruki, but it was Teira's hand that had caught it. The water demigod's face appeared astonished by this, but only pathetically. It was almost as though he had been waiting for the god to strike him, or more accurately, to attempt it. "Do you not see? A god that's meant to protect his people seeks to harm them," he said and held out his hand. "Aid us, people of Lucus and our king, Zyair. Humans will become powerful, none of us weak or useless again!"

As silence befell the group of soldiers, Kye witnessed Sage—who hadn't previously been with the other three—grab a man and suck every last bit of oxygen from his lungs in the midst of the crowd that had gathered.

As if it were a signal, Teira grabbed a shard of glass from the floor and stabbed it into Cyero's chest. He wheezed and choked on his own blood. Pain exploded inside of him but somehow he had managed to grab her arm and freeze her in place by her feet. This ice created fractals that reached Chasaka, Ruki and eventually Sage, who had been hiding in the crowd.

"Kill them," Cyero rasped from the ground where he lay, his body going completely limp as his last bit of energy was exhausted from that simple command.

Kye laid in his own slowly-forming puddle of blood in the midst of battle, his wounds had become too much to bear.

Blood and ligaments splattered everywhere, the attack; ravenous. But Kye recalled losing consciousness soon after being struck by Teira's weapon.

The execution ended with the coming of dawn, dried blood and broken glass left in its wake.

* * *

Kye opened his eyes, snapping out of this memory when he felt a hand fall upon his shoulder. He craned his head around only to lock gazes with the king himself.

"Your highness," he said as he felt his heart drop from a quick bout of fear. What did the king want to have left the capital just to find him? "To what do I owe the pleasure?"

"Kye, we aren't before an audience, there is no need to be so formal...however, I've come to you with a rather pressing matter," he said.

That was when Kye's expression changed to one which held a bit more concern, even if Zyair couldn't see it behind that mask of his. "What is it?" he asked.

"The two demigods, the ones who were exiled twelve years ago—"

"Rose and Amaya."

"They've escaped."

Kye could feel his stomach turn when his friend spoke these words. He knew the day would eventually come. Isolation was no place for a human being to be, even if the two had had each other. But where would they go?

"I've sent out some soldiers to patrol Aessatia and have sent word to a few of the neighboring towns and villages to keep an eye out for them. The only problem is that we will have no idea what they look like until the soldiers who found them can give a description to the forensic artist," Zyair explained.

"The forensic artist...you say it as though they're criminals. They haven't done anything wrong," Kye replied.

"They were banished from the kingdom and sent to Tochfuyu for their exile with no permission to be released," Zyair pointed out.

"I don't see how you could have expected them to stay. You were worried about them being corrupted, do you not think their exile could have done the very thing you were trying to prevent?" the other asked him.

"I order you to find them and return them to Tochfuyu." This time, the king spoke with a bit more of an authoritative tone. No longer did Kye feel like an equal when speaking to this man. Zyair was above him.

His eyes lingered on the king for a long, drawn-out moment before a sigh exited his lips and his eyes shifted back toward the gurgling waves in front of him. "I'll set off as soon as I can."

3: Blood Drawn From Thorns

Nineteen years ago

Teira worked as a maid at an inn after the demon war was over. It was the only job she could have hoped to get around that time, since her mother owned the place. It was peaceful only a few days, and she wished those times hadn't been so scarce for her. Being a woman made her a minority—and that simple, unchangeable fact made her life that much more miserable.

She wished she could have been as strong as her late father, but she wasn't. And so she fell prey to many. The only reason for which Teira would be called was when a man was feeling rather lonely. A sad but very true fact.

Teira remembered the first time she had ever been taken advantage of. It was a slow night at the inn, and her mother had been asleep. The young girl was grieving for her father that night. She had known no greater sadness in her life. Though she may have understood the reason, nothing could have prepared her for the news or the harsh truth of it.

One of the men who had been staying there was quick to try and comfort her. He led the young girl to his room and began to kiss her deeply. His lips were rough and cold, scraping her with his stubble. The more she tried to resist, the more difficult it became to struggle away. Red marks blossomed over her body. He had bitten and sucked her skin as though he were an alpha wolf dragging away the carcass that she would become.

He shouted in her ears, telling her she was a monster and she deserved the pain she felt when he forced himself upon her. Her ears rang, Teira couldn't move, couldn't breathe. Everything hurt and she bled. The world felt as though it was crashing around her. "When will it ever end?" she found herself thinking.

Her mother was a cruel woman. She couldn't hope to tell her about the encounter, at least if she had hoped to accomplish anything in doing so. It was pointless.

From that day onward, she became the reason the inn was popular among men. It was how she made a lot of her money.

One night, a boy around her age had entered. That gender had become a monster to her. But she recognized him as the aqua-haired boy she had seen the day her father was lynched. He had been watching with tears in his eyes as a woman who looked just like him was hanged before his eyes.

She recalled having brief words with the boy while she watched him tear a piece of his mother's red dress and tie it around his neck after the crowd had dissipated.

Ruki, she believed his name was.

The boy was in tears again, and part of it pained her deeply—but she was too timid to approach him.

"Is there anything I can get you?" she asked him with shaky hands.

"I hear that you keep great company if I purchase a room here," he spoke as he tried desperately to wipe his tears.

She thought to herself, *So this is it then? He's just another filthy man?*

Despite this, she nodded her head slowly, and he placed a bag of money in her hands. "Keep the change," he said.

Teira widened her eyes at the bulky baggage and thereupon walked to the inn's kiosk to give him a room key. Quietly, she led him to the room he would be staying in and shut the door behind them.

With an emotionless look across her face, she began to slowly unzip her maid's dress and slip the straps off her shoulders. This had become routine for Teira, so it rarely bothered her.

"What on Earth are you doing?" Ruki snapped at her in shock.

Teira froze in her incomplete action and stared at the blue-haired boy. Then, she understood. "Oh, I'm sorry, did you want to undress me by yourself?" she asked.

"Why the Hell would I want to undress you? That's disgusting. Did your mother teach you no decency?"

Teira's pink eyes could only stare in bewilderment at this boy. Had he not talked about her keeping him company? What was going on? She spoke not a word and began slipping her outfit back over her body. "I'm sorry that you're repulsed by me," she mumbled.

Hearing him say this made her somewhat sad, despite having been told the same thing by people before.

Ruki rolled his eyes as though he was annoyed by her. "I'm not repulsed by you; I'm repulsed by what you were insinuating just then. Who do you think I am? Some dirty sex criminal?" he asked.

Those words rang in her mind. Is that what those men had been doing to her? It had happened many times, she couldn't fathom the reality of it all.

"Quit thinking about yourself for just a second. I told you I needed your company, did I not?" Ruki asked her.

Teira simply nodded her head and approached the boy with azure eyes so that she was in front of him.

What he did next surprised her. She could hardly even process it fully with his arms wrapped comfortably around her waist as though they belonged there, his head rested on her chest. She could only stare at every little strand of hair that poked from his scalp with her hands up as though begging for mercy as he was seemingly attacking her.

But Ruki did nothing of the sort. He simply shed tear after tear while keeping that position as his shoulders trembled. This boy was truly sad when he had walked into the inn that night. She knew she had seen it, even if only briefly.

"What is the matter?" she dared ask.

"My father told me that I'm no longer welcome into his home," he answered almost immediately.

Teira was unsure of how to answer this or of how to even attempt to comfort him. But she offered him a quick pat on the head and said, "I'm sorry."

Ruki pulled her down onto the bed with him and she tensed at the action. She knew it was too good to be true—there were no good men.

But his hands didn't wander, his legs didn't dare go near the places that she feared they would. That night was merely spent with her listening to his soft sobs and sniffles as he explained to her what had happened before he had entered the inn that night. He did this until he fell asleep, holding Teira in his arms.

* * *

Three days and three nights had passed since the two ambitious young girls had set out for a village known as Dufmoore. Amaya was finding it rather unbearable to continue walking with her arm in the condition that it was. The bone was still exposed and had shifted into a position that made it hard to sleep. Worst of all, their rations had run dry.

Rose still had high hopes at finding this place. After all, this was the first of the outside world they had seen in years. Though it may not have been much to look at, given that spring had only just begun, it was still a very new and almost foreign experience. Amaya couldn't say she was the most thrilled about it, however. She seemed more paranoid after their exchange with the soldiers from the Lucian territory.

The sun was just setting below the horizon in front of them, and with it they could see the silhouette of some sort of establishment. It had to be Dufmoore. As soon as Amaya had seen it, her slouching had stopped and her aching feet, which had been crying out for a rest, no longer bothered her. "Is that it?" she asked, pointing off in the distance at the figure.

"It must be; I'm sure we have been walking in the right direction," Rose answered.

An hour passed before the two travelers came upon the village, passing a small sign that read "Dufmoore" along the way.

But Rose couldn't get excited about this. A few feet back, she could already tell that something was rather off-putting about this place. The buildings looked unkempt and its atmosphere held an air of sadness. When they passed through the entrance, it only made it easier for Rose to deduce that the village and its people weren't in the best shape, and she couldn't help but wonder why.

Amaya could feel sadness about herself as well when she walked through the village beside her friend. Some people sat outside houses, but aside from that, the place may as well have been completely vacant as far as they could see. Another thing that she noticed was that upon entering the village, the grass that grew outside of it faded into packed dirt, as if crops—or any kind of greenery, for that matter—simply didn't exist there.

Of the few people among that rundown place, Rose took it upon herself to approach one, a woman who sat on the ground, leaning against a fence post. Amaya hung back a bit as her friend did this; she didn't feel comfortable speaking to this random person. She knew it had to be done so they could find the help they needed, but it was nerve-racking.

"Excuse me, miss. Do you happen to know where we might find a medic?" the young woman asked the older one.

Her eyes met Rose's upon her approach, and the whole time, she just stared. "We have a medic, but I doubt you will be serviced by them very quickly," the woman replied. Her voice was dry and raspy, as though the back of her throat consisted of sandpaper, yet she still appeared to be rather young.

Rose only gave the woman a look of confusion in response to what she had said. Before she could open her mouth to ask what she meant, the woman spoke again. "You both seem to be travelers," she said. "Many of our village's people are sick. We have a limited supply of drinking water, much of which is either owned by our farmers or very expensive. But I'll save you this sad little hamlet's life's story..." the woman trailed off before pointing a shaky finger down the path that had once been in front of the two girls. "It's that way; you can't miss it."

Rose nodded her head at the woman and offered her a smile of courtesy. "Thank you, miss, I appreciate it," she said.

At that, the two began heading down the path that the woman had pointed toward. At the end of it, a building could be seen with far more people either standing, sitting, or even sleeping in front of it. Rose could feel her chest swell at the sight of such despair. From what she could vaguely remember from her youth in the kingdom, she only saw folks who looked like this in the first district of the kingdom where all the commoners lived. Even then, there weren't this many people.

As they walked carefully through the sick people they tried to avoid eye contact with any of them, but they could feel their eyes upon them the whole time. It was heartbreaking. The inside of the structure was almost completely opposite of the outside: empty. This allowed Rose to take a breath which she had been holding in ever since they came across the crowd of people in front of the building. "All those people...I feel so terrible for them," she whispered.

"They're like us. With nothing," Amaya told her.

"Yes, it's very sad, isn't it?" a voice echoed from somewhere, causing both their heads to focus on the direction it seemed to come from. There, they saw a man come out from one of the rooms branching off from the main hallway.

Both girls felt a quick rush of fear surge through their bodies before relaxing to see someone who wasn't nearly on their deathbed. "Are you the medic here?" Rose asked the man without regard to what he had said. Amaya's arm needed to be fixed, and quickly.

"I am. My name is Soren. And how can I help the both of you?" he asked.

From under the hooded mantle he wore, his shoulder-length, deep navy-colored hair spilled over his shoulders and out of the hood. In fact, he almost looked like the epitome of a coming storm with his eyes of gold. Yet despite these jarring features, he looked young.

After hearing the man called Soren's question, Amaya pulled back her fur cloak to show him her broken arm, at which he pulled a shocked expression. "Oh my, that's quite an injury. Come this way," he said, beckoning the two of them down the hallway from which he had first emerged. He led them to a room and motioned for Amaya to sit down on a chair which allowed Soren to do his work.

"This is going to hurt, but I have to align the bone properly before I can begin," Soren said to the red-haired woman.

Amaya nodded in understanding. The wound had been killing her for the past few days, so she was sure the quick stab of pain wouldn't be so bad in comparison to having to walk around with the bone sticking out the way it was. "Just do what you have to do," she replied, mentally bracing herself.

Soren allowed Amaya a few seconds to prepare for the pain, and then an unsettling crunch resounded in the room, followed immediately by the injured girl screaming in pain. Rose ended up looking away, covering her ears as her friend screamed. When it was over, she looked back to see that the bone had now retreated to the inside of her skin where it belonged.

"My, this truly is remarkable, how did you receive such an injury?" Soren asked the girl.

"A bear attacked us," Rose answered him.

"A bear? Really? You both must not be from around here... I've never seen a bear anywhere near here." After having set the bone, the man began to wrap the girl's arm in bandages, being sure to mind the wound.

"Where are you two from?" he asked to change the subject, which immediately caught their attention.

"We're just travelers," Amaya answered hastily.

"Oh, really, I most definitely couldn't tell," Soren replied, his voice dripping with sarcasm. "Well, you must be from somewhere," he said.

"You're just a doctor. We don't need to tell you any of that," Amaya replied with an edge in her tone which caused Rose to look at her with a warning glance.

"We're from Lucus, actually," the blonde girl spoke up, ignoring her friend's clear want for anonymity.

But this response earned a curious look from the man. Neither girl could read the emotion it held. But the room grew silent for far too long after that.

Soren returned his focus to wrapping Amaya's arm. "It's all right, I wasn't going to force you to answer," he said.

No other words were spoken after that, and after just a few more moments, Soren stood from his kneeling position, signaling that he was finished with the young woman's arm. "That should do it for now, but you should at least keep yourself from moving it, since I don't have a means of splinting the arm," he said.

When the man's hands slid off of her, Amaya looked up at him. "Thank you for your help," she said.

"So, Lucus, you said, right?" he asked. "You might want to be careful around here...you look an awful lot like the two girls from the wanted posters." He had gone over to a wash barrel to clean off his hands from the blood which poured out after having set the bone.

Amaya and Rose both felt their stomachs drop in an instant when they heard the medic say this. "Wanted posters?" Rose asked him.

"Mhm," he confirmed as he began to dry his hands with a rag. "There are two girls hailing from Lucus, Barness in particular. Imperial guards came through from Folkvangr the other day and put up the posters around town. I guess the two girls are supposed to have been banished all the way to Tochfuyu."

"I see...well, thank you. We will make sure to watch our backs," Amaya said as she and Rose moved to exit the room.

"Hold on just a moment," Soren said, causing the girls to freeze out of fear. Was he going to turn them in? "You know, I'm going to need compensation for my work."

Rose and Amaya turned their heads to look at the man, relieved to hear that he wasn't interested in their bounty. "Compensation?" Rose asked.

"Money, of course. I don't work for free," Soren replied pointedly.

Amaya and Rose shared a look with one another for a brief moment before looking back at Soren. "See...we don't have any money," the redhead of the two confessed.

Soren sighed, feeling stupid as he placed a hand over his forehead. "Silly me, I should have mentioned there would be a fee...I apologize, I assumed you knew," he said with a groan. "Listen, I don't normally do this, but I'll let it slide as long as the two of you stay here and work for me for a day or so."

"What? But we don't know you, and we must go," Amaya argued with him.

"You will be considered thieves if you leave now," the man pointed out.

"Amaya, it's all right. We aren't in any rush, we can stay for a while and help. It's the least we can do. After all, he *did* help you with your arm," Rose explained to her friend.

Amaya kept her gaze on Rose, her eyes riddled with what appeared to be anger. It was clear she didn't want to do this, but Rose couldn't tell why. After all, it wasn't such a big deal, considering that he had helped Amaya with her arm.

"Very well, I'll expect the two of you back here by sunrise tomorrow, and don't fret, I promise not to make the work too taxing," Soren replied, a smile gracing his lips whilst Amaya still looked visibly annoyed by the whole idea of it.

When the two young travelers left the medic's cabin, they set out for the streets of Dufmoore again. Since money had all at once become a factor in their lives, they realized they wouldn't be able to sleep in any kind of inn, and wound up choosing a space in the brush just outside the village. It didn't bother them, however, considering they had spent most of their lives living like this. It was surrounded by trees and relatively hidden from passersby. They started a fire between them, and once they got settled in, Amaya and Rose began to murmur amongst themselves.

"Why did you tell him we could do that?" Amaya said, at last addressing the subject that had been on her mind ever since Rose had offered to work as compensation for Soren's help.

"It was the least we could have done," the blonde answered.

"And you didn't find it at all concerning that he mentioned those wanted posters?"

Rose pursed her lips after listening to her friend's question and her stomach suddenly dropped. "I...actually hadn't thought of it that way. I'm sorry," she said.

Amaya sighed, placing her hand over her face before sliding it down. "I was getting the feeling he knew who we were right from the start. What if he just wants us to come back so he can turn us in? You have to take these things into consideration," she said.

The other young woman groaned a bit and placed her chin on her knees and wrapped her arms around them. "I know, I know," she whined. "What are we supposed to do? If we just leave, we could get into even more trouble. They won't take us back to Tochfuyu; they could put us in jail!" Rose said as her head surfaced from the sea of arms encapsulating it.

"We risked this from the start. I say we just leave at daybreak," Amaya replied.

Rose knew that that was probably their safest option, but deep down, she felt wrong about just leaving without compensating the man who had been kind enough to help them. Amaya could feel her distraught, in essence, radiating off of her, and got up only to sit again beside her. She placed her uninjured hand onto her shoulder and craned her head around to look at her friend directly. "Your heart is in the right place, I know. But our situation is a bit more dire than that. Maybe someday we can find a way to come back and return the favor, okay?" Amaya said, trying to be reassuring.

Rose's blue irises didn't peel away from the fire, they only watched, its orange flames dancing in their reflection before she closed them. "We already have so much against us, I just want to make a better profile for ourselves, and then maybe people will see that we aren't as bad as they think," she said. She laughed, but not because she found anything humorous about the situation. "Hell, we don't even know why they hate us. Part of me just wants some answers, while the other just wants this whole thing to be behind us."

"Let's not think about it too much, we would find it hard to sleep," Amaya replied. At that, she scooted back a bit so that her back would lean into the tree standing behind them.

Rose found it more comfortable to lie flat against the ground on her side. But she doubted there would be any sleeping to come.

Hours had passed into the night, and the young woman's suspicion ended up being true. Sleep hadn't come. The fire had long since died out, which made her eyes dart around the darkness, searching for movement within it. That fear of hers had been around for as long as she could remember. It was normal for a child to be afraid of the dark, but she had never gotten over it.

She always thought of one memory whenever it was dark. A tall, black demon coming into her bedroom in the dead of night and reaching for her. The scenario had been replayed in her mind so many times that she could no longer deduce its reality. All she knew was that she was afraid of the unknown that lurked in the dark, and if she ever told Amaya about it, she knew she would be told that it was a foolish thing to be afraid of. After all, everything was the same in the dark as it was in the light.

In her paranoia, Rose actually *had* managed to catch some movement in the brush surrounding their little campsite, which caused her to raise her head up to focus her eyes to where she had seen it. Upon listening closer, she could hear murmuring and could understand now that they were humans.

Quietly, the blonde rolled over toward her slumbering friend and nudged her with her elbow. "Amaya, wake up, someone is coming," she murmured in a hushed tone, causing Amaya to groan a bit before opening her eyes.

"Huh...? What do you mean?" she said groggily. She sat up carefully to scan the surrounding area, trying to find the reason her friend had awoken her so late in the night. Upon not hearing or seeing anything, she sighed and laid back again. "Rose, you're just being oversuspicious. Calm down and go back to sleep," she said tiredly before closing her eyes once more.

The girl craned her head around a few more times, trying to listen for any unnatural noises. But to her dismay, she neither saw nor heard anything in the vicinity.

Sighing, she laid herself down once more, beginning to doubt her suspicions. Perhaps it really had just been paranoia.

Within just a few minutes, she heard the rustling again. But this time it sounded like it came from multiple directions at once—and really close. She shot up from her once-lax position, only to be too late to even react. Two tall figures had grabbed Amaya, causing her to awake and scream out of both fear and pain from her wounded arm. Just as soon as she had seen this, Rose was being held against the ground by someone who had been standing over her.

"That's them!" rasped a familiar voice.

Turning her head, Rose could see the dimmed face of the woman they had come across hours earlier. She felt hurt and betrayal ravage her all at once, shock filling her expression. "How could you?" she growled at the woman as she tried to struggle from the grip of the one holding her in place.

She knew the woman probably didn't have an ounce of remorse for this. After all, it was a much-needed payout for her.

"Shut it!" the voice above Rose hissed at her. She was now certain that it was a man holding her down. The next thing she knew, something slammed against her head, making her yelp in pain and causing her vision go blurry.

As Rose's eyesight began to flicker and eventually fail her, she could see Amaya trying to fight the grip of those holding her hostage. She couldn't stay conscious long enough to see if she had actually won that scuffle.

Within moments, she was out cold.

4: Blood in the Water

Ruki's Journal

Water.

The key element to the survival of human life. And yet, it was the downfall of my own. This magic—this curse that I possessed—had turned the people I once called "comrades" into monsters. Going out of the house became a warrior's task, and returning home turned into a war field in itself. I'm a demon, my father would say to me.

My eyes and my hair had been the same color as the very element everyone so despised. Not only me, but those other three who had watched their parents die at the gallows, apart from the woman who had been killed in a hunting trip by a hungry grizzly. I couldn't recall his name, but I was sure her son was suffering just as I was. Not only for the painful sting that death wrought, but for the awful descrimination perpetuated by those who lived among the major kingdoms and empires. Folkvangr included.

After the lynching of my mother, my father fell into a deep depression and met a woman at a tavern one night. This woman became my hellish nightmare. But he loved her. His love for her couldn't compare to his own for me.

I grimaced at the thought of him loving a woman who hated his own son—and so soon after my mother was killed. Everything that had ever been tied to my mother became a disgrace to him. Including me. His love for her was drowned in the stigma that now surrounded the demigods, and he punished himself heavily for it—for the fact that he was still in love with a monster.

Nothing I did was ever good enough for him. That's why he never listened to me when I told him that the woman he had grown to love anew was hurting me. Even with physical proof, I was a liar. I prayed to the gods that I was no longer sure existed. No answer came to me. But because of the power in my body, I knew the gods were real. They were ignoring me.

That was when I realized that I was truly a disgrace. Relying on the gods to fix my problems was indeed disgraceful. So I decided instead to fix it all myself.

I drowned that woman in an encasement of water while my father was away. I watched her with unfazed eyes as she struggled to escape the imprisonment of water that was around her head. It felt good to see her struggling to breathe and finally die. To know I had done it by myself was an even greater feeling.

That night, my father returned and discovered what I had done. I made no effort to hide it.

"Is this not what you wanted, father? To see your son become an honor and not a disgrace? I've erased my problems with my own hands. Am I still a disgrace to you, father?" I said while I watched him scream at the unmoving corpse before us surrounded in a puddle of the water I had created to drown her.

Remorse often stung me in the days—no, the months that had followed her death. But it could only get easier, taking lives to get through my own, it became my justification.

He forced me to leave that night with nothing but the clothes upon my back and some money I had gotten from a few tasks during the day. I used them to stay at an inn for the night where I met a woman.

She, too, had a story to tell, just like the rest of us.

* * *

U mber eyes fluttered open, only to take in their surroundings—four cobblestone walls. They noticed the various nicks in the stones which had started to erode either from time or from previous prisoners. There was nothing to help alleviate the stench of the sewers that Amaya was likely near. It was no brighter inside than the gathering gloom of dusk—even at midday. But with no windows, it was impossible to tell how much time had passed or what time of day it was. It was suffocatingly quiet, except for the distant dripping of a dingy pipe. The prison cell was a hollow cube of cobblestone, one way in, no way out. It was disorientating by design; purposefully.

Given enough time, a person could forget their own name in here. The isolation was total and the stimulation was zero.

Her friend was nowhere in sight, which made her begin to worry. Amaya stood up and rushed toward the door, only to trip. She was anchored down by something heavy and felt a sharp pain enter her ankle. Thankfully, she hadn't fallen on her injured arm, and after scraping against the rough floor, Amaya grunted and looked down to see what had caused her to lose her balance. Apparently her foot was chained to what looked like a heavy, immovable ball of black iron.

Was she in Barness? Dufmoore? Or someplace else completely? Wherever she was, she knew she needed to escape. "Rose!" she called out.

"Hey, quiet in there!" a gruff voice snapped back at her.

Amaya maneuvered her head to try and see where the voice had originated. Around the cell's right wall, she could just barely see a person standing vigil by her cell.

She looked around once more. Would this be her life from now on? Death surrounded by four blank walls? Certainly not. She hadn't been bested yet. "Let me out! Let me out!" she yelled, determined somehow that this would get her anywhere, even managing to just barely reach the cell bars and pound on them with her good fist.

This quickly brought the attention of the guard outside the cell, who now readied a sword. "Hey! Get back!" the man said, clad in armor. His sword lashed out, swinging at her through the cell's bars, slashing her shoulder and causing her to fall back, growling.

"Your king will be here tomorrow to retrieve both of you... peh. I shouldn't even say he's your king," the guard mocked.

Amaya stayed on the ground where she had collapsed. "How long have we been here?" she asked before slowly sitting up.

"Three days," answered the guard, sheathing his sword as he did so before reclaiming his position beside her cell.

The king would be there soon, what did that mean for their fate? Where would they end up from there? Amaya couldn't spend her days in exile anymore, nor did she want to spend even another moment in prison. She would have a lot of questions for Zyair once he arrived.

"Where is—"

"Silence!" the man shouted before she could even ask her question.

Being forced to remain quiet, silence ate away at the young woman. She was never one to simply sit doing nothing. Minutes passed by, feeling like hours. A soft patter of water slapping the floor as it fell every few seconds was the only noise left to keep her sane. Her legs were restless, shaking from side to side as she sat in the cell.

A crash sounded against the floor. The noise caused Amaya's body to start, and she lifted her head, trying to see what had brought it on. Within moments, a figure appeared before her cell door with Rose beside it. She swore she could recognize that fabric upon the hooded character's body. But her excitement to see Rose and being freed from the person unlocking her cell and then her chain was enough to distract her. "Rose, how did you get out? What is going on?" she asked her.

"No time for that; we need to get out of here," said the figure beside her friend.

Now she was sure she knew who this was.

"Soren?" she asked. A grin appeared across her lips. "You were really eager for that payment, huh?" she joked.

The figure looked fully at Amaya, his face only proving her suspicion to be true. "As I said, there is no time for that. We need to go," he said. There wasn't a single hint of amusement on his face from her comment, and with that, he turned to the exit of the cell, only to run off in the opposite direction from which they came, Rose following after him.

Amaya was quick to do the same, but not before catching a glimpse of the work Soren had made of the guard who once was in front of her cell. He was on the floor, unable to move but still alive. It appeared he had only been stunned.

The three of them made their way hastily through the cobblestone passage. There were torches posted on the wall to their right, lighting the way through. At this point, Amaya heard the sound of clanking metal growing increasingly closer to them. Her heart rate sped up. She couldn't let herself be caught again. She couldn't go back to that lonely cell. Adrenaline rushed through her veins, which may have been the only reason she was able to keep pace with the other two beside her. Her body still ached from the battering it was put through over the last few days.

Their journey developed into a plethora of twists and turns as well as stairs going upward and downward. At last they came across a sewer system, which was where the faint smell was coming from.

"We will have to escape through the drainage system," Soren said as he turned to the two of them.

The thought was far from appealing. The arch of Amaya's upper lip and Rose's furrowed brow was more than enough to hint that neither wanted to set foot into such disgusting water. But with those shouts to stop and the clangorous sound of metal fast approaching, Amaya didn't take long to think through her decision. Wading through sewage was definitely more ideal than spending the rest of her life in a cell. Rose followed after her, with Soren right behind them both. As they fled the stronghold, Amaya could faintly hear a man in the distance shout, "they're escaping through the sewer!"

They kept going for a while without speaking. Once they were sure they were no longer being followed, the three of them slowed their pace a bit to catch their breath.

"Thank you for saving us," Rose said between pants.

Soren returned a courteous smile. "You're quite welcome," he answered.

"But why?" Amaya asked him. "What do you benefit from saving us? Our bounty would have been helpful to your village," she said.

"Dufmoore isn't my—" Soren cut himself off before he could finish and heaved a sigh. "There is much to discuss...I'll explain everything once we aren't knee-deep in scat-ridden water."

Amaya pulled a face at hearing the man say this. She had been trying not to think about her feet sloshing in feces, but now that he mentioned it, it was all she could think about. "Yes, good idea," she said, stifling a gag.

Rose, Amaya, and Soren then traversed the remainder of the sewer system until they made it out through a drainpipe into a grass field. Suddenly they were surrounded by guards from the stronghold, all with swords and lances pointed at the three of them.

"Stop, we have you surrounded and outnumbered!" one of the guards yelled.

"I'm afraid I can't," Soren answered them. His posture brought forth a firmness; he didn't look like he planned on giving up so easily.

Amaya looked over toward Rose, a worried look in her eyes. When the blonde caught the movement, she, too, looked back with the same expression. Both were in mutual agreement that there was no way they were getting out of this, not even with a stroke of good luck. With Amaya's arm in the shape that it was, she wouldn't be able to even injure a single guard to allow them to escape, let alone a miniature army of them. The guards had taken their makeshift weapons as well, leaving them defenseless.

"You're serious? With so many disadvantages, you still choose to stand against us?" the guard asked.

Without another word, Soren drew a dagger from the sleeve of his cloak and began racing toward the crowd of guards. Rose knew she couldn't leave the man to fight on his own, and decided to try using her bare hands, leaving Amaya feeling absolutely helpless. They had managed to push the guards back a little bit, but this feeling of power over the tide of battle didn't last for very long. Their quantity was able to overpower them within moments of starting the fight. Soren, Amaya, and Rose had all been restrained.

"All right, you two, I'm going to need you to get serious with me for a moment," Soren said as though he had been referring to something. Amaya and Rose had absolutely no idea what he was going on about, and looked at the hooded man with pure confusion.

The guard who was restraining Soren pushed his metal boot against the hooded man's head, pressing his cheek into the mud. "Silence!" the guard snapped. "Don't be naive. We have you now," he said.

As the guards lifted the prisoners off the ground, rain began to fall from the cloudy sky, signaling that a storm was imminent. Fighting the grip of the soldiers, they were each dragged farther and farther from freedom.

At that moment, a sound like cannon-fire ripped through their ears, followed by yet another. A flash blinded the guards, the sound making their bodies rigid. A tree blooming near them had been struck by lightning from the storm, alighting it and causing it to collapse right toward them, the crunch of the trunk snapping was almost as loud as the thunder that followed the strike.

The soldiers scattered away from the flaming tree, which, upon falling, ignited the dry grass around them, causing the guards to drop the prisoners out of fear.

Rose and Soren quickly got to their feet and were about to flee from the fire that would likely consume them. Having landed on her arm, Amaya couldn't bring herself to get up, groaning in pain as tears stung her eyes. "Wait! Help!" she yelled after them.

Soren turned his head upon hearing Amaya's plea and rushed back through the growing flames to help the young woman to her feet and aid in her escape. Gently, he grabbed her uninjured arm and slung it around his neck to support her. "Can you walk?" he asked.

Amaya pulled her arm from him and glanced back at the fray of soldiers, who were still trying to reach them in spite of the rage of flames that couldn't be quelled by the falling rain.

"I'll have to." She took off in the direction Rose had gone with Soren quickly following her.

"Are you all right, Amaya?" Rose asked once she caught up.

"Yes, I'm fine," she answered. Still, she winced as she ran but Rose decided to say nothing more of it, knowing her friend would insist, even if she tried.

They stopped not too far away from where they had escaped, hiding in the cover of some trees since the rain still hadn't ceased.

"That was quite lucky, the lightning striking that tree," Rose said.

Their ears still rang from the encounter.

"Nonsense, it was the god Rotos who answered my prayer," Soren said.

The conversation was less important to Amaya. What she noticed first was that their current location certainly hadn't been Dufmoore. "Where exactly are we?" she asked as she took just one last glance around to make sure she wasn't mistaking her surroundings.

"I'll explain later. For now, you must come with me. There is something I need to show both of you," Soren replied.

Again, the two were being led away from where they had stopped. An annoyed groan rumbled in the back of Amaya's throat, refusing for a moment to follow. "Could it not wait? I'm tired and horribly starving...not to mention that I'm injured, as well," she complained.

Rose didn't want to say it outright, but fatigue and hunger were beginning to catch up with her too, infringing on her drive to continue on.

"It's very important," Soren urged, "afterward, I'll take you somewhere where you will be able to rest your heads and fill your stomachs."

The compensation seemed well worth the journey, and their curiosity to discover what this stranger had in store for them was enough to force them to go on a bit longer.

The path going forward was covered in foliage and fallen trees, giving them plenty to walk beneath and climb over, even avoiding some of the poison ivies along the way. Eventually, they emerged from the wayward trees and set foot upon a trampled path leading both left and right. Soren led them to the right. Rose noticed that with each step they took, the packed trail was at an incline.

They soon came upon a forest glade surrounded by lush greenery. In the middle of it was a good-sized rock formation which the path led up to. Rose and Amaya admired a beautiful, yet small waterfall that spilled from the top of the structure into the small accumulation of water below. Lily pads with black lotuses atop them were scattered about the surface of the peaceful pond.

However, Soren gave them virtually no time to take in the sight before coaxing them up along the path which would bring them to the top of the formation. Once they reached the top of its peak, they could now see that there was a red-leafed tree. Upon closer examination, they could see that it was starting to wither.

There was shallow water in front of it, the dying leaves that often fell from its branches littering the water's surface. Somehow, it managed to not dry up completely.

Soren looked up toward the canopy, the spaces between offering to the forest shafts of gallant moonlight that extended upon the structure they stood atop. Suddenly, the wind began to pick up around them, rustling the branches of the tree and rippling the water in front of it. The ground shook beneath their feet, a presence of heaviness falling over Rose and Amaya. It didn't seem to bother Soren, however, as though he were used to it.

Another giant sound ripped the sky and cleared up the clouds above, still spilling gentle tears down upon them, misting their skin. The moon that was once eclipsed by the clouds now outlined a large figure flying down through the hole in the canopy and perching itself on the side of the mass. Its giant claws outmatched a human body. The creature's large wings folded behind its back and its white scaly face came into view. Its body was massive, beyond anything the two girls even knew existed.

Behind them, another creature appeared, wingless but with similar features as the one that came from the clouds. Its colors deeply contrasted the white dragon, matching the color of the black lotus and making it almost impossible to see in the blackness of night now that the other creature blocked the moonlight above.

Amaya and Rose were frozen in fear. With a dragon in front of them and a wyrm behind them, they were trapped and hopeless for escape. Amaya silently cursed them for agreeing to stick close to this man while Rose's mind remained devoid of thought—a product of the fear instilled by these beasts.

"Buhus…" Soren uttered before dropping to one knee with a hand across his chest. He stood again and turned to the wyrm, taking the same position as before, saying, "Vadu."

Amaya and Rose looked at each other, searching for affirmation of this event. For neither the dragon nor the wyrm lashed out to claim their meal, in fact, their eyes didn't hold any bloodlust. To Rose, they almost looked pained. Not that she was any expert on reading the emotions of large, carnivorous creatures—especially dragons.

"Don't fear, small ones," the white dragon said to them. His voice was raspy, as though he had swallowed a hive of wasps. But this assurance didn't completely relieve them.

Vadu crawled around the side of the place they stood atop to perch beside Buhus. Their bright green eyes watched them.

Soren placed a hand upon Amaya's and Rose's shoulders, causing each of them to jerk as shock went through their bodies. "It's all right," he reassured them. "They're Buhus and Vadu. You may have heard stories of the great twin gods of earth, but their existence is no myth," the man explained.

"I've never heard their names in my life," Amaya replied. "I didn't know such creatures existed."

"I can't say I have either," Rose said. The two had heard the man mention that these creatures were gods, but even though their appearance was grand, they still found it hard to put faith into that claim. "I didn't know gods were real," she added.

The white dragon shook his immense head slowly, closing his eyes before they focused on Soren. "They know not of our presence in the world?" he asked. "That's surprising to hear.

There is no mistaking the two of you are the demigods who were sent into exile by your kin in years past."

Both Amaya and Rose's eyes grew wide at hearing the word "demigods."

"Someone explain what is going on! Why did you bring us here, Soren?" Amaya's voice had an edge to it as she spoke. She was growing tired of the ceaseless danger and mystery she'd been put through since leaving her snowy home in Tochfuyu, and she could sense that Rose was feeling the same way.

"I wasn't being completely honest with you when we first met one another," the man replied. "I'm a prophet hailing from an empire called Folkvangr; a messenger of the gods. When you entered my cabin, I could tell almost immediately that you were the ones the prophecy spoke of—the two demigods," Soren explained.

The lack of certainty remained across the young women's faces. Amaya craned her head up toward the man with golden eyes. "Prophecy?" she asked. "What prophecy?"

"One prophesied by a man named Asabüro, lo, twenty-two years in the past," rumbled the deep purple-colored wyrm as his eyes flicked over toward the dying red-leaf tree. One of his giant claws reached toward it and grabbed a crumbling leaf from a singular branch. "Back then, demons from Hell had invaded your formal home and were driven back by Aessatia's forces, including a clan which has since died out, the Astral Clan," Vadu explained. "Asabüro died along with them and left one final message for the world: one moon after the discovery of two in the snow, betrayal shall be uncovered where once was hope and faith, tainted by heavenly blood. They will be the ones to break the cycle." His claws shredded the leaf that once had been between them, its remnants falling to the ground below.

"I believe those 'two in the snow' are the both of you," Soren said.

"But...demigods? Do you truly believe that we're demigods?" Amaya asked him.

"We don't need to believe," Buhus rasped. "We can feel it running deep within your veins. You're the reincarnations of Noctis and Avius; the heroes who founded the Lucian bloodline, and the daughters of Chasaka, Ruki, Teira, and Sage," he explained.

Amaya went rigid upon hearing the names of hers and Rose's parents.

"Our parents are demigods?" Rose cut in. There was a feigned look of confidence in her eyes that evaporated as she remembered them. "What does this mean?"

"The full contents of the prophecy aren't yet fully clear... but as of late, well, I'm certain you must have noticed the dying trees and the shortage of water in Dufmoore—all of those sick people I had been treating," Soren said. "They're all the result of the gods' powers slowly diminishing, growing weaker with each passing day," he explained.

Rose looked down toward her feet as Soren spoke. "I noticed...but I simply thought it was the fault of spring only just beginning," she said.

As if to demonstrate her mistake, a bout of coughing erupted from the white dragon. When he was finished, he spoke once more. "We're no longer able to assume our mortal forms," he said.

"I believe it's your duty to restore their vitality," the prophet said to them.

All at once, their hearts sank low in their chests, pressure welling up within them. "Hold on, how are we meant to do this? You only seem to be sick," Amaya said. "And even still, Rose and I are in danger of being captured and returned to Tochfuyu. We can't hope to scour the world for some sort of cure, if that's what you're suggesting."

"If it were that simple, I don't believe the prophecy would have specifically called for you both," Soren pointed out.

"I don't know what will happen in the days to come, but should something happen to us…" Buhus trailed off. "The world may be thrown into complete chaos," he said

"You can't force us into this," Amaya said. "So what if you're sick? Why should we help? We were locked away in Tochfuyu, abandoned for years. Where were you so-called *gods* when we were suffering, freezing, and nearly starving to death?" Her tone was abrasive and filled with remorse. It had caused even the two gods to watch her with what appeared to be guilt.

Rose's eyes wandered off to the side after her friend had spoken. She felt it too; the exact thing she was feeling. That feeling of dereliction, one they had felt almost their entire lives.

"You're obligated by fate to do so. The leaves will fall where they may. They can't avoid that which awaits them." He analyzed the cold expression on Amaya's face and the distant look in Rose's eyes. "I can see that within the tarnished layers of your hearts lies a core that's pure," Buhus replied.

Amaya thought for a moment, her eyes focusing on the ground beneath her feet. "We were promised a place to stay if we came along with you, Soren," she said.

Buhus closed his eyes, disappointment contorting his scaly features. Vadu moved his ears back and began crawling back down the landmass.

Soren studied the girls' faces, but for now held little worry in Amaya's silent decision. However, he was discontented at Rose's silence in the matter. From what he had gathered, she put kindness and care into her decisions, even if it meant putting herself in danger. "Of course, I'll keep my word. Head down the path, and I'll catch up to you," he said.

Without a word, the two of them began backtracking down the structure. They were both quiet as they walked.

Soren turned to Buhus, who had opened his eyes to look at the prophet. "Worry not, Buhus-Vadu. They will undoubtedly rethink their decision, if they're the right ones," he said.

"There is no 'if,' dear Soren. I felt it deep within them. I just plead that it won't be too late by the time they realize their decision was a mistake," Buhus replied.

The prophet nodded his head. "Put your fears to rest. I won't allow this disease to fester far enough to kill you," he said.

The dragon closed his eyes and flexed his claws into the hillside as another bout of coughing fell over him. Buhus didn't reply after this, but extended his large wings before taking flight, ascending toward the clouds.

Soren closed his eyes and tightened his hold on the dagger in his hands. *Please let them be the ones,* he thought before reopening them and beginning to walk down the spiraling path to flat ground where Amaya and Rose awaited him. He glanced between their dismal faces. He decided not to prod them all too much, knowing it may simply agitate them. Instead, he gave a smile. "Brekka is this way. That's where we will be staying for the night," he said.

The girls noticed him suddenly and looked up at him, simply nodding their heads before he began leading the way toward the place of which he spoke. It was in the general direction of where they had come from.

"Why are we going back? Especially with the king of Lucus on his way," Amaya asked.

"They will probably let him know that you've escaped. The village would be the last place they would think to look for you since it's so small," Soren answered. "It's likely they will search the houses once they arrive, but we will have a safe place to hide."

It didn't take long to reach the village they had been imprisoned near. The houses were set up neatly along the path that ran through; all its citizens tucked away for the night, leaving it empty.

"What is this place called again?" Amaya asked the hooded man.

Soren turned his head to her as they ventured farther down the path and replied, "Brekka. This place has been around just about as long as Lucus."

This rather saddened her, reminding her that they had been sheltered from the world for so long and barely knew the land upon which they lived. "I see," Amaya replied. But just before the conversation could again fall silent, she asked, "where will we be staying?"

"With someone very dear to me. She helped me at a time when I didn't have a place to go. So there is no doubt in my mind that she will be willing to help again," Soren answered.

They approached the front door of a rather cozy-looking cabin. The outside was decorated with flowers which—judging by the dewdrops upon their leaves—had been freshly watered by the rain that had finally cleared. Outside the window beside the door was a flower bed with pansies growing inside. They were a small detail, but added to the welcoming feeling the place instilled inside of Rose.

She noticed to their right in the distance was a building made almost completely out of cobblestone, save for some metal bars that dappled the outside walls. One could only assume it was the prison inside the village. It looked so small compared to the hidden caverns she remembered traversing not an hour before.

Soren knocked gently on the oak door, and a woman even shorter than Rose opened it. She looked rather old, so her height could be excused by that alone.

The woman's wrinkled face lit up when she saw Soren standing before her and said, "Soren, my dear. What are you doing so far from Folkvangr?"

Soren flashed her a warm smile. "It's good to see you, Ms. Ayita. I'm here on some rather important business, and came across these two. They're very tired and hungry. You wouldn't mind letting them stay for a night, would you?" he asked.

Ms. Ayita smiled warmly at the prophet. "Of course, dear, I wouldn't mind at all. I'll get the spare room and some cots set up for you," she answered cheerfully before allowing the three of them into her abode.

Amaya cocked an eyebrow at how welcoming the woman had been, allowing two strangers into her home without question. Did she not consider the possibility of them possessing weapons? Of course, she didn't have any ill intent for this woman and wouldn't question her unmarred trust in them.

The old woman shuffled to another portion of the house, leaving them to let their eyes explore. "You can each help yourself to some rice, tea, and dumplings. I had made extra," she called out to them from the other room.

Soren led them to the kitchen table. "Sit, I'll get you both something to eat."

Rose smiled and thanked him, Amaya offering her own quiet thanks. The blonde girl thought it kind of him to get them each a plate of food and a cup of tea. He served it to them accordingly before spooning a small portion for himself. The girls ate enough to fill their small stomachs and left quite a bit on the plate, both of them seeming apologetic for it.

When Ms. Ayita came from the spare bedroom, she smiled at them. "I hope that you both enjoyed it. Your room is all set up for you," she said. Her wrinkled eyes then looked at the dark-haired prophet. "Soren, I set up an extra cot in there if you're at all interested in staying as well."

Soren nodded to her and returned the kind smile. "Thank you, Ms. Ayita, I'm indebted to you," he replied.

"Nonsense. You owe me nothing, boy," she answered.

"Thank you for the food, Ms. Ayita. I would have eaten more if I could. It was really good," Rose said, offering her own gesture of kindness.

"The same goes for me," Amaya said.

"You both are welcome any time. You should get some rest. You look like you haven't slept in ages," she scolded them playfully.

Rose smiled for having been shown the consideration and stood to her feet, as did Amaya. The two of them walked to the spare room from which they had seen Ms. Ayita emerge, and chose two cots beside one another.

Meanwhile, Soren stayed awake for just a bit longer to share words with the old woman while she cleaned up from the meal.

"Do you think they're the ones?" she asked him.

Soren nodded his head in response to this and said a simple yes, knowing she was busy tending to the dishes to see his gesture. "Buhus-Vadu sensed the power deep within them. Sleeping, perhaps, but still very much existent," he said.

"I have faith in you, Soren. You've never been wrong before," Ms. Ayita said.

"I do have one concern though. It was clear to me they were reluctant to accept this task, and after tonight, I'm unsure of where they will decide to go," Soren replied. "If we miss this opportunity, it could mean the end of the gods. They're growing sicker, Ms. Ayita, and my clarity of what to do is failing me," he said, his voice devoid of hope.

"Don't fret, Soren," she said and walked over to the man before brushing away the hood from his head to fully reveal his deep navy hair. "You've made mistakes in the past and I believe that the course your life is now taking is aiding you in atoning for those mistakes," she finished.

Soren looked down as anguish filled his topaz orbs. "Even if they do accept my proposal to save the gods, I haven't the slightest clue on where to begin," he replied.

"Might I suggest the Ice Sanctum in the kingdom of Lucus?" Ms. Ayita said to him. "It holds all the knowledge known to mankind. Perhaps there is an account of something similar to this taking place, and it may even hold a cure or a clue as to where to go next," she explained.

"I suppose it's worth a try, but it will be difficult, considering their situation. They're the two demigods that Lucus is after, you know," Soren said.

"Yes, my dear. But no one ever said such a task would be easy. Now, why don't you head to sleep? I assume you have some sort of traveling to do tomorrow, so you will want to be well-rested," Ms. Ayita said.

The dark-haired man smiled. Nodding, he pulled his hood back over his head upon standing to his feet then said, "thank you again for everything, Ms. Ayita. You're very kind."

Ms. Ayita smiled and replied, "You're welcome, dear, goodnight."

Thereupon, Soren headed into the bedroom where the two girls were mostly pretending that they had fallen asleep. When the prophet fell asleep on his cot, it was almost instinctive for the girls' eyes to flutter open when they were sure that he wouldn't hear their soft whispering.

Rose was the first to speak up when she whispered Amaya's name.

"Yeah?" Amaya responded.

"What are you thinking about?"

"You mean about this whole thing?" Amaya whispered back.

Her friend nodded back to her. "I'm starting to think about it more. What if we really are the only ones who can save the gods?" she asked.

"So what? What have they ever done for us?" Amaya replied almost bitterly.

Rose looked up toward the ceiling and sighed. "Still, I can't help but feel we should do something," she said.

"They can find a cure themselves," the redhead replied sharply.

There was no further dialogue between them after that, but Rose still lay awake for a while longer, her mind dwelling on the outcome of such negligence, were they to truly do nothing about the predicament.

* * *

When morning rose in the sky, Amaya and Rose began tidying the room they had stayed in. Soren was in the other room talking to Ms. Ayita while they did this, and within mere minutes the girls were heading toward the exit.

"Girls, please do stay for breakfast," the old woman called to them before they had a chance to set foot outside the door.

Soren had still been contemplating what he could say to convince them to reconsider helping him.

Not being in too much of a hurry to leave, they decided to stay, and quietly ate the food she served them. The silence between them was rather awkward. Neither Amaya nor Rose dared to speak a word.

It wasn't silent for long, because soon Soren spoke up. "Are you sure there is nothing I can do to convince you to help?"

Rose's kind heart wanted to try, but Amaya spoke up for both of them, with her own reasons driving her response. "I'm sorry, but no. We have made up our minds," she said.

Soren fell quiet after that. He could only hope and pray to himself that something might avert their decision. But some of that hope began to die as he watched their feet step out of the door after finishing their food and saying their goodbyes.

5: BLOODLINE

"NOTES ON NATURE'S PARAGON"
EXCERPT FROM PAGE 58

She was a special breed of human. One like no other.

Some folks say that she had been isolated in her youth and grew to learn the pain of humanity at a young age. But through that pain, she found growth and learned self-sufficiency.

In a culture surrounded by people who believed the gods would bring about each of their desires, Elise was different. She was convinced that humans could be self-sufficient, as she had been. She was the second queen of Lucus and ruled alongside a man who didn't share her beliefs.

King Altus believed in the gods, as did many of her subjects. Around her, she noticed a pattern. It felt like "sheep upon an endless flourishing pasture," she wrote in one of her journals. Her subjects didn't witness enough suffering, she thought, because the gods had always been there to protect them in each of their endeavors.

At the time, it had only been around twenty years since the passing of our ancestors Noctis and Avius, who had bestowed the powers—which had been granted to them by the gods—upon five people, which would thenceforth continue within their bloodline until it ended, where then a new generation of demigods would be reincarnated. They were the only ones with the power to break this deadly cycle.

However, Queen Elise refused ever to use those powers, even if it meant her life. She wouldn't progress upon the leash slung around her neck by the gods who so desperately tried to tug her back into their control.

After her dethroning, Elise held a vendetta against the demigods within the kingdom and sought to rid the world of them, which she did after she and some of her followers went through with a coup d'etat of the royal military.

They were exiled from Lucus, and thus set out on a journey, seeking the power that exceeded what was believed to be human potential—and they found it. They discovered it residing deep within the very fiber of every human being. They called it "evolution." The ability for humans to adapt over time to any circumstance, where the weak die out and the strong survive.

After that journey, Elise began her journals, which are now kept by the leader of Nature's Paragon. "Aessatia needs a cleanse" (Journal 1, Pg. 23), she wrote. "There are far too many humans relying on the power of those fictional animals residing in those little sanctums scattered about. They're unable to comprehend the true capabilities of the human body. It's capable of healing without the use of the herbs growing from the earth or the healing of the gods. I wish they would all open their eyes so they could see how being complacent caused them to submit themselves fully to those who have made them lazy."

Alas, her reign ended, and so, too, did the era of peace from the demigods she had brought an end to. Time gave rise to reincarnation, and they returned—still Aessatians beneath the spell of false glory, and each time praising them. For what did they deserve that praise? They hadn't worked hard to attain those powers. They may use them for good, but a birthright is nothing to celebrate. Even the very ones who created this bloodline relied on power beyond what they were given from birth.

They were weak—and thus our work has surrounded the redemption of humanity.

END OF EXCERPT

* * *

Nineteen years ago

Sage looked up toward a sea of stars as she walked along the stone pathways. She could feel a soft breeze on her skin and even caught a whiff of the marketplace smells and heard the faint murmurs of citizens as they milled about in the second district of the kingdom.

She always found the nebula of lights to be a work of art every night. It distracted her from the troubles of the day droning on behind her, whispering chest-tightening doubts into her ear.

Suddenly a man shoved his way against her, nearly toppling her to the ground. "Gh! S-Sorry," she apologized quickly to the unfamiliar face, even though the incident hadn't been her fault.

"Hey! Watch where you're going next time, why don't you?" the man said. His breath reeked of alcohol. He was clearly drunk. "Huh...aren't you one of those half-breeds?" he asked almost to himself as he pulled Sage dangerously close.

He tugged on her hair, squeezing a yelp from her throat. With fear in her grey eyes, she raised her hands in front of her face in defense. "P-Please don't hurt me, I hadn't meant to be in your way, sir," she pleaded.

The drunk pulled a scowl and shoved the girl off to the side, where she then fell to the ground with a grunt, scraping her arms on the cobblestone pathway. Sage took a moment to calm herself from the encounter, watching the man walk away out of the corner of her eye. She wiped her hands together to brush off the dirt that had gotten onto her now-raw skin.

Her eyes darted to the side as she noticed something she hadn't seen at first: a pair of shoes standing beside her.

"You're really going to treat a lady like that?" the voice belonging to the pair of shoes called after the drunk.

Looking up, she saw that the man who had said this donned a pristine white cloak. She recognized his accent to be Folkvangrian. The drunk turned to him with the same scowl on his face as when he had left Sage. He stumbled toward them again and the hooded man stood firm, staring back at him challengingly.

"And what are you supposed to be, some knight in shining armor? A lady's man? You belong in the third district with all your rich friends. 'Sides, this isn't a lady; she's a monster," the drunk growled at him.

"She didn't ask to be born into such a horrid bloodline, now did she? It would be people like you who would turn her into a monster."

While the two argued with one another, Sage took the opportunity to slowly back away from the two, crawling on her hands and knees.

"See? She's running away without even thanking you," the drunken man said as he began to trek toward Sage. However, the man who had stepped in to defend her drew a sword.

"I'm going to have to ask you to step away, sir. You're in my personal space," the man in the white cloak said.

"Bastard…" spat the drunk as he gave one last spiteful look toward Sage before walking away.

The man in the white hood turned toward Sage, stopping her before she could get very far. "I'm sorry you have to go through things like that. It's not your fault you've got such inhuman blood running through your veins," he said.

Sage only nodded silently, doing her best to avoid eye contact with the man. "Not much of a talker, hmm?" the man asked. "Say…are you tired of being pushed around like that?"

Sage figured that had to be a given and wondered why the man would ask such a question with an obvious answer. Unless, of course, he had something else to say after that.

"See, I'm part of a little group called Nature's Paragon. I think we may be able to help you," he said, despite the girl's silence.

She remained quiet, which caused the man to chuckle to ward off the awkwardness.

"If you're interested, you can meet me in the main courtyard by the fountain two days from now, understand?"

The man received another nod from Sage, and that was all she saw of him. Then, just as soon as he had shown up, the man was gone.

Who could blame a young girl—especially one existing within a minority—for taking up the man's offer? As was agreed, she met the man two days from that night by the fountain in the courtyard. She never saw her father; her home; the outside again after that day.

This man she met lured her away to the lair of his cult. She spent four years imprisoned where she was injected with strange things and was experimented on. But no amount of tests or modifications could take away the curse she was born with.

However, she developed a sort of Stockholm Syndrome for the man who had captured her. He always assured her that she would be cured soon. The cell she was kept inside held no windows or doors so there wasn't a shred of light. She knew not how long she had been kept in those walls. But one day the man told her they were going to perform something on her that he was sure would work, a statement he often said—and Sage always fell for it.

The faceless members of the cult tied her up like a hog on a wooden stake. Below her, she could see them spilling ashes of some sort, likely gun powder. They told her that it was a sacrifice to the gods, that it would strip away her powers and leave her with a mortal body. But deep down, Sage knew she was going to be burned alive.

But she couldn't fight it. It made her feel that perhaps at last she really would be free of the burdens of being a demigod placed upon her back. She could only look upward at the night sky as she heard them preparing to burn her. That sea of stars made her smile—something she had been unable to do for a very long time.

Suddenly, she saw a flash out of the corner of her eye that hadn't been the twinkling of a star within the thick band of them above her.

Sage's head lowered to see where such a phenomenon could have originated. When she looked down, she saw fire—lots of fire. Flames swayed, eating up the grass, cinders flying, lighting up the darkness very briefly before dying away, the wind carrying away the ashes left behind, never to be seen again.

She saw two figures dashing around the cult members, fire flashing before her eyes at times, creating a glow off her skin while at others, she could see the glittering of what sounded like water sloshing through the air, soaking its opponent. Suddenly, the rope tying her down to the stake was set ablaze, causing her to gasp. She began to thrash as she saw it eating away at the rope and inching closer to her skin. Yet, after the fire had consumed the rope, she felt water splash onto her as she began to fall. She hit the wet earth below her, trying to catch her breath from panicking.

She heard that fire swallow up the air again with a roar. It was close and caused her to quickly lift her head from the ground. She could see a half-lit face above her, the eyes a deep crimson surrounded by blackness where white should have been. From the light produced by the flame, she could also see his hand held out. His features were carved into some kind of scowl, but it didn't seem like it was meant for her. Somehow, she saw heroism in those eyes, even kindness.

"Get up," his deep voice ordered her.

She was unsure of what was happening. All she knew was that there was a chance to be free. Her pale hand reached up toward the man's, which then pulled her to her feet. But it didn't let go after that; instead, he pulled her along, away from the site as screams of "get them!" echoed around her through the darkness.

Sage panted once more as they ran through the woods, eventually stopping at a safe distance. The fire that had once been in the man's hand had returned, it had gone out while they were running so as not to leave a trail. Looking over, she could see another shadow, which she presumed to be the one who had been using the water beforehand. Sage knew she heard another pair of footsteps beside them, but she had been too shaken to look over.

"You both...you saved me," she said breathlessly.

"We couldn't abandon one of our own, could we?" the redhead asked her.

"That would be a bad tactical move on our part," the other darkened figure said.

"What are your names?" Sage asked.

"I'm Ruki, and he's Chasaka," the man replied.

Sage looked between the two of them before releasing a laugh, which was out of character for her. "S-Sorry...I just wish I could see who 'Ruki' was," she said.

She could hear the other scoff before grabbing Chasaka's arm and pulling it toward himself. Now she could see that he had blue eyes and blue hair with a lighter complexion than the one beside him.

"How did you both find me?" she asked them.

"Coincidence," Ruki answered simply in response. Though it did sound a bit sarcastic. "But never mind that, let's get out of here before those guys catch up to us."

Eventually, Sage was led back to Barness, the home she never thought she would see again, and into a house after following some back streets.

Once there, they met with a fourth demigod where Sage was pushed to explain her situation and how she had been persuaded to fall for such a trick. But then she said something that made each of the other demigods perk their heads.

"It was terrible, but I won't lie. I think I believe some of the things they talked about...maybe Aessatia really does need a cleanse."

* * *

A void filled the hearts of the two young girls upon leaving that village. Though what they had been through may have been memories any normal person would want to forget, Rose and Amaya couldn't help but long for more adventure. Not only that, but now that they knew they were demigods, the thoughts of their choice—or rather, Amaya's choice—wouldn't leave their minds. But neither could speak of it. However, it was painfully obvious they were thinking about it.

Rose's eyes would linger upon each tree that looked even slightly dead as they passed it, her mind taking heavy note of the fact that she couldn't find any budding flowers anywhere.

"Are you sure we should have left?" the blonde asked, letting her thoughts get the best of her.

They had only been but a few minutes out from Brekka, wandering the lands aimlessly, and already Rose couldn't help but bring up the looming burden swirling around them.

"Yes. We had to assert ourselves. Just because some prophecy says it, doesn't mean we have to be the ones to fix this whole thing, if it even has any credibility anyway," Amaya answered her.

"But...this is the fate of Aessatia we're talking about. What if it really is right? Then what?" the other pressed.

"Then we die."

Amaya could hear her friend's footsteps cease from pressing into the dirt path they had been following, which made her turn to look at her. What she found were eyes staring at her in astonishment. The two shared gazes with one another, one indifferent, while the other held worry within it.

"What?" Amaya spoke to break the uncomfortable silence.

"Are you okay with that? Just accepting death?" the other asked in return. "Not only of yourself but of everybody else?" She paused for a moment to wait for an answer that was never to come. "That isn't the Amaya I grew up with...you've always helped me with everything; you've always been there for me," Rose said.

"This is no fool's task! The *world* is at stake, Rose! I'm not ready to stick my neck out for something like this!" her red-haired friend finally argued with her.

"And yet you choose to ignore it. What have we got to lose? We're wanted and probably dead anyway if we don't try!" Rose shot back at her.

"Well, nobody ever said we had to stick together."

Rose's expression filled with bafflement once more. She couldn't understand why Amaya was lashing out so uncharacteristically. But it angered her, so her shock contorted to hooded eyes of betrayal and anger. "Well, if that's how it's going to be..." the blonde trailed off. She turned on her heel and began walking back in the direction she came. "I'm going back to Brekka."

Amaya felt a woozy feeling hit her stomach as she watched her friend turn her back on her and start to walk away. Throughout their days, the two had never really been separated like this. But maybe it was for the best if they split up. *We're both adults, we can handle ourselves,* Amaya rationed with herself.

While Rose walked along, she, too, had that uncomfortable feeling within her stomach and even considered turning back, or at least hoped her friend would do the same. But as the minutes passed, she realized that neither of those things were happening. No distance seemed safe enough to turn her head, for she feared seeing that her friend was no longer following in her tow would make her want to turn back. Just as she had suspected, upon turning her head to look back, she saw that there was nobody behind her.

When she came in sight of the gates of Brekka, she noticed a group of horses trotting in neat lines with gilded passengers on their backs. In the front sat one individual who stood out from the rest. He wore white robes lined with silver, upon which sat a fur mantle to shield him from the breeze. At his side was the scabbard containing the royal family's sword, not that she could recognize it of course, but she would never forget the armor on each of their bodies. She recalled from her days of youth that her parents had donned the same armor as well as those who patrolled the streets of the third district where her house had been stationed. Her memories from that time may have been faint, but she could remember those few distinct details.

Within those few moments it took for her to identify these horsemen, she could deduce that they were Lucian guards who were looking for her and Amaya. She watched the horses file in through the front gate of the village and then stayed a safe distance behind them, hiding in the trees surrounding Brekka until she could reach Ms. Ayita's home, hoping that the prophet she had met days before would still be there. Unfortunately, the group of men on horses had stopped just slightly before her destination, so there was a good chance someone could see her if she tried to walk inside. However, each of the guards were preoccupied with whomever they were speaking to, most likely one of the higher ups from the prison.

Rose pulled the hood of her clothing up over her head and began to carefully venture out toward the house, hoping she wouldn't be noticed. She didn't hear any sort of urgent yelling, so she assumed that she was safe. She had been so worried about being caught, however, that Rose had forgotten to knock on the door and barged right into the house. When she did, Ms. Ayita gasped at seeing her.

"Oh my, dear! Don't come in so suddenly like that, you scared me nearly to death," the older woman said.

This reaction shocked Rose as well, not registering for a moment what she had done. "Oh, I'm sorry, I didn't mean to; there were guards out there so I rushed in, I guess," she said.

After having gotten over the initial shock of her walking in, Ms. Ayita became more concerned with why exactly she had come back. "Well, did you forget something?" she asked.

"Is Soren still here?" Rose asked in response.

She nodded her head before walking toward the threshold of the hallway in her house. "Soren, dear, one of the girls is back here looking for you!" she called to him.

Moments later the hooded prophet emerged from the hallway. He was a bit confused to see the blonde girl standing there without Amaya beside her. "You again? Where is the other one?" he asked.

"Ah, it's Rose," she answered. "And her name is Amaya. I'm sorry, we were never properly introduced."

Soren furrowed his eyebrows a bit, no answer leaving him. He was curious as to why she would be introducing herself.

"I—" Rose had been about to speak until a knock was heard at the door. Panic set in like a live wire. "There are Lucian guards here, we have to hide," she said quickly.

"Oh, go on and hide in the cellar then, you two. I'll stall them," Ms. Ayita said after hearing her speak.

The prophet's golden eyes got wide at this. "Come, this way," Soren replied as he pulled her down the hallway from which he had first emerged. He led her swiftly down a stairway and into the cellar. Above them was a vent that Rose took quick notice of, since it allowed the sound of the door to travel to her current standpoint.

"Hello there, young man. May I help you?" Ms. Ayita asked the visitor.

The voice that was heard after the question brought a familiar air with it, at least to Rose. She couldn't see the face, but she could almost immediately deduce who it belonged to.

"Hello, I was wondering if there was a girl who had entered your home," the man said.

"I apologize, you must be mistaken, I live here alone," the older woman replied.

Rose began to panic for a moment, her mind going to war with itself as she was faced with the dilemma of whether or not to chase that voice or hide from it.

"Are you sure? I'm certain I saw her run here. I don't mean her any harm. I just want to talk to her."

Rose broke from Soren's side and made a break for the cellar's stairs. By the time the man noticed, she was already halfway up. "Rose, where are you going?" he whispered with urgency.

But Rose didn't stop, she continued up the stairs until at last she could be seen by the man at the door. His mouth was agape once he laid eyes on her.

"Rose, dear, what are you doing?" Ms. Ayita asked, unaware of the situation. As far as she knew, she was supposed to be hiding her from this man.

Upon hearing the name exit the old woman's lips, tears came to the soldier's eyes behind his helmet. "Rose, is that truly you? Look at how much you've grown..." he said.

Rose could see the unmistakable tendrils of red hair peeking from beneath the soldier's helmet. He ran into the house and embraced the young woman, regardless of the fact that he had just broken in.

Rose had never seen the man's face before, but that made his voice that much more distinguishable from any other. Now she knew for sure that the man she was hugging was Amaya's uncle, Kye.

"Kye..." was all she could manage to say before her own tears began to pour down her cheeks. The man had been like a second father figure to her, from what she could remember of him. He had been the one who led her and Amaya out to that barren wasteland. "A-Are you not going to turn me in? Is that not why you're here?" she stammered through her occasional sobbing.

Kye pulled away from Rose before removing his helmet and letting it drop to the floor. She was slightly shocked to see that beneath it was a half-scarred face coupled with a gentle pair of umber eyes that held a striking resemblance to Amaya's.

"I take it you must know this man?" the old woman asked from behind them as she closed the door to the house.

"This is Amaya's uncle," Rose answered.

Kye shook his head in reply to her initial question. "I'm not going to turn you in. And I'm very glad to see that you're alive and well," he said. "Where is Amaya? Isn't she with you?" he asked, looking around as if to see his niece.

Rose looked off to the side where Soren was now entering the room, trying to formulate her answer.

"Why don't you all sit? I'll fix some tea," Ms. Ayita said as she hobbled her way into the kitchen.

"Amaya and I were together, but we split up—it's a long story," Rose said as she sat down at the table.

"The two of you split up? Why?" Soren asked as he, too, made his way over.

"I came back because I would like to try and help you. She and I weren't seeing eye-to-eye so she suggested that we split up," Rose explained.

At hearing this, Soren felt a bit downtrodden, but still held hope that at least one of the two demigods was interested in helping in the midst of the crisis. "I see..." he trailed off.

"I see you've met Soren," Kye cut in.

"You know him?" Rose asked, turning her head to the soldier.

He nodded in response. "I met him not long after I brought you and Amaya to Tochfuyu. He was working as a traveling medic to the different villages and kingdoms. Small world, isn't it?"

"Yes..." Rose said. There was a long pause in the air, with only the sound of the whistling kettle breaking the silence. "About that...we've been wondering for a long time; why were we forced to live there? What happened to our parents? Did they abandon us?"

Kye parted his lips and inhaled deeply as he looked down at his folded hands on the table. After looking up, he and Soren shared a glance with one another before his eyes returned to Rose. "Listen, I can't stay here long, or the others will get suspicious of me. However, since the king believes that the two of you escaped from Brekka's stronghold, I'll be heading out for the Empire of Folkvangr. I'll wait for you there—and I promise I'll explain everything to you then," he said.

Rose felt a strange mix of both disappointment and hope surge through her. "Okay."

Kye excused himself from the table, taking his helmet into his arms where he then placed it over his head again. Before he left the house, he turned back to Rose and asked, "if you come across Amaya again, could you please tell her that I miss her dearly?"

The blonde froze before giving him a warm smile. "I'll make a note of it," she replied.

With that, the soldier left the house.

Ms. Ayita returned not long after with three steaming cups of tea. "I take it the soldier left?" she asked.

"Yes," Rose answered as she took a teacup.

"I suppose this one will be for me then," Ms. Ayita said, referring to the third cup.

Soren turned his head to look at Rose after taking a sip of his tea. "So you're serious about wanting to help find a cure for the gods then?" he asked.

The young woman nodded in response. "Someone has to. Besides, I'm wanted to be thrown into prison and I don't have a home, so there is no reason why I couldn't at least try," she said.

"I plan to head to Barness from here. The Ice Sanctum is a repository, so I was hoping that we might find some kind of medical cure, or anything that might point us in the right direction regarding what caused this," Soren explained. He could see the immediate discomfort in both Rose's body language and her facial expression. "I know what you're thinking. But I'm sure we will find a way to convince the king to let you enter," he added.

Rose shook her head. "It's not just that, I want to meet up with Kye again. I need to find out what happened to our parents. I need to know why Amaya and I were sent away to Tochfuyu," she said.

"Yes, I understand that, but—" Before Soren could finish his statement, he felt the ground rumble. Looking into his cup of tea, he could see ripples coming off its surface. He grunted before grasping his head with both hands. His once-serious face twisted to reflect the excruciating pain.

Ms. Ayita gasped as she was knocked from the chair she was sitting in by the shockwave. She grunted and cried out, her hand reaching toward her hip.

"An earthquake?" Rose yelled over the sound of the rumbling.

Soren got out of his seat, doing his best to shake away the pain in order to help Ms. Ayita from her fallen position. Tears were coming from her dried-up face. "They've never been this strong before," he muttered to himself. "Are you all right, Ms. Ayita?" he asked her.

The old woman waved her hand at Soren as the shaking continued. "I'll be fine, you must go to soothe them, dear," she said.

The prophet's eyes lingered on the condition of the old woman's leg, tears stinging at them. "Rose, start heading to the forest where we met with Buhus-Vadu. I'll get her to a safe place," he said.

Rose nodded her head and started to run toward the door, minding the walls and fallen objects. Outside, she found people taking cover and running to try and get to their homes. Trees were being uprooted and the ground beneath their very feet was beginning to split open.

Her heart raced as she saw all the panic and heard the screaming. Whatever it was, she knew it must have had to do with the earth gods and it was that, coupled with the condition of all those sick people in the village of Dufmoore, which made her realize the severity of the situation at hand.

Carefully, she began making her way along the path through the forest. She could hear distant trees beginning to uproot, the sound like a large door slamming. She made sure to mind each tree she passed.

As she ran, she could see the ground of the forest begin to split apart in the distance, knocking over a few more trees. She noticed one of them had barged right into a thinner tree—which was now heading straight for her. Rose shrieked in fear and dropped to the ground, covering her head. There was no way she would be able to outrun it.

When the noise stopped, she could see that above her, the tree had just barely stopped from falling on top of her, having wedged itself between the ground and another, more sturdy-looking tree. But she didn't wait around to find out if it would stay. Instead, she scrambled to her feet and continued to run toward her destination.

6: Dragon's Blood

Thirty minutes had passed since Amaya had split up from Rose and the whole time regret coursed through her belly. She was beginning to worry about her friend. As much as she was opposed to the idea of them risking their lives for these gods, she knew that Rose being by herself for something so dangerous was bound to get her killed, even if Soren would be alongside her.

She tried not to give in and turn around, and she was even about to do so until she felt the ground beneath her feet become unstable. It felt like there was water below the surface of the earth. She stumbled, trying to keep her balance until the shaking grew more violent and forced her to the ground, crying out in pain as she felt the broken halves of her arm force against one another. Blood seeped into the bandages it was wrapped in.

Fear coursed through Amaya, her hands gripping tightly onto the dying grass as though she were trying to stop the quaking and the pain. But it didn't work, of course, and she was left lying on the ground, hoping that it would stop soon.

Across from her, Amaya could see a tree being ripped up from its roots and slowly topple over, a loud cracking sound accompanying it. The next sound orchestrated for her ears was one similar to this. Not too far from her, she could see the ground beginning to split open, as though it were a demon trying to swallow up the land in its wake.

Amaya started to panic as she saw the gaping gorge in the ground getting closer to her and even attempted to crawl away from it. Alas, it would prove to be futile as the crack eventually inched its way toward her, splitting wide apart and leaving her only with a patch of dead grass to hold onto. She screamed as this realization smacked her in the face. She couldn't pull herself up with strength alone and was left to hang there, her broken bones now stretching and morphing incorrectly, the stress of falling into the abyss of blackness weighing heavier on her minimal strength with each second.

"Help! Someone, please help me!" she screamed, hoping someone would come along to save her. Fear overcame her though as she began to process that there couldn't possibly be anyone walking out in the middle of an earthquake—and it was becoming increasingly more difficult to hold on.

Amaya started to cry as the fear of death overwhelmed her. She started to repent for all of the things she had ever done wrong, mentally cursing herself for having split up with her best friend, pleading that Rose wouldn't meet the same fate. She thought about Lucus, her parents, and her uncle, and wished that she could have spent more time with them. She wished most of her life hadn't been wasted away in Tochfuyu.

All of this happened within seconds, her dull life seeming to flash so quickly before her eyes that she wasn't even sure if it had happened or not. It disoriented her more than the ceaseless shaking ever could.

All of a sudden, Amaya felt something sharp dig straight into her arm, causing her to scream out in pain. When she looked up, she nearly passed out when she locked eyes with a huge lion. Since her arm was within its maw, she could feel it growling since she couldn't hear over the sound of the cracking earth, the toppling trees, and the ringing in her ears. By now, she was almost certain that she was going to die—if not by falling, then by the jaws of this beast.

But the lion wasn't trying to eat her, it was starting to pull her, making it feel much easier to climb out, even if the pain was unbearable. Perhaps it was a farfetched thought since her adrenaline was pumping so hard that it was making her think outrageously, but it almost seemed like this green-eyed beast was trying to help her.

At any rate, she wasn't going to fight against it. Amaya worked with the beast, and with both of their strengths combined, the young woman was, at last, able to climb out from the crevice.

"Are you all right?" the lion asked her.

Yes, the lion had spoken to her and it took Amaya a moment to fully comprehend this, but when she did, she deduced that this must have been a god she was speaking to. There were a pair of swords atop his back, held in place by leather straps.

"Y-Yes, I'm all right," she answered in spite of the fact that her arm was still on fire from the pain delivered by the animal's teeth.

"Get on my back if you want to live," the lion growled in an almost-threatening tone.

Too scared to argue, Amaya did as he asked, climbing atop the back of the proud creature, holding onto his shaggy mane so she wouldn't fall as he bounded along with the shaking earth. His movements were so swift that it didn't seem like he was running at all—more like flying.

She was still disoriented by all that was happening, but Amaya could piece together that they were heading back toward Brekka.

It didn't take them long to reach that familiar forest just outside the village, which the lion leaped straight through. This was rather nerve-racking since the redhead could already see that some trees had uprooted. One of them could have fallen on them. But they were going so fast that it was the least of their worries.

The lion leaped atop multiple felled trees along the way, and as they approached the horizon, they could see dust and debris flying everywhere from the hilltop Amaya had once visited. The friendly twin dragon gods that Amaya and Rose had met only a day ago were now tearing into one another.

Large teeth bore into the reptile's bodies past their armor and pared the flesh, spilling purple blood and fragments of scales over the plateau like an overfilled cup. The once-clear water below was now stained cerulean, dotted with white scales, while his brother chomped at the base of his wing.

Not only did Amaya bear witness to such violence, but off to the side, she could see Rose standing there watching, mouth agape too. "Rose!" The redhead didn't hesitate to call for her friend, quickly dismounting the lion to run over to her.

"Amaya! What are you doing here? Is that a lion?" she yelled over the roaring and shaking.

"There is no time for that, do you know what the Hell is going on?" Amaya shouted back at her.

"I don't know. Soren said he would be here soon. I'm sure he will know what to do!" Rose replied.

The young women watched in awe as the deep purple wyrm wasn't only attacked by his brother but was also battling against him. Their faces were distorted by the dust cloud created by their quarrel, but when the eldest of the two, Buhus, bellowed a roar, the soundwaves ripped through, causing it to clear. This allowed them to see that the flesh of their faces appeared to have been torn off, revealing bare skulls with a coating of thick purple muck.

The dragon's eyes that were once gentle were now beat red with rage.

"I'm not sure what happened to them, but they started attacking one another out of nowhere," the lion told them after bounding over.

"What do you want us to do?" Amaya asked him quickly.

"I can't hurt them, but they will kill each other if they aren't separated soon," the animal replied.

Rose's eyes got wide. But before she could open her lips to speak, a huge boulder landed right in front of them, causing them each to start.

The proud animal leaped onto the fallen rock and roared at the brawling siblings. "Stop it, you two!"

This brought their attention toward the lion. His lips drew back to show his teeth, and both dragons snarled back at him. The white dragon took flight while the other set off on land to chase after the beast, which was smaller than them by far.

Rose closed her eyes in fear for what would become of the poor animal, while all Amaya could do was stare in shock. *Please don't let him die!* Rose thought. The fire that the blonde had expected to come from the dragon's mouth and scorch the lion had, in fact, come from the lion to drive back the pursuing twins.

Suddenly dark fabric distorted their view. It was the cloak that they recognized Soren to have worn when they met. "Thosus! Look out!" he called to the lion.

At the moment he had let his guard down to look back, a crack in the earth had begun inching its way toward him until it finally split open to reveal lava below, nearly singeing the lion's fur before he leaped onto a tree to the side of the rock, which was quickly swallowed by the earth.

Soren held out his arm and gripped it with his free hand. This bound the two dragons with one another and put a stop to all the violent shaking.

Rose and Amaya could only stand there with shocked expressions as this wonder appeared before them. They stared at the panting Soren. His hood had flown off at some point and now a birthmark was visible on his forehead in the shape of a star, uncovered now that his bangs were frazzled.

Thosus' green eyes gaped as they stared at the mark. The cursed mark of the Astral Clan that had committed a heinous genocide long before the demons of the tower had attacked—the same clan that he was sure had died out. Yet, here this man was before him. Not even the gurgling growls of the bound dragons behind him could take his eyes away from that one mark. In retrospect, the mark had held no significant meaning, but to him it was a disgrace.

When Soren felt those burning feline eyes upon him—more specifically on his forehead—he pulled his hood back up to cover up. He cleared his throat in a vain attempt to ward off the brief silence that followed. "What happened?" he asked.

Thosus didn't answer him, only narrowed his eyes, creases forming across his masculine feline face. His tan fur bunched along lines that had been formed from years and years of stress. The lion felt betrayed. He knew this man well, but never knew of this mark he bore. His maw nearly parted to speak to him, to question him about the mark and to then take out his rage upon him. But alas, Amaya had spoken before him to answer the question, turning the prophet's attention toward her.

"They were fighting, isn't it obvious?" she asked.

"Could this have to do with the sickness?" Rose asked as she turned to Thosus.

The lion's ears, which poked out from his broad mane, perked up as the girl spoke to him. "Plausible," he replied. Really, he had wanted to say more, but his urgency to answer had caused him to respond only with the single word. Again, he tried to speak, but was this time cut off by the prophet.

"Do you not see now that your aid in this is important?" Soren asked the two girls.

"So they were fighting, don't all brothers?" Amaya asked defensively.

Soren's eyes narrowed and it was then that his patience had run thin. "I didn't risk my life, nor did I take precious time that could have been better spent finding a cure for them, just to see that you're nothing but a selfish brat who hasn't been taught the values of life and its importance!" he snapped at her. "Your blood is special and it, surer than Hell, holds a power that's foretold to save the gods, the ones who protect this land—the same land upon which your feet rest! Perhaps they couldn't prevent whatever strife makes you so reluctant, but they make this land called Aessatia a place to live! That power put into rage as you just saw would devastate a metaphysical balance and ultimately destroy the world," he continued.

Lava ran through his veins. But as if water had cooled it to obsidian, the angry creases in his features calmed and turned to a deadpan. This was caused by the swords that suddenly appeared between the three of them. His neck was encapsulated between two blades, making any maneuver ludicrous. Soren stared off to the side at the man who stood in place of the lion, his eyebrows raised over his icy green eyes curtained by burnt locks.

The blades' cold edges gently kissed the prophet's neck. Visibly, he stiffened. The swords were white steel, beautiful and glimmering, its base filigreed with gold.

Rose gasped at the sudden action and began to imagine Soren's blood slowly gushing down its grooves. The lion was no longer there, so she was left to assume that he was now the stoic man before her. He was clad in a fine, gold-laced mantle patterned with deep red.

"You shouldn't shout at them." Thosus' green eyes flecked with gold stayed on him while his lips pressed together. "However dire they may be to the prophecy, they can't be forced. It isn't their duty to protect the gods, nor is it your own to make them feel as such!" he growled.

Messenger of the gods or not, the prophet was human. Sword would still pierce his flesh and loss of blood would still bring his life to an end. Soren's body trembled visibly. Amaya saw the fear in his eyes and could almost feel how cold his blood ran. "Thosus, don't hurt him!" she yelled.

The man chuckled, his laugh warm like a fire crackling in its pit, the swords hissing as they re-entered the scabbards which were now at his side. "It was merely an empty threat," he responded.

All at once, the other three let loose a tentative breath that once begged to be released as relief washed through them.

"I apologize," Soren said once his heart had finally finished the marathon it was running inside his chest cavity. "The gods are very important to me and so...I ask that you respect my urgency toward the issue at hand and accept my apology for my words and actions," he said.

"Yes, but you're right," Amaya said. Her eyes shifted toward the ground as shame washed through her. Hearing that she had been selfish upset her. Her long red hair slipped over her face as she lowered her head. "Understand that my life hasn't been handed to me on a silver platter thus far," she began. "It's hard to throw my struggles away so quickly. Even after all of this, I'm still reluctant. It will be dangerous, and I'm still young yet. Furthermore, we've never been faced with an ordeal like this before and are really quite inept as for what to do or how we fit into this elaborate painting," she said as her head lifted to lock eyes with the prophet.

"But know that if you don't help, there may not be a painting for you to fit into," Soren replied.

Rose bit her lip and looked to her friend. "We have to do something, Amaya. I can't bring myself to ignore this. We have to try."

Again, Amaya lowered her eyes, focusing on the blades of grass in front of her before lifting them past the men to look at the struggling dragons that had been bound together inside a red-hued magic. Their occasional growls and roars as they fought against their binds had narrated the scene for the past few minutes.

She studied the eyes of the mythical reptiles; red and still very much filled with hatred, they stared with intent. This intent was deep. Never had she felt something so dreadful, like their eyes would lash out and devour her. She felt vile; invaded; tainted; violated. Those eyes held only one thing: *bloodthirstiness.*

She studied the dragon's flesh as it peeled away from their muscles and vanished into thin air, and shivered slightly as she pictured how much pain they were in but with no way to express it. It seemed that all the beasts could do was kill. It was pitiful and she thought, *Can we really fix this? We're just a couple of girls, neanderthals, had we not known any better.*

Finally, she took a deep breath and brought herself back to reality as she collected her thoughts. "I'll help," she said.

Again, relief and a bit of happiness washed over Soren. "My debt is to you. I'll protect you both with my life," he said as his hand reached across his chest to bow. When he rose again, he looked at the girls. "We will be heading for the Ice Sanctum, its knowledge has been around the longest, so I believe we might find some sort of cure within the scrolls containing medicinal practices," he explained.

At the mention of this place, Thosus grimaced. "I'll travel with you as far as Folkvangr. From there, you will be on your own," he said.

"So then we will be heading there after all?" Rose asked with a surge of hope.

"Yes, it falls upon the quickest path to Lucus," Soren replied.

"Wait, Folkvangr? Isn't that another big kingdom? What if we get taken in again?" Amaya asked.

"It's an empire. As long as the two of you are with me, you will be honored as special guests of Folkvangr," Thosus replied.

"And what about Lucus? We would definitely be recognized there," Amaya asked.

"Don't worry. I told you that I would protect you, didn't I? I plan to hold true to my word," the prophet replied.

After that, Rose's eyes shifted back toward the two dragons. "Will Buhus and Vadu be all right being bound that way? I mean, they can't escape, right?" Rose asked him.

"The seal will hold only as long as the magic is stronger than what is being kept inside. This should enable us some time, but not too much, I fear," Soren answered.

Amaya lifted her head. "Then we will leave now," she said.

After gathering their wits, Soren, Rose, Amaya, and the god of fire, Thosus, had set out toward their next destination. Along the way, Rose began to speak to Amaya.

"When I went back to Brekka to find Soren, there were Lucian guards out looking for us," Rose began. "I wasn't caught, but one of them saw me," she said.

Amaya looked over toward her friend. "What? So they know we're close? What if they find us?" she asked as worry and even a hint of anger began to fill her. But Rose shook her head.

"It was your uncle."

Amaya's jaw dropped after hearing this. She wasn't sure how to feel about that bit of information and glanced off to the side. "He's the one who took us to that wretched land, why is that so significant...?" she asked grimly.

"Because he's on our side. He told me that he would be waiting in Folkvangr for me so he could tell me what happened," Rose explained.

"What? What if it's a trap then! Why do you not think these things through?" Amaya yelled at her.

Then she felt a hand on her shoulder, causing her to look at who it belonged to. Soren was looking back at her. "It's not a trap, I can assure you of that," he said. "I've known Kye for many years, and I can tell you that when he met me, he was very distraught about having to abandon the both of you."

After connecting a few dots, Rose's own head turned to look at the prophet. "Wait, does that mean you know what happened all that time ago? Why did you not tell me?" she asked.

After a long pause the hooded man replied, "I think it would be better said by someone closer to you than by me."

His answer caused a bit of angst to build up in both Rose and Amaya. They were so close to uncovering the enigma that was their past and the whole reason they had been brought to the present, and yet this man was keeping it from them. It was frustrating, but his words carried with them a heavy weight. One look shared between the two young women helped them decide to refrain from pressing the subject; they would rather hear it from Kye than Soren. But it did increase their determination to reach their destination.

As the sun walked its path across the sky, the four of them found themselves in a forest of white dogwood trees. The frost-colored leaves glimmered in the setting sun as they rained down from the treetops. The forest stretched for miles with only the steps of past travelers to guide them through. The forest canopy was just thin enough to allow heavenly beams of light to shine through, bathing the trees in their rays.

Some of the trees had been pushed straight from their stumps as though they were snapped like twigs, leaving them felled or just barely clinging to their stumps.

But the travelers had a hard time appreciating the beauty of this place, the pain in their feet and the emptiness in their bellies took precedence. But none would openly complain. Soren had been their savior. He knew that they ached and their stomachs begged to be filled, so he suggested that they stop for the night.

"The Silver Timberlands are no place to be resting for the night. There is much nocturnal fauna that would feed on human flesh if given the chance," Thosus replied.

"At least allow us the liberty of resting for a short while. We're hungry," Rose replied.

Thosus scanned the skies before nodding his head, though reluctant. "We have until the sun dips below the horizon," he compromised.

"I'll search for something to eat," Amaya said as the other two rested atop a worn felled tree. It grew moss and mushrooms from its old trunk, and the occasional vine crawled across it.

"I'll follow you," Thosus replied. "This place holds many dangers, even what it reaps can be deceiving," he said.

And so they set off into the thicker portion of the forest that wasn't guided by a path. They searched around logs and in the brush for any edible berries or mushrooms, or even some small animals. They had spent quite a while searching with hardly anything to show for it, but it was just enough to get them by.

A chilling breeze caused the branches of the dogwood trees to shiver. But this gust felt different, at least to Thosus. His head craned toward the red sky which was beginning to shine its brilliant stars as it started to turn to navy. Suddenly the coo of an owl echoed.

"Get down," Thosus barked to the girl. His sharp, green, feline eyes saw the flapping of albino wings. *Large* albino wings. Talons glinted in what was left of the sun.

"What? Why?" Amaya asked as her chocolate eyes lifted to follow the lion man. But as soon as she could see it, its talons were already tearing through the canopy, taking branches and large tree limbs with it.

"Amaya! Look out!" Thosus called to her.

Its cry hurt her ears. She had to cover them.

The beast landed on top of Thosus, pushing a plume of white leaves aloft before they would inevitably trickle down to the cold ground. It was a white owl that had struck down the man and an unnaturally large one at that. "Thosus!" Amaya screamed. She wanted to rush to his aid, but knew that she couldn't—the beast had its feet pressed against Thosus' head, forcing it into the ground, its claws digging into the soft dirt.

She had no choice but to run deeper into the forest and farther away from Rose and Soren. The boots that had once helped tread the snow in Tochfuyu, now only served to kick up moss and dirt, keeping her from sprinting. Amaya tried to hide behind some foliage from the beastly owl, and each time she heard its huge talons stomping against the fallen leaves, she knew that they were for her. She couldn't stop, she told herself that she had to keep moving.

Branches crunched beneath its feet, the daunting sound growing louder and louder. Amaya's heart thudded against her chest as adrenaline coursed through her veins. It made her faster, more quick-minded. She froze when she could no longer hear the pounding footsteps.

Again, she hid. She cowered in the underbrush, sitting as close as she could to it. Perhaps the owl's eyes had left her and had found another animal to prey on. She peeked around the foliage, searching for the creature, and waited a few moments, her suddenly in-tune hearing had confirmed that the beast was no longer stalking her. *Please be all right*, she thought as she started to race back toward Thosus.

Inwardly, Amaya groaned, not realizing until then how far she had truly run while panicking. She had to stop again when she heard churning in the air above her, which she knew was caused by huge wings. It had to be.

Before she could grasp a chance to hide, the owl landed in front of her. Its deep red eyes bore into her, its frost-hued wings just barely spread. Its skin was peeling, just as she had seen with Buhus and Vadu. Purple muck dripped and bubbled beneath it, the owl's crimson eyes dilating as they watched her every move. They couldn't be natural. There was no doubt in her mind that the white beast before her was a god—a sick one.

Its head jolted and jittered from side to side as it slowly approached her. Amaya tried to hold out her hand to calm it as she slowly backed away. "Calm, please, please calm," she whispered so quietly that she herself could barely hear it.

She tried not to show it fear; she tried to keep herself together; she tried to be brave. But the farther back she tread, the farther the owl followed. Both froze when her boot landed on a stick and crunched it. Bricks of ice formed in her stomach and she paled when she saw the bird's pupils dilate again. It screeched and fluttered its wings in order to gain level on her. All she could do was scream to combat the terrible shriek.

Amaya was frozen, she couldn't even struggle when the bird of prey grabbed her and took flight.

* * *

"Was Ms. Ayita all right when you left her?" Rose looked toward the prophet, oblivious to the situation that would soon occur.

Soren's eyes were downcast when she asked this question. "Judging by the condition of her leg when I left her...it's likely she will never walk again..." he trailed off.

Rose pursed her lips, her brow furrowing in sadness. "She must be important to you," she said. "After all, you did mention that she helped you."

The man nodded his head and didn't speak for a few moments. "At times I find she's even wiser than I," he said in a hushed tone. It was silent once more after that, but only for a few seconds until they could hear the sounds of Amaya's distant screams.

"Is that Amaya?" Rose asked, panic quickly setting in.

Soren looked around before they found the sky as the screams ascended. "It could be a bird...It seems to be moving about the sky," he said.

The blonde furrowed her eyebrows as she watched the sky. The screams continued. She could swear she heard words embedded within them but she couldn't make them out.

It had indeed been Amaya. She was screaming for help.

* * *

The vice grip on Amaya's torso was beginning to fade, the owl descending below the treetops again. It was anything but gentle, and it seemed as though the bird was struggling.

With panic clouding her judgment, she couldn't begin to imagine what could possibly be making the owl struggle so much, let alone what may become of herself once she hit the ground. Would death greet her as she had feared earlier? All of the feelings and crossroads her mind had come upon in the moments where she had been struggling to hold onto the other side of the crevice once more returned to her—a feeling she'd hoped to never encounter again—yet here she was, descending so fast and so slowly all at once.

Suddenly, she dropped from its grasp.

She saw the owl god thrash its wings to stay up. She watched the white dogwood leaves grow farther away. She felt the lash of their branches against her back. She felt the blunt ground hit her head. Nothing would cushion her fall. Nothing but the cold, hard ground accompanied by blackness.

7: Lion's Blood

One-thousand-six-hundred years after the creation of Heaven and Hell, there arose a breed of humans like no other. They held something that the gods had never thought of before: determination. They found it in Noctis and Avius.

After a fight had ensued between Rotos and Cyero, the demons of Hell had been released upon the overworld. The aforementioned two wanted to put an end to the years of suffering the demons had unleashed upon the land due to the brawling siblings, and they called out to the gods of wind, water, ice, fire, lightning, and earth—who bestowed upon them gifts of their power in an effort to bring a stop to the Armageddon.

The first of the two, Noctis, had received the powers of wind, fire, and ice, while Avius gained the powers of water, earth, and lightning. These elemental powers were capable of creating weapons respective to their element. Fire created Sacris Ignem, a sword made of a holy alloy that was unbreakable by human hands and untouchable by evil. Water created Diluvium, a bow and arrow with darkness-purging abilities. Wind created Ventum Praesidium, a silver shield that offered divine protection. Earth created the Blade of Keshō, a slim, branch-like scimitar which, even if broken, could regrow another of itself from the pieces. Ice created a scythe, that was nameless but its power was absolute. Lastly, lightning created a lance called Fulgur, that could summon the wrath of the sky within each swift blow.

Thus, a great battle had ensued, and the end to demon rule upon the surface had been brought.

Noctis and Avius were from then on viewed in a new light as heroes of the surface. But the gods had grown weak from their time on the planet, and told the man and woman to keep their powers for use in the lifetimes to come, or to break the cycle that retold their existence again and again, inscribing it into the fabric of reality; a cycle of reincarnation, lest the surface world fall into imbalance again.

* * *

The burning light of the morning sun hurt Amaya's eyes, and the pounding in her head didn't make the sensation any better. Hunger ripped its way through her empty stomach; blisters stung her feet from walking and running the day before. The young woman's body ached.

She was conscious, that she knew, but she couldn't open her eyes.

She heard rustling, not from the trees she knew were above her, but from the leaves that had fallen. They were blunt, sharp rustles. Like footsteps. Still, she couldn't find the strength to open her eyes.

She felt something cold and wet upon her cheek. Breathing huffed in and out. Indeed, it had been an animal. But what animal?

The animal barked. A wolf?

"Ao, what is it?" a voice asked.

No, this was a domestic dog. More barking.

She forced herself to finally open her eyes, squinting as the light from the torn branches above her flitted through onto her still body. She lay in the middle of the descending beams of light and on top of branches that had left the hole in the canopy above.

"Hello? Are you okay?" the voice asked her.

Amaya raised her head slightly as she slowly started to look around.

A gasp came from this male voice, and he dropped to his knees beside her. "Miss, your head is bleeding; are you all right?" he asked as urgency sprung from his tone.

"Where...am I...?" she whispered. Her mind hazed a bit before her memories came back to her.

"You're in the Silver Timberlands. What happened? Can you remember?" he asked.

Amaya slowly shook her head yes to avoid hurting herself more. Pain exploded even though she moved cautiously. "There was an owl...I fell," she muttered.

The man sighed and picked her up gently. "Well, good thing my dog found you. You sound delusional," he joked. "Do you know your name?"

"Amaya," she replied. Her eyes watched her surroundings dissolve into nothing but clear skies. It took her a moment to realize that they had exited the forest. "W—Wait, Thosus, and Soren. A—And Rose...Rose!" she started to comprehend.

"Did you just say, Thosus? Geez, you really hit your head good," he said.

"L—Let go of me, my friends are back there, we have to go to Folkvangr," Amaya argued with him.

The man had to keep himself from laughing at her asinine remarks. "You aren't friends with Thosus."

"Why will you not believe me?" she asked.

"Mostly because your head is bleeding, as I said before, and Thosus is the name of the fire god. We're heading to Rivervein; that's where I'm from," he said.

"But what if the owl got them?" she asked.

The man sighed again and looked down at his dog. "Ao, go sniff out her friends and bring them back to the village," he said.

The great dane beside him barked just as Amaya had heard when she first awoke. She could hear his footsteps bound off in the field back toward the forest. A small bit of relief went through her, but not enough to completely rid her worry.

She looked up at the man who was carrying her and noticed his appearance. He wore a white mantle over his broad shoulders and had a stoic face. His eyes, hazel, and his hair, dark, which complimented the brighter colors he wore. She felt they signified his personality somehow. "Who are you?" she asked.

"I'm Daniël Auber, master of the five dogs making up the White Fang," the man answered her.

"The White Fang?" she questioned.

Daniël nodded at this inquiry. "They're the dogs that protect Rivervein, ordered by the wind goddess herself, granting me the power to speak to animals and understand them. She told me this one day when I was a small child that the dogs and I are to protect the village I live in, so that's what I've done since then," he explained.

"All right, I *suppose* that answers my question—" Amaya replied as she looked at the man.

"What, were you expecting something else?" he asked her, interrupting with a smile.

The redhead gave a blunt chuckle and a grin formed across her face despite the pain lancing throughout her still-bleeding head. "I didn't exactly ask for your life story," she answered.

The man only laughed at this and stayed quiet afterward.

When they arrived in Rivervein, Amaya took in the sight of it. A straight path ran through the civilization—or at least what was left of it—and made an abrupt decline in the distance where a grand structure stood at the end of the pathway. From what she could see, the building had been torn apart, much like a lot of the other buildings in the area. A few smaller pathways branched from the main one, and a nearby stream ran just in view past the houses and various trees, some of which had toppled over onto them.

It looked a lot like Dufmoore, with people benched on the streets, satchel bags standing open in front of them, waiting for passersby to drop change inside. She tried to disregard this, of course. It was simply too sad.

"The infirmary isn't too far from here, we will arrive soon," Daniël said as he carried Amaya along the path.

"What happened here?" she asked. She had forgotten to acknowledge his statement.

"Adione," he answered.

"I'm sorry, what?"

"Adione happened. You said you ran into a huge owl? Well, that's the goddess that protects this village. Or at least she used to," Daniël explained.

Amaya winced a little bit, knowing why it had happened.

"Everyone's saying she turned on us for whatever reason. Some say it's a punishment, others say it's part of the coming of humanity's divine retribution for all of our sins," he said.

"I'm sorry, Daniël. That's terrible," she replied.

Looking up, the young woman caught a glimpse of an expression that she couldn't at first recognize. He seemed deep in thought, in another place far from the present.

But just as soon as she had noticed it, it was gone, and his expression returned to normal, to which he then spoke, "So... Amaya, was it?" He was looking down at her. "Where are you from anyway?"

Now it was Amaya's turn to zone out. She really didn't want to answer this. From what this man had told her, he owned four other trained dogs besides the one he had sent out to find her friends, so if he really knew where she was from, he could have her jailed—or worse, even killed if he saw her as enough of a threat. And thus, she pretended to lose consciousness again.

* * *

The forest canopy outside of Rivervein rustled in the morning wind, which woke Thosus from his injured state. He heaved a shaky breath and stood to his feet, hoping that Soren and Rose hadn't left their spots. He had shifted into his lion form in order to make a quick return to where he and Amaya had first entered the deeper part of the forest.

To his dismay, Rose and Soren weren't there. Only a charred fire pit remained and a couple of patches of grass that had been flattened; presumably where the two had lain.

Thosus pushed his snout against the ground where the indents had been, attempting to catch a whiff of their scents. Faintly, he could smell Soren's scent, given he recognized it more clearly. He started to follow along the trail, making sure to move where the scent grew stronger.

A grunt exited his lips when a branch brushed across his back. The pain stung as if his entire back were skinned and exposed to the open air.

He rolled onto his side in order to see what was causing the stress. When he peered over his shoulder, his stomach sank and he could hardly move a muscle as he stared at what had been there. It was a deep wound left by the owl's talons, bones exposed and covered in that same purple muck that he had seen on his brothers.

"Well, what do you know...she infected me," Thosus said, and closed his eyes as he sighed. The lion flexed his claws, digging them into the soft dirt in order to pull himself up. He tried to bear with the pain as best he could. It was strange, however. Almost as soon as the explosion of pain had presented itself, it left as though it never existed.

Not minding that fact, he began to sprint along the trail again for fear of the sickness manifesting any further. Relief washed through him as he sensed Soren's scent growing stronger. When he rounded a bend in the path, he finally came across the two. He could sense the worry in their demeanor as they scanned every bush, tree, and log. When they heard him bounding up behind them, they turned to look at him.

But just as soon as their faces showed relief, their expressions quickly turned to horror. The girl with blonde hair covered her mouth at the sight of the lion's wounds, having recognized the sludge which flowed beneath his skin. "Thosus, what happened? Where is Amaya? Is she okay?" she asked.

The green-eyed beast shook his head in shame. "Regrettably, no. I believe it was my sister, Adione, who attacked us," he said as he lowered his head, ears flattening. "I was hoping she had found her way back to the both of you, but I seem to be mistaken," the lion continued.

He wished not to remain in beast form for much longer, wanting to test the limits of the disease he had contracted.

"And your back?" Soren pointed out as Thosus shifted into his human form. The wounds couldn't be seen in this state.

"She wounded me, unfortunately. I believe I've been infected," Thosus said.

"Damn," Rose spat under her breath.

Soren looked at their surroundings as though he were trying to facilitate some kind of plan. "We must get Thosus away from Folkvangr if he's been infected. Regarding Amaya, perhaps she made it to the next village already," the dark-haired man said.

"Or maybe she's still out there and hurt. You said you were attacked, right?" Rose replied as her face scrunched up with anger.

"Hush," Thosus snapped harshly as his beastly eyes dilated. He glanced around the area, looking through the brush and felled trees. They flicked over to some greenery that had grown enough to cover a hiding animal.

Slowly it trekked out of the brush, showing them its face. It was the dog that Daniël had sent after them. It barked wildly when it found them, seeming to demand that they follow along.

Soren glanced over at the lion god as if waiting for confirmation to follow the dog. Thosus nodded in response then waved them off. "You two go with the dog. I need to get away from here," he said.

"But what about Amaya?" Rose said, her words giving the impression that her feet would be firmly rooted to the ground until she knew where her friend was.

"The dog says he's found our friend and that we must follow him," Soren replied.

As soon as she heard this, her expression turned to a confused one. "How could you understand him?" she asked.

"I can understand his language. It's the same that the gods used to speak a coon's age ago," the prophet replied before looking down at the dog. "This is no ordinary dog," he said.

"Well then, we should get going," Rose said. Then she turned to Thosus. "Take care, Thosus, be safe," she said.

"Of course. And, Soren?" the fire god said, his green hues slowly shifting to him. "Please protect them with your life," he said.

The prophet nodded and then got down to one knee, placing his hand on his chest. "You have my word," he answered.

Nodding back at him, the god returned to his beast form and proceeded to bound off in the opposite direction. With that, the two followed the great dane through the remainder of the white dogwood forest.

It didn't take long to reach the civilization they had been seeking. Through the village, Ao led them toward his master's location. But this gave them time to take in the devastation around them.

Rose had to cover her mouth; it was absolutely terrible. "Oh, Soren, this is awful," she whispered.

"I know," the other replied. "But don't worry; soon Adione, Thosus, and all the other gods will be cured," he said.

There was a swinging wooden door just big enough for the canine to fit into built on the entrance that they had approached. When they walked in, they continued to follow the dog through the building until they were stopped by a woman.

"Excuse me, are you two visiting someone?" she asked.

Rose's eyes shifted from the dog and up to the woman. She suddenly noticed her attire and a feeling of fear washed through her. Knowing the woman was dressed like a medic, she could only imagine the state that owl had left her only friend.

I knew I heard screaming, she thought as she mentally scolded herself for not following those faint pleas for help the night before.

"Yes, we're here to visit someone named Amaya. Is she here?" Soren spoke up as Rose was in the midst of a mini heart attack.

"Yes, she is," the woman answered then turned to the great dane who was sitting patiently at the start of the hallway for the two. "I assume Ao was taking you to her?" she asked.

Soren gave a quick nod, and the medic smiled, allowing them to continue following him.

The dog led them down the corridor and into the room where the redhead would hopefully be. Rose's jaw hung open when she saw her friend, almost as though she hadn't expected her to be there at first. She had an ice pack over her head with bandages wrapped around her forehead and fresh ones around her arm.

"You're both okay!" Amaya shouted as soon as she saw them from the bed where she lay. She was about to get up before being gently stopped by Daniël's arm.

"You shouldn't move yet," the man warned.

Rose gave him a curious look. He didn't seem like a medic or anyone who even worked at the place.

"Where is Thosus?" Amaya asked, doing her best to disregard the man's prodding.

"He's all right for now, but he was hurt quite badly by the wind goddess. He went off to ensure he wouldn't hurt anyone," Soren explained. "I see you've come across Daniël."

Daniël stood up from the wooden chair upon which he sat. "I found her passed out in the Silver Timberlands. Must've suffered some kind of concussion. I didn't expect you to be one of the people who had been with her," he explained. He appeared rather disgusted as he looked at Soren.

"On a need-to-know basis, it's my duty to stick by her and Rose," the prophet replied as his lips drew back a bit.

"Hah, just like the reason your clan received those powers was on a 'need-to-know basis,'" Daniël shot back.

"It has to do with the gods," Amaya said in order to break the tension she could feel was slowly rising between the two men in the room. "The ones that are getting sick; we're trying to find a cure."

The look that the dog trainer gave lingered but a few more moments before his gaze turned to Amaya. "Is it true?" he asked.

The young woman nodded her head. "Apparently so," she answered.

Then, Daniël looked at Rose. "You will be able to save Adione then?" he continued with hope in his hazel eyes. Though, it seemed to be faltering.

"I'm afraid we will have to be saving more than the wind god. The twin earth gods, and, more recently, Thosus are infected," Rose replied.

Daniël's eyes widened as he heard the name of the fire god. It was as though some kind of wake-up call had alerted him to this disheartening truth. "I would be honored to help you in any way I can," he said.

Rose smiled a little at this. "We will need all the help we can get. Thank you."

Daniël crossed his arms and a more serious expression grew across his features. "I had a feeling the god of fire would be infected at some point. Adione has been terrorizing Folkvangr during the night. In fact, you'll find it empty when the moon rises, other than the dogs and I. We've been doing our best to lead her away, but she always comes back. I've been losing quite a bit of sleep," he explained.

"I suggest that we head off again then," Soren said before walking over to Amaya to examine her wounds.

After gaining clearance from the medic, the four of them left the infirmary in order for Daniël to collect his other dogs. There were four other dogs aside from Ao. There was also Hiro, a husky, Rex, a pitbull, Chio, a samoyed, and lastly, Milo, a shepherd dog. Both women found it particularly difficult to ignore their presence. Though it held strength and dignity, it brought them peace and a bit of happiness through all of the despair they had witnessed.

They walked on for a few hours along a beaten path that led into a small wooded area. By then, the sun had risen high above the travelers' heads. Not only that, but they had also worked up quite the appetite. Their feet carried them to the edge of a tiny lake surrounded by the trees they had previously been walking through.

"Would we be able to take a short rest here?" Rose asked.

Turning back toward her, Soren replied, "Yes, I was just about to mention it. You all must be hungry."

The four of them came across a worn down campsite. There was a stick pitching up an animal skin tarp, most likely to shelter from the elements, with a few logs surrounding some charred pieces of wood.

"I'll see if the dogs and I can catch some fish. The rest of you get the fire going," Daniël said. He gave a quick whistle before the five dogs began following him toward the water.

"Let's try to find some sticks to start the fire," Amaya said to her friend.

"Hold on," Soren said before they could walk away. "I feel it may become increasingly imminent for you both to start using your powers as demigods," he began, causing the girls to return confused looks at him. "I wanted to see if either of you would be able to start the fire without the use of sticks."

Amaya and Rose shared a look with one another before looking once again at the prophet who had spoken to them. "If I remember correctly, I believe it was my dad who was able to use pyromancy," said the redhead. She leaned down toward the pit of fire, examining the birch wood that had been used as fuel for the fire from the previous camper.

Soren's eyes watched her, curiosity filling his pools of gold. Her hand hovered over the wood for a moment, her mind doing its best to concentrate on creating some sort of flame or even just a little bit of heat.

Even after all she had been told, Amaya's body still started a bit when she saw a spark spring forth from the palm of her hand. Before then, the idea of being able to create elements out of thin air just seemed like part of a fantasy, but now that she had witnessed it with her own eyes, it felt empowering.

It caused Amaya to even laugh at it. "Rose, did you see that?" she shouted, just to be sure she hadn't been imagining it.

A smile had appeared across Rose's lips as well. "Yes, I saw it! You did it, Amaya!" she cheered with her.

"Wait! Do you remember when that bear tried to attack us when we were trying to get away from Tochfuyu? The wind? What if that was me?" This was the most excited that Rose had seen her friend in a long time. It gave her much joy to see such a broad smile on her face.

"I would imagine you must be right then," Soren cut in. "If you possess wind and fire, then Rose must have water and earth," he said.

"I guess I'll have to try my luck at it then," Rose said.

Amaya placed her hand over the wood once more in an attempt to create a flame. This time, she managed to light the wood, a fire beginning to consume it.

"Why don't we search the area a bit to look for something to go with the fish. We'll stick together this time so we can prevent another dangerous run-in with Adione," Soren told them.

Amaya stood once again and looked off toward the trees. "Sure, and we should probably find something to put water in as well," she said.

Nodding, Soren waved over toward Daniël. "We're going to look for more food! We will be back!" he called to him.

The man raised his hand, showing he had heard and acknowledged him.

Thereupon, the three of them set off into the woods again.

At some point into the walk, Amaya and Soren had begun to speak to one another about topics that were a bit mundane to Rose and, distracted, they didn't notice her wander off to a nearby tree. It was far enough that she could no longer be seen by the two, but still close enough for her to hear the faint sounds of their voices. Beside the tree was a dense thicket covered in ripening strawberries, which was shocking to see—considering what had happened to Buhus and Vadu. The girl gathered ones which seemed ripe enough not to cringe from their sourness. When she finished, she looked overhead, noticing that the tree she was beside housed a plethora of Cornelian berries.

Living in Tochfuyu hadn't taught her much about edible and non-edible flora, however, so she couldn't be certain if they would poison her or if she had just struck gold. Figuring Soren may know something about them, her eyes began to size up the tree. It wasn't immense, so she knew climbing it wouldn't be too much of a task.

Her arms reached up with ease to a nearby branch, using it to hoist herself up. From there, she moved from branch to branch, picking as many ripe-looking berries as she could fit into the makeshift pouch she had fashioned of her shirt. Once full, she realized she would have to scale down the tree with only one hand. If she didn't, all her hard work would go tumbling to the ground, soiling it.

Rose's eyes were glued to the ground for a moment. Even if she did take a fall from that height, it wouldn't be enough to harm her too bad physically, but she didn't want to risk it. "Amaya? Soren?" she called. But there was no answer, bringing her to the conclusion that she would have to make her way down the tree herself.

Taking in a deep breath, the young woman began to slowly inch her way down from the bark-covered limbs. Inevitably, she ended up slipping, yelping as she quickly registered this. She held her breath, bracing for an intense impact and for her harvest to fall to the ground with her. But when no impact came, she felt her body start, opening her eyes. What she saw were a pair of golden eyes gazing back at her through strands of tousled blond hair. They weren't familiar at all, even though seeing those eyes made her believe for a quick moment that it had been Soren who had rescued her from her demise with the ground. She was quick to deduce that she had never met this person before falling, and she hadn't heard him approach either. But there he was, and in her makeshift pouch, all her berries were intact.

Blood quickly began to rush to her cheeks as she laid eyes on the rest of this man's features. His face barely held a single flaw. His lips were slim, yet enticing, which made his words easy to follow. On top of it all, this man gave off an almost overwhelming aroma. Rose couldn't put her finger on what exactly it was, but it smelled captivating.

"Be careful there," he said.

Rose finally let go of the breath she had been holding in since the start of her fall. "I'm so sorry, I slipped by accident." The more she looked at the man, the more blood rushed to her face. She needed to get out of this man's arms.

As though he had read her mind, the man placed her down beside him, catching a berry as it nearly fell from her shirt and placed it back inside.

"Hungry, are we?" he asked her.

"Er...no, they're not all for me, actually," she replied.

The man tilted his head a bit, wondering who else the food could have been for. But it wasn't his business so he didn't ask. "Are you out here all by yourself, young lady?" he chided playfully.

Rose brushed a few strands of hair away from her face, keeping her gaze downward since she was unable to follow his out of embarrassment. "Ah, no. My friends are near here. There's a lake back that way, we're traveling and stopped there so we could eat," she explained.

"I see. Allow me to accompany you back then?" he asked.

"Well, thank you kindly, but I don't even know your name."

"Of course. It's William. But call me Will. And what might yours be?" he said.

"Rose," she answered.

The man's lips creased once more. "That's a unique name...it does suit you," he said.

A small laugh came from the young woman. "All right, Will. You can walk me back," she said.

Will walked beside her as she started to lead him back toward the direction she came from. Rose knew Amaya and Soren would eventually find their way back as well and didn't bother trying to call out for them.

They soon reached the clearing where Daniël and his dogs had already begun cooking the fish they had captured.

When he heard their footsteps, his eyes lifted to look at them. "Hey, where'd the others go? And who's this?" he asked.

"They're still out looking for food. This is Will," Rose answered.

Golden eyes locked with hazel ones for a long moment before one broke away from the other to look at the girl beside him. "She'd have lost all those berries if I hadn't caught her from falling," Will said, gesturing to the red berries in her shirt.

"Oh, that reminds me," Rose said as she walked over toward Daniël. "These berries, are they poisonous? I've never seen them before," she asked as she held up one of the unknown berries for him to see.

Daniël examined it briefly, not having to look for very long to know the answer to this question. "Ah, these are Cornelian berries. They're edible. But I would wash them off first," he said.

"Right," she said before heading over toward the water. She wanted to attempt to use her powers to do it instead of dunking her shirt into the water to wash the food.

Will had stayed back, hanging by Daniël so that the two could share a conversation. "Do you know the area very well? Rose mentioned you were traveling. I'd be happy to assist if you can't find your way," he said.

Daniël gave the other man a suspicious look, his eyes narrowing. "I do know the area well, actually," he said. "We're on our way to Folkvangr," he said.

"Oh, really? I am as well. Why don't we all travel together?" Will suggested.

"What are you—"

"I did it!" they heard Rose yell, causing their heads to look over in unison at the girl who had one hand up in celebration.

Will's eyes returned to the brown-haired man for only a second before standing up to join the girl. "What did you do?" he asked with a friendly smile on his lips after approaching her.

Rose started a bit upon seeing Will appear beside her. She thought he must have left by now, yet there he was. However, this raised the question. Should she tell the man what she really did? She was still wanted, after all, and if the man knew she was a demigod, there was no telling what might happen. "Oh, heh...I just washed the berries, that's all," she said.

Raising an eyebrow, Will gave a slight chuckle at this. "Well, that was an awfully enthusiastic reaction for something like that," he said.

Before Rose had a chance to explain herself, two other pairs of footsteps entered the area. "Rose! There you are, you can't just wander off like that!" Amaya scolded as she made her way over to them. She hadn't noticed the man beside her at first, but when she did, it caused her chest to swell as she, too, was captivated by his handsome features. "Uh...Rose? Who is this?" she asked.

"My name's Will," the man replied before Rose could even open her mouth.

"I see...well, I'm Amaya, nice to meet you," she said.

"Would it be all right if I came along with you all? I spoke with your other friend and he says you're all on your way to Folkvangr, right?" Will asked.

"You can come with us. We could always use the extra hands around here," Rose said without even giving a second thought to it.

143

This caused Amaya to widen her eyes. "Um...Rose, why don't we go over to the fire and get those berries into the leaf bowl I made."

"Oh, yes," her friend answered, sending a smile in Will's direction before following Amaya.

She rushed Rose to the fire before Will had the chance to catch up with them. "What if he knows who we are?" she asked. "We can't keep inviting all these people to go around with us; we're still wanted, you know."

"I know, but it's only until we get to Folkvangr. I'm sure we can just keep quiet about all of that stuff until he leaves. Besides, he's really nice. If he did know who we are, I'm sure he would have made it clear by now," Rose said.

It didn't take much to convince Amaya and eventually Soren to let the newcomer tag along with them until they reached the capital of the empire. They all sat down and were just finishing up the meal they had all helped to prepare.

"There's some leftovers, Will, are you hungry?" Rose offered him.

"No, that's all right. I've already eaten," the blond man answered.

Daniël interrupted as he stood up. "Well, we're on a bit of a time schedule, so if everyone is finished here, we should be heading off. We've got quite a bit of ground to cover if we want to make it to Folkvangr by tomorrow."

After setting off again, nighttime soon dawned upon their backs, the moon rising behind them, indicating that they would have to set up camp for the night. Time found that Amaya,

Soren, Daniël, and his dogs would fall asleep, leaving Rose and Will awake.

However, Rose hadn't realized he was awake until she felt him sit down beside her. She turned her head to the side so that she could see who it was that had sat down. "You're still awake?" she whispered.

"I could ask you the same thing," Will replied.

Rose looked forward again, avoiding the man's eye contact as she sighed. "I've always found it hard to fall asleep..." she trailed off.

"How come?" he asked.

Rose fell silent for a few moments, wondering if she should fess up the truth to the man she had just met. She tapped her finger against the ground a few times before curling her body a little more as she lay against the ground. "Do you promise you won't laugh if I tell you?" she asked.

A rush of air came through Will's nose as he let out a very slight laugh. "I promise," he answered.

Again, she was quiet until her heart finally grew the courage to speak. "I'm afraid of the dark..." she whispered.

"I see..." he trailed off. "You know, the dark is no silly thing to fear," he assured her. "Especially when you're sleeping out in the wilderness like this. There are plenty of animals...or even demons who would love to feast on someone like you."

What he said caused a chill to scrape its way down her spine. She couldn't answer for a few moments. "That doesn't help..." she said.

A slight chuckle left his lips after that. "Don't worry, I'll protect you...You know, when I was a kid, my mom used to sing me songs to help me fall asleep," he said.

"Oh, what, are you going to sing me a lullaby?" Rose teased.

"If it would help," Will answered back with a stone-like look on his face.

This caught her off guard and her laughing fell silent. "Oh... well, I guess it can't hurt to try," she replied.

Will said nothing more after that. What she heard was a series of deep humming coming from his throat. It sounded more soothing than she expected. As she closed her eyes to try and fall asleep, all she could seem to picture was his face accompanied by that gentle voice.

It didn't take long for her to fall asleep. A few minutes had passed, and looking down at the girl, Will stopped his humming. "Rose?" he whispered so as not to wake her if she really was sleeping.

A grin slipped across his lips as he stood up. From the clothes he had been wearing, Will pulled out two knapsacks and began to unfurl them. He slipped the first around Rose's head and carefully began tying her wrists and ankles together with some rope. Once that was done, he snuck over and cautiously began to tie the other girl as well.

Once he had gotten them all bound together, he was able to easily pick each of them up, throwing them over his shoulders as he began to walk away.

"Stop," a low voice said.

Instinctively, Will stopped in his tracks.

"Put them down, demon." He had begun to hear growls coming from behind him.

Will's eyes flicked off to the side, and his grin spread from ear to ear. "I really thought I would get away with it without conflict." He released a sigh, dropping the two girls to the ground, causing a yelp to come from the both of them as they hit the hard surface.

"Dammit! Did we get captured again?" Amaya's yell was muffled due to the fabric over her head.

"You haven't been captured," Daniël answered her. All the growling coming from the dogs and his voice had awoken Soren too.

"Yet," added Will as he finally turned around.

Rose's eyes grew wide from within the darkness of her own knapsack. She could recognize that voice, having just heard it lull her to sleep. She had hoped her ears were deceiving her. Will had been so nice to her before.

"You really thought you could hide behind that smell? The scent of evil transcends any spell, including your own trickery," Daniël said. "Now step away or they're going to tear you apart." He nodded to the dogs standing beside him.

"Is that what you think? Well, suit yourself..." Will replied. From his crossed arms, the demon raised one of his hands, waving it around a bit. When he did this, the five of his companions whined softly, their heads hanging low as their bodies grew weak. Within mere moments, the canines dropped to the ground.

"Bastard," Daniël spat before drawing something from behind his back. What he took was a crossbow, an arrow nocked between the limb and string. He aimed the equipment at the demon, pulling the trigger just as soon as he released the safety lock.

Hissing, Will flinched back as the arrow struck him in the shoulder, burning his skin. His teeth were clenched together, his face scrunched out of pain. Grunting, he ripped the arrow from his shoulder and looked at the liquid running from its side-notched tip. "Repythil...?" A feeling of dread went through Will's body and a growl left his throat as he was struck with yet another arrow.

The material running from the arrows was paring his flesh, peeling it away while he felt its lash.

Will hissed once again before a pair of wings shot out from the back of his clothes. He took to the skies, prying the other arrow from his body then tossing it away. While struggling to escape, the demon could hear a few more arrows zip past his head, and one even struck his leg. But he didn't stop to soothe the pain, only kept flying until he was out of Daniël's range.

Once the man was finished with his target, he placed the bow back into its holster and rushed over to the two who had nearly been captured, helping Soren while he cut away the rope and uncovered their heads.

"Are you both all right?" the prophet asked them.

"We're fine...aside from having been dropped on the ground," Amaya answered.

But Rose looked not to be so relieved. "I'm so sorry. I shouldn't have let him tag along," she said.

She felt a hand land upon her shoulder which made her lowered head raise a bit to look at its owner. "You couldn't have known, besides, if he was that persistent, he likely would've followed us anyway," Daniël said assuringly.

"What I don't seem to understand is why a demon would want them. I suppose they're demigods, but at that point, why not just kill them right there when he had the chance?" Soren said.

Amaya shuddered a little bit. She knew that that could have been a very real possibility. The dangers of this journey had truly begun to show itself at that point. "We had better not stay here, he could come back," she said.

"He already knows we're heading to Folkvangr, so trying to rest any further ahead would be futile," Daniël replied.

"We will stay," Soren cut in. "I'll stay awake and keep watch of you all while you rest. If he returns, I'll take care of him."

"Ah, and how do we know *you* wouldn't attempt to kill us in our sleep?" the other male asked with accusation in his tone.

"Listen, I don't know what happened in your past to make you so hostile toward Soren, but he's helped us a lot, and we owe him our lives. I trust him. So you should too," Amaya said. "We're all too tired to go anywhere else, so if you have a problem, we have no problem with letting you go back to Rivervein."

Daniël sat with his mouth hanging open. He hadn't expected the girl to retaliate with such words. But he regained his composure quickly. "Well, I wouldn't trust anyone with an alias," he said softly.

Without another word, he returned to where his dogs were lying. After checking to be sure that the demon hadn't killed them, he lay down. But this didn't stop the looks from being shared between the remaining three people.

The air held too much tension to mention what had been said.

8: Owl's Blood

Morning brought with it newfound energy to face the day, and by afternoon the four travelers had, at last, arrived in the courts of Folkvangr. It was a lively place in spite of all that was happening on the outside. People were bustling about the cobblestone paths that had both shops and houses lined up all along them.

"I reckon we ought to find these two a disguise. I'm certain the folks around here wouldn't be too pleased with their presence," Daniël said.

Amaya exhaled an exasperated breath. "I almost forgot, Thosus was meant to be our guide through here, but I suppose now that has been ruined," she said. "Hold on, how did you know?" she asked quickly.

"I knew you looked familiar at first, and after all that's happened since I've joined with you, it's been easy to deduce. I knew it had to be the both of you," he replied.

"Then you aren't interested in turning us in?" the red-haired girl asked.

"Your intent is to save the gods, who are in a detrimental state. What you did before now is none of my concern," Daniël said.

"Hmph, I wish that little rule of thumb applied to all of your circumstances," Soren muttered.

"What was that, Soren? Did you say something?" Daniël asked in a warning tone.

"Why don't you go on and purchase an inn for us to stay the night. I'll see the girls through the shopping district to find them some more suitable clothing," the prophet said.

Without another word, Daniël and his dogs parted from the group, leaving the remaining three to traverse the shops lining the streets. "Try to stay as hidden as possible until the both of you are able to change," Soren said to them as they began browsing about.

"There is something I've actually been a bit curious about," Amaya said.

Turning around, Soren looked down at the young woman. "And that is?" he asked.

"Your relationship with Daniël. Why are the two of you always so hostile toward one another? And about that alias he mentioned the night before," she explained.

"Amaya...maybe he isn't comfortable explaining—"

Soren raised his hand to the midsection of his body. "No, I do owe it to you both...after all, there is a chance that we could be spending quite a bit of time together, and I see no reason why you shouldn't know who I really am. Just...perhaps this isn't the place to be saying it," he said.

With respect to his wishes, neither of them said anything more about the matter until the next hour brought them to the inn which Daniël had taken them to once they met up with him again. After finding the proper clothes, Amaya and Rose were now just a bit less recognizable, at least by the common folk.

As promised, Soren was prepared to reveal to the two girls what he had been hiding. "My name isn't truly Soren. What Daniël said was no lie," he began. The other man sat across the room, his arms crossed as he listened to what he had likely already known or been told. Soren removed his hood. "The mark upon my brow is the mark of the Astral Clan who possessed the technology to reach places we're forbidden from ever speaking of outside the ears of our kin. Shortly before the demons attacked the surface, we discovered a people whose powers mirrored that of the elements of water and earth. Our clan slaughtered them and left none to survive, having been told the lie that they would be a threat to our people. The rumor was given by your grandparents, Tobias, Vincent, and Elaine, and they were convincing. As a result, my clan received those abilities from those they had murdered. The Astral Clan's death became a death to my pride as an Astrian, and so I faked my own death and became Soren," he explained. "As for my real name...well...I would prefer to keep it hidden for now. I hope you can respect that, since I prefer my alias anyway."

The two young women listened as the prophet told his story; they felt wrong for having edged him into talking about his past. Thinking of how long ago the siege had been, Soren couldn't have been any older than a teen at that time, which meant that he didn't have a say in what his clan decided—no, what they had been manipulated into deciding.

"I'm sorry that I doubted you before and that I forced you to share that," Amaya said.

But Soren shook his head. "You need not apologize. You were right to be suspicious of me after what Daniël had said. He and I used to be friends until I told him the truth," he said as he looked at the brown-haired man. "I've begged for his forgiveness, but have been unable to attain it."

Daniël interjected, "Perhaps it could have to do with the fact that you are undeserving. You and your people were ruthless murderers and if you weren't, you would confess your sins, accepting what you did. Even now, you're a coward and refuse to even tell them the whole truth of who you are," he finished bitterly.

"I can't ignore the screams of that day so long ago. They exist, and I can't rid my mind of them. I've tortured myself in the hopes of purging my body of them, but to no avail," Soren argued. He could feel his chest pounding and his blood beginning to rise as he tried desperately to defend his intentions.

"Soren," Rose said quickly in order to prevent any more tension from forming between the two. "It's all right, if you don't want to tell us who you are, we're fine with that. Some people simply weren't meant to see eye to eye."

"As much as I wish it weren't so..." Soren answered after taking a moment or so to calm himself. "Fine then, we should spend the remainder of our time searching for Kye. The night will be upon us soon. And I'm not certain how long Adione will be able to yield us by the time dusk begins to fall."

Rose felt excitement go through her body. She had almost forgotten that her friend's uncle had been waiting for them to give them the truth of what had happened so long ago. "I agree. Where do you think he might be?" she asked.

"The palace, perhaps. If the king sent him anywhere, it would likely be there," Soren said.

"Yes, but if he was trying to talk to us, don't you think he would stray away from the people who have the ability to imprison us?" Amaya asked.

"Then where do you propose we look?"

"Let's just start anywhere for now. We're burning precious time waiting around here," Daniël cut in.

And so they did. From the inn they were staying at for the night, the four of them set out to search the aristocratic portion of the populated capital. They walked cobblestone paths and avoided eye contact with the noblemen and ladies. So as not to attract too much attention to themselves, they each agreed to travel sparsely. But as the gorgeous elegance of evening painted its way across the sky—signaling bright weather by morning's arise—Amaya and Rose were beginning to lose hope.

They stopped at a botanic recreational ground, sitting down near a fountain. The gentle noise of the running water beckoned to drown out the worries and sorrows of the two demigods. "Are you sure he's even here? Maybe he forgot about us," Amaya asked, sighing as the rest of them took in the fresh air.

"Don't worry, I'm sure he didn't forget about you. That isn't like Kye. He will keep his word. But I'm afraid if we don't find him soon...well...we can't afford to waste another day here," Soren replied.

Rose's eyes watched the slowly dipping sun as darkness began to swallow it. With it, her faith was consumed by hopelessness.

But a ray of hope soon shone upon her. It was small, but touched her shoulder, causing her to turn her head. There she could see a mask looking back at her with recognizable long red hair pooling from behind it. The sight made her gasp. "Kye!" she exclaimed and bolted to her feet. "We have been looking for you all day!"

Amaya turned her head when she heard the sound of her friend yelling her uncle's name. Her eyebrows raised up high as she stared at the familiar figure, her mouth agape. That crimson hair was a trademark to the Achyra family. The young woman could feel her chest swelling. She was excited but almost fearful of this man, and thus frozen in place on the ground.

"I'm sorry. The emperor and empress ordered a garrison search around the capital's border," Kye said before his eyes caught sight of his niece. A smile came to his lips. "Are you just going to sit there, Amaya?" he asked. Tears began to well in his eyes, causing the same reaction from the girl in front of him.

The two men sitting aside couldn't help themselves from smiling at such a heartwarming reunion. The girl had sprung from her seat on the edge of the fountain and embraced her uncle tightly. Her sobs were muffled from the fabric of the man's clothing. This was her only remaining tie to her family. Suddenly, the enigma of her past felt so much closer to the light.

Kye's hands entangled themselves in the locks of the young woman's hair, holding her small form as though she may float away if he didn't.

"I've missed you so much, Uncle Kye," Amaya said softly through her sobs.

"I've missed you as well. Not a day has passed that I didn't think of you," the man with long hair replied.

Looking up from her head upon which his chin rested, he locked eyes with Soren in his spot on the ground. The two shared this gaze for a long moment, Amaya's sobbing narrating the scene.

"Kye...I believe you have a few things to be sharing with your niece and her friend," Soren said.

Taking a deep breath, Kye pulled away from Amaya and placed his hands on her shoulders. "If the both of you wouldn't mind, I would like to speak to them privately," he said to the two men.

"Of course," Soren replied. He stood up before nodding to both girls individually. "Amaya, Rose, we will be at the inn. Be sure to rendezvous with us once more when you are finished," he said.

Daniël stood with him, waving to the two before heading off down the path with Soren. Kye watched them go, waiting until they were gone from sight completely as if to stall what was to come. It was true that even though Rose and Amaya had grown into fine young women, he still felt pain lance through his chest when he looked at them, knowing what he would have to share.

"Come," he said once his gaze returned to them. Without a further response, he began walking toward Folkvangr's western gate, motioning for the two to follow him. It brought them to the capital's outskirts, a beaten path in the forest. "I suppose we will begin with the both of you asking questions. What do you want to know first?"

The question left much open to discussion and inquiry. But one thing needed to be established first: "Why were we exiled to Tochfuyu?" Amaya asked.

Kye watched the different grasses of the forest as they blew gently in the breeze. He watched insects flutter by as if trying to find a happy place before his mind returned to the darkness. "It's the fault of your parents," he said. "They tried to murder the god Cyero, and were plotting treason against Lucus. Because of what your grandparents did twenty-two years ago, Lucus didn't want to risk the corruption of yet another generation of demigods. At first, they wanted to kill you, but I convinced the king to spare your lives. After all, killing you wouldn't have broken the cycle of reincarnation."

"And what of our parents? Were they imprisoned?" Rose quickly asked.

Kye stopped in his tracks, and Rose and Amaya stopped behind him, anticipation building in their bellies as they waited for the man to speak. For a moment, the only sound remaining was the rustling of leaves above. He turned to them and lifted his mask, once more showing his half-scarred face to Rose. This was the first Amaya had ever seen of her uncle's actual face. His umber eyes were red and riddled with tears as he started to cry.

"No, they were killed, Rose," he said finally. He could see the wonder on their faces quickly turn to what appeared to be horror and sadness and anger.

Rose's eyes stung and her skin paled. "So it's true then. They're really dead?" she asked, her voice shaky.

"They wanted tyranny—"

"Our parents weren't tyrants!" Rose yelled childishly as though she were in the midst of a petty argument. "They were good people and they loved us so much!" she continued.

Amaya's own strife began to surface, but she couldn't show it. She could feel it there, like a boiling bubble doing its best to rise to the surface and burst. A bubble thick like tar, hot and black. But she wouldn't allow it. However, she wasn't completely willing to dismiss the thought that her parents weren't good people—at least not to others.

"I can't express how sorry I am. I wanted so badly for you to know what happened all this time. But I couldn't bring myself to tell you until now," Kye said.

"You are a coward, Kye! It's been twelve years! For twelve years we were left wondering why we were so alone all because you couldn't give us the truth!" Rose yelled at him. Her legs felt weak and caused her to fall to her knees on the ground.

Amaya knelt down with Rose to keep her from collapsing completely. She held Rose's head against her chest, rubbing her back as she tried to comfort them both. "Rose...it wouldn't have been any better back then than it is now. We would only be so much more confused if he had told us so long ago," she said, trying to be assuring.

Rose tried to shove her friend away, her breathing becoming erratic as she sobbed and cried. "G—Get off me!" she shouted.

Amaya loosened her grip and let go of her friend. She watched the blonde stumble to her feet before running off once more to the capital. When she did, the red-haired woman caught sight of the dipping sun and she gave a brief scan of the sky. She knew of the creature which may soon slice through it and was already beginning to see clouds roll in from the distance.

"Amaya," she heard her uncle say, which caused her turn her head to him once more. "Are you faring well...?" he asked her.

"It's...devastating..." she said. "But somehow I already knew it in the back of my mind, so this merely confirms my suspicion."

The older man approached her, placing his hand on her cheek as he brushed away some of her straying hair. "Amaya... you've always been so independent and strong. I see a lot of the personality reflected in the heroes of old in you—more now than ever," he said. "But I can tell this still wounds you deeply, even if you don't show it."

"Of course," Amaya replied. "It 'wounds' me more than you can possibly imagine. To know that there is so much Rose and I missed out on in our lives. More importantly, I've watched Rose struggle with crippling loneliness and try to hide her sadness from me. Uncle Kye, all I've ever wanted was for her to be happy. That's why I agreed to leave Tochfuyu with her. At first I wanted nothing to do with this. I wanted to stay there where it was safe, but now, because of everything that has happened to us, we have seen more of the world than I ever thought we would. And though we have faced hardships, with many more to come, it's all been so worth it," she explained before pulling away from the man to face the distant palace. "Daniël told us that the wind goddess, Adione, has been terrorizing this place. And before we came here, I was nearly killed by her. Did Rose tell you about this prophecy we're supposed to fulfill?" she asked.

Kye could feel pride welling up inside of him as his niece spoke such insightful words, but upon hearing her question, he answered, "no, she didn't."

"Soren believes we're supposed to save these gods from getting sick and attacking all of these innocent people and destroying Aessatia, but we have barely even the slightest idea about where to start. We will be off to Barness after this, which is utterly terrifying and..." Amaya heaved a great sigh and entangled her hands in her hair.

"Amaya," Kye said in a low tone, "this is a tremendous burden...one which you and Rose don't have to carry alone. Would you allow me to return to Lucus with you? Whatever it is you are looking for, maybe I can help you find it," he said.

"Soren mentioned going to an Ice Sanctum of sorts," she answered.

The reply caused Kye to tense and his eyes shot to Amaya. "I'm afraid you may be out of luck."

"Why is that?" she asked, looking at him.

"After your parents tried to kill Cyero, he forbade any mortals from entering the sanctum from that day forward. We haven't seen him since then," her uncle replied.

"Great, so we're going somewhere to find a place we likely won't even have access to," she said.

"Perhaps given the severity of the situation, he will make an exception," Kye tried to assure her, unsure himself.

Amaya's eyes returned to the sky when she felt something wet drizzle upon her arm. As expected, she could see a figure heading for the capital from the distance while thunder began to growl, its counterpart lighting up the darkened clouds. "We need to head back. Adione is coming," she said, pointing to the movement that she was seeing.

They began to run from the pouring rain, which got heavier with each step they took. "Are you sure you're equipped to fight in your condition?" Kye shouted over the torrential downpour, glancing at her injured arm.

"I'll have to be!" Amaya yelled back at him.

Amaya led him to the inn where Rose, Daniël, and Soren were already waiting outside. They all wore hoods over their heads, the fabric getting soaked along with their hair. Daniël, however, wore only his mantle, the rest of him drenched from the deluge.

The streets were quiet—void of people—while only the patter of water hitting stone could be heard. Another bolt of lightning lit up the sky, the gurgle of thunder coming quickly after it. One by one, the dogs making up the White Fang began to growl, their ears twitching as they saw the silhouette of the giant owl whenever the sky lit up. "She's here," the dog trainer said as raindrops fell from his lips and nose.

Amaya looked at Rose, hoping her friend was prepared for this, when in fact neither of them could say they were. Truthfully, they were both frightened by the idea of battling a god. Before, Thosus and Soren had done all the work to subdue Buhus and Vadu.

"What is the plan? Do we evacuate everyone first?" Amaya asked.

"Soldiers have already begun doing so; there is no need. Even if they hadn't, there wouldn't be enough time," Soren said.

"We need to lure her away to keep as much of the capital intact as we can," Daniël said. "Amaya, you might do well to stay out of this fight. You're still injured."

Amaya looked down, feeling a bit useless, but at the same time knowing he might be right. "I can't bring myself to simply do nothing."

"Daniël is right. I know it may not be ideal for you, but in your condition, you would do well to stay safe. After all, if you were to get hurt even more, you wouldn't be able to help in the future," Soren pointed out.

Amaya's eyes were downcast after this; she wanted badly to help, but knew that her presence in a fight against a corrupt god would only be a burden. "Fine...but at least allow me to watch from the capital," she said.

Soren looked to Daniël before sharing a nod of agreement with him. "Very well, but no matter what happens, you must not rush in. Understood?"

Amaya nodded back, and with that, she took refuge in a nearby hovel while the others prepared to fight. Daniël removed his weapon from its sheath and aimed it at the bird creature. His arrows laced with Repithyl usually worked to drive back the beast until she came around again.

In the moment before he pulled the trigger, the goddess and the man locked eyes with one another in a tense glare. Once the sound of the trigger being pulled hit his ears, soon, too, did the screech of the struggling owl whose left flank had been struck directly by the quarrel. A series of shrieks echoed through the skies of Aessatia. Adione flapped her wings wildly to stay in the air, causing feathers to be set aloft in her wake. The nearby trees started to rustle, wind whipping through them while rain pelted their leaves.

Daniël pulled out another trinket just after he was sure his arrow had hit. A silver whistle was what he had grabbed and placed to his lips. It made hardly any noise upon being blown, but all of the dogs had responded to it at the ready. He and his canine companions rushed out of the town, encouraging the goddess to follow them.

Seeing this as a signal to move along too, the other three ran off in the same direction.

The owl dived down at Daniël, outstretching her talons to attack him. Luckily, he had already mounted another quarrel to his bow and had it aimed at Adione's wing. Firing it, he prepared to have the goddess come crashing down and darted backward, but the wind had knocked the quarrel off course, allowing the bird to begin a tangle with the man to scoop him into her claws, opening her talons once more.

Before she could even scrape his skin though, Rex leaped up and sank his teeth into the goddess' thigh. His jaws were tight around it, even as Adione writhed to shake herself free. Blood escaped the deep wound, littering Rex's teeth.

It quickly became evident that Kye and Rose would need to play their own parts in attempting to subdue the owl so Soren could trap her within his barrier. Kye pulled his halberd from its sheath and readied it to strike when the time was right.

Within those short moments, Daniël had shot thrice more at Adione with his arrows while Rose tried to use the falling rain as projectiles to make it more difficult for the goddess to move about the sky. She was a bit sloppy with her techniques, of course, having only just learned to use water the day before.

Kye soon joined in on the action, his eyes scanning for an opening; but alas the owl, though struggling, was far too high in the air for him to possibly land a hit on her and attempt to drag her down.

Adione's sharp red eyes flicked toward Kye, the rain causing a thick bog to spew from her open injuries. Her screech sounded once more, and within seconds she was diving toward him, causing the pup that had been dangling from her leg to fall to the ground below, lying still after landing. Chio, another of the dogs, had rushed toward him to help.

Kye was quick to react to the bird nose-diving toward them. Before she could reach him, the man thrust his halberd into Adione's skull and used its mast to launch himself onto Adione's head, stunning her. He then removed the halberd's blade from her head and began to slice at her infected skin.

The goddess bucked about, trying to shake him off, but he was persistent, and the blade of the halberd once more sunk in. Her wild thrashing had caused Kye to slip down her head toward her wings, where his halberd blade finally ceased cutting into her flesh. Feathers once more rained down from the sky. But now the goddess was close enough for the other three dogs to jump up toward her and start weighing her down.

"Soren, now!" Daniël yelled to the prophet.

Soren held out his hand to begin putting a barrier over the goddess, but in the mix of all the chaos, they each had failed to notice Rex and Chio. Both had gotten back up, and before Soren could secure a barrier over Adione, they had turned and attacked Soren, piquing the interest of both Daniël and Rose, who had watched the strange occurrence unfold.

"Rex! Chio! Heel!" Daniël shouted over the patter of rain all around him. He pulled out his whistle, blowing it to try and get them away. But the dogs didn't respond to him, only continuing to maul Soren.

Daniël was conflicted, he didn't want to have to shoot them, but if he didn't act soon, Soren would be hurt; and for the sake of Rose and Amaya, he couldn't allow that. He had aimed his crossbow at Rex, pointing it at his shoulder so it would subdue him. It held them just long enough for Soren to retreat from the fray quite a ways. Now Daniël could see that these weren't the sweet dogs he knew so well; neither of them had black fur before now; he remembered one with a pristine white coat while the other was speckled with brown and grey. Now they looked like Hellish demons with beady red eyes.

"This is bad. Daniël, be careful! They've been infected!" Soren yelled.

Adione began to bristle, like anger was consuming her. Her fur and feathers had ruffled up like that of a threatened beast. Kye—who was still atop her neck—and the dogs that had been attempting to drag her down could feel themselves begin to lift from her body before being blown off of her, each tumbling to the ground with a grunt or yelp of pain.

Hearing this, Daniël turned to look at what had happened, keeping his crossbow aimed at the corrupt dogs to caution them from approaching him, should they escape.

It was overwhelming him. The battle seemed more difficult than any previous incursion with Adione had been. He had never even had to use his dogs before now; usually, the quarrels were enough to keep her away. *What changed?* he wondered.

While he was distracted by the event, Rex and Chio had recovered from the wounds caused to them by the crossbow, and attacked the weapon, causing Daniël to turn back toward them. He hadn't heard them with all the wind and rain in his ears.

"Off! Off!" he shouted to no avail.

Just as he said this, the wind began to whip again, this time slicing each of them at random like tiny knives flying through the air.

While they were staggered by this, Adione landed directly on top of Daniël. Her screech was loud and so close to him that it had burst his eardrums. Blood ran from each canal, and everything sounded like loud ringing. He could only see her beak outstretched as the air in his body began to constrict and rot inside his lungs. He couldn't pull it in anymore. His chest burned as the air was forever kept out of it. His skin turned pale at a rapid rate.

"Daniël!" Rose yelled as she dashed toward him to try and fight back the goddess, even with her pathetic knife. But as she did, another infected canine jumped onto her. Her head didn't turn more than an eighth of the way around before a pair of incisors chomped down onto her shoulder. The weight of the brute force toppled the young woman. But she wouldn't soon fall prey to the dog, as Kye rushed over to help her fend him off.

Soren's eyes were wide at this display. Rex had attacked her. His eyes darted about in the midst of all the carnage that had just taken place. One of his only friends—though they didn't get along well—had just suffocated right before him. He closed his eyes briefly, knowing that he couldn't allow this to stop him. When they opened once more, he looked over to check if Ao, Milo, and Hiro had also become infected.

Thankfully, they each appeared to be acting normal, recovering from their injuries as best they could.

When Adione had finished off her prey, she turned to the others with deadly intent in her eyes. Milo and Ao were the next to charge, without a second thought to the outcome. They sprang onto the grounded owl, jaws ripping and tearing into her flesh, feathers flying with each bite.

But they, too, were shaken away with ease. Like Rex, they both lay across the ground, which told Soren that they would also turn.

"Now!" Soren shouted and held out his hands to enclose the god in a barrier, hoping to bind Ao and Milo as well. Just then, the owl stretched her wings to take flight again, but before she could, Kye had slung his halberd toward her right wing after having fended off Rex from Rose.

"Trap her now, Soren!" Kye growled as his eyes glared daggers into him. Again, he readied himself to get the job done, but was stopped yet again by Chio and Rex, who had begun to pursue him.

Hearts sank with worry. Now Milo and Ao were getting ready to attack Kye and Rose, while Adione fought against their grip, and Soren was being mauled by the other two dogs. Hiro was all that remained to be unaffected.

Kye rushed to Soren's aid. As much as he wanted to ensure Rose's safety, without the prophet, the goddess and the demonized dogs would never be sealed—and could end up killing them all. He rushed toward them, and though defenseless, began to fight off the dogs with his bare hands, knuckles bloodying from such intense blows.

Without his help, Rose was quickly prevented by the other two dogs from getting any closer to the goddess. It was like the dogs had completely changed sides. They had no interest in each other nor Adione.

With Milo and Ao in her pursuit, Rose began doing her best to fend them off with her measly knife, all while attempting to use the rain to keep them from harming her. But this wouldn't last long.

That was when Amaya rushed in, screaming. She held her wooden lance in her hands, charging at the two dogs attacking her friend. It did well to keep them at bay for a little while, but her poor arm couldn't long withstand the pressure of such forces against it.

"Amaya! What are you doing here?" Rose shouted, alarmed.

"I couldn't just watch any longer!" she replied, her teeth clenching between her words in order to quell the pain in her arm. The husky that hadn't become tainted by the infection rushed over to them to help Amaya, and was doing his best to defend the three of them from the ravenous Ao and Milo. Both dogs frothed at the mouth, their backs haunched as they slowly paced toward them. But now Adione was after them, too. Her talons tried repeatedly to grasp at least one of the three, but they dodged each swipe. Eventually, of course, their bodies would tire; Rose's before Hiro's. Finally, Adione was on top of the blonde.

"Rose!" screamed Amaya. Milo snapped his jaws at her, but she needed to get to her friend as fast as she could. It may have been a torrential downpour, but now she was trying to create flames as adrenaline flooded her veins. Not only had she created flames, but they were white and had tempered a blade straight into the grasp of her fingers.

She could hardly bring herself to care how it had happened or to be amazed by it. Her legs pumped faster than before—even faster than when she was running from that bear in the forest. Sword in hand, she charged with fury in her umber eyes. She swung the blade at the goddess's flank, drawing her infected violet blood as it singed away some of her feathers. Though her broken arm shifted in the process, somehow that pain didn't register.

Rose was stunned, unable to move. Swinging the blade ineptly, Amaya began to fight off the two dogs and the raging goddess, who were beginning to surround her. She blocked a flying talon one second while she slashed the muzzle or shoulder of a dog the next. This pattern would soon grow far too futile, and now Rose and Amaya were at the mercy of death's clutches. Now Hiro lay still, his fate imminent like his siblings.

Just then Soren rushed in front of them, having left Kye to fend off the other two dogs, callous as it may have been. Amaya and Rose witnessed him pull a cylindrical object from the small of his back, one which they had seen there before, but had never paid close attention to. When he did, its shape changed, elongating into a lance that was even longer than himself. It had a blade on each of its ends, one larger than the other.

Soren held the lance ready in his arms, but though he seemed adept at using it, he was frozen. He couldn't bring himself to use the object, even as Adione was diving toward them—leaving the ones he was protecting to wonder why exactly his feet were failing him. If he were to stay frozen as he did, they were all sure to be doomed.

Adione charged forward, the wind so sharp as it flowed around her bleeding body that it could be seen with the naked eye. Her huge form sent all four of them to the muddy ground. Their ears rang, the only thing they could hear was the sound of her immense wings flapping as she recovered from the attack while their eyes witnessed Ao and Milo slowly approaching.

A bellowing roar ripped through the darkened sky. Flames blazed through the pitch-black air.

Rose saw this and knew then that it would be their end. But when she expected to be torched by the lion god from whom she knew had emitted this sound, she caught a glimpse of his green eyes. They glowed against the light of flying flames as it lit up the surrounding darkness.

At that moment, Adione had been about to dive at them. But then a wall of flames shot out in front of them, forcing her to charge right through the burning wall, catching fire as she did. She fluttered her wings to halt herself in an attempt to quell the flames that burned her.

Having stopped her, Thosus was free to leap onto Adione, clawing and biting to bring her down.

Though they were close to one another, Soren knew he needed to seize this opportunity as Thosus held the goddess still and, mustering the rest of his strength, he stood up to accomplish the task they had expended so much energy to achieve.

Finally, a barrier was placed around the two, and with the five corrupt dogs lying still enough, he was able to place barriers around them as well. Relief flooded the four of them remaining as they fought to calm their racing hearts which pounded like thunder in their ears.

Rose and Amaya gasped for air as they watched the trapped dogs try to scratch free of their imprisonment.

Taking advantage of the moment of peace, Soren had collapsed from exhaustion and Rose didn't even attempt to get up from having been knocked to the ground.

"Amaya...you made a sword..." the blonde said, still panting.

"Never mind that, are you all right?" the redhead replied as she looked at the others. She tried not to wince from the throbbing pain in her arm.

Slowly, Soren sat up and groaned in pain as it lanced through his body.

"I'm okay," the prophet said.

"I'm doing fine as well, only a few scratches is all," said Kye, who was now only a few feet from them, even though it was clear to see that mere scratches weren't all he obtained from the fight.

"How did they all became infected? I thought this sickness only affected the gods," Rose finally asked after giving a nod to let her friend know that she was all right.

"These are no ordinary dogs. There must be a sort of divinity to them. But we can't worry about that now," Soren said as his eyes stayed on the trapped dogs.

Amaya lifted her head as she heard this. "That's right... Daniël told me—" she cut herself off. "Where is he?"

Soren lifted a hand shaking from adrenaline toward his friend, unable to bring himself to look yet. "She killed him..." he muttered.

Amaya followed his arm toward where the man lay, covering her mouth as she laid eyes on his unmoving body. "No..." she whispered, covering her mouth.

Soren closed his eyes, unable to stand the sorrow in her voice as she looked at him. "He fought well," he said. "We will head back now...our job is done," he added before turning his head to look at his fallen friend, whose head was surrounded by blood. He felt it only right to give him a proper burial. At last he stood, though his footing was a bit wobbly at first before he found it.

They used the last bit of their remaining strength to dig a hole for Daniël to be buried within, and sadness filled the eyes of all who witnessed his burial. But Soren was the most torn about the situation.

* * *

Quite a bit of time passed before Kye decided to part from them and report what had happened to the emperor and empress. Though it had been a sad and unfortunate death, Rose and Amaya were exhausted from the battle which had ensued, and hoped Soren would finish his grieving soon.

"How close were you and Daniël before he began resenting you?" Amaya asked him. By then the rain had mostly stopped.

"Though we haven't been close for the last few years, Daniël and I were once the best of friends—he was my *only* friend," Soren explained. "I have many fond memories of him...I wish I could have protected him from this fate."

Rose looked down and to the side. "That reminds me...that lance you pulled out in the middle of the battle...why did you not use it before?" she asked.

This caught the man off guard and he couldn't speak for a moment. "I...saw no reason to...I saw Thosus coming to our aid... and I sort of froze," he said.

Amaya didn't buy the excuse and looked at him suspiciously. "If you had a weapon like that, why did you not use it even before then? You may have prevented Daniël from dying."

Soren whipped his head around to look at Amaya, and right away she realized her mistake in her choice of words. Before he could say anything he might regret though, Rose put her arm between them.

"Amaya, don't be so insensitive. How would you have felt if I had died?" she asked.

The other woman quickly bowed her head. "Right, I'm sorry. I didn't mean it that way...I was only curious about the lance," she apologized.

Soren took a deep breath, blinking slowly. "It's late and our efforts were rigorous...let's head back to the capital and get some rest..."

With that, he was the first to leave the burial site, only to be followed by the two sympathetic girls.

9: Kin's Blood

The capital was bustling with news of the previous night's battle as the inhabitants of Folkvangr began milling about. At first, the buzz seemed to be good news, knowing the citizens felt safe; however, Soren was beginning to fear that it might draw too much attention, should people find out that these "vigilantes," as they called them, were really the demigods that most of Aessatia wanted dead.

"It would probably be best to get going as soon as we can," Soren said while they were in the marketplace searching for materials to buy for the rest of their journey. They had been waiting around that area for Kye to return since Amaya had mentioned something about him accompanying them to the kingdom.

"Shouldn't we keep waiting for my uncle?" Amaya asked as she handed a small bag of fruits to the prophet.

"I would like to apologize to him as well," Rose cut in.

Soren gave a distasteful look. It was clear that he wasn't in favor of the idea, even if it was of importance. After all, Kye *was* from the kingdom, and he would be a helpful ally if they ever hoped to make it past its borders.

"I understand, but we can't spend too much longer here. We need to reach Lucus as fast as we possibly can," he said.

"He said he would be returning to the palace to tell the emperor and empress about what happened. He would be there, right?" Rose asked him.

"I suppose," the prophet replied.

"He's right, Rose. We can't afford to waste any more time," Amaya said.

A sad expression met the blonde's face as she gave an "okay" of agreement.

With everyone on the same page, the three of them finished gathering their rations and began to head for the capital's eastern gate.

They descended the stone steps leading into the fields—or at least that was what had been listed on Amaya's map. She wanted to know just how far they were from Lucus, and at their pace, it appeared they wouldn't be reaching it anytime soon on foot, which was disheartening.

They made it to the bottom of the stone steps when Soren stopped, having heard a sound. He turned around only to see where the hasty pattering was coming from. Once it registered in the others' ears, they, too, turned, just in time to see Kye rushing toward them. "Wait up!" he yelled.

"Uncle Kye, there you are," Amaya said.

"The Emperor Arthus and Empress Helena said that they would like an audience with whomever it was who prevented the attack last night," the man replied.

All three of them shared a glance amongst one another, each wondering the same question: was that really a good idea?

"I'm unsure. Are you sure they really should?" asked Soren.

"I haven't revealed your identities, but I think it would be beneficial for you to meet with them. Perhaps they will be appreciative, even if...you are seen as enemies," Kye answered.

"Or *perhaps* they will send their guards to imprison us before we even get a chance to speak," Amaya replied. She was fine with people knowing *someone* had saved their people, just not knowing *who* this someone was.

"I wouldn't let that happen," he said.

"I think it might be worth a try. If we do, we could gain some supporters, and maybe we can stop worrying about so many people breathing down our necks constantly," Rose said. Then she turned to the man and said, "Also, I'm sorry for how I acted yesterday; it was out of line."

Kye waved his hand and shook his head. "No worries," he replied. "So then, will you come?"

"I'll leave that up for the both of you to decide," Soren said, referring to Rose and Amaya.

They eventually came to the conclusion to agree to the audience with the emperor and empress, and allowed Kye to lead them toward the palace.

Upon reaching the palace, Kye escorted them past the guards. It was nerve-wracking to walk past them, and they half expected for them to try chasing them, but were relieved when they heard no footsteps but their own.

The palace was beautiful inside, its walls lined toward the upper trim with marble carvings of what looked like lions and humans bowing to them. There was gold encrusted in some of them, and above the stained glass told a story about Thosus. The structure clearly had taken a lot of time and funds to build, it was no wonder royalty lived in such a luxurious place.

Eventually, they came to a large corridor with a set of double doors at the end. This was the colloquium room, where generals and the emperor would come to discuss matters of war. This was where Kye had been told to take them.

"I'll stay out here and listen in. Just yell if there is any trouble," Kye offered.

"Thank you, Kye," Soren replied.

As the three of them entered, they were met by two pairs of eyes staring at them, as though any move they made would count badly against them. Each of them took their seats across from the emperor and empress.

"Well, I certainly didn't expect two Lucian demigods to have prevented the befellment of my capital, the two demigods, mind you, who illegally escaped the imprisonment of Tochfuyu...and who have left countless of Aessatia's people fearing their lives," Emperor Arthus said.

He wore a proud suit of armor over his body and an ornament on the side of his head of a gold flame. It mimicked Folkvangr's crest, one they had seen many times on the banners of the capital.

"Please don't hold such heavy judgment against them, your majesty. Hear what they have to say," Soren cut in.

Neither Amaya or Rose looked prepared to speak for their position before such important ears. But the blonde young woman took it upon herself to begin. "We fully accept the punishment we had received and the reasons for which we—"

"No," growled Amaya. "I don't accept it. Did anyone ever stop to consider that the punishment we received may have been inhumane? Yet the line across which a human must not set foot seemed to have been rather diluted when my kin decided that two girls no older than six years should be subjected to life in a frigid prison with no knowledge of reasoning and with no one to keep them safe. To outcast them from the world because of a heinous sin that their parents had committed—the parents they began to think had abandoned them after years of loneliness and slowly fading memories—who unknowingly had been slaughtered by their own kin." Amaya's blood started to boil. After hearing the truth from Kye about their past, it was only her right to display anger to outsiders who had no idea of the situation and wrongly accused them of being dangerous. "Yes. We escaped that awful place without permission from a higher power. But by now, Lucus has made it clear that its only intentions involving us have to do with exiling us. So why should we walk by its commandments?"

The four others sitting at the table stared in bafflement as the young woman spoke her mind. Rose was in utter disbelief. Her friend had been so worried about being detained ever since their departure from Tochfuyu, and yet here she was—defying an emperor.

Now Soren took a turn to speak. "It's become their divine duty to break free from their imprisonment. If they hadn't, Folkvangr, and likely the rest of Aessatia, would be in ruins. You must be aware of the dangers of a god lacking self-control by now, yes? Lives were lost in the chaos of such a battle." Soren's own heart began to pound in his chest as the loss of his former friend came quickly to mind. He ripped off his hood. "So as an Astrian prophet, I order the voidance of their capture!"

The emperor and empress sat with looks of astonishment across their faces. But when Soren spoke, Arthus' features contorted to anger. "The Astrian name lost its authority when its people were eradicated twenty-two years ago," he growled.

The empress placed her hand atop her husband's softly. "You must digress, Arthus..." she said. "We can't ignore that it's their sovereign blood that saved our city from another attack," she said. "I'm Helena, and as the empress of Folkvangr, it's within my authority to bestow upon you all the means of completing your quest as hastily and as safely as possible. Where is it your feet will have you next?"

The emperor looked at Helena with wide eyes, not expecting her to side with the travelers.

After taking a moment to calm himself, Soren answered her. "Lucus. We're hoping to search its repository for an answer," he explained.

"Then I'll see to it that you are provided with armor, horses, and enough rations to see you through the journey," Helena said.

"Helena! You can't give concessions such as those!" the emperor yelled at her.

"If they were proper soldiers, would you have said the same?" she asked, to which she received no response.

"Thank you, your majesty. Your kindness won't be taken for granted," Soren said.

The meeting was adjourned, and time found them in the eastern courtyard once more. On the way, they explained to Kye what had happened, which hardly needed to be done considering he had heard most of the spiel through the doors.

They were given four horses, one for each of them, so that they could travel faster than they would have if they were on foot. Each horse was equipped with a saddlebag containing plenty of fresh rations to get them through their journey. Amaya and Rose had never ridden horses before, so it was a bit terrifying, to say the least, to be atop the towering creatures.

Helena had wanted to give them a proper send-off with a whole ceremony commemorating their efforts so the empire would know their name, but Soren insisted that time was imminent and that it could be saved for another occasion. For now, she agreed to take their faces off the wanted boards around the empire.

When first setting off, it was hard to get used to controlling the horses, even if they stayed on the path. Because of their varied experience with riding, they were traveling at different speeds, which was hard to keep pace with, and staying balanced while the horses galloped was rather difficult for the inexperienced riders. However, after a few hours the girls became more accustomed to their new method of travel.

They rode on for a day with only a night to rest their aching bottoms.

They were off again by the following morning with full bellies, a feeling they hadn't been able to enjoy recently.

"On horseback, around how long do you think it will take to reach the kingdom?" Amaya asked. The horses had slowed to a gentle trot so they would have the chance to rest a bit from galloping. Because of this, she was able to look at her map, examine her surroundings for landmarks, then back at the parchment to check where they were going.

Soren looked over to see the paper in her hands, and as Kye was about to answer her, he cut in. "Normally about twelve days. However, I know of a...secret passage which may get us there a bit faster. It would bring us closer to Lucus and keep us from having to traverse a forest along the way. But we will have to scale a mountain...if we don't wish to waste time going all the way around it," he said.

This answer confused the male redhead in their group. There weren't any shortcuts along the way that he was aware of. The fastest way to Lucus was always by way of the main roads.

"I'm not quite sure I understand," Kye replied.

"You will all see once we get there," Soren answered, giving no further information on the matter.

They were soon led to a forest shaded by dense trees. They were expecting to be taken down the seemingly endless path ahead of them, but Soren stopped them dead in their tracks and dismounted his horse.

Beside them was a large rock which the prophet approached. He stood in front of it and removed his hood, brushing his bangs to the side so that the mark on his forehead would show—a mark none of them had formally seen. The rock suddenly glowed bright green and a beam of light shot from it and ran over Soren's face before disappearing.

He pulled his hood back up, letting his hair fall back over his forehead. While he did this, the rock began to turn by itself and face another direction, one where no trees grew. Then the ground fell away, revealing steps in its wake that led beneath the earth. With that, Soren mounted his horse again and steered the stallion to the daunting staircase.

While all of this was happening, the other three were absolutely astounded by what they had witnessed. It was unlike anything they had ever seen before. Soren waved his hand, saying nothing as he beckoned them forward.

They were hesitant at first, but if it really was a shortcut like Soren said, it had to be safe. Upon entering the cave-like structure, the earth closed behind them, leaving them in the darkness.

"Amaya, would it be possible for you to create a flame?" Soren asked. His voice echoed in the tunnel they were in.

The girl held her hand out, making sure to let go of her horse's mane before she did so as not to set it ablaze, and made a flame from the palm of her hand. This made it only slightly easier to see. Soren was off his horse again and searching about the walls for something. Once the area was lit up he was able to easily find what he was looking for. To the others, the object was completely foreign, but it was clear that Soren knew the object well. His fingers tapped on it and the object lit up like a screen. Then he tapped on characters which had appeared on the object. After doing so, the walls of the cave lit up that same emerald color they had seen on the rock before.

Figuring that was what the flame was needed for, Amaya put it out, allowing the lighted walls leading them down the cave to illuminate the way instead. Again, Soren mounted his horse and kept a steady trot as they descended.

Their eyes couldn't focus on any one thing at once—it was all so foreign and beautiful. Surrounding them were stalactites and stalagmites lining the sides of the cave which glittered from the minerals inside of them. But this beauty was nothing compared to what would come next.

Farther into the cave they could hear the faint sound of running water. Soon the cave grew brighter and the crystals lighting up the cave weren't needed. They stepped inside an underground air pocket which was composed of a wasteland of crumbled buildings and other such structures along with some unrecognizable objects. There was a system of canals that ran through the wreck, its water apparently coming from the source of the noise they had heard, which was actually a waterfall running from another portion of the cave high up on a nearby wall.

The others were awestruck while Soren wore a melancholy facial expression.

"Soren, what is this place? It's absolutely gorgeous," Rose said, her tone sounding breathless.

It was true, the area, despite its desolation, still held a natural beauty to it. A cool draft blew through and mist sprayed them from the spilling waterfall. The air inside the huge cavern felt so fresh, like unobstructed wind on a brisk day in the middle of a boundless field.

"This is my home," answered the prophet. "This is the former capital of the Astrian Empire, Agartha," he said.

Kye's jaw was agape. He had only ever heard stories of this place. It was secret to anyone who didn't belong to the Astral Clan by blood. Its innards had never been seen by anyone other than the Astrians.

Soren spoke again, "But it was destroyed twenty-two years ago by the demons, along with all of my clan."

"Why did you bring us here?" Amaya said, being the first to notice the pained look on the prophet's face.

"Well, as I told you, it's a shortcut. Agartha had many underground systems through which we could traverse the world on foot. Though many were destroyed in the wake of the battle, I know the one leading to Shadow Peaks is still intact," he answered.

But Amaya couldn't help but feel that perhaps there was something far deeper going on inside. After all, this was the place where Soren had grown up; where he surely had friends and family and many people who loved him. They were his kin, and had been gone for so long.

"It's sad...what happened to them, I mean," Amaya said.

Soren cleared his throat in order to ward off the lump he had been starting to feel in his throat. "Yes, well, there's no time to be wasted dwelling on it," he said. He lightly whipped the reins on his horse, and with that, he led the way again through the ruins of the once-grand city.

Both Rose and Amaya took notice of the way his eyes would linger on some of the unrecognizable wreck as the horses picked their way through it.

"I feel bad for him," Amaya whispered to Rose, having brought her horse up beside her friend's so that Soren wouldn't hear her.

"So do I. In a way, isn't he just like us?" the blonde whispered back.

"Yes, it's a sad and terrible sight, isn't it?" another voice interjected.

This voice caused them all to pull back their horses, halting them quickly.

A flash appeared suddenly, causing the horses to rear back onto their hind legs and knock their passengers to the ground. After recovering from the fall, their eyes fell upon the figure who appeared before them. It was the demon—Will.

Amaya ached from her earlier wounds, but still found the courage within herself to draw the sword which she had made a couple days before, doing so with her left hand. "What are you doing here?" she growled at him.

"A sword, huh? I don't see my dear Rose with any kind of weapons. That's a bit unfair, isn't it?" Will purred with a grin as he began to approach the blonde.

Amaya stepped in front of him before he could get closer. "Did you honestly think you could get away with trying to capture two demigods? And then you have the nerve to return and try again?" Amaya asked as she pointed the blade at Will's face.

The demon raised his hands to show forfeit. "Woah! Hold on! You don't wanna go pointing swords like that, you don't know where they might end up," Will said. He carefully placed his finger on the tip of the sword and tried to avert its path away from himself. Instead, he hissed and shook his hand as the sword burned him.

Two grunts were heard. First from the girl and then a loud groan of pain from the man. Amaya had plunged her edge deep into the demon's gut, burning him. He let out repeated grunts and groans through gritted teeth as blood trickled down his burning hand after trying to pry away the blade from his midsection. "O—Okay...I get it..." Will grunted as he slowly backed himself off of the sword. He brought his hand to his lips to wipe the blood that had sprung from them.

Amaya froze. She'd never stabbed someone before. She had killed animals for food, but had never mortally wounded another person. It was gruesome. Just knowing she had that kind of power was near sickening.

Now the crimson liquid was clotting in his throat and he started to cough it up.

"Oh, my..." Amaya mumbled to herself. She couldn't blink or look away as she stared, wide-eyed, at the demon. She knew he was against them, but this? To do this to someone? *How do people go to war?* she wondered.

Noticing her unrest, Soren placed his hand upon her shoulder. "When faced with a ruthless demon, you must not show weakness or you will be killed," he said.

"Wait!" shouted Will upon hearing the man speak. "Let me explain...please!" He put his hands up to show mercy—for the time being.

All four pairs of opposing eyes stared at the demon accusingly as they awaited a reasonable response, as if anything could excuse trying to kidnap them. "Oh, all eyes on me now, huh?" he asked, his demeanor changing as he kept his hand against his wound.

"I don't think you are in any position to be acting cheeky," Soren threatened.

Kye didn't know who or what this was, but from how the others were acting, it was clear to him that he must be an enemy.

"Yes, fine. Have you heard of the demon called Waru?" Will asked them.

"Hell's ruler; everyone knows that name," Kye replied.

"Well, before you youngsters were born, your parents murdered mine. I'm not gonna go into it, but long story short, I'm trying to get my soul back. And bringing you two to the big man in Hell is the only way I can do that," he explained.

"Unfortunately for you, we can't let you do that," Amaya replied as she pointed her sword at Will once more. She may have disliked the way she felt when stabbing him, but defending themselves was far more important.

Soren also drew something: a dagger he kept at his side.

Will narrowed his eyes, annoyed by their resistance. "You may have had me cornered before...but this time...you're mine," he growled. Just as Soren had seen before, the blond demon's wings flung out from his back and—unlike the last time—a pair of horns grew from his temples. He took off into the air to gain level on them.

They had no idea how they would get away from this creature without a fight.

Rose's face contorted uncharacteristically to one of utter anger. "You won't get away with this!" she spat.

In the short distance from them to the running waterfall, a crash sounded as a torrent of water rushed through the gaping hole in the cave where it came from. It broke open an even larger hole, sending shards of rock and crystal flying down into the pool below it, while the immense energy coursing through the water surged straight into Will's body, knocking him out of the air. The demon grunted as he slammed against the cave floor. Soaked, the demon growled and shot up once more. His target: Rose. His body slammed into hers, taking her to the ground.

They skidded across the rocky cave floor from the aftermath of the force exerted against her. The slip of rock against her clothes and her body being forced the other way caused her clothing to rip, scraping her skin.

"I guess you're first then!" he sneered.

His clawed hand reared back to strike, yet in a quick moment, red-hot pain shot through his arm, stopping him from completing his action. Amaya had slashed him with her sword, shoving him over afterward. "That weapon's getting annoying," Will said from his place on the ground while Amaya helped her friend to her feet.

"If you don't want to be hurt, then stand down," Kye stated firmly.

"That would defeat the purpose. It'd make me look a bit foolish, wouldn't you think? Besides...I'm not done yet," the demon answered.

Will spread his arms wide apart, yet his core was tight. Still, for Amaya, he was an open target. She rushed forward and swung her edge once more, mere inches from his arm until she froze. She couldn't move. She could hardly breathe. Darkness slowly encapsulated her, as if all the lights brightening the air pocket they were in just went out.

"What have you done to her!" Soren shouted at the demon as Amaya's body fell.

"Merely reducing the threat is all. Now this should be easy," Will said.

An ear-busting shriek came from the girl who had collapsed to the floor, so loud that even the chasm shivered. By now, Rose was against the ground too, piling up beside Amaya, who was still screaming.

Soren looked up as he saw something shimmer in front of his face. Looking above, he saw the ceiling was cracked from its wear—and realized that what he saw was a stream of dust falling in front of him.

"Dammit," he spat under his breath.

He broke into a run and kneeled beside Amaya, not caring that he was in Will's immediate crossfire should he do anything. "Wake up, quickly!" he shouted, trying to wake both girls.

"It's useless, you know. It's impossible to wake up from your worst fears," the demon told him. The chasm shook more. By now, Will had taken note of what Soren had seen above them. "Move off, I've got to take my leave," he growled and raised his leg to slam his foot into the man, kicking him aside.

"No stop! Calm them first!" Soren yelled immediately upon regaining himself. More rubble from above rained down as Will gathered the writhing girls into his arms. But just as he did, the roof of the cave came tumbling down. "Look out!" Soren shouted.

Then there was a flash that couldn't be registered by anyone still conscious at the moment. A deafening sound blocked their hearing with a continuous and nagging ring. They were all blown to the ground and they stayed there for a long moment, allowing their bodies time to recover. Will's body was wounded by the heat of the explosion, causing him to drop his former captives.

Kye did his best to shake away his blurred vision. There wasn't much to be seen, however. His surroundings were filled with black smoke and debris. He couldn't see where such a blast could have come from, but he had to leave that for later. For the moment, he leaped through the smoke in search of his niece and her friend. Kye eventually heard light coughing and groans of pain, which led him to find Amaya. Carefully, he scooped her into his arms. A faint voice was saying, "Rose, are you all right?"

He couldn't make out the response. He couldn't see Will through the remnants of the explosion, but that was of no importance. Kye hurried back to where they had dismounted their horses and carefully placed his niece atop hers, trying to calm it as it bucked in fear of the explosion.

Soren soon found his own way over to them with Rose at his side. She held something he couldn't see against her chest.

"Come on, we have to get out of here—quickly!" he yelled at them as he mounted his own horse.

The horses were a bit rowdy from the blast but were able to navigate the travelers through the wrecked civilization. Part of Rose wanted to look back at the sight, but she couldn't bring herself to worry about someone who had tried to harm her.

The four of them rode away on their horses without speaking for a while.

When they emerged from the other end of the chasm, they allowed themselves to take a short break. "What in Hell even caused that explosion?" Kye asked.

"That place has wasted away since I last visited...it's likely the rocks above fell onto something and triggered it," Soren replied. He then turned his head back toward the two girls. "Are you both all right? What did he do to you?"

"I don't know...all I remember is seeing him kill Rose, but... it almost felt like a hallucination, looking back on it now," Amaya answered.

"I couldn't see anything, it was pitch black," Rose said.

"He did say something about not being able to escape your worst fears. Perhaps he used your fears against you to subdue you," Soren replied.

"I'm just glad we got out of that alive," the young blonde girl quickly said. Obliviously, she had just exposed her childish fear to the others. But perhaps they hadn't noticed. "I found this book after the explosion. I'm not sure where it came from, but it doesn't look very old."

The others examined the book closely, including Soren. "It doesn't look like anything the Astrians would have written, perhaps it belongs to Will," he said. "You should hold on to it for now."

Soren had been about to wave them onward when suddenly a voracious pounding began in his head. A groan left him and his body began to wobble a bit on his horse's saddle. "Gh...now...?" he grunted to himself.

"Soren? Is everything okay?" Rose asked him.

She received no response, causing the rest of them to share a look with one another. But as they did so, there was a thud. Upon looking over, they could see that Soren had fallen off his horse.

"Soren!" Kye shouted. He dismounted quickly and rushed over to the stilled prophet. The other two did so as well, and collectively they kneeled down beside him.

"I don't understand. What happened? He was fine moments ago," Amaya said.

Kye made haste to turn the man over onto his back and felt around his wrist to check for a pulse. Fortunately, there was still blood pumping against his vein, and upon further inspection he was still breathing as well.

Moments later Soren's eyes reopened. With a soft grunt and a hand to his head, the prophet eased himself upright, his face scrunched in a wince.

"Are you all right, Soren?" Kye asked, concerned.

Soren's eyes flicked over toward the man. He looked a bit shaken and didn't respond for a good moment or two. "Yes, I'm fine. Let's get going," he said before slowly rising to his feet.

Kye watched, hesitant to his reply, while Soren climbed up his horse, perching himself atop its saddle. He wasn't convinced, and looked with a scrunched brow at the back of his head. "Are you sure? You gave us quite the scare just then," he said.

Soren turned his head, his eyes meeting with the other. "Don't concern yourself," he said. "We need to go." With that, he faced forward once more and jostled the reins of his horse before it began trotting forward. The others were soon to follow suit.

The day drew on after that, soon fading into night. Soren had mentioned riding on for the whole night, but after quite some time had passed, they each found themselves growing weary.

The whole time, Soren hadn't said much. Even when asked questions, they found themselves given short answers by him. It seemed he was only physically present and mentally, he was elsewhere.

"Come on now, we've been riding for hours," Kye complained. "We're all tired, hungry, and our arses hurt!" he shouted.

Upon hearing his complaints, Soren turned his head and looked shocked for a split second before softening. "Oh, yes, I'm sorry. I wanted to keep going until we reached the foot of the mountain but..." he trailed off as he looked at Rose, Amaya, and Kye. "Well, it seems it's not the most optimal decision. I didn't realize how late it had gotten."

They each pulled up the reins on their horses and dismounted in order to set up camp for the night.

"We covered a lot of ground," Rose said as she looked off in the distance. Beneath the illuminated moon and stars, she could see the faint figure of a structure far off. "Is that it?" she asked, pointing to it.

"Yes, that's the Shadow Peaks," Kye replied.

"So...I've been wondering, what exactly is the plan for getting us into the capital?" Amaya spoke up as she lay down.

"I'm a knight, remember? You will act as my prisoners. Zyair is the only one who can grant us access to the sanctum, because he holds the key," Kye explained.

"And how exactly do you plan on getting it from him without us being thrown in jail or executed? I mean, who knows what will happen to us once he sets even one eye on us," his niece spoke nervously.

"Don't fret about it, I'll figure things out."

"Great, so you don't even have a solid plan for this."

"Relax. If push comes to shove, we will get inside on our own," Soren cut in.

Amaya looked between both Soren and Kye before heaving a sigh and rolling onto her side. "I hope you both know what you're doing..." she trailed off.

While the others began to settle in for the night, Soren remained awake and sat up with his eyes focused on the distant mountains. After a while, he closed his eyes, trying to meditate to the soft sounds of crickets chirping in the night air. Meditation proved far too difficult, and upon opening his eyes he looked at each sign that the gods he held so dearly to himself were dying.

He could see the branches of far-off trees but no leaves, the grass around him looked like bales of hay, and he couldn't feel the breeze that would normally kiss his skin on such a calm night.

Soren drew in a deep breath and dragged his fingers through his hair, trying to think of any possible solution to this catastrophe; yet, like many other times, he could think of nothing. "I hope this journey won't be for naught..." he murmured under his breath while staring at his lap.

He heard a rustle beside him and alerted himself to it, looking over to see Rose sitting there. "Huh? What are you doing awake?" he asked the girl.

"I couldn't sleep again. Anyway...you haven't been acting yourself since you passed out earlier. Is everything okay?" she asked.

Soren's eyes lingered on her for a long moment before showing confusion. "You would worry yourself with that? Even when struggling with a bout of insomnia?"

"I'm supposed to be saving the world. Or...at least trying. How could I bring myself to say that if I can't even concern myself with your needs? You are a friend, after all," Rose explained.

This brought a smile to the man's lips before turning his head to look down once more. "Your heart is very kind, Rose," he said. There was a delay in his words before he spoke again. "I had a vision back then," he said. "And it's been troubling me."

"A vision?"

"Yes. I'm a prophet, remember? Each time I receive a prophecy, something to that effect happens to me. It happened in Brekka when the earthquake struck."

"I see."

"Anyway, the vision was of Will. I believe he's supposed to aid us somehow," Soren explained.

"What? But he's been trying to capture us, how is that possible? Are you sure?" the young woman asked.

"I've been trying to deduce that all day," he replied. "But it seems to be the most plausible."

"What did you see?" Rose asked him.

"We were fighting. I couldn't make out against what it was, but we were fighting alongside him."

"Well...if that's what you saw...perhaps it's meant to be then."

10: FORTHRIGHT BLOOD

When afternoon came the next day, the travelers were already well on their way toward Shadow Peaks. The clear, open fields of the kingdom territory which they had entered soon faded into the verdant trees covering the mountains. There were no paths to tell them where to go, making the journey all the more ominous. But what made it more menacing was the comment Kye made just as they could no longer see the foot of the mountain they had begun to climb.

"I've heard stories about this place from a few of the soldiers and even some from my days of patrolling the sea with the armada," Kye started. "Many said that those who don't traverse these mountains through the valley end up being taken. Some say creatures ate them, others say there is a group of barbaric people who cannibalize them. Sometimes the stories were horrific. I've only traveled through the valleys, mostly because they're easier to traverse on horseback than through the trees...but the valley is miles from here." The other three listened intently to Kye's story while he told it.

It filled them with a sense of unease, even though such stories were likely folktales to keep people from being foolish enough to fully scale the mountain. Soren noticed the nervous look on Rose's face and quickly cut in. "You know, it's probably mountain lions they're speaking of. We just need to be careful once night falls," he assured her.

Kye turned his head to look at the girl. "Oh, I didn't mean to scare anyone, I was only telling stories, is all," he said. "I'm sure most of them were untrue, anyway; the sea does get quite boring when a boat surrounded by water is all there is to occupy your time."

"Ah...of course," Rose answered.

There was a few moments of silence before Amaya spoke to Soren. "I was curious about this sword I had made," she said. "Since you seem to know more about these powers than I do."

Soren looked down at the girl whose horse fell into step beside his own. "Ah, well, what do you want to know?"

"How did I make it in the first place? The most I had ever done with fire before I made it was making a spark within my hands."

"These powers have always been awake and alive within you and Rose, as you said, there were even times when you used them by accident. Each demigod is capable of tempering the weapons used by the gods. But yours was actually forged originally by Noctis himself, it's called Sacris Ignem," Soren explained.

Amaya looked at the hilt of the sword strapped across her back for a long moment before her gaze returned to the man beside her. "Noctis...that's the name of one of the demigods' ancestors, isn't it?" she asked.

"Yes, he and Avius were the two original demigods. I'm actually quite surprised you have been able to wield it with your arm in the condition that it is. You keep getting injured," Soren said.

The girl looked off to the side with a nervous grin. "Well...I suppose I've simply been biting my tongue when I used it...but it hasn't been hurting too much lately, at least when I'm not using it," she explained.

"Of course, how could I forget. With holy blood, your wounds heal much faster than a normal human."

As Amaya was about to reply, a loud rustle and then a yelp stopped her from speaking. She gently pulled the reins on her horse and turned her head to see what the noise was caused by, as did the others.

Rose had dismounted her horse and was now being held up by a net.

Kye got down from his horse and examined the area around where Rose had fallen victim to the net. "A trap...?" he murmured to himself. Carefully, he began kicking away some leaves to search for any more traps. "We had better be careful; this place is littered with traps."

"Traps? That's strange...this place is usually remote," Soren said as he, too, dismounted his horse.

"Why did you get off your horse in the first place?" Amaya asked.

"I dropped something and went to pick it up," Rose said. "Could you please cut me down?"

Without a word, Amaya got down from her horse and drew her sword, reaching it upward to try and cut the rope. "It's hard to cut…" she complained as she worked away at the thick rope.

While Rose watched the endeavor, she failed to notice the figures approaching, which within moments covered Kye's mouth and restrained him before he disappeared into the trees without a sound.

The others whipped their heads around to where the man had once been. They didn't see him leave but heard the rustling and knew he was missing. "Kye?" Soren asked.

One by one, the remaining two on the ground were taken into the silence of the Shadow Peaks' forest. Within moments, they vanished without a trace, with only their horses to signify anyone had even been there. But they, too, were led away along with Rose, who the captors had cut down from the tree and dragged off.

* * *

Rose was the first to awaken an hour after they were captured. Panic quickly set in as she realized that she was tied with her back against a tree, but as she calmed a bit, she realized that there were quaint houses around her and an overall tranquil scenery. There was no way they weren't still atop that mountain, but where exactly upon it, she was unsure.

The ropes stung against her healing wounds, but she held in her expression of the pain they caused. Looking around further, Rose discovered that the others were also tied to their own trees separate from hers. As they began to wake and lift their heads,

Rose called to Soren, whose tree was the closest to her position, "What happened?"

"We have been captured, but by whom, I'm unsure..." he said.

Before either of them could blink, the tip of a long blade was being held against Soren's throat, attached to someone dressed in a sleek black suit. Most of the person's face was covered, save for their eyes—which were glaring daggers into Soren's.

"Explain your business on our turf, or you will be killed." The voice he received was that of a man's.

Rose saw the fear well up in Soren's eyes as he registered what had just happened. He rarely looked afraid. He always seemed so determined—so ready to face any obstacle thrown at him—but now he was showing something completely different. "Please have mercy on us." Hearing him beg for his life was even more horrifying. It made her question whether or not they would make it out of this situation alive. "We were only passing through Shadow Peaks to reach Barness, we didn't mean to intrude on your territory. I was unaware that there was a settlement all the way up here," Soren explained.

"Why did you not take the valleys?" the man asked accusingly, the point of his blade starting to dig into Soren's throat, causing him to shut his eyes tightly.

"We're very short on time, and the valley was miles away from where we first began climbing the mountain." Soren's voice was filled with fear and nervousness, he knew not if the sword pressing against him would end his life the second he spoke a wrong word.

The back of the man's katana pressed against the underside of Soren's chin and a suspicious look met his face. "Time? What for?" he asked with a tilt of his head.

"Perhaps if you weren't holding a sword to his face, he could answer you more clearly," Amaya interjected from her own tree.

The man's eyes darkened, but he removed the sword from Soren's neck, only for one to immediately be brought against Amaya's. "Don't disrespect our leader," a female voice commanded from behind her.

From what Rose could see across from her, the woman was wearing similar attire to the man in front of Soren. "Please forgive her," Soren said hastily. "She's only worried. You see, we were on our way to Barness to see if we could find any information about the gods becoming sick."

This seemed to strike something within the man because he immediately sheathed his sword. "That can only mean one thing..." the man trailed off, his suspicion quickly disappearing. "Release them at once, they're the ones from the prophecy."

At his word, the ropes began falling from the bodies of the four travelers, leaving them all confused as to the sudden change of attitude. "I deeply apologize for how we have treated you. You see, we're religious followers of the gods. We have been waiting for the day the sovereigns would come to cure them, and since the gods have become sick, we have been on edge about who walks upon our mountains. But when we caught wind of merchants in the valley talking of demigods escaping the tundra, we were hopeful again."

"Yes...but who exactly is 'we'?" Amaya asked.

From behind the trees, three more soldiers dressed almost exactly like the man stood beside him. "This is Altona Village, where the vigilantes of the kingdom all live. Where there is injustice, we seek to put an end to it. I'm the leader of this establishment. You may call me Lou," he said.

The four of them got to their feet. "Your horses are tied up near our coup and your belongings were put in the treasury."

None of the others, including Soren, were satisfied with the things this man was saying, and their disapproving faces made it blatant. Lou bowed his head before fully getting onto his knees and bowing to the four of them. The other three standing beside him were quick to bow down as well. "Please forgive us for your ill-treatment. If need be, we will offer hospitality for the night and food and water," he said.

Soren held his chin before looking up to the sky. "The day is already almost over, and to get to Shadowcrest would take at least another full day..." he said. "Very well, we will accept your offer." Wasting the remainder of the day wasn't the most optimal decision, but it would save them the trouble of having to travel late into the night or settle in the open fields to rest their heads, vulnerable to attack at all angles. Though it wasn't the fastest option, it was definitely the safest.

Lou rose from the ground along with the others beside him. "Thank you for your mercy, how may we refer to you all?"

"I'm Soren, this is Rose, to her left is Amaya, and to my right is her uncle, Kye," Soren said, motioning to each of them with his introduction.

"We're very honored to have you here with us. Allow me to show you around our beloved home of Altona." With that, the other three vigilantes dispersed and allowed Lou to lead their guests along the quaint little paths of their village.

He first led them to the stables so they could see their horses were all right. When they got there, a little girl was standing beside one of the stallions, stroking him gently as she stood behind the gate.

"Agnes, I told you not to touch the horses." Hearing Lou's voice caused the little girl to start, her head turning swiftly toward them. "I do apologize," he said to the four travelers. "This is my daughter, Agnes."

Rose smiled at the display of the little girl petting the horse. "That's quite all right, she seems harmless enough," she said as she approached the girl. "So your name is Agnes? Do you like horses?" Rose asked.

"Papa, how come she's not from here?" the little girl asked. She completely ignored Rose's question and looked over at Lou.

"Come now, she's an honored guest; you must be kind," he answered and walked over to pick up his daughter. When she was in his arms her eyes trailed over to Rose before shaking her head.

"She's a princess, Papa!" Agnes exclaimed.

"A princess, huh?"

Agnes nodded her head rapidly, smiling widely.

"If she's a princess, I wonder what that makes the rest of us," Soren whispered in jest to the others standing beside him.

"You're always so vivid and colorful, you know that, Agnes?" Lou said.

But the little girl pulled an upset face. "I'm not imagining today, Papa. She's really a princess!"

"Sorry, she has quite the imagination, she always has," the man replied with a smile.

Still, the girl looked rather unhappy. "Papa, can you please put me down? I want to go to the flower field." Once set down, the little girl rushed off.

Rose watched as she ran off before turning her attention to Lou. "She seemed quite upset..." she said.

"Yes...see, Agnes tends to get quite frustrated when I call her imaginative. I never really understand it..." Lou said. "Anyway, shall we continue with our tour?"

"Actually...I think I would like to go talk to Agnes. Would that be all right?" Rose asked.

Lou was confused as to why the girl was so concerned, but didn't see it as a problem. "If...that's what you want. We will be in the village's center when you return," he said.

Rose nodded. "Thank you...could you...erm...point me in the right direction?" she asked.

"Oh, of course. The flower field is that way," the man pointed. "As long as you keep walking straight, you can't miss it." Rose wandered off in that direction while Amaya, Soren, and Kye continued to follow Lou.

"That was a little odd," Kye said quietly to the others while they walked.

"I agree...she seemed very genuine about her words," Soren replied.

"She's just a little girl. Her father was right, she's only pretending," Amaya cut in.

When Rose found her way to the field of flowers, she saw Agnes sitting in the middle of it all, almost as though she, herself, were a flower among the rest. She sat on her knees, face downcast toward a flower pinched between her small, delicate fingers while her other hand gently peeled away the petals, letting them fall wherever they floated.

Rose approached her quietly so as not to startle her and kneeled down next to the girl. "Hello."

Agnes looked up to the older woman and smiled a little upon seeing her there. "Hi," she said timidly.

Rose wasn't sure how to begin to speak with this girl. She had never dealt with someone whose age was once her own and deduced it must be best to deal with her carefully. After all, she didn't want her to run off again.

It was a good feeling to see youth in such desperate times. How could a child like her be so blissfully ignorant that it kept her happy even when the world around her was in shambles? Rose wondered if she was aware while she, too, began absentmindedly picking away at a dandelion. "Does it anger you when your father doesn't believe you?" she finally asked.

Agnes pulled a crestfallen face, her head anchoring down a little more. "Nobody ever believes me," her somber voice muttered.

"Well..." Rose was uncertain of how to approach this, since she didn't know how to accommodate what a child needs to hear. "As you get older, there may be a lot of people who don't believe you." She couldn't bring herself to leave off the response there. It was too vague, too unsatisfying, even for herself. "But you have to remember that even when they don't, you should always stand by what you believe in." Rose felt more proud of the rest of her reply. It seemed like just what the girl needed to hear, and she even earned a smile from Agnes.

"If you ever become a princess again, I think you will be a kind and fair one, just like in the stories Papa tells me before bed," she said.

Even Rose found herself able to smile. "If I ever become a princess, I'll be sure to keep you in mind."

The two spent a while longer out in the field picking flowers and arranging them into bouquets and weaving them into crowns and rings. When Rose found it time to be heading back to the establishment, the two were adorned with many pieces of flower jewelry.

"I feel bad for taking all the flowers," Agnes said as they headed down the lightly trampled path.

"Why might that be?" Rose's eyes didn't remove from the path ahead while she spoke, she could see the glimmer of a fire in the distance with more than a few people surrounding it.

"Because Buhus-Vadu tried very hard to make them, even though they're sick."

Rose felt her heart sink, her attention immediately being grabbed by the little girl. "Oh...so you know about them?" she asked.

Agnes nodded her head. "It's a shame you guys had to lock them up...now the flowers won't bloom anymore."

The woman's mouth hung open as she watched Agnes run off toward her father. She missed the conversation between her and Lou about how she should probably be getting to sleep.

To be fair, the evening sky was just starting to darken over the mountains.

When Rose returned to her group of comrades, she found a seat between Soren and Amaya, but she still couldn't shake the impression left on her by that little girl who Lou had already taken to his home to go to bed.

"Is something the matter, Rose?" Soren asked, immediately noticing her expression.

She would have answered him were it not for the faces of the other villagers looking at her, having heard Soren's question.

Rose's posture retreated back a little, as though she had been snapped from her thoughts. "Oh, no. I was only thinking." Amaya read the lie from her friend without even looking at her and decided to ask her about it later when everyone else was absent from the conversation.

"If it's so," Soren answered her and went back to eating. "There is food if you're hungry."

This brought Rose's attention to the fire burning between her and the rest of the people who had joined together. She supposed she was quite hungry and decided to have some food for herself.

Lou returned shortly after she took her seat again and began to eat. "And just like that, the little one is fast asleep," he said. "Sorry for the delay, you three seemed interested in the story."

Rose knew the man must be talking about her comrades, but of the story he spoke of, she knew nothing. Wanting to escape from the confusion caused by that little girl, she inquired. "What story?"

"Ah, Lou was telling us a wonderful tale of how this village was founded," Kye answered. "Apparently when the demons attacked all but twenty-two years ago, he defeated the ones at the base of the mountain singlehandedly!"

"Correct, and since that day, I vowed to bring justice to humanity," Lou finished for him.

"Still, it's hard to picture that after so much time has passed, demons still lurk atop these peaks," Soren said.

"Even if they're far and few between, demons do linger here. But sometimes I worry about them because the ones that usually come around are underlings," Lou replied.

"What are they?" Amaya asked him.

"Underlings are the ones created by the king of Hell, Waru, or so they say. They're his servants that bring him meals. When they kill you, they bring your soul to him, where he then devours it. That's how you wind up there. But we're usually able to keep them at bay, even when night falls."

And thus night fell upon them. Rose's mind was either focused on Agnes or the fact that a demon might barge into the travelers' sleeping quarters and devour them all. Needless to say, night would bring more sleeplessness. Her insomnia was becoming debilitating. She hadn't mentioned it to anyone else, but her energy was waning with each night that sleep neglected her.

She needed fresh air, but was afraid of leaving the house they were staying in. Everyone else was well on their way through a land of dreams and fantasy while she stayed awake in a reality of nightmare. Worst of all, there was nothing to arm herself with.

Even still, she needed to steel herself if she wanted to escape from that stuffy little cottage and breathe the open air...even if the altitude made the air thin.

Soon she found herself wandering the empty village while her mind wandered the crowded, spaceless confines of her head. The scenery around her blurred into the thoughts of what may come of the world if she and Amaya were too late to save it. Prophecy or no prophecy, they weren't immortal—and that fact was constantly prominent on her mind. Even if saving the gods was something feasible, she feared the ones who had lost their minds would destroy them before they could set any kind of plan into motion.

Facing Adione was terrifying and being thrown in jail was a very real threat as Amaya had always proven to her. She wished there was a way to feel confident in herself. After all, Rose never expected to be taken on such a journey, and sometimes she wondered if she was burdening Amaya by having convinced her to leave.

She had thought of it for years of their time in Tochfuyu, but never said a word to her friend of it until the day she had had enough of it.

But even if the journey so far had caused so much hardship, Rose couldn't help but feel it must have been fate for them to have left that wasteland of snow just when the world was falling into its perilous state. Or perhaps that was an overstatement—it was children like Agnes that gave her hope, if only a little, that Aessatia was still okay. The sky wasn't falling, the lands weren't burning. Sure, the gods were sick, but that was what she and Amaya had set off to fix. Perhaps things weren't as hopeless as her mind made them seem.

Rose breathed in the fresh night air as relief—at last—fell over her.

Suddenly, a certain smell turned her expression sour when she inhaled again. It was metallic and so thick that she could almost taste it. Shaking her head from her reverie, she realized that she wasn't in the village at all anymore, but had wandered mindlessly to the flower field where she and Agnes had spent all afternoon into the evening.

Scattered within the petals of the few remaining flowers and among the green blades of grass were dribbles of deep red that were recklessly left behind by what she could only assume was an attack. The droplets were scarce until Rose looked farther ahead, where the color became thicker and denser, turning into a trail that led into the trees on the other side of the field.

Regardless of the fear gripping at her insides, Rose's legs carried her forward along the trail of blood.

As she reached the edge of the forest, the smell became much more potent than before. And now she was beginning to hear screaming, which made her feet move even quicker. She came to an abrupt halt where her path ended between a toppled tree and a trunk covered in moss.

The creature before her stood on eight pale arms which ended in hands. Blood covered two of them, likely originating from the source of the trail she had been following. She leaned quietly around the beast's massive body, her heart pounding in her ears harder and harder the more she saw. Beneath the towering stature of the horrific being was a child, bleeding profusely from multiple wounds on her body. It was difficult to imagine that so much blood could even come from a child that size.

Rose could feel uncertainty welling up inside her mind while her fear met its brim. Her hands shook. Her legs almost gave out more than a few times. She didn't know how to save this child. But there was one thing she did know—that she needed to detour the demon, even if it was toward herself.

She was about to move, but was stopped by a voice calling out for her. "Rose! Please help me!" Though it was distorted and overflowing with fear, there was no mistaking that voice; it was Agnes.

All at once, that voice replaced her fear with determination and rage; replaced her shaking hands with steady ones, and her trembling legs with the strength to charge forward. Without thinking, Rose grabbed a branch from the ground and raised it above her head before bringing it down on the creature that was two times her size. It screeched and whipped around to face her, ignoring the girl it once preyed upon. But now that its hungry eyes were looking at her, Rose's fear returned with a vengeance—and any thoughts of being able to actually fend off the demon fled.

Its head jittered as it approached her slowly, its movements unpredictable. It wasn't long until the demon backed her against the moss-covered log. Now there was nowhere left to run. *Is this where I meet my end?* she thought to herself. She looked around the creature, seeing that Agnes didn't have the strength to get up and run. After the demon feasted upon Rose, it would only return to Agnes once more.

The creature's hand lunged forward, its unnaturally long nails slicing open her shoulder. Then its mouth parted, huge, bloodstained teeth glaring right into Rose's eyes as they came toward her.

"No!"

The girl rolled to the side, dodging the creature's quick movements despite its massive size. *I can't let Agnes die...I can't give up...My ghost would never part with this place knowing the sadness I caused someone because I didn't try.* Rose pulled the wooden dagger from her waist satchel and held it ready. The blood from her fight with the bear and the goddess of wind was still smudged on its dulled cutting edge. It was undeniable proof that she was capable of winning against the beast, even if her comrades weren't there to help her.

Rose stared at the beast, now recovering from the missed blow that had sent its jaws into the felled log. It left a huge mark in the wood, causing just momentary relief that it hadn't been her head in place of the log, but fear took its own role in reminding her that if she wasn't careful, it *would* be her that the demon took a bite out of.

She ran forward, taking a swing at one of the demon's arms, and, to her own surprise, actually landed a hit. But joy quickly drained away as she realized that the knife was only capable of nicking its flesh, leaving a measly scratch that quickly healed on its own. Just a moment later, that same arm swung upward, knocking the weapon from Rose's hand. The knife flew up, but didn't come back down. She chanced a look upward to see why her knife hadn't fallen back to her, only to realize it was ensnared within a web, likely woven by that very demon.

Within moments the demon was pinning her, the large body towering over her while its huge arms surrounded her on every side. Rose shut her eyes tightly, bracing for the pain she knew would come to her and shrieked as loud as her lungs would allow when the brooding creature's teeth took a chunk of flesh from her shoulder. Her blurry eyes opened to see what would happen next, fearing the worst. But instead she felt something cold and wet touching her hands until it melted away, becoming solid. When she looked down, she saw that in one hand she held a bow and in the other, an arrow.

Rose had never shot a bow before, nor had she ever nocked an arrow, but the demon was so close at that point that she was able to stab the arrow into the demon's chest, causing the beast to scream out of rage and pain. This allowed her enough time to escape and properly examine what she had done. *Is this similar to what Amaya had done?* she thought to herself.

When she looked down to see the bow, she noticed a quiver filled with arrows like the one she had wounded the demon with. She used the opportunity presented by the struggling demon to shoot another arrow at it, not caring where it might strike. In the rush of the fight, she didn't even have time to wrap her mind around the fact that she instinctively knew how to load and shoot the bow. She shot a few, only because she missed the second and the third struck somewhere non-lethal.

Each arrow caused more and more pain to the demon as their tips seared its skin. The beast collapsed against the forest floor, leaving a rumble in its wake. Then Rose dashed toward Agnes. Her throat constricted when she saw the mess the demon had left her in. It was gruesome—she could hardly keep her eyes on it.

"P-P...Princess..."

"It will be all right, Agnes, I'm going to bring you to your papa, okay?" Rose choked on her words. She was doing all she could to hold back her tears and remain strong for the little girl. "I'm so sorry..."

Rose put her arms around what was left of the little girl and picked her up, even if the pain in her shoulder was explosive. Blood spilled from both of them; more from Agnes than herself.

She donned injuries from head to toe, ranging from huge lumps of missing flesh to deep slashes—she would be lucky to live through such an attack.

When she turned to rush the girl back to the village, her stomach sank upon seeing that the demon she had struck full of arrows was standing once again with eight blood-thirsty eyes glaring at them.

"Please...!" Rose cried as if the mindless fiend would understand her plea for mercy. But it just kept on trudging toward her and Agnes.

Four of its hands whipped at her, and before she could even blink, she was screaming in agony. Webs suspended her body in the air, binding her. It felt like thousands of tiny knives digging into her flesh and making her bleed more. Her blood dripped like rain off her body and stained the grass red. It left Agnes on the ground, alone and shaking.

The spider-demon thundered toward her, hands outstretched to take her.

The young woman's eyes widened, her mouth ajar. The sound of a crash followed by a thud hit her ears, both sounds mingling with one another as it happened so fast.

A figure had leaped from the trees above and struck down the beast, but what confounded her was that the person who had caused the demon to fall wasn't anyone she would have ever expected: it was Soren. He stood atop the carcass as it seized beneath his weapon, the one he refused to use against Adione. It must have been what was causing the spider demon to jolt so violently since electricity was coursing down the mast of the lance.

She was both relieved and astonished all at once.

When he was sure the beast wouldn't recover from the blow, Soren removed the lance from its body and leaped toward Rose, using the weapon to cut her down but catch her before she could hit the ground. He placed her down beside Agnes. "You shouldn't have wandered off on your own, you could have been killed by that thing," he said.

"Save your scolding, Agnes needs medical attention immediately," Rose answered.

Nodding, Soren put his weapon back into the holster on his back, returning it to its discreet form then took Agnes from the ground carefully. Then they both rushed to return her to Altona.

Rose's whole body was on fire, cuts and slashes decorating her skin, stinging against the cool night air.

They weren't allowed to accompany the now-unconscious girl while she underwent the procedures to save her life. Forced to wait outside, neither of them spoke to one another for a few moments.

"I see you awoke Diluvium," Soren finally broke the silence, glancing at her bow.

"Soren...who are you, really?" Rose kept her eyes focused ahead on nothing in particular. When she received no response, she spoke once more. "That lance is no ordinary weapon, is it?"

From the corner of her eye, she saw Soren lower his head and heard a hushed sob leave his chest. "It's true..." he answered after many more moments of hesitation. "The lance belongs to me...I created it myself...because I, too, am a demigod."

Rose turned her head to look at Soren. Some things made more sense to her now, but she ceased the many questions that were begging to be asked and allowed the man to explain.

"My real name is Liland, son of Asabüro, the former emperor of the Astrian empire...and I'm the demigod of lightning. Once word got out that demigods were disliked, I faked my own death and became a new person."

"Soren..." Rose's eyes were filled with tears. "You shouldn't have had to hide your identity out of fear, I'm so sorry."

Soren shook his head. "You should go back inside and ask them to treat your wounds...but Rose," his eyes pleaded with her, "I ask that you please keep this information to yourself. I don't feel comfortable sharing it with the others yet."

"But you must, they deserve to know who you are. They will understand, just like I do," Rose argued.

"I will eventually," Soren confirmed. "I'm not yet ready for anyone to know who I am...so please..." he trailed off.

Rose was silent for a long moment until she found it in herself to answer him. "Very well...I'll keep your secret."

Soren nodded, clear relief in his demeanor. "Thank you... now let's go inside and get those wounds wrapped."

11: Liar's Blood

When the dawn of the following day arose, the travelers were making preparations to begin the rest of their climb up the mountain where they would eventually descend. As they mounted their horses preparing for departure, Lou approached them before abruptly dropping to his knees in front of Rose's stallion.

"I'm forever in your debt, Miss Rose. You have my deepest gratitude for saving Agnes' life. If it hadn't been for you, she would have been killed."

No one had been notified of Soren's assistance in the matter, so Lou didn't mention him, which was completely fine with Soren.

"Please, Lou, stand," Rose insisted. "You don't have to bow to me; I just did what anyone else would have done."

At her request, Lou returned to his feet then looked at the rest of them as a group. "I wish you all safe travels. Are you sure there isn't anything else you need before you go?" he asked.

"No, thank you. We appreciate your hospitality," Soren replied. "We will be on our way now."

"If you insist, safe travels all of you."

Lou and a few of the other villagers waved to them as they went, but Rose's horse was stopped, followed by the sound of Lou's footsteps behind her. "Agnes! What are you doing out of bed? You should be resting." When Rose looked down, she saw it had been Agnes who stopped her, her body very bruised but bandaged, and she was standing so that had to be a good sign. Seeing her one more time alive and in better condition than when she last saw her made Rose smile.

"I wanted to give you a crown, Princess Rose," Agnes said with a bright smile.

She held up a woven flower crown like the ones they had made the day before. "Mama said she pressed them so they won't die," she said.

Rose smiled more, fighting away tears as she took the crown from her. "Thank you, Agnes...I've something I want to give you too, actually," she set the crown onto her head and pulled out the stuffed cat she had dropped the day before. "This is Mer. He means a lot to me. You will take good care of him, right?" Rose asked as she handed it to the girl.

Agnes stared at the toy in her hands. "I will," she promised and then looked back up at Rose. "I hope you see him again soon."

Mishearing her, she replied, "I hope I see you again one day as well. And be careful from now on, okay?" Rose smiled fondly.

Agnes nodded slightly, likely because she was in pain. "Me too. And I will!" After that, Lou put an arm around his daughter, coaxing her back to their house so she could rest.

"Thank you again," he said as they left.

Soon they were a ways out from Altona, feeling the sun's warm rays as they shined through the canopy above. "It seems you left a pretty good impression on that village, Rose," Kye said.

"I suppose, but they already liked us to begin with," Rose reasoned with him.

"It was nice to see a change of tune," Amaya said.

"Actually, it's not as surprising as you think. Outside the capitals of both Lucus and Folkvangr, the demigods are still worshipped just like any other god," Soren cut in.

Amaya pressed her lips together, her expression resembling one of annoyance. "I think the concept of it all is just the byproduct of stupidity..." she murmured. The comment caught the attention of the others, which caused her to tense uncomfortably. "I just think too many see us for what we are, and not for *who* we truly are."

"Sad as that reality may sound, it's the truth nonetheless."

"But you shouldn't let that discourage you, few as they may be, there are still some who look past what you are," Kye cut in. "Like myself, and I assume the rest of us as well."

"Absolutely," Soren said.

Amaya gave no sign that their responses were very convincing. "Can that be enough?"

"Enough for what?"

Silence befell them until they came to the mountain's crest. What lay on the other side stole away their attention from the conversation. It was vastly different from what familiarity had already presented itself to them by the northern side of the mountain. The south showed a steep descent with a craggy surface, a near-impossible feat on horseback. The sheer slope seemed hopeless. But even if they didn't have to reach the snow-capped peak to get around it, the air from their current standpoint was still rather thin.

Within moments, the four of them had all but forgotten their discussion. Regardless of the despairing descent, a large establishment was visible from the height at which they stood, silhouetted by the rising sun which had begun to paint the blue-black sky a rich orange. It was still quite early. But at the forefront of the territory sat another settlement, and it looked like they could reach it before the day ended—given they didn't plummet down Shadow Peaks and get buried within a landslide first.

"That must be Barness, right?" Rose asked, her finger extending toward the distant unrecognizable place.

"Indeed. But we will likely rest at Shadowcrest once we make our way down the mountain," Soren answered her.

"That little hamlet down there?"

"Right."

"That is, of course, if we can *survive* making our way down this mountain," Amaya cut in. "Whose idea was it again not to take the valleys around this thing? Sure, perhaps we could make it on foot if we were careful, but with horses?" Two of the horses whinnied, clearly daunted by the task of having to scale down the landmass.

"Horses are actually the safest option; they may be heavy, but they can maneuver steep surfaces relatively well," Kye answered.

Amaya let loose a sigh and placed a hand on her head, her mind thinking up multiple horror scenes of someone getting hurt on the way down. "Well...I guess we have a long way to go," she said.

Step by step, the mountain slowly revealed how treacherous it was outside of looks alone. Unstable rocks slid the horses further down and onto cliffsides which gambled life and death each time weight pressed upon them. Hours of dodging slopes and plenty of scares led them to a larger, more stable platform where they decided to stop and rest for food. A lone tree clung to its edge, roots overlooking the rest of the descent, which was filled with jagged rocks extenuating that one slip would mean death. Needless to say, they stayed close to the mountain face.

Fear-inducing as it may have been, it provided a breathtaking view of the other two sister mountains—which still looked just as perilous—a deep grey mingled with the blue and green of the surrounding scenery. One spilled a stream of water from its face while the other seemed just as bland as the one they were upon, though it played its own part in the elaborate setting.

Soren dished out food for everyone that didn't have to be cooked. Once they were all served, he chose a spot beside Amaya, who sat slightly away from everyone else, eyes glued to the capital peeking over the horizon.

"Hello, Amaya," he greeted her cheerfully, hoping it might lift her spirits a bit. But her eyes looked back at him, unenthused. She gave him a nod, acknowledging his existence at the very least before distracting herself once more with the silhouette of Barness. "Does it worry you?"

Soren heard a crunch as Amaya took a bite from the apple she was eating and waited patiently for her answer. "A bit...but that isn't what I'm thinking about," she admitted. Soren stayed silent, knowing that if he did, she might eventually force herself to answer. But he was wrong. She played along with his game, causing Soren to release a sigh.

"Well, what *are* you thinking about?"

Her look gave Soren the impression that she felt antagonized. "Awfully pushy, aren't we? For someone who is lying about who they are, that is."

It was evident—at least to Amaya—that years of being alone had influenced Soren's once-sculpted ability to talk to women. The comment dealt a heavy blow to Soren's self-esteem. "I can see you're not interested in talking," he said.

"Shocking that you needed me to say it before getting the message."

Soren stood after that, respecting her wishes to be left alone. But before he could make it very far, he was stopped by the feeling of her hand grabbing his pant leg. "Wait," she said, causing him to look down. "Sorry...I'm having some troubling feelings is all." Amaya averted her gaze while she explained herself.

He couldn't just walk away from her after hearing that, and sat down again, a little closer this time. "What is bothering you?" he asked.

Amaya traced the outline of Barness with her eyes, distracting herself just one more time before having to face reality out loud. "I'm angry," she finally said.

"About?"

"When my uncle told me what happened to mine and Rose's parents, I..." she trailed off, struggling to find her words again. "I felt this boiling...rage deep inside me. They're dead, but somehow I can't bring myself to forgive them."

"Forgive them for what?"

"For leaving us alone with all the problems they created for us to live with," she admitted. "Looking at the capital, I can't help but reminisce on the few memories I have of it. I always cherished all of them, doing my best throughout the years to hold onto them. But it feels like they were all lies...knowing now that my parents were terrible people is a staggering blow. It feels like what I remember and the truth are so different from one another that I don't want to lump them together."

"You don't want to...but you do," Soren replied.

"Exactly...and I hate them because of it," she admitted.

"Even if they were bad people, I don't think you should hate them."

"Why not?"

"Because they gave you life, didn't they? And you shared fond memories with them."

"That's what makes me wonder why they had me, then." Her eyes fell into her lap and she played with the apple core in her hand, doing anything to avoid looking into Soren's eyes. "And I wonder about the life I could have had, were it not for their choices. I wonder who I was meant to be."

"Don't you see? This is what the gods had intended for you. What you are now *is* who you were meant to be," Soren tried to assure her, but she looked displeased with that answer.

"If all I was meant to be is a distrusting person filled with strife and anger, then my existence to them must be nothing but a joke to laugh at," she bit back.

"Is that all you see in yourself?"

"Well, what do *you* see?"

Soren looked up, tapping his lip as he gave the question some thought. "Well, I think you're a caring person, at least from what I've seen with your interactions with Rose. You care deeply for her since you two are so close," he began. "Oh, and courageous too," he added quickly. "You were quite reluctant before, but when the stakes are high, you don't seem to mind risking it all for those you care about."

Amaya saw some truth in his words, even if only some, evident by the smile that made its way onto her lips. "Thank you, Soren. I needed that," she said.

"Of course. Sometimes a pick-me-up is all you need when you're feeling discouraged." Soren gave a smile of his own and the two went on eating.

When their bellies were full and the horses were given adequate time to rest, Amaya, Soren, Rose, and Kye set off down the safest route. It was harder to judge which rocks were the safest, considering being atop horses made it hard to test their stability before treading on them.

Soon they came to a rather tapered ridge that was just graded enough to traverse. At this point, the horses began stepping along it as carefully as possible. The animals huffed nervously every once in a while and since their hooves would slip more than often, it was difficult to know whether or not continuing forward would mean their end. But it wasn't as though they could necessarily turn back. They were close to another patch of flat ground provided by a rock jutting out, however, and it was just far enough away to make it seem hopeless.

"Are you sure we won't fall before we reach that landing?" Amaya asked Soren, who had been leading the way.

"I don't know...let's just say that if there is a next time, we will definitely be using the valleys to get through."

Tailing them was Kye, whose horse seemed to be the most nervous of them. His horse whinnied—and that was when it happened. The others heard Kye yell, followed by the horse's hooves clanking against the ridge once. But by the time they turned their heads to see what was the matter, Kye was already halfway through his fall.

"Dammit!" Soren spat before dismounting his horse as quickly as possible on the precarious rocks. "Both of you stay up here and try to get to the landing! I'm going down there."

Kye landed with a thud against the crumbled rocks while Soren did his best to make his way down to him quickly but cautiously. While the girls kept moving, Amaya couldn't help herself from staring down where her uncle had landed in the rubble below. Worry was eating away at her, but she wasn't showing it as outwardly as Rose. "I really hope he's all right, I want to go down there too." After that, she got off her horse as well and began making her own way down.

"Rose, you shouldn't! It's dangerous," she warned, but by that time, Rose was already halfway down. In retrospect, it wasn't the biggest distance from the ridge to the place where Kye had landed, but it was full of jagged rocks that could have pierced him.

After carefully making it across the ridge, Amaya looked down to see if her uncle was all right, worry stinging her like tiny bees.

When Soren reached the lower ground from the ridge, he saw Kye lying against the hard ground, gasping for air, which had likely been knocked straight out of him upon landing. "Are you all right, Kye? What happened?"

Kye tried to shake the blurriness from his vision to look directly at Soren, but it took a moment for it to correct itself. "I...am not sure. But something must have spooked her." He looked up at the mare who waited idly atop the ridge as though she hadn't just sent her passenger plummeting to the ground; so ignorant.

"Kye, can you stand?" Rose asked once she arrived as well.

"Rose? What are you doing here? I thought I told you to stay on the ridge with Amaya," Soren scolded.

"I was worried. I apologize..."

"No need." Soren looked back to Kye, offering his hand.

Once to his feet, Kye looked up once more to his horse, squinting from the sun, trying to see what caused her to act out, but he could see nothing but endless rocks and slag.

"Are you able to climb back up?" Soren asked, bringing Kye's attention back to himself.

"Oh, of course."

When they reached the top of the ridge once more and Kye mounted his mare, he noticed a few flower petals that had drifted softly to the ground in front of his horse. Rose and Soren had already begun moving as he looked around with squinted eyes. There were no flowers or budding trees anywhere near them. *Could the wind have taken them this far...?* he thought.

Within moments the thought was gone; akin to the day. They reached Shadowcrest when night fell and hunkered down at a cheap inn since their funds were decreasing and, of course, there was a fee for keeping their horses at a stable. After all, Soren hadn't earned much from his days of being a medic, as much as the job should have paid him well.

Outside the inn sat a quaint stone well where Soren and Rose were murmuring amongst one another until their fatigue caught up with them.

"I know it's fresh and all...but I still feel they have a right to know," Rose told him. She was referring to the details she had learned the night before.

Despite Amaya's distrusting behavior, Rose found it far easier to trust other people. Even so, she couldn't put her finger on her reasoning for that. Perhaps it had been her longing for a closer bond with someone—anyone—that she put her feelings on display, even to a stranger. She remembered Will for a moment and how she ignorantly told him about her fear of the dark.

"I know I must eventually...but give me some time. Even telling you was a challenge; I had no other choice because you saw it, but I can assure you that it still rattles me. The anxiety of not knowing what you could do with the information—or even what you yourself think of it—is something my body finds difficult to stomach." Soren fiddled with his fingers to keep himself from making eye contact. It was strange to see the normally-dignified man in such a vulnerable place. "It's as though I've been lost inside inescapable darkness. Having to hide who I am from the world around me has become something I'm more comfortable with than my true self. In that way, I empathize with you and Amaya. Living in fear isn't truly living, it can't be; yet you've done it, as have I."

Rose's heart ached for the man. She thought him a friend and didn't know how to release him from the pain he had been repressing. "Even so...it's important that you be yourself no matter who opposes you," she said.

A small smile creased his lips as he stared down the foreboding well. "Thank you, Rose, I'll keep that in mind." He took a breath and added, "I'm going to head in for the night...you shouldn't stay out too late. We will reach Barness tomorrow." Soren turned from the well to face the inn.

"I'll be in soon, I was just going to stay out a little longer," she answered.

She turned to watch him go, only to see him brush past Amaya, who was now walking toward her. He paid her presence no mind, but Rose had other thoughts. There was no question that her friend had caught wind of at least *some* of their conversation. A bit cruel—a bit petty of her, but she wished she knew how much of it she had heard so she could avoid telling Amaya what she knew.

"He's quite the character..." she trailed off, approaching her. "A man with an alias. There are so many possibilities as to who he might be...and yet you trust him so...effortlessly. I've felt off about him ever since the day we met him. Think about it, he's leading us straight to Barness, the place where the kingdom will be most alert to our presence...has that thought not crossed your mind?" Amaya asked.

It was hard not to completely defend the man, since that was what he deserved. She trusted what Soren—or rather Liland—had told her, and Amaya had the wrong idea. He really did want to help them. So now the question was; how she could defend him without seeming like she really did know something. "I..." she trailed off, "no, I hadn't thought of it like that."

Then again, perhaps Amaya has a point. After all, is there truly any definitive evidence to say he isn't lying? Rose's thoughts drifted away from Amaya. *But why would he make such an elaborate lie? Is Soren truly the type to risk all of this just for a bounty?*

"But why not? How do you *know* he's not lying to us?" Amaya asked.

"I don't," Rose replied more sharply than she meant to. She paused. "I can't say without a shadow of a doubt that he isn't a materialistic man searching for the bounty attached to our names, but he deserves a chance. Without him, we would still be wasting away in a cell."

"What are you hiding?" There was no more dancing around the obvious reason she came to speak to Rose. Amaya wanted answers. "What do you know?" she asked with eyes narrowed, and her voice oozing with blame.

The questions weighed heavily on Rose's chest. She swallowed the ball of thorns in her throat and proceeded to answer her calmly. "I'm not hiding anything." The lie stung her.

"Please, don't think I'm oblivious. I know Soren told you his little secret."

"And what makes you think that?"

"That conversation you two were just having. About him having to hide from the world. So just tell me, who is he really?" Amaya was getting fired up now. She was prepared to beat the answer from her, at least that was how it seemed to Rose.

"Even if I knew, I would let him tell you first. He was simply telling me how unbearable it's becoming to keep it from us. He's trying to gain the courage to do it," Rose said.

"I find it strange that you put so much trust in a stranger, and yet you're losing your trust in me," Amaya hissed. She turned to go back in after that, leaving Rose to herself.

She never knew that keeping a secret that wasn't her own could be so difficult or of the weight that it carried. It seemed simple enough: let no one know. And yet it had escaped to Amaya's ears: the one whom she had spent most of her life telling her deepest thoughts and feelings.

Soon she found herself staring down the well too, the stagnant water below almost as black as the sky above. She gazed as if the answers to her questions would be revealed if she only stared long enough.

Then something whirred past her line of sight, her head lifting to follow it. Walking down one of the paths through Shadowcrest was a woman with short brown hair. When she squinted, she could swear she saw brown appendages and even flowers coming off her body. Was she dreaming in wakefulness? Was she hallucinating? Her feet carried Rose toward her as she neared a corner and turned out of sight. But in the split moment, she caught sight of the side of her face. Her eyes were a gentle pink hue and her face held so much familiarity.

Rose picked up her pace and soon rounded that same corner. She half-expected her not to be there, but there she was, heading farther down the path. She couldn't be dreaming. Rose chased the woman down the winding streets of the village, dodging the straggler passersby. "Wait!" she shouted after her, but the woman didn't notice her.

No matter how fast Rose went, she couldn't catch up to the woman, and eventually she lost her. Even so, Rose kept going, trying to stay on her trail, which eventually led to a graveyard.

From the distance, the moon silhouetted a figure. It was the woman. Rose ran faster even though her legs were tired and dodged the headstones scattered about and crashed into the woman, her arms falling around her. "Mother!" she shouted.

She felt the figure stir in her grasp before it hugged her back. "I knew I would find you here," The voice she got in return wasn't the voice of her mother—but Will's.

Rose didn't hesitate to yank herself out of the demon's grasp, her eyes glaring at his. "Will?"

"Yes, yes, it's me. Are you surprised?" he asked.

"How could you? You disguised yourself as my mother just so you could capture me? And you led me all this way...why? Why do you need Amaya and me so badly?"

"Listen, I've no idea what you're talking about. I was going to come looking for you, but I guess you just couldn't resist, huh?" Rose drew Diluvium and slid an arrow from the quiver in response. "A fancy weapon..." Will approached her slowly; confidently. "But can you use it without your pathetic human fingers quaking?" He was inches from her body now, her efforts to pace backward; futile. "It's awfully dark out, you know."

"Stowe your mockery," Rose hissed. "If I were you, I wouldn't be standing so close, where even my 'shaking hands' could strike you." Her eyes were daggers.

Will chuckled. "It's just like a delicate rose to hide behind her thorns." He leaned down to her level. "But what happens when I pluck them away?" Rose felt Diluvium splash through her grasp and soak into the ground beside her feet. He began to cite some sort of incantation and Rose shut her eyes, bracing for something to happen. She didn't know what to expect, since

Will could be unpredictable. But when nothing happened, she opened her eyes.

"Shit," he spat. "Of course I would do it wrong right when it counts..." Rose furrowed her brow. "When we met in Agartha, I lost my spellbook, so I guess it looks like I won't be capturing you tonight. What a shame."

"You have to be the worst kidnapper I've ever met...you're terrible at this," Rose replied, using her water to create Diluvium once again just in case Will decided to do anything. But she took note of his mentioning of the spellbook. That must have been the leather book she had picked up after the explosion.

"What do you mean? I think I'm doing fairly well," Will replied.

"You could be doing anything else to capture me, but you just gave up." Rose gave him an unamused look.

"I think it's more fun this way."

Rose found it strange that the demon thought of this as a game. She certainly wasn't having fun playing if so.

"Or maybe I'm just going easy on you," he added.

"And why on earth would you be doing that?" Rose asked.

Will turned to the graves they had been standing near. Both of them had names she didn't recognize etched into the stone. One read "Blaine Avery" and the one to its left read "Amelia Avery." "Wouldn't want my old man to see me hurting a lady," he said, but his voice sounded somber. "And I'm sure mom wouldn't be too proud of that either."

"I had almost forgotten you told us your parents were murdered. You live here then?" Rose asked. She felt a little sympathetic toward the man, even after all that he had done.

"Used to. Before I lost my soul and all that. But I'll spare you the details," Will answered.

"So my parents killed yours. Did they kill you too? Is that why you're trying to get your soul back?" Rose asked.

Will shook his head. "No. But...in a way, you could say they did...I tried to get revenge, but it didn't work out."

Rose felt bad for the demon. Even if he had been trying to capture them, deep inside, he was just a small boy trying to feel some relief from the sadness left behind by her own parents. She thought back to what Soren had told her, about how he would fight alongside them.

"Well...what use is trying to get your soul back? You could be focusing your efforts on a greater cause than this. You could help us cure the gods."

A smirk flashed on Will's lips before he shook his head. "You're so innocent, Rose, you know that? But it's not that simple. Again, I won't go into it, but you and I can't be friends."

"Pity, I almost felt bad enough to submit," Rose replied and turned away from him, her arms crossing.

"That'd be boring anyway," Will said. "Now why don't you scurry on back to your friends. Oh, and don't look sad—this won't be the last time we meet."

Rose gave a huff. She could have taken arms and stopped Will once and for all. But in reality, she wouldn't be able to do something like that, not after what he told her. They willingly spared one another that night. Even with her back toward him, Rose trusted he wouldn't take her by surprise.

The tangle of houses and other buildings had the girl lost within minutes. After all, she didn't remember how it was she got to the graveyard in the first place. But as she walked, Rose pulled out the spellbook that Will had been missing. She figured it might be better in her own possession, just in case he truly hadn't been as adept as he had at first made himself out to be.

She began to look through its worn pages. It seemed to be an older book. How old, she couldn't tell. A few pages caught her eye, but only because there were scratchings of what she assumed to be Will's handwriting beside them. The book was written in an unidentifiable language. She noticed a few notes such as "disguise scent" and "immobilize." She had to assume Will must have been using the spells against them.

It was a shame though, Rose's first thought had been to learn some of the spells, but now she couldn't.

It was a while before she eventually found the well in front of the inn and she hurried inside. The night brought with it a chill, so Rose was glad she wouldn't be spending the night in it.

When she entered their room, she found Soren and Kye asleep, but Amaya was sitting up on her cot, observing the night sky outside. But when she heard Rose's footsteps, her attention was on her friend.

"What took you so long?" she asked.

"I was just thinking," Rose answered before making her way to her own cot. She still felt guilty for lying to her friend and appreciated Will for a brief moment for having taken her mind away from the mess, but now it was all she could think about.

Amaya didn't speak to her after that, leaving the tension between them quite prominent. Needless to say, Rose spent hours worrying about what would become of them before her fatigue finally won over the battle between it and her anxiety.

12: Cauterized Blood

Eighteen years ago

Encased in a blackness, there are two flames, both meant to warm the one who is imbued by it. Swayed by the empty winds of solitude, one alights and loses control, burning what lies in its path, scarring all it dares touch and fears the water. The second flame remains delicate and is feared by none. By use of another wick, it can travel miles all while maintaining its control, never once fanned to create the embers of death.

By now the first flame has burned out and killed itself, all but life in its wake. But soon the ashes will be devoured by the earth, fruit for the new pastures that will engulf the lands, spreading beauty. Yet the small flame remains; traveling, but confined in isolation, never to change, never to unleash the capabilities of its potential; breeding possibility, but leaving them all yet to be seen.

And perhaps all life can be so compared to it. Destructive and fleeting, yet leaving experience to what it bears, or contained and benevolent, to be squandered and forgotten.

Some say fire has no preference to what it burns, whether it be meaningless things like wood, dried grass, or leaves—or those that would inflict sorrow, such as the family pet or the mother and father who used to tuck in a child before bedtime.

But Will was older now, he was less naive than he was as a child. He knew that tampering with magic used by dark lords was forbidden in the past, and that his family often took retribution for it. But his parents were good people, that much he knew—even if others didn't think it so.

It was the afternoon of his eighteenth birthday when his parents finally decided to allow him to look in the pages of the book they held so close among the rest. It was sought after by many people who still practiced the dark arts. He would normally have to wait until he was twenty-one to begin trying, but was surprised when they offered him the chance to learn some basic spells.

His father was usually strict about the rules regarding magic, something Will admired about the man, but was glad he had a sudden change of heart for his birthday.

They had gone out to the spot where he would watch his father train at on occasion, and though his teachability was quite laughable, Will managed to perform a few spells. When Will became frustrated, they decided to call it a day and head home to prepare lunch.

"You did well today, Will. But you know, magic takes a lot of patience to master. If you give up every time you get frustrated, you'll never learn it," his father said.

Will had been walking ahead of them, his hunger driving him forward. He looked back to speak but noticed a worried demeanor on his mother's face. "Mom? Something wrong?" he asked.

She looked toward his father without a word, and he feared for a moment that perhaps her faith in him had diminished. He wondered if she truly thought he wasn't ready to practice magic.

"Mom, if you're worried about me not being ready, I—"

"Will," his father said in a low voice and pulled his son close to him. Will scrunched his eyebrows at his father's sudden offish behavior. But his eyes became wide when he felt his father's spellbook being placed into his hands. Was he finally going to give this to him to practice on his own? His heart raced with excitement and a smile started to form on his lips.

"Dad, I can't believe—"

"Take this and hide in the woods."

Will's heart sank and he could feel the warmth drain from his face as he looked up into his father's eyes, which matched his own. "What's going on?" he asked.

"Don't ask questions, just go," he ordered him.

Strict as usual. But it was always for a good reason. Without another word, Will took the book firmly into his hands and headed toward the path leading through the woods. He passed a few skinnier trees before reaching a thicker one, further shielded by underbrush and other foliage. He heard footsteps along the path he had just come from and turned his head so his ear would face that direction.

"Have you considered our offer yet?"

The male voice that spoke sounded familiar, yet he couldn't remember for sure who it belonged to.

"The decision was final the day you came beforehand. We can't give you the book," his father responded.

Now he remembered. Four people had come to his home a couple weeks prior asking for the book. It belonged to his bloodline of mages. It wasn't something that could be sold or given away; doing so would be taboo. His father made sure to drill the idea into his head. That was why most of the magical books had been lost. They were burned once the family name had died completely.

"I don't care about your family's lineage. Where is the book?" the other male voice demanded. He remembered two men and two women out of the four of them.

"We don't have it! Now leave us!" Will's mother shouted.

"She's lying," one of the female voices said in a dull tone.

"I can see you have no intention of making this easy for us," the first male voice said. He heard the sound of flames being set alight and the soft clink of metal. "I guess that means we will have to search for it in the remains of your dead bodies."

Despite the ambient temperature, Will's skin grew cold and his heart raced. He swallowed a thick nothing that had formed in his throat, trying to ease the tense muscles within. He heard a blade sink into its victim's flesh and then his mother's scream; her guttural choking mixed with her agonized cry of pain.

"Amelia!" His father's devastated scream echoed into the woods.

Will stared blankly at a tree in front of him, his vision blurring, his ears ringing, forced to listen to his mother being murdered.

"Get away from her, you bastards!" his father screamed, just barely audible over his deep heartbeat and the deafening ringing.

Will felt thick hot tears start to pour from his eyes and down his cheeks as he heard his father start to choke too, just after attempting to cite an incantation. He had tried to fight back, but lost before even being given a chance.

"What a shame..." Sage sighed as she stared down at the pair of dead bodies that Chasaka had been forced to kill.

"It isn't with them," Teira said, kicking one off to the side after searching through them both.

Ruki gave a grumble at this. "We'll search their home, then. Let's go."

The four made their way to the village from the path where they had taken the lives of Will's parents. He followed them there, using the trees as cover until they reached the village, where he hid from a distance.

He watched them enter his home as if it were their own and from there began to rummage through it. They searched all the bookshelves and tore through his father's belongings to little avail.

"I've found something," Ruki announced to the others from the study of the home. It contained four bookshelves all lined with books which he had begun tearing through one by one and was now holding one of the larger ones in his arms.

Chasaka rounded the corner first and entered the room to see what he had happened upon. "What is it?" he asked.

"It's filled with prophecies and there are notes written on the pages up to future dates," Ruki said.

Teira entered the room next and crossed the mound of discarded books toward the desk where he stood. "Those books were written long ago. My father told me once that they were written by a group of psychics who could tell the future. That's why the gods were the only ones allowed to look through them and could impart knowledge of their choosing onto the prophets from the Astral clan," she explained.

"Lucky find then," Ruki replied as he flipped through the contents of the pages.

Sage soon came into the room holding a scroll in her hands and joined the others, who gazed at the book which Ruki had placed onto the desk.

"Hold on," she spoke just as he had been about to turn the page and placed a finger on one of the written prophecies with notes scribbled beside it.

Sage read the note aloud: "foretold by the prophet Asabüro shows the technical descendants of Noctis and Avius—who are written to have the power to end the demigod's cycle of reincarnation—will be born when the blood of the four base elements has been combined."

"This could be exactly what we need to end the reign of gods over humans," Sage said.

"The four base elements being wind, water, fire, and earth, correct?" Teira asked.

Chasaka reached forward and took the page of the book before tearing it carefully from its binding. "Then it's settled... we must have children in order for this to work. The plan will take time, but it's a necessary step we must take. If we don't break the reincarnation cycle, then killing the gods will be for naught."

* * *

Will slammed the door behind him, breathing heavily. He scrambled toward the desk in the corner and threw the book open to the section at the end. "Come on, come on, there's gotta be something..." He flipped hastily through the pages, scanning each spell quickly before moving on to the next. Finally, his eyes fell upon what he was looking for: summoning spells. He grabbed a pen and began scribbling notes, flipping from the page he found and the back of the book, where his parents had written out a translator for him. The book itself was filled with large blocks of text and other notes written in a dinosaur language, one long forgotten since times of old. The translator was like a key, allowing him to understand the words that had been written by the old mages and warlocks.

When he found the spell he was looking for, Will circled it several times before ripping the page out, shoving it in his pocket. He grabbed the book and stowed it away in a secret compartment behind the desk's shelves to be sure that no one would find it, and with that, he left.

* * *

As night fell upon the land, Will made it to his destination. He stood before the bodies of his parents, glad that the growing darkness kept him from fully seeing their unsettling condition. But he could still smell the stench of their blood as it blanketed the area. Like nothing more than dead animals, which he tried not to think about—but the reality of it all would soon hit him like a tidal wave.

He took the ripped page from his pocket and squinted in the darkness, barely able to make out the words. He spoke the incantation, once, twice. On the third iteration, the ground began to tremor, cracks forming deep in the earth's surface. Thick black smoke began spilling up through them, forming in front of Will. The crevices glowed a deep red, which surged into the cloud of smoke. Two blood-red eyes appeared in the haze, boring into him menacingly. "Why have you called me here, mortal?" a voice growled in Will's head.

Will stared at the apparition, struggling to keep his composure. "I want to make a deal with you," he managed to say.

"You don't have the grounds to be making deals with the king of Hell," the voice boomed in his head.

"I'm willing to give up my soul," Will offered quickly.

This seemed to pique the phantom's interest. "The soul of a mage...what is it that you desire?" he asked, eyes narrowing.

"I want you to bring my parents back," Will gestured to the bodies lying behind the figure.

The king of Hell remained silent for a moment, as if in thought. "Then I'll take your soul and you will serve me. If you violate the terms of this deal, your soul will be consumed and you will become a poltergeist. Is that agreed?" he asked.

Will nodded his head.

"Very well, then the deal is made," the king answered. Without another word, the smoke began to swirl and a shadowy hand protruded from one side of it, reaching out to Will. It came to his chest and swiftly dug into it. Instead of piercing his skin, the claw phased through him, though he felt as if it had physically clawed his body. Will groaned in pain, falling to his knees as smoke billowed from his chest, encapsulating him completely. There was a flash, and as quickly as it came, the smoke left him and flowed back into the cracks in the ground, carrying a wisp of light with it. "A pleasure doing business with you," the voice echoed before the smoke disappeared and everything fell silent.

Will slowly rose to his feet, breathing heavily. He looked to his parents, who remained unmoving. "Mom? Dad?" he whispered, moving toward them. Suddenly the two began to stir, much to the relief of Will. He had begun to worry that the demon had tricked him. He knelt beside his parents to help them stand, but froze. Something was wrong, he could feel it. His parents stood, turning to face him, and it was then that he knew what. The whites of their eyes were black, their irises glazed over. He didn't know what the king of Hell had done to them, but they weren't his parents anymore, not fully, at least. They were empty shells, filled with darkness.

The two staggered toward Will, instilling fear in him with each step they took. He could see the cold, voracious look in their eyes, even in the darkness. "Stop, please! I can't fight you!" Will begged, backing away. His mind raced as he thought of the spells he had been practicing earlier but thought of nothing he could use to help himself. "This isn't what I wanted," Will whimpered as his parents drew closer. He lost his footing, falling backward, and his parents began scrambling toward him.

Tears ran from Will's eyes as he spoke out an incantation as fast as he could. He shut his eyes as he did, the smell of necrotic flesh bursting into his nostrils. He kept his eyes shut, as he felt their cold blood suddenly speckle the parts of his skin that met the air. Will couldn't bring himself to open his eyes, knowing he wouldn't want to see the state his parents were left in after citing the spell for spontaneous combustion. He was just glad he didn't have to hear their screams of pain once more as they died for the last time.

He got to his feet quickly after that and sprinted from the scene as fast as his legs would carry him.

In doing so, Will had left behind the page he had used to summon Waru.

Those who had watched the gruesome event unfold emerged from within the trees and picked up the bloodied paper from the ground.

"If nothing else, at least we will come out of this with one page," Chasaka said, trying to smear away the blood. "How nice...it appears they left translations for us to read," he said as he browsed through the three spells that were on the torn page. "'Antithyl:'" Chasaka began, "'unlike Repithyl, used to subdue demons, it's a substance used to weaken the power and mentality of divine beings'... there appears to be a warning at the bottom... but, well." The man gave a chuckle.

"What other spells are on it?" asked Ruki from beside him.

"A summoning spell. I assume that must be the one he used to summon that demon from before," the other man replied.

"Well then, shall we give it a try? Perhaps we, too, can manage to strike a deal with him," Sage said.

Chasaka turned to an open space and began to recite the incantation translated beside the spell. He spoke it three times just as Will had done, and on the third, the ground shook as it split open once more, a plume of blackness spewing from it with two slices of red within the bog. "Why have you called me here, corrupted demigods?" The demon's deep voice filled their minds, overwhelming like a heavy weight on each of their chests.

"We wish to make a deal with you."

* * *

Present Day

The gates of Barness felt tall and foreboding, at least for Amaya and Rose. Its shadow cast over their person, shading them from the sun, even though they were still quite distanced from it.

They were tied up by their hands with a rope that Kye had fastened. Their weapons were put away. Each step their horses took toward the gate gave them a hollow feeling within. When Kye passed by the guarded gate, the soldiers who stood there sent a glare to both tied up girls.

It was a rather long walk to the castle. The passing stares of others made time fall short of its normal pace.

"I'm not sure I can handle much more of this."

Amaya looked at her friend who had spoken. Her expression was crinkled in discomfort like her own.

"What is the matter?" Kye asked. He must not have been paying attention to the people they had walked by.

"Everyone is looking at us like we don't belong here," Amaya answered.

"We're almost to the castle, pay no mind to the gawking faces," Soren told her.

Had this been his attempt at comforting them? If so, neither of them felt it. In fact, being told to ignore it only made them want to search for those judgmental eyes more.

The four dismounted their horses outside the palace gates before being led in by Soren and Kye. Amaya recalled running around the palace halls with Rose back when their parents would have important meetings, soldiers chasing them to get them to stay still. She could almost see their younger selves whizzing past, bringing a breeze with them as they ran.

The memories faded when she saw the matured face of the king. The young face she recognized so long ago was beginning to wrinkle a little, and were those strands of gray-silver peeking from beneath his crown? *What had caused them*, she wondered. *Old age? Stress?* Amaya almost felt happy looking into his handsome blue eyes. But what stared back were emotions hardened by routine and law. Zyair didn't need to see the drawn-up wanted posters to know who was standing before him.

"Your highness, to you I have brought the demigods." Kye kept a respectful demeanor, knowing the king might be upset to see their faces.

"And why would you do that? These weren't your orders. I told you to return them to Tochfuyu, did I not?" Zyair's eyes narrowed, scowling.

"Please listen to me before turning me away," Kye pleaded.

But Zyair didn't silence himself. "Kye, you already did your part in defending these lives twelve years ago. This isn't about your personal feelings, it's for the safety and well-being of Barness—no—*all* of Aessatia. They were blessed as it stands not to have been executed."

Amaya was clenching her teeth down against her tongue to keep herself from speaking out of turn. The only thing holding her back was his social stature. Rose was holding tightly onto her pinkie, knowing personally how much his words pained her. *Are our lives truly meaningless to this man?* she thought.

"Sire, if I may speak," Soren said.

"And who might you be?"

"My name is Soren, hailing from Folkvangr. Surely you must be aware of Aessatia's current situation and with how her gods are falling ill, correct?"

Zyair bowed his head slightly, curious as to where this man was going with mentioning this.

"We have journeyed all this way to find a cure for them. Our hope was to enter the repository so it might give us some information," Soren explained.

Zyair pinched the bridge of his nose, his eyes squeezing together. "While I understand that your cause is noble, I simply can't allow Amaya and Rose to—"

"Your highness, please! You've become so dogmatically entrenched in the so-called safety of your people that you've forgotten your compassion. You banished two girls at the age of six!" Kye cut him off

"They're a potential danger to—"

"They're innocent!"

Kye's voice echoed throughout the throne room, bouncing off its tall, empty walls. Even filled with antiques and riches, what were they truly worth?

"I understand that my brother and his accomplices did blasphemous things, but they received their punishment with their death. Amaya and Rose may be their offspring, but why is it that they must suffer the wrongdoings of the dead?" Kye said. "They've done nothing to prove they may be a danger to Lucus or Aessatia. You're simply afraid of the possibility that they *could* be harmful to others, and for that fear they faced a life of hardship and loneliness. No king of mine is capable of such selfishness."

Zyair's eyes were glued to the man he called his friend. He never knew Kye could be so passionate. He was always laid-back, quiet, never spoke out; a follower. "Very well, you've been heard. Speak." He looked at Rose and Amaya, awaiting their response.

Silence befell the throne room, even Amaya was scared to speak. But all eyes were upon Rose when her soft-spoken voice rang out.

"I believe I speak for both of us when I say life in Tochfuyu was hard. But that's a drastic understatement. Though, despite our reservations created by such unnecessary punishment, we have dedicated our efforts to make it this far so that we may save the lives of those who have endlessly shown the extent of their hatred for us since our escape. We're constantly regarded as objects and dangerous weapons. I believe it may be these discriminations that caused our parents to act the way they did when they were alive. I suppose part of the reason this is all so important to me is because I want to restore the honor that was lost to the blotted past of my kind."

Amaya tasted blood in her mouth; she had bitten down so hard now that she caused herself to bleed. Rose's words were too kind for her liking; too noble. Amaya wanted to speak her mind, but for the sake of what they wanted to accomplish, she stayed silent. After all, they were already standing on unstable ground regarding the king.

Zyair stood and pulled something from his robes. "This is the key to the Ice Sanctum," he said. He walked down from the dais upon which the throne sat, and suddenly he seemed much more equal to them. "Follow me."

With that, Zyair led them to the castle's second floor by way of a grand spiral staircase. It ushered them through a set of double doors that led to the balcony. From the balcony was a path that went off in different directions, but the king steered them left. When they rounded a bend in the path, they discovered a gorgeous structure colored with a gentle blue and silver. It was tall with windows all over it. But the panes were covered in fractals of ice so there was no way to see inside. The structure itself was maintained as best as the citizens could keep it, but the evidence of what had happened twelve years ago would stay stained in how secluded it was. They had passed by a lot of guards before reaching it.

Zyair turned to the four travelers. "Long ago, Cyero forbade me from allowing any human to enter and gaze upon the contents of his library, so I can't say what will happen once you enter. Be cautious." He looked and sounded serious when he spoke. Still, he placed the key in its respective lock, fumbling with it a little before finally hearing a click. Thankfully, the lock wasn't frozen shut.

Anticipation began to build when Zyair started yanking on the handles of the sanctum. At last, a loud crack was heard and one door came open slightly, releasing a plume of cold air. It took a bit more prying to open it, but at last, it screeched apart wide enough for them to fit through. "I'll stay here, you all go inside," he said. And so they entered.

The interior of the construction was frigid, covering their bodies in goosebumps. The Ice Sanctum was immense, seeming almost bigger inside than outside, but it was crowded with bookshelves and archives stuffed full with knowledge. There was a huge silver clock embedded in its polished marble flooring, which served as the structure's centerpiece. But most notably, there were no patrons and no gods in sight.

Kye felt his stomach begin to fill with a nerve-wracking feeling. He could remember Cyero's specific orders the day after it all happened. "No human shall ever be allowed to enter this place of sacred knowledge again. Anyone who fails to abide by this shall face divine retribution," he had said.

Kye closed his eyes and looked over to his niece and her friend. He suddenly could picture the walls covered with the blood of his people. He remembered the purple blood of the ice god running onto the floor.

"Hello?" Rose called out, her voice echoing through the empty walls.

But Soren quickly hushed her. "It would be best not to draw attention to us. If Cyero really is against others entering this place, he may force us to leave if he finds us. We should just search for what we're looking for and get out," he said.

"Are you sure he's even here? This place is completely empty," Amaya pointed out.

"We shouldn't assume anything," Kye warned her. "This place is incredibly massive despite its quaint appearance outside. So why don't we all split off into groups? We will accomplish more that way."

"What exactly are we searching for again?" she asked.

"Anything that has to do with the gods falling ill and becoming hostile like this or any kind of medical archives," Soren answered.

With everyone on the same page, they split off from one another, Kye and Rose went off together while Soren and Amaya parted ways.

Amaya wandered the aisles of bookshelves, searching for labels and titles that might be useful in gathering information. Of what she spent time looking through, none of the documents had recorded such a strange phenomenon as the one they had faced. She felt her hope waning. She sighed and walked along the maze of bookshelves as clinical records eventually turned to historical plagues, wars—and then she found something that piqued her interest. The title on the binding simply read *History of the Lucian*. Intrigued, she picked up the book and turned to the first page.

LONG BEFORE THE kingdom of Lucus had been established, Noctis and Avius were regarded as the greatest mortal warriors in Aessatia. They conquered many foes in their time, but they held a sense of compassion with a deep faith in the gods. They were described as exemplary humans and many respected them. Those who dared defy them quickly met their end.

But soon they met their match. One fateful night when the snow and thunder fought against one another, their battle struck a hole into Hell atop the Tower of Twilight. The ruler of Hell, Waru, alongside his accomplice, Tokiwa, led their masses into the overworld. They caused destruction anywhere their feet stepped, killing all who stood in their way. Families were massacred, homes destroyed, even Noctis and Avius were no match for the demons.

They always had a strong connection to the gods and called upon them for help in defeating the evil that had plagued Aessatia. And so they received their blessings. Noctis received Ice, Fire, and Wind, while Avius received Lightning, Water, and Earth. With them, they created holy weapons capable of slaying the demons and driving them back into Hell. They did so single-handedly, and when it was all over, the humans who remained, amassed into what we know today as our beloved kingdom.

The warriors were permitted to keep the abilities gifted to them, lest the humans become extinct. This is where the cycle of reincarnation began for the demigods. Furthermore...

* * *

When Amaya looked up from the book she felt enlightened, as though she knew something that others didn't. But it also raised suspicion within her. What if these demons, Waru and Tokiwa, were responsible? Perhaps their lives had returned with a vengeance.

Carefully, she slid the book back into its place. Beside it, she found a brighter and more beautiful-looking book that was much larger than the one she had picked up.

It was titled *History of the Gods*. She slid the book out of place and took a moment to admire the gold-laced binding and the shining corners also containing gold.

She took the cover and began to flip it until a hand reached forward and snapped it shut, causing her to start while a shiver clawed down her neck. Amaya looked at the pale hand that had done this and followed it up the arm it was attached to, which was clothed in plush white and whose neck was wrapped in a velvet red scarf.

Eyes so icy-blue that they could almost be silver stared down at her. She found them to be extraordinary. So silvery, yet flecks of blue still resided within them. His white eyebrows were knitted and those very eyes were ablaze with anger. Atop his head of white hair sat a pair of ears akin to that of a wolf.

"Who sent you? What business have you within these walls?" his cold and raspy voice boomed. Amaya was too shaken with fear to reply. "You weren't given permission to read the knowledge in these texts," he said and pulled the book from her almost non-existent grasp, putting it back in its place. "Now stand, child, and speak your business." He fully stood and crossed his arms expectantly.

With fear in her eyes, Amaya stood, never leaving his gaze. She was paralyzed by that stare after that, mostly forcing herself against the bookshelf. "A—Are you...a demon?" she stuttered, fear binding her stomach.

"If I were a demon, I would have killed you already. Why do you not answer my question?" he spoke coldly.

Some of the fear inside of her had quelled enough to finally respond. "I came here with a few others seeking knowledge."

The albino stared at her for a moment, eyes moving along her body as if trying to read her. He then shut them and lowered his head slightly. "I know what it is you seek, but you won't find it here," he said before fixing those glaring eyes of his on her again. "My name is Cyero. Clearly, you weren't aware that humans aren't allowed here, so I'll let you and whoever you came along with leave without punishment."

Amaya clenched her fists firmly and shook her head. "We can't leave. You're the god of ice, aren't you? You know better than I that this information is vital to everyone. We came all this way and can't return now. Time is running out. We came here to find an answer, and we won't leave until we get one," she said.

The ice god scrunched his eyebrows just a bit further from their default state. "As I said, you won't find what hasn't been written. Now take your friends and get lost," he growled.

"Please," Amaya said desperately. "If you know anything about the disease, please tell me what you know."

Cyero gave a sigh of defeat as his face softened. "This disease—as you may call it—is called the Taint. You won't find within these walls its cure or a way to stop its spread," he said.

"Do you know what is causing it, then?"

* * *

Rose had decided to stay alongside Kye as they made their way through the aisles of the huge archive units. She had some questions she needed answers to—and she couldn't rest or continue her search for this information until she had them.

But she didn't dive in straight away. "Do you think we will really find any kind of information about all this?" she asked.

"I can't be sure. I don't recall there ever being something like this that has happened. The gods don't simply 'get sick,' it's unheard of," Kye said.

"I wish I had known that sooner," Rose said solemnly. The older Lucian turned to the girl and tilted his head in confusion at her tone.

"Kye...who were my parents? And Amaya's? Did they just... not love us enough and decided that committing a crime would be an easy way out?" she asked.

Kye went dead silent upon this question. He lifted his mask to show his chocolate eyes and look properly at Rose, whom he had always done his best to protect alongside his niece. She deserved to know the truth. "I don't know what your parents' true intentions were, but even leading up to their deaths, they loved you with all they had. And I know Amaya's parents loved her too," he began before placing his hand on her shoulder. "But they weren't fond of the gods like both of you are...they were plotting to murder them all, not only that, but the entirety of the human race with them. The first phase of their plan began here in this very sanctum, as far as I know, where they threatened Cyero's life. So the soldiers executed them and banished the two of you for fear that you may have been corrupted by their ideals, or would eventually become clouded. It killed me to have to make both of you leave all on your own at that age. I'm sorry."

Rose had her head down as she heard a watered-down version of the story be retold to her. "We did inherit their powers. But we aren't corrupt like everyone thinks we are. There must be some way to clear our names," she said. "Never mind that." She shook her head. "What really happened the night they were killed?"

"Your father and mother along with Amaya's father came to the Ice Sanctum, demanding that Cyero tell them where they could find a place called the Tower of Twilight. I don't know where they heard of it. Even I didn't know of its existence until they spoke of it. But they were going to kill him if he didn't tell them. That was right about when I walked in and stopped them. They were talking about these horrible things like bringing salvation to our capital through the death of the people. Then

Amaya's mother joined the mix. I passed out during the fight, but I woke up to blood lying everywhere, and then I was told that they were killed," he continued.

Hearing this sent some clarity to Rose. Not that the information was pleasant, but it gave her peace to know the whole truth. "I always wanted to see them again, you know? How could I've known this is how they had been? Nobody ever said anything."

"Yes, and I'm so sorry. I really would have said so sooner, had I been thinking it would affect you so much later on." Kye sighed shamefully. "It was stupid of me," he said.

"I forgive you. It's okay; you just wanted to protect us," Rose tried to shed some light on the dreary mood.

* * *

"Their names are Chasaka, Teira, Ruki, and Sage," the ice god said to the girl as he closed his eyes. "The day they threatened my life was the same that they escaped into the Hell and began building their empire, one that stood against us."

A feeling of dread washed through Amaya's body upon hearing this, for she knew those names all too well. They had been the names of hers and Rose's parents. She thought of what brought them to this point. "So all this destruction has been caused by dead people? Are you saying that in order to pursue the slaughterers of the gods, we must bring back the dead? If that's so, why are we the ones still taking the fall for their mistakes?" she asked.

"Because your mothers and fathers still breathe," he answered. "Every now and again, I can see their figures leaving the tower from my observatory. To the people of Barness, you were both still capable of hurting them, with the powers that you inherited. After what Tobias, Vincent, and Elaine—your grandparents—had done, in addition to what your parents did, king Zyair had to make the decision to exile you for fear of another attack against the world."

All of this information was being shoved down Amaya's throat so fast that it made her stumble back into the bookshelf behind her. She nearly collapsed from shock and the way it made her heart pound in her chest. The god of ice leaned forth and helped her steady herself.

"Are you all right?" he asked her as his head tilted a bit.

Many questions raced through her mind, but the first that had managed to verbally come out was, "What am I supposed to tell Rose?"

Assuming that had been the name of the other daughter, he replied, "Well, keeping the truth from her wouldn't help anyone."

Amaya shook her head at that. "I suppose what I meant was, *how* do I tell her?" she said.

Just then, Rose walked over with Amaya's uncle. "Tell me what?" Rose asked with a rather confused tone, given that she had heard their last few pieces of dialogue from the other aisle, which had drawn the two of them toward the god and the human girl.

That familiar voice alone was enough to give Amaya a start, and her heart raced even faster as she looked into Rose's eyes. There was no way of getting out of this at all. "Rose, our parents are alive," she said, despite every emotion that raged inside her mind.

Kye was the first to respond to this statement, and with his mask off, it was clear to see the look of horror that crossed his features. "You—you must be joking, right? All of the capital's guards saw them die," he stammered around his nervousness.

"They aren't dead," Cyero replied. Kye's face went pale when he heard the ice god speak. "It's been made apparent that they had stolen spells passed down from the Avery family, one of the only remaining families of mages remaining during this time. The books are normally to be kept in possession of the next of kin. I have my theories that they must have used that knowledge as well to create this 'Taint' that has begun infecting the gods."

Rose's eyes widened when she heard the man explain this. The book she had in her keeping was definitely the one he had mentioned. She recalled visiting the graves with the demon who had been tailing them since the start of their adventure, the graves of William Avery's mother and father, Blaine and Amelia Avery.

Kye had been the most shocked out of them all. "If what you say is true, then that would mean that the king has lied to me. Why would he do that?" his words turned into angry growls with each one.

"He never told me," Cyero answered him. "They faked their deaths that night. Zyair was the only one who knew of it until he told me the truth. Since then, we have been at a loss for what to do. Since Chasaka and the others never returned to the capital after that night, we assumed that perhaps they had gotten lost in the forest trying to find the Tower of Twilight. But now that the gods have begun to get sick, there isn't a doubt in my mind that it has to do with them." Cyero looked at the frightened human man, feeling sympathy for him. "Ignorance can be a cruel thing once the truth is learned, I suppose."

"We will find them and put a stop to this once and for all," Amaya spoke with a dark look on her face.

"Or we could negotiate with them somehow," Rose offered.

"I'm afraid it won't be so easy," the ice god said in a downtrodden tone.

"You don't know your parents as well as you think that you did," Kye added to his comment. "Each and every one of them has gone through their own personal Hell, which drove them to this point. Of Chasaka's, I know the best. As for the others, to have joined him, they must have gone through something equally as terrible," he said.

"Not only that, but they must have done something terrible to my brother, Rotos, to have managed to get into Hell. His lightning is the only thing that can open the gate from atop the tower. If you so wish to continue and travel there, know that it will be a dangerous road ahead," Cyero said.

"With all due respect, we have made it this far, I don't see what makes you think we would give up here," Amaya said.

"Very well, then I would be honored to escort you toward the Tower of Twilight where your parents are hiding," the god replied.

"Let's get Soren then and tell him the news. I'm glad this didn't take too long," Amaya said.

"It was nice to see you both again. But I'm afraid I won't be joining you; I have to speak with the king now that I have this information," Kye said. The look in Amaya's uncle's eyes was grim and filled with hurt. She wondered what her uncle had been through before she was born to hold such fear toward his own brother.

The girls nodded in understanding, and after saying their goodbyes, they set off to search for Soren. It didn't take long to find him, and when they did, they explained all that had happened and what the current plan would be.

While they had set off, however, Kye stayed behind so as to consult his king—no—his friend, about what the god had told him.

So there he found himself sitting in the intimidating presence of Zyair, balancing his shaking body on one knee as he kneeled before him. "Zyair," said the man when at last he rose to his feet.

"Yes, Kye?" he asked as he stood from his throne.

Kye's lips trembled. He felt like a child again, cowering in fear of his superior brother. The longer he waited to speak, the more his words choked and strangled him. He tried repeatedly to swallow the rocks in his throat. The vengeful thoughts he kept for that man who he thought for so long had been eradicated from this land were flourishing underneath his skin. Chasaka had taken so much from him.

"Why didn't you tell me that my brother was still alive?"

Zyair found himself rooted to the floor hearing this question, his heart catching on a snag, horror running through his body. His mouth hung open and his hands hung still at his sides before he nervously brought them up before his body and played randomly with his fingers. "Kye...I..." he trailed off. "How did you find this out?"

"Irrelevant! I demand an answer!" Kye wasn't normally the type of man to anger so easily, but his lid had been blown at that point. He didn't care who he was talking to, he just knew that this particular person kept vital information from him. "You knew he was alive all this time, and did nothing to stop him from doing such terrible things!" He trembled in anger as he spoke.

"Relax yourself this instant!" Zyair spat back at the man.

"That man was the bane of my existence. You knew how much he destroyed me, Zyair! So, why? Did you think I wouldn't eventually find it out myself? Were you intending to keep it from me forever?" Kye was livid; breathless.

"I know how much Chasaka hurt you. Even uttering his name was enough to make you shudder. But don't you see? It was to protect you! I didn't want you to know the truth of what happened that night, because perhaps you still hurt even after he passed, but you were far more at peace! You were no longer obsessed with knowing exactly where he was at all times," Zyair's blood, too, was beginning to rush, making his head feel light.

"And what of it then? You let him escape, and now he and his accomplices are the ones causing all of our gods to get sick! Don't you feel any remorse?" Kye couldn't lower his voice anymore.

"Of course I feel remorse, but there was nothing that could be done! They made off with the information they were seeking. I was put into a corner; I didn't know what else to do! There were times when even I had convinced myself they were each dead. I wish they were, but they aren't! I may be king, but I don't have the answers to everything—all I can hope to do is try to protect my people, including you!" Zyair explained.

His steps came barreling down the stairs that led to his throne before swallowing his dear friend in a tight embrace while he wept. His arms stayed around the man.

Guilt sizzled inside of Zyair. He had made so many wrong decisions—from banishing Amaya and Rose, to keeping the lives of Kye's brother along with Ruki, Teira, and Sage a secret from him.

"I wish I were a king with all the right choices, but I can't be. Please forgive me, Kye," Zyair said to his friend.

"Well, this certainly wasn't how I pictured our reunion in my head," said a voice.

Kye's entire body went numb and he felt like he couldn't breathe. Zyair slowly pulled back from his friend, preparing to meet the eyes of that voice's owner.

"Then again, this is how you've always been: a small, helpless weakling, cowering in someone else's shadow. I don't know why I was expecting any different," he said. "Actually, I came to help you, Kye."

"You aren't welcome here, Chasaka," Zyair growled firmly at the man, stamping his walking stick against the marble flooring.

"I welcome myself anywhere I please. This is my world, after all."

"You're delusional."

"What's wrong, Kye? It's rude to ignore someone," Chasaka mocked him before looking to the king. "I'm a bit saddened that you were the one to reveal the truth to him before I could."

Kye felt sick, like he was going to lose whatever was in his stomach right then and there. His fingers clutched the fabric of his clothing and he kept his breath inside.

"You look surprised to see me, even after you already knew the truth...you see, after we killed that Avery boy's parents, we came across some useful spells that just happened to help us formulate this little plan. One of them would explain the reason

I'm still alive...the king of Hell sure loves making deals." Chasaka shook his head and began approaching the two of them calmly with a snide smile on his face.

"Guards! Seize him now!" But fear washed over Zyair as he remembered that he had sent all the guards away in order to speak with Kye alone.

"Looks like the cavalry isn't coming for their king. You know, I heard what you said; about how you're not a king containing all the answers. But you know something, you're worse than that. I suppose it's simply heritage for every king to be a fool. Taro could have prevented the massacre of the Astral Clan; could have prevented the death of thousands of his people, and yet, as fate would have it, he didn't," Chasaka explained. "And *you* managed to allow your people to freely discriminate against the demigods after Tobias, Vincent, and Elaine were killed. Well, I would say that has to be your *first* mistake in all of this."

Grimacing, Zyair drew the broadsword hanging from his side, made from the kingdom's finest alloy. It was a family heirloom, one which had won many past battles.

Chasaka's lips grew into a twisted grin before a bout of chuckling burst forth from his throat. "Don't humor me with such foolish gestures! A sword? You must be JESTING!" At his final words, his own sword was out. It was another Sacris Ignem, akin to Amaya's, or rather, Amaya's was akin to his. "The four of us are here to ensure more mistakes don't occur in the future, so that a less power-hungry world can exist, leaving the previous one behind, never again to be remembered."

"Such hypocrisy...I would imagine a man with such strong beliefs of Nature's Paragon wouldn't be using holy weapons,"

Zyair growled at him. "Enough talk. You wish to invade my kingdom, so be it. I'll protect it."

"Please, you're nothing more than a twig in my way," Chasaka replied. "I'm here on a personal note, a little revenge that I grew impatient for."

Zyair didn't even have time to register his blow. Any hint of emotion within Chasaka's features was vacant when he swung his sword outward. It swung in such a way where in its wake was Zyair's throat. The blade cut through the man like a simple twig, like he had said.

Kye took two steps back as he saw his friend's body drop to the floor, his head rolling beside it. He screamed in horror. He couldn't stop. He could have deafened himself with the sound of his own screams. He held his head and dropped onto his knees, his clothing getting soaked in the growing pool of blood.

It was the most horrific sight he had ever laid eyes upon. His nausea, at last, got the best of him and he emptied the contents of his stomach all over the floor.

"How indignant for the new king of Lucus," Chasaka said. He picked up the blood-soaked crown from the former king's head, not bothering to wipe it clean before placing it on his brother's head, who continued to sob, scream, and weep. Then he picked up the walking stick from the floor, thick, crimson liquid oozing down its shaft.

Kye raised a shaky hand to push away Chasaka's offer of the stick that his friend once held. "N—No!" shouted Kye.

"Hush up, it's a gift. You're the king now. Zyair would have wanted you to have it," his brother replied.

Seeing that Kye still refused to take hold of it, anger contorted Chasaka's face and then he forced the end of the walking stick through Kye's hand, causing him to collapse in a bout of screaming again. "Take it!" Chasaka yelled at him.

Kye writhed on the floor, trying to ease his pain. The pain that moments ago felt like a horrible burn dissolved into numbness. Black filled up the edges of his vision and he was deaf to everything but the beating of his own heart. Kye could hear the call of faint voices without discernible words. He didn't know what made him think so, but he assumed they were trying to help him. But any fool could tell there was no saving him from his demise.

Chasaka beat him nearly to death when they were younger. Now that his brother had taken lives to achieve his goals, the feeling was familiar and didn't seem to bother him much. There wasn't a doubt in Kye's mind that his brother was going to kill him. A dark part of him wanted to smile when he finally figured it out and looked his brother in the eyes with his fading vision. If Chasaka killed him—when Chasaka killed him—he could finally leave behind all the pain he had inflicted. Now he could only pray his brother wouldn't torture him first.

Chasaka kneeled down in the pool of blood and lifted his weeping brother a bit. "D—Don't touch me!" screamed Kye as he flailed away from the man. Despite his twisted thoughts, his body still begged him to do whatever it took to keep him alive

"Oh yes, I almost forgot his highness' heirloom," Chasaka said and stood once more. He took hold of the sword which Zyair had so pettily drawn at him.

"I was considering sparing your life. It feels so good to be in control, you know, I wanted my little brother to know just what that was like for once in his pathetic and miserable life. But here you lie. It's all being handed to you, and even now you still writhe like the pitiful worm you are," Chasaka said.

He raised the sword over his head, both hands firmly on the hilt, eyes dead as he prepared to end his brother's life. With one swift movement, Kye caught the sword by the blade. The velocity at which it moved had been enough to lob off one of Kye's fingers, but it still kept the steel from bringing him death. He tried to stifle the pain dealt by the sword, but more tears soaked his face.

"You've grown far past cruel...not even giving me my final words before you put an end to my existence," Kye said shakily, his nose running.

"You were so muffled by your own screams that I assumed you had nothing left to say, Kye. But I'm glad you aren't as naive as you used to be," Chasaka replied. "Unlike your friend there, it appears you've finally accepted you're going to die with everyone else."

"You won't win...Your children are coming, and they're going to destroy all of you," Kye growled at his brother.

He smirked at such a foolish choice of final words and shook his head. "Doubtful." With that, he plunged the steel into Kye's skull.

"Long live Lucus' king."

Chasaka breathed in softly as he stood on the balcony of the castle, watching the ignorant noblemen and women below him mill about the capital. The bodies of the king's guards lay beside him and his head leaned into his hands. "Now that Lucus' king is dead, I suppose that concludes the start to this world's anarchy."

Teira appeared beside him. "I've finished in Folkvangr and am heading back now," she said.

"Go on without me...I'll catch up."

13: Blood of the Vengeful

Kuba Documents (Translated roughly from ancient High-Speak) (Excerpt from Pgs. 129-131)

It was a vast expanse of beauty surrounding my very being. None back in our caves would even be able to comprehend it. Trees sprung up in almost every direction while the sound of water running could be heard almost anywhere. In all my days of this journey across the land and in all of the places I've so courageously mapped out, none have been so beautiful as this. Were I talented in the art of sketching, perhaps I would have doodled it, but I'm afraid that even then it would do the place no justice.

Like in other of these expanses I've been so graced as to happen upon, I came across those little toadstools, so named because I came across a few toads perched atop them.

Some places along the wooded area happen to be hillous and slippery. I nearly busted my face trying to scale one. But I just had to see something.

A structure of stones, unlike any natural thing I've ever seen before. It seemed to stretch onward toward the clouds, taller than any cliffside I had ever set my sights upon.

I reached the top of the stones after what felt like an eternity and examined the structure. Small but very soft grasses grew along it. I'd made it a point earlier to take some from a tree that I had found some growing on much earlier in my travels. I had decided that it was as good a time as any to sample, so I placed it in one of my satchels which had some free space. But then I realized that I was running low on space and promised from now on to only grab hold of items that interested me the most. It would be a hard decision to make.

Enough rambling, upon reaching this strange landmark, I decided to mark it on my map and allow myself to rest for the night since it had turned to twilight by the time I reached it.

However, when I woke the next morning, the structure had vanished into thin air, almost as though I had simply fabricated its existence from delusion. After searching around the area and finding nothing, I erased the mark on my map.

This was a truly captivating place and I felt like I could spend my entire exploration just covering the area. But by the time the sun set once more, I came across that structure again. I wanted badly to explore it, but was so exhausted that I allowed myself to camp at its base once more. It was strange though. This strange structure hadn't appeared in the same place I saw it before. I marked it once more on my map and let sleep fall over me.

When morning rose, it was gone again! I was baffled by nature's mysteries before, but this truly was something for which I could find no explanation. I decided to keep the mark upon my map and would mark it again if and when the structure were to appear again.

As the days passed, I couldn't be sure if the thing was following me, or if I were following it.

* * *

T raveling to the tower would begin immediately the next morning. But since their horses would do them no use in Hell, the travelers left them behind, which meant that it would take a bit longer for them to arrive there. There was a small town on the way which they decided to rest in before they would search for the tower.

The town they were heading to was one Amaya identified on her map as Silkmaw.

The path steered them through a sparsely wooded area, where dirt paths soon turned to cobblestone. It didn't take long for a pungent odor to strike them once their feet landed on Silkmaw's roads. Not only had this smell begun to violate them, but so, too, did a white substance sprinkle from the sky.

"Snow...?" Amaya asked to break the silence caused by the confusion. The air felt too warm to prove her suggestion even remotely true.

Cyero held out his hand to capture some of the white flakes drifting down. He stared at them for a long moment before he raised his eyes and glanced all about. "These are ashes." He turned to the rest of them. "Look around. It's everywhere."

Amaya looked to the cracks in the path and lifted her feet to see the ashes stuffed inside them, only then had she noticed the various scars on the few trees surrounding them. "A fire..." she said. A sinking feeling settled in the pit of her stomach and suspicion took hold of her. She ran forward without another word, leaving the others behind.

"Amaya, wait!" shouted Rose.

With that, the rest of them began trailing her as fast as they could, even if her head start gave them a disadvantage. The closer they came to Silkmaw, the more that smell stung their noses, and the more recognizable it became. Amaya didn't need to see the origin of the substance to know what had happened; the village of Silkmaw had burned to the ground. But the significance of the sight was something that took her aback. Nothing could have prepared her eyes to see it. The others pulled up short to where she had stopped, now viewing the sight for themselves.

Black and white ash lay in large heaps, the paths invisible. Homes were withered away, only their broken remains standing. The ashes were still hot with embers glowing inside them while smoke rose from their core.

Rose placed her hand over her mouth before it slid down to her aching chest. "How atrocious..." Her whispering voice sounded like thunder to the silence of Silkmaw. "I hope everyone made it out alive." It was hard to find the faith that even some of them had.

"Even if they did, where would they go after this?" Amaya shook her head. "Come on, we have to find at least one survivor." She stepped forward again. The rustling ashes beneath her feet unsettled her. Each one was someone's personal belonging; someone's home; someone's father; their son or daughter; their wife.

Soon they came upon someone alive in the disaster, but she was trapped underneath the remnants of a collapsed home. In fact, the only reason they found her at all was because of her constant rasping for help. Her face was barely visible beneath all the ashes, as she, too, was covered in them.

Amaya began cutting away at some of the wood with her sword while Soren and Cyero lifted it and Rose struggled to pull her out from the house's foundation, propping her up gently as the ash-covered woman muttered soft thank yous.

It was hard to be certain, but the woman appeared to be middle-aged. "Miss, what happened here? Are there any other survivors?" Soren asked.

The woman lifted her face, baked with soot, to meet Soren's gaze. "No," she answered. "At least as far as I know." She looked down at her folded hands. "It was the demigod of fire who came from Barness. There were rumors for many years that he had died with the others of his kind...but no...he burned this village—"

"Did you see him?" Amaya cut her off, eyes serious.

The woman nodded her head. "I don't know why he did it...but I do know that it was him. He had that unique red hair, those deep black and crimson eyes. It was no doubt his fire that reduced this village to nothing..."

Amaya's ears blocked out the conversation after that. It was hard to hear the battered woman speak of Chasaka's wrongdoings. She was still trying to comprehend him still being alive—and now she was witnessing his work.

What is this vile feeling inside of me? When the woman referred to Chasaka—her father—her veins became hot like the surrounding embers. She opened her hands and gazed at them before balling them into fists. "Don't worry," she said. "He will pay for the things he's done in due time. I'll make sure of it."

The woman looked hopeful in her final moments.

Their stay in Silkmaw wasn't long, and the travelers walked onward. But Amaya walked with newfound determination in her steps, falling ahead of Soren and Cyero. But Rose tread beside her with much on her mind. She looked at her friend, pressing her lips together. "What did you mean when you said that to her?" she asked.

Amaya didn't take her eyes off the path ahead. "We're going to train as hard as we can and we will hang their heads from the gates of Barness for all to see," she muttered. When their eyes finally met, Rose looked mortified. "What did you think we were chasing them into Hell to do?"

"Amaya, we were going to bring them back to Barness so that the king could decide what to do with them. We can't defeat them, are you mad?" Rose shouted, catching Soren and Cyero's attention.

"Maybe," her friend answered. "Do you truly think some steel bars could hold monsters like them? No. The only punishment for a crime like theirs is death."

"Must it end in violence?" Rose snapped back. "I'm tired of you taking things into your own hands, thinking all your choices are righteous. Can't you listen to me for once?" Rose's veins felt hot, her body shaken. The last thing she wanted was to kill her own parents—especially after spending so many years hoping they weren't dead. "We can't kill them; it isn't our duty to take their lives into our own hands."

Amaya stared dumbfounded at her friend. She had never heard her speak so heavily before. "And what? You think they will follow us blindly out of Hell?"

"I don't know what the future will hold. I just know that violence isn't the only way to solve this. Just think rationally, please," Rose begged.

Her friend sighed. "Fine...but if all else fails, we will have no other choice."

The day went on as they left Silkmaw and headed for Carawe Forest. Amaya didn't speak for most of the day thereafter, but as night began to approach, Cyero stopped them before the wooded area began.

"What is going on? Why are we stopping?" Amaya asked.

"Well, the reason the Tower of Twilight received its name is that it's only visible from the outside at twilight," Soren told her. "It would be safer to sleep out here for the night so the dangers of Carawe wouldn't easily find us."

"I hate to be the bearer of bad news, but I...am not feeling so well," Rose said softly. Her complexion was paler than usual and her eyes were glazed over. Whatever was wrong, it couldn't be good.

The others looked at her, concern in their eyes. "What's the matter?" Cyero asked.

"I'm finding it hard to breathe," she said.

"It's probably from breathing in all the ashes from Silkmaw, you had better get some rest for now," Soren said as he helped her lay down.

Amaya gave a sigh and turned her head to look at the near forest. It was within reach...but if there was no way to get into Hell anyway, she supposed it wouldn't be rational to go in hastily. And now Rose wasn't feeling well.

She helped set up the fire to keep them warm in the cold night. But even as all the other travelers drifted into slumber, Amaya stayed awake, her mind racing with thoughts that ranged from confronting her parents to ultimately ending their lives, which she knew was inevitable. It made her blood rush with anger, thinking of all the despair they had left in the wake of their selfish plans.

Amaya grew tired of tossing and turning and rose. As she did, a gentle sprinkle of rain began to mist her and her comrades, causing the fire between them all to release steam.

Heaving a sigh to relieve the pressure on her mind, Amaya set out for the forest which they could have reached had their group just continued on for a little while longer. Her plan was to walk a little ways into the forest to hone her proficiency with the sword. She began just by swinging it at some trees, but then went on to slice smaller, thinner trees in half.

She swung her sword and continued to put herself through vigorous physical exercises until the blisters on her hands began to bleed and her chest ran dry of air. But growing tired as she did had caused a wave of anger to flow through her. Picking up her sword whose shaft was buried halfway into the damp earth, she swung it once more, doing a spin until she was facing the direction behind herself.

Amaya's body was about to give up just then and collapse, but something kept her legs from giving out. She found her sword pointed directly at the chest of a living person, and she quickly retreated back to see who it was she had nearly impaled. But when her eyes lifted, they filled with surprise.

"Amaya?" the person asked after a moment's hesitation. Their voice was warm, inviting, and ran plentiful with nostalgia. In fact, it even took a few moments for the girl to even recognize this person or how they knew her name.

She, too, was hesitant to speak, but forced herself to do so. "Father...?"

Faces so similar in semblance looked upon one another, neither knowing what to do or say to the other.

"This...is quite a sight for sore eyes," the man said.

Amaya's face slowly began to contort, her eyebrows furrowing, her lip quivering as tears stung her eyes, and her sword dropped from her fading grip, plunging its blade once more into the dirt.

"All I've ever wanted...was to finally see you and mother once more, so that maybe...just maybe...I could be happy again as I used to be. But as of late, it seems everywhere I turn I'm hearing one bad thing after another about you, including laying waste to that entire village, burning it to ash." Amaya wiped away her tears as best she could, but the rain falling from above would only soak her cheeks once more. "I don't care if every one of my comrades and the many innocent people who have become your supposed victims are all lying to me, but please...tell me it's all untrue. Because when

I heard, I was filled with a wave of anger that I couldn't quell, I fantasized my blade causing your flesh to bleed until you suffered more than I or any other you have brought harm to. But now... standing before you...all I can feel is anything but those things."

Chasaka cast down a gaze of sorrow and sympathy for his grieving daughter. "Amaya...for your sake, I wish I could tell you they were all liars. Leaving you and Rose was the hardest decision I, your mother, and Rose's parents ever had to make...but it had to be done in order to fix this broken world. You and I aren't so different, you know. We both have withstood pain and suffering, we both desire peace, but you search in the wrongest of places," he explained.

"You're wrong!" Amaya snapped back. "I'm nothing like you; I'll never be like you! The only reason I ever felt such pain was because you left us behind to fall within the aftermath of your sins! And all you could think of then was yourselves! I don't think any of you ever stopped to consider the consequences of your actions. But that's just what I would expect from someone who takes part in impetuous and pointless murder." She took up her sword and used every ounce of her waning strength to try to cut through her father. But her blow was met with a clang that momentarily drowned out the sound of the pelting rain. Her eyes, filled with rage, were met with ones so far in contrast to her own that she was unsure if they had ever truly held anything but mercilessness. "Mark my words. If it's here upon this very soil, I'll be the one to shed your blood, and never again will you terrorize another innocent soul."

Within moments after Amaya finished speaking, the two became entangled with the blades of one another, exchanging blow after blow, flames flying and disappearing just as soon as they had appeared in the rainy night.

Amaya's exhausted body couldn't long withstand to block her father's swings, and eventually she was shoved back into the mud on the ground, a sword identical to her own being pointed at her face. "Aside from your mother, you were the only individual in this world for whom I ever held compassion. But if you ever turn your blade against me again..." Chasaka leaned down toward his daughter's face. "...I'll kill you."

To expend her last drop of strength, Amaya lifted her sword once more, its blade slicing cleanly across her father's cheek. In the recoil, Chasaka swung his own sword, only to slice Amaya's right brow with the very tip of its steel.

Gritting his teeth, Chasaka finally sheathed his sword and turned from his ailing daughter, only to disappear into the darkness of the forest.

Amaya scrambled to her feet, but her body was too tired to pursue, so she was left holding the wound delivered by the man as she stared into the trees that had swallowed him. After bringing her hand away from her face to see the blood that stained it, Amaya turned around and began running the other direction, even if her legs screamed in agony. She made it back to camp faster than she had left it. Out of breath, she knelt down and began jostling Soren to wake him.

"Soren, we must gather everyone and go now!" she told him urgently.

The prophet groaned himself into wakefulness, Amaya's jostling shaking away his grogginess. His eyes caught sight of the cut across her face and the condition of her overall physique. "Amaya, what's happened? Calm yourself," he said.

"My father...I came across him at the edge of the forest. He's alone. We must take advantage of the opportunity and pursue him!" she yelled, causing the other two to awaken.

"What is all this ruckus? I had just managed to fall asleep," Cyero complained.

The only way to signal Rose had awoken was the fact that she erupted in a fit of coughs before ending it with a sneeze.

"Amaya...let your body rest, please," Soren told her, trying to calm her down as he grabbed her hand with both of his own and then sat up.

But the girl looked at him dumbfounded instead and did just the opposite of his intentions. "You can't be serious! We've been handed the chance to take down one of these awful people, and you want to simply rest?" It was clear how miffed she was by how loudly she was raising her voice.

Soren finally stood, towering over the young woman before placing his hands upon her shoulders. "If you ever hope to take down a man as powerful as your father, you—along with the rest of us—are going to need sleep! Rose has fallen ill, and we all are exhausted from traveling the whole day. So please, do all of us a favor and give it a rest!" he snapped.

The look Soren got in return from Amaya may as well have stabbed him straight in the chest, and the blood dripping off her brow and mixing with the rain falling from above caused her to appear even more frightening. She knocked his arms away with her own and turned her shoulder to him. "Am I the only one who is taking any of this seriously? Fine. If you all won't help me, then I'll go kill him myself," she growled before turning and beginning to walk away.

Soren stepped forward after her though and reached his hand toward her. "Please wait, Amaya!" he said.

The shriek of steel sounded within the rain hitting the mud puddles beneath their feet, and Amaya turned suddenly, the point of her blade aimed at Soren's face, the rest of the sword directly parallel to his arm. The two shared gazes for a long, hesitant moment, one pair of eyes in shock while the other scowled. "You wish to stop me, and yet you refuse to aid me—even when time is running out for this opportunity...tch." Amaya sheathed her sword once more before turning away for the last time and running off.

She was certain that with enough determination, one more clash with her father would bring about his end as the tides of battle turned in her favor.

Soren watched her go, worried, his feet begging his body to run after her. Cyero was beside him suddenly, causing him to turn his head. "Don't worry...she won't be able to find the tower without my guidance. The forest is the farthest she will get into this fatuous endeavor of hers," he assured the man.

Releasing a sigh to further relieve himself of doubt, Soren sat down once more. "First Rose falls ill, and now...I fear Amaya is growing more consumed with revenge than an actual desire for peace," he explained while Cyero seated himself beside him.

"Deep down I know she means well, even if her behavior is reckless and unsympathetic. But she must be shown some kind of light to help her see in this dark place. While she goes about expressing it in the worst ways, she's hurting," he answered softly.

While the two talked, Rose lay beneath the lone tree she had chosen to rest near, their words causing her heart to quiver with distress. She hoped her friend wouldn't fall down such a dark path as they were suggesting.

14: Blood of the Hydra

When morning came, Rose, Soren, and Cyero wasted no time getting on the move. First, they needed to find Amaya. However, it wouldn't prove to be a very formidable task, as she hadn't made it very far before her tired body collapsed just before the forest's edge.

Rose kneeled down and shook her friend gently, trying not to cause her pain. "Amaya...? Are you all right?"

The young woman's body started as she came awake. She rolled over, noticing all the faces looking down at her. She knew they had to be upset by her actions from the previous night, and there was some guilt for the way she had spoken to them. But she couldn't lose sight of her goals. "Morning," she grumbled before getting to her feet. Her whole body ached from her battle with Chasaka, but she did her best not to show it. "Well, let's keep going then."

Amaya decided not to mention anything about what had happened. She didn't feel an apology was necessary, after all.

Rose, on the other hand, had been astonished by this other side of her friend which was beginning to bare its ugly head. *I hope she's all right,* she thought.

When they set foot into Carawe, ambient sounds welcomed them. The leaves of the tall canopy above rustled only occasionally, creating a gentle silence. Somehow it was still lush despite how long the twin gods of earth had been corrupt. But Soren had told them once that the seal on them could have halted the process of all plant life decaying.

There were sounds of distant crickets singing a drawn-out song, ceaseless but never louder no matter how far they walked. There was no path to follow, so they dodged bushes and other foliage growing on Carawe's floor. Whenever a subtle breeze would budge through, Carawe would lean away for its presence to fill its vegetation with life.

The trees ingrained in the surface reached skyward, all of them skinny and crooked, covered with umber bark, verdant moss, and lichen. None looked the same with their mostly short, spiny branches extending toward their brothers. But to the mindless traveler, they all blended together, disregarding how many footsteps the traveler would take to lead him further in and never let him emerge. If he looked behind him, he would see a completely different place than when he had walked past it.

The constant nagging sound of those crickets carried them further into the directionless tangle of underbrush.

"Are you sure you know where you're going?" Amaya asked Cyero. The sound of Carawe was beginning to drive her mad.

"The tower has a strong spiritual connection to my brother, so even though it's currently invisible to our eyes, I can sense it," he answered.

"Do you know the approximate location?" Soren asked.

"It will appear next on the southeastern shore of the Black Mire," Cyero answered.

Soren's eyes trailed over toward the god upon the mentioning of this place, and both Amaya's and Rose's faces registered confusion.

"Black Mire?" Rose asked.

"Yes, not only are its waters the new home of Dytia, but they're filled with a hallucinogen designed to shove away any who try to cross it," Soren answered.

"Is Dytia the name of another god?" asked Amaya.

"The goddess of water, yes," Cyero replied.

"She chose to lock herself away from Dufmoore in order to protect her people. She and Adione were close with one another, so when Dytia found out what had happened to her and began exhibiting the same symptoms, she left the village," Soren explained.

"Are you sure there is no other way to get to the tower?" Rose asked.

"I suppose we could probably go around the lake, but we may be cutting it close on time. It's a long way around," Cyero replied.

"What? If it's easier just to cross, then we should," Amaya said.

"The lake is very dangerous, especially with Dytia roaming through the waters. We're going around," Soren answered firmly.

"Then have fun going around without me, because I'm going through." Amaya walked ahead of the rest.

Rose sighed and placed her hand on her head. "I'm sorry...she isn't usually so reckless," she told Cyero. "I don't know what has gotten into her, but we can't let her go by herself."

Upon agreement, the conversation stayed quiet, the only thing narrating them became the dull wind that rustled the dying trees around them. The silence allowed thoughts to ease their way into Rose's mind. She thought of her parents and what Cyero had said a day back. Ever since those memories of her parents had been lost, she longed to meet them again. Part of her had always hoped that they abandoned them, so at least there was a chance of seeing them again. Once they believed they were dead and that hope was gone, but now they were alive and were working against them. As disheartening as it was, she hoped they might listen to diplomacy if it came from their own children. But now Amaya was beginning to concern her—she seemed bent on wanting to end their lives.

Morning became afternoon as they walked, and an eerie feeling fell over them as they passed through some trees which were twisted and gnarled to create an overhang that adorned a tunnel. The path looked as though it were seldom walked upon, as the grasses and moss which grew throughout it were unkempt. In fact, the area would be easily missed had Cyero not led them to it.

"Are we almost there?" Amaya spoke up in the dead silence.

No birds sang their songs and the chirp of the crickets had dissipated, there was only the bristling of the tall grasses around the four of them which tickled their legs as they walked.

Soren nodded his head. "This feeling, it's a sign that we have nearly reached it," he said.

Rose looked at the prophet with an eyebrow cocked when he mentioned that the feeling would stay. This wracked her nerves even further, since the deeper they ventured into the tunnel, the dimmer it became. The only source of light was the sun's rays that flitted through the leaves.

Anxiety filled her mind as darkness covered the four of them. Her eyes glanced around every few seconds and her palms became sweaty. She was on the verge of a full-on panic attack until something touched her shoulder. It was nothing to fear, however—it had only been Cyero, who had sensed her fear. She smiled a little when she realized this and hoped that her nod and lingering smile would be enough thanks for his sympathy.

The sky remained dark when they emerged from the tunnel. Amaya and Rose both looked up to see what had happened to the sun that once shone effortlessly across the sky. The blockage was caused by black clouds in the sky which became a silhouette from the sun that was attempting to shine through them.

Before them was a lake that reflected the color of the clouds above, and the fact that the trees surrounding them were rather dense caused the area to appear that much darker. "Didn't you say that this was a mire?" Rose asked the prophet as she did her best to take in the area, even given that there wasn't much to behold.

"The word *mire* has two meanings. One represents the area of land while the other represents fear."

It was then that the two understood why the feeling around them was of significance to the area. "The tower will appear on the other side once twilight rises. We will need to take the boat across," Cyero said, pointing to a boat which was stationed at a rickety, broken dock. The boat itself was nothing to look at either; a simple wooden canoe with a mossy oar inside of it. It was unknown how much time had passed since the thing was last used.

"I thought you were going to be taking the long way around," Amaya said and crossed her arms.

"We can't just leave you by yourself, so we're going with you, whether you like it or not," Soren answered, earning an eye roll from Amaya.

Reluctantly stepping into the barely-stable boat, Amaya could feel just how worn it was from the water eating away at it. Once they were all in the boat, Soren took the courtesy of rowing them across the lake, which didn't go by all that quickly given the vastness of the body of water.

"So what kind of animal is this water goddess?" Rose asked in an attempt to quell the building fear within her.

"Dytia is a white koi fish," Soren answered. Then there was silence again, aside from the sloshing of water as he paddled them along.

The water intrigued Rose, as it always had, and she couldn't help but to dip one of her fingers into it and allow it to be dragged along as they moved. But upon placing her hand in the water, she quickly jerked it away and yelped when a burning like acid met her touch. "What happened?" Amaya asked, whipping her head around.

"I'm not sure," the girl replied as she examined her hand for any wounds. Surprisingly, she saw none and scrunched her brow.

"Be careful!" Cyero scolded her and took the young woman by the hand. "This place is cursed, you mustn't touch the water with your bare hands," he said.

Before Rose could even open her mouth to reply, a churning began within the depths of the lake.

Though the churning came from the boat's front, Soren didn't stop rowing. "Even if it's her, we must keep going," he told them. With the bank of the far shore in sight, relief filled each of them.

Then, something large bumped the underside of their vessel. The knock was bad enough to send Rose plummeting into the depths below with a splash.

"Rose!" her friend shouted after regaining her balance. Panic set in when the blonde didn't surface after a few moments. She could almost sense that she was in danger, and didn't hesitate to jump in after her.

"Wait! Stop!" Soren yelled to try and stop her, but it was too late by the time his warning reached her. She had already dove into the lake. The prophet dropped the oar into the boat and moved to look over its edge. Silently, he cursed the black water which gave him no visibility of what was happening.

They could feel their skin burning as though being enveloped in the fires of Hell. Rose opened her mouth to scream when she tumbled down, but when she did, the acid-like water burned her throat. The pain ate away at her body, and her mind fought to reach the water's surface, but she couldn't move at all. She was tiring from moving, even though she hadn't made any progress toward the surface. It was as though the water had seeped into her skin and ignited her from within.

Amaya's case had been no different, each suffering in agony below the silence of the water. She knew opening her eyes would be torturous, but she had to, just to know if she could see in the murky water.

When she painfully opened her eyes, she was surrounded by absolute nothingness. Below her, she could see something very faintly. She did her best to move closer to it, but her body weight was the only thing pulling her down. As she descended, she saw that it was the friend she was trying to save.

Rose tilted her head up to look at Amaya, her eyes opened as well as she tried to swim up toward her. Had she somehow figured out how to move? Amaya tried to reach down to grab Rose's hand but her body wouldn't respond. At this point, she became the one who needed saving.

Rose must have realized what had happened and was swimming up, reaching for her friend, but she grabbed Amaya's foot instead of her hand. She was dragging her further under. She wanted to struggle, but again, she couldn't. Furthermore, Amaya was starting to run out of air.

Suddenly, Amaya heard a loud splash of water beside her, which exploded like cannons in her ears. Then she felt something grab her wrist, pulling her up toward the surface.

Once there, she saw it was Cyero who had rescued her, the god having pulled the young woman into his chest to prevent her from sinking below the water once more. He lifted her back into the boat and immediately dove back into the depths to retrieve Rose.

Within moments, he surfaced with Rose in his arms and leaped from the water and back into the boat. The force of him landing in the boat had sprung a leak in the boards making it up.

"Dammit," the ice god spat and began glancing around.

Something came into his view in the water, something milky white—and it was big. His eyes flicked back toward the hole in the boat, which now was flooding.

"Cyero, what do we do?" yelled Soren.

Ice fractals shot from the palm of the ice god's hand. It plugged the hole in the boat. Not only that, but it began freezing over the entirety of the lake around them.

"There, we will be safe now," Cyero said.

The abrupt silence that came over them after was terrifying considering what had just happened.

"What just happened?" Rose asked.

It all happened so quickly that nobody had the time to register it. "It must have been Dytia. I don't doubt it. In fact, I don't even think there is anything in the water that could have caused a tremor of that magnitude. At least not in a lake this size—or of this consistency, for that matter," Soren said.

"Well, now the boat is frozen. Are we supposed to walk to the other side of the lake? We will break all our bones before we even make it half the distance," Amaya said.

While each of them was distracted by conversation, Cyero's eyes had been glued to the rear of their boat. The ice there was beginning to crack, and below the jet black surface, he could see that milky white color.

"Get on," he said.

The others looked at him with confusion as to what he was talking about.

Before anyone could even blink, they were all hurled into the air by the god of ice. Behind them, they could briefly see a huge mass, the size of a whale leaping out of the ice, shards like glass flying in every direction around it. Before they could fall, they landed on something else, which was also white—but it was furry and felt muscular.

Each held onto it tightly as the furry, white creature landed atop the ice. Regaining their composure, they could now see that what had caught them was Cyero, whose paws were now racing against the surface of the ice. Behind them, the huge fish which had burst through it was chasing after them, breaking up the surface of ice as it swam.

The way Amaya had landed, she was facing backward, watching the horrifying fish plow through the ice after them, decaying scales flying off because of the velocity at which it swam.

Upon reaching the shore, the white wolf leaped from the ice and lurched his body backward, causing the three humans to go tumbling to the damp earth below while the wolf completed his somersault and whipped around to face his pursuing sister.

The koi fish jumped from the water, but was stopped by the wolf slamming into her—paws forward and silver eyes blazing.

The strength of the blow alone was enough to send the fish hurtling back toward the water, landing in it with a sound like a clap of thunder as her immense body smacked its surface.

Most of the ice had all been broken by now, so Cyero was left to swim the short distance back to shore, panting a bit from his strenuous actions.

"Are you all right?" Cyero asked upon returning to his mortal form.

"A bit of a rough landing, but I think we're all fine," Rose answered.

"Yes, thank you for saving us," Soren added.

Amaya said nothing in regards to any of this.

They stayed a distance from the shore while they awaited the tower's appearance in order to avoid any further conflict with Dytia. By the time the sun dipped close to the horizon, the travelers, namely Amaya, were beginning to lose hope that this really was the correct location of the tower, or that it even existed at all.

But as time would tell, the Tower of Twilight truly did exist, as its immense being loomed before each of them within a literal instance. It didn't erect from the ground, nor did it magically build itself up from foundation to steeple. It was large and it was dangerous. It shoved trees out of the way and left a dust cloud in its wake. But when it all settled, it was something marvelous to behold. Moss crept up its beaten stature and even vines entangled it, stemming from an unknown source. Just barely in view was a single dungeon-like door, and its height nearly reached the clouds. Needless to say, it wouldn't be a short climb.

"So what exactly should we be expecting when we climb this?" Amaya asked. She was determined almost as immediately as the tower had appeared.

"It's the home of the portal to Hell, so it's likely we may come across some demons. I would say the hydra may be a problem, but regarding your parents, I don't know what has become of it," Cyero explained.

"The hydra?" Rose asked him.

"The hydra is the surface's guardian, chained to the depths of Hell to protect the surface from any demons who manage to escape his labyrinth alive."

"Well, we should get going then," Amaya said as she began walking toward its entrance.

With that, it was time to make the trek up the tower which housed absolutely no windows. The interior of the structure included multiple floors through which the five of them would have to navigate in order to reach the top where Cyero had told them that the lightning god would be.

But the inside didn't include a simple ascent of stairs—instead was a spire of death waiting to kill them. It included obstacle after obstacle and those which didn't include obstacles were crawling with ravenous demons from the rift they sought out.

They were about halfway up the tower when something stopped them dead in their tracks. Amaya grunted, Rose letting out a gasp as she saw her friend receive a blunt strike to the head.

She passed out on impact from the blow. Behind her, a creature was snickering in the shadow of the walls. Its eyes lit up in the darkness in the room. Upon hearing the crash of Amaya's body hitting the floor, Cyero and Soren turned around, wide-eyed.

Cyero looked closer at what had attacked her. He was able to scope out that its ears were feathered and cat-like, its body bulky and masculine, and it donned rather large claws. "Athelstan..." Cyero whispered, his ears flattening straight against his head.

Rose was about to venture forward to help her friend, but the tone of Cyero's voice shook her to the core, as though this were something she shouldn't be tampering with.

The glowing eyes slowly approached Amaya's unconscious body, and fear brimmed inside of Rose. She tried to run forward to remove her friend from the situation, but was pulled back by her stomach, firm arms keeping her in place. "Rose, stop." It was Soren who had stopped her.

Out from the shadows came a lynx. Its eyes were a yellow-green color surrounded by deep black, and were deep-set, which brought out the striking color of its eyes even more. Not only that, but it held a rather snide and threatening look on its face.

Cyero stepped forward through the group, shaping an icicle before shooting it at the lynx. Athelstan was able to dodge it easily, leaving it a mere puddle on the ground. The god narrowed his eyes down at this. "Follow the path to find Rotos; I'll stay here," he said without taking his eyes off the target.

"What? I can't just leave Amaya!" Rose shouted before being pulled back yet again by Soren. She was still having a bit of trouble with breathing from the night before and wheezed a bit when he pulled her.

"She will be all right, rest assured. Time is wasting, we must continue," he said to her.

Still, the blonde fought against the other's grip on her body. Cyero stepped in front of her and pushed her back, causing her to lose her footing. From there, Soren carried her away from the scene despite her resolve to escape. As cruel as it was, they truly didn't have time to waste on watching the battle unfold. Plus, there was no saying what Athelstan was capable of. Amaya was clearly his prey, and the fact that he was able to knock her out with one blow was a thought to consider.

Soren apologized to her the whole way through to the final floor. The man found it rather hard to climb the stairs while holding her, as she still squirmed despite knowing she was way out of her sorts in this instance. She pleaded with him to let her down, but all Soren could do was apologize to her.

Reaching the outside of the building led to a staircase which gave rise to the top of the building. Here, Soren finally set Rose down. "We need to go back for her, she's hurt! What if she dies?" she shouted in a panic.

"Do you honestly doubt that Cyero will keep her safe?" Soren asked her, making sure to be ready if she happened to make another attempt toward escape.

Rose kept quiet at that and folded her arms, but the silence didn't keep her mind from raging with worry for her friend.

But this worry suddenly dissipated when her eyes beheld a beast in front of them. Soren looked mortified by this and was breathless. "What is that thing doing up here?" he murmured in horror.

"Is that the beast Cyero mentioned earlier?" Rose asked him.

"Yes," Soren replied. "It's supposed to be in Hell guarding the portal from that side. But it's here, and Rotos is nowhere to be seen," he said.

Looking across the clearing atop the tower, Rose suddenly understood what that statement truly meant. She could hear and see that the beast's rightmost head was struggling physically to breathe, as though something was caught in its throat.

"In the esophagus," Rose said. "The god has to be lodged in the beast's throat," she said. "Is there some kind of dagger or sword that could cut him out?" she asked.

"Perhaps this," the prophet answered as he pulled out his dirk. "The skin may be too tough to cut with this alone, but it's worth a try," he said.

Rose took the dagger from him and walked cautiously toward the three-headed beast. Its rightmost head hindered the other two from moving. But she still didn't wish to startle it. When she reached it, she stabbed the hydra in its corresponding neck. But the dirk didn't completely pierce the hide. After a bit more effort, she discovered that any more time wasted doing so would be futile.

"Soren, I'm going to do something that's probably completely crazy," she called over to the man. After doing so, she walked toward the face of that singular head.

"Just be careful," he warned her, though, he had a slight suspicion of what the girl might do.

Feeling the creature's eye on her from above created a nervous lump in her throat. Its maw opened a bit to growl at her and its claws flexed, showing the hydra's interest in tasting her flesh; a desire which she appeased by slipping in through the gap in the creature's mouth. She nearly gagged at the awful smell of its breath. Because of its position, the pathway down its throat was relatively flat with no decline. Then she found something deep black toward the middle.

When it opened its eyes, they glowed in the darkness of the moist chasm. The hydra roared from its middle head, causing Rose to cover her ears. Then she could faintly see the muscles of the throat contracting under the plentiful glistening saliva as it attempted to swallow. She toppled over as the ground beneath her feet shifted her straight into the lump in the beast's throat. "Are you the god, Rotos?" the young woman asked.

But the beast roared back at her, a shiver scratching its way down her spine.

"Oh no..." she murmured. "Soren! Help me!" Girl and beast struggled with one another, the god snapping and clawing at her, while the hydra kept trying to swallow, growling as it felt the god's claws against its flesh.

Alarmed, Soren looked around, hoping Cyero would take longer to deal with the demon. He pulled out his lance and ran forward, carving up one of the hydra's heads in an instant. Rose and Rotos tumbled out of what remained of the dragon's neck in a clot of saliva and blood.

Even though he was covered with blood, Rose could now see that Rotos was a sphinx. He got up more quickly than she could register and swiped one of his large paws at her, but Soren pushed between them and swung his lance upward, the edge slicing it off cleanly.

But Rotos didn't seem to be so concerned with his wound, and went on trying to attack. Meanwhile, the hydra was beginning to regain its strength and stood up onto its legs. A clap of thunder shook the sky before lightning, its counterpart, struck down the hydra immediately.

Rotos growled, and thunder that rushed through the open sky boomed louder than Soren's lightning. The man closed his eyes and took a deep breath. He felt the lightning's presence surging through the clouds, knowing that Rotos was trying to strike him.

And he let it.

Rose screamed in horror when the lightning touched his body, but he felt alive, unfazed by the powerful force. The amount of electricity coursing through him lit up every cell in his body, and once it entered him, Soren reached out his hands and aimed them at Rotos, striking him with his own lightning. While he recoiled, Soren bound him in a seal.

Once it was over, the rumbling thunder faded into silence. "Soren, that was incredible!" Rose said in awe.

Soren sighed softly. He was visibly shaken from the whole thing. "I haven't felt so empowered in a very long time." He looked at his hands and then to Rotos, who had begun to growl and grunt. "I hate it." His golden eyes drifted toward Rose. "But because of this...I now have to use my powers to open the portal."

* * *

Within the tower's stronghold, a fierce battle of wits and strength had already begun. Even with only one opponent, Cyero was hardly a match for the demon lynx; it was becoming a hopeless battle. Athelstan had the ability to walk through shadows, which gave no opportunity to attack him. He was silent and his agility was a force to be reckoned with.

"Athelstan, stop this madness at once!" Cyero called out.

The lynx appeared out of thin air at the call of his adversary. "Have you had enough? I can't allow myself to have mercy on you," Athelstan replied.

Cyero narrowed his eyes as he watched the ruthless demon begin to circle around his bleeding body. He, too, had suffered a few wounds, but it was nothing he couldn't heal. "Cease your attacks, Athelstan," Cyero said rather confidently.

The lynx looked at the owner of the voice which spoke to him. "I have a proposal," the ice god said as he stared into the yellow-green eyes of the demon.

Athelstan growled at him. "I seek no deal with a god," he sneered.

"Hear me out. We wish to reach Hell on account of the humans who have been traveling to and from there for the last twelve years. It's my understanding that you're rather satisfied with living. Should that be the case, we have a common enemy. Join us, Athelstan, and we will take them down together," Cyero replied.

"And for what purpose would I ever unite with you pathetic little earthworms?" the lynx spat. "Besides, if I so wished, I could take them out on my own accord," he added.

"You and I both know that you're no match for those humans, their abilites far surpass any shadow-hopping magic you were thinking of using against them. I advise you to quickly rethink the offer," the wolf god said.

Cyero slowly rose to his feet, getting ready to attack should Athelstan deny the proposal. "Very well then..." the lynx said. "I shall join you, although I'm unable to traverse through Hell as of this moment, as I've some other duties I need to attend to," he added. Then, a sort of necklace appeared shrouded in black shadows with a single fang on the end of it. "However, should the time so arise that you're in need of my assistance, use that. Having said this, should you call upon me in a situation that isn't so dire, I'll see to it that all of you're utterly destroyed beneath my claws. Is that understood?" the feline beast asked.

Cyero nodded his head curtly and took the object from the air. "Your alliance is greatly appreciated," he said.

But Athelstan didn't acknowledge the appraisal, rather giving a slight growl before slipping away into the shadows without giving the god any indication as to whether he was still among them or not.

"I'm surprised...I never knew he would take an offer like that," Cyero said to himself as he walked toward Amaya, who was still unconscious on the floor. He slung the necklace around her neck before kneeling down in front of her motionless body.

Cyero held his hand out in front of him, creating a small flurry of snow that crystalized into ice on his palm. He took her hand with his.

After a second, Amaya's eyes opened wide and she bolted upright, letting out a yelp of distress due to the freezing cold enveloping her hand. She looked around quickly, obviously confused as to where she was. She looked at the man above, and then finally at her hand, which was holding Cyero's tightly. She looked back up at him slowly, redness spreading across her cheeks. "Um..." was all she could manage to say before snapping out of her trance-like state and instinctively pulling her hand away from his to hold her injured head. "Thank you, I guess," she said.

"Of course, but we need to get to the top of the tower with the others." Cyero got to his feet after that and offered his hand to the young woman, which she declined silently by standing on her own.

He said nothing in that regard and awkwardly lowered his hand back down to his side. They moved toward the top of the tower, but as they did, the very core of the tower shook violently, dust showering down from the stairs above them. "Come on, they must be fighting with Rotos!" Amaya hurried forth, being sure not to trip on any stairs as she drew her sword.

When they reached the top, they saw that the job had already been taken care of. Soren and Rose were standing in front of the hydra's large carcass and the god of thunder had been sealed with the same red seal as all the other gods.

Rose breathed a sigh of relief from seeing that both Amaya and Cyero were all right. "I guess we're all ready then, right?" Soren asked. He seemed uneasy, and though Rose understood why, neither Amaya or Cyero did.

"Does Hell scare you?" Cyero asked.

"No."

Soren looked at the middle of the tower's surface, knowing what needed to happen. "Amaya...as you know, I haven't been truthful with you," he said.

Amaya narrowed her eyes and furrowed her brows. "Yes."

"I told Rose who I was before I told you...and I'm sorry for that. For a very long time, I was terrified of being who I was—no—who I am. But...I've begun to realize how important it is to accept who I am, just like you and Rose do...no matter who is against you," Soren began. "So here I am...the man before you is Liland von Estan, former heir to the Astrian throne. And I'm the demigod of lightning. I no longer hold fear of judgment... this is who I am, and I can't change it."

"So you could have been helping us this whole time," Amaya said. Rose's stomach dropped. She knew Amaya might react this way and she didn't want it to discourage Liland. Even if he had claimed to not be afraid of discrimination, she still knew he was. Amaya continued, "When we were all in danger, you could have done something. When we fought Adione, you were going to pull out that lance. You had no idea if Thosus would come to the rescue. You were willing to throw all our lives on the line because of *your* fears."

"Listen, you're one to talk!" Liland bit back. "If I recall correctly, you wanted to put all of our lives in danger by going after your father when you proved to yourself already that you weren't strong enough to face him! You were being reckless!"

"That's different! At least I'm trying to do something about all of this in a more timely manner instead of just waiting for us to get to their base, where they will all be together!"

"Please, don't fight!" Rose tried to step between them as they began inching closer to one another, but Amaya shoved her away.

"The one thing I can't stand is a liar," she hissed with her blade, which she removed from its sheath.

"You can't seriously be drawing your sword," Liland said. "I don't have any intention of fighting you."

"So what if I am? You've been useless to us this far, we don't need you anymore." She swung her sword horizontally at him and Liland thrust forth his lance to defend. But Cyero stepped between them and took hold of their weapons by their blades. Purple blood spilled from both his hands, but within an instant, the weapons dissolved into nothing.

"How can you hope to accomplish anything if you both end up killing one another? Does the concept of companionship mean nothing to either of you?" Cyero asked them.

"Perhaps not to Amaya," muttered Liland.

"Shut it. You don't know anything about any of us," Amaya shot back at the god.

"I know enough to know that if you don't stop fighting, you will kill each other before you even reach your parents," Cyero chided her.

Amaya gritted her teeth and let out an exasperated "tch." "Let's just go," she said. Deep down, she knew Cyero was right, but was reluctant to admit it.

"Amaya! What has gotten into you these past couple of days?" Rose finally broke out. "You're acting completely irrational!"

"The gods are going to break out from their binds soon, and you're all concerned with going slow, yet I'm the irrational one somehow." Her eyes flicked toward Liland. "I'll kill them for everything they've done; for all the pain they've caused. And if you're all too weak to join me, then I'll enter this portal on my own!"

Liland shook his head. "You're not doing anything on your own. You will stay with us at all costs, no matter how slow you think we're going. We're not putting all of our lives in as much danger as possible just to reach them at a more convenient time."

"Just open the portal," Amaya hissed back.

Liland held back everything he wanted to throw at her; stowed the vile words boiling up. He took a deep breath and looked to the tower's roof once again before reaching his hands toward it. Even if he had already let his facade fall away, it still made his body shake, knowing there were eyes watching him. Finally, he let down a bolt of lightning which exploded into thunder and busted open a deep, blackish hole in the surface.

"I don't know how long it will stay open," he said, hesitating a glance at the others.

"Let's go, then," Amaya said. There was still an edge to her tone. She was the first to walk through, and within moments they were all enveloped by the darkness of Hell.

15: Demon's Blood

The other side of the rift was vastly different from that of the overworld. The group of them had originally intended to jump into the portal since it was positioned flat against the roof. However, gravity behaved rather strangely and weighed them down to a sideways position when they reached the realm of darkness.

The atrium into which they had wound up was large and barely visible. To enter was disorienting, almost as though they had forgotten how exactly they ended up there. It didn't take all that long to remember though.

Below Rose's feet, she could feel something almost moist and it crunched beneath her steps. The smell was putrid, and when she spoke, it was the first thing she addressed.

"What is that awful smell?" she asked with a hand over her nose and mouth as she spoke.

"I believe that would be rotting flesh, Rose," replied Liland. She couldn't see him, but from the sound of it, he was most likely holding his nose.

"Without a doubt," Cyero added.

"I can't see anything; where do we go?" Amaya asked.

"Look off to the right, do you see flickering?" he asked.

"Yes," she answered upon turning her head.

There she saw patterns of repeated flickering lights almost like torches up against a wall.

"It looks like we will have to pick one of the exits and get lucky," Liland said.

"That would be the case," Cyero spoke up.

Whilst heading toward the lights, a deep jingling was heard in the darkness, followed by a yelp and a thud. The sound originated from Rose who had tripped over something that she couldn't see. Upon landing, she was revolted by the feeling of slippery bones on her bare hands.

"Ugh! What was that?" she asked and reached her hand back, hoping and praying she wasn't about to feel something dead or mutilated. Fortunately, the sensation which met her hand ended up feeling cold and metallic. She heard footsteps come up beside her, and someone knelt down to touch what she had been touching.

"These feel like shackles," Cyero's voice spoke. "They must be, since this is likely where the hydra was imprisoned to stop the demons from getting to the surface."

A thought came to Rose as she slowly stood and brushed herself off. "They must have used it to keep Rotos at bay while they infected him," she said.

"It's possible...the hydra nearly killed Rotos very long ago, so if that's the case, then I'm sure the struggle must have been brutal," Cyero said.

"All right, well, it's too dark in here," Amaya said. She held out her hand to create a flame. But when she tried, it failed. "Huh? Why aren't my powers working?"

"What do you mean, they aren't working?" Rose asked.

"I'm trying to make a flame and it won't work."

"It would be useless to keep trying," Cyero told her. "This is a labyrinth meant to keep its prisoners inside and lost forever. It suppresses physical and mental prowess...including my own powers."

"We can just use the torches, let's go," Amaya replied.

They stopped at the five openings on the other side of the atrium, eyes gazing over each as they tried to choose the best one to go through, as though one were a more obvious choice than another. But in truth, they all looked maddeningly similar and held no evidence to suggest one choice might be more favorable than another.

Cyero looked through each darkened tunnel. "Standing here trying to decide won't help us," he said, and then pointed to a random one. "Let's go through that one," he said.

They didn't have any evidence to otherwise prove that any other passage would be better than the next, so they each agreed to follow this path. Upon walking through, they heard a deep rumbling behind them and the ground shook beneath their feet. Looking back, they realized that the passage had caved in.

"What do we do now? We won't be able to get back," Rose said, her nerves starting to eat at her. Though there may have been lighting upon the walls, it was still dark and the path ahead was unclear.

"This is a labyrinth built to confuse those who enter, and thus it's ever-changing so its path can't be memorized. If you don't get lost and die in here, you do when you get to the other side where the hydra once was," Cyero explained.

Rose shuddered, worrying they may be stuck in Hell forever.

"No sense in dwelling here since we can't hope to move the rocks," Liland said, almost as though he had read her mind.

Then they came to another fork in the road, this time with two breaks in the road instead of five.

"Which way shall we go this time, Cyero?" Liland asked.

"You seem to be having a bit of trouble deciding. Allow me to help you with that," a chipper voice sang from behind them.

A hand went to push Cyero forward into one of the branching caves, but he quickly turned his body to grab onto it, staring coldly into the golden eyes of Will.

A smirk grew across the demon's face before his foot launched forward and kicked him, finishing the job meant to be completed by his hand. The force caused Cyero to release his hand, and within the split second of turning his head, Rose's bow was already drawn, Amaya attempting to rush the persistent demon with her bare hands.

Will brought up his other leg instinctively and kicked the girl out of the way, sending her barreling in the same direction

Cyero had been pushed just as the tunnel caved in, trapping the two of them.

The demon was visibly enraged by his own actions and clenched his teeth. "Great. I came for both of you and now I'll have to find her," Will growled. His eyes fixated themselves upon the two that remained. "I suppose it'll have to do. After all, I won't have a god trying to meddle in my business," he said.

* * *

Cyero and Amaya were now on the other side of the caved-in tunnel. Amaya was trying to scrape her way through the fallen rocks to the other side, only managing to rake her fingertips in the process from their roughness. "Cyero, do something!" she yelled at him.

"Stop. It's useless," said Cyero. "They aren't moveable."

The girl dropped to her knees. "What do we do? He's going to capture Rose!" she exclaimed. Her brow wrinkled with worry as she placed her hand onto a rock, like a lone pup attempting to escape the confines of its prison.

Cyero knelt down beside the girl and placed a hand upon her shoulder. "Even so, we must continue," he said.

Amaya's head turned in his direction, her face clearly showing that she was unsatisfied with this response. "We just leave them here to die then?" she asked defensively, her body jerking away from his touch.

"What else do you expect us to do?" His tone had begun to raise from the naivety of this girl, and he spoke more firmly toward her. He didn't replace his hand, knowing she wouldn't accept it. "I know that they're your friends, but you must understand the severity of the situation. Not only that, but you need to grasp the impossibility of reaching them."

Amaya stood, looking down at the god of ice with even colder eyes than his. "I'm starting to see a pattern of you giving up when the going gets tough, after all, you probably watched my father burn that village—among other things—and did nothing to stop it. Some god you are. Maybe we should have left *you* behind instead."

With that, the girl turned and began pressing forward through the cavern. There was no point in continuing to try prying open the blockage to the other part of the cave from which they were separated. There had to be another way around—and she was going to find it.

* * *

On the other side of the blockage, another sort of battle was ensuing.

"So, you've managed to find us once more, have you?" Liland said in an almost congratulatory way. It was all to mock him though. The prophet glanced over at Rose, and she knew just what this look meant. But she wasn't sure how she felt about it. She was hoping to have come to terms with this feeling of betrayal deep within her before seeing the demon again, but she couldn't find it within herself to do so. It was a strange feeling to hold reservations and grudges toward a person because she had never done it before. But in a way, she was beginning to understand how Amaya felt toward Liland.

"You don't sound shocked. In fact, you sound almost as though you expected it; rightfully so," Will said. His happy-go-lucky grin turned dark in a matter of moments. "But I've waited far too long to waste time talking to you both."

The demon spread his fingers, within them forming a deep blackish-red substance that went hurling toward Rose after he whipped it at her. At that moment, she was drawing her bow and had started to mount an arrow to it.

When this substance hit her, she expected some kind of pain or to be taken aback by it. But instead, she was met with a rather underwhelming feeling falling over her body, like she wasn't herself. At the very same time, her bow, Diluvium, had splashed into a useless puddle of water onto the ground beside her feet. "What? How can you use spells in here?"

"It's been tough up to this point, it really has," Will said as he began to form another ball of magic in his hand. "But when it comes down to it, you guys don't put up much of a fight, do you? It's like the tides always seem to turn in your favor at the last second."

This time, the ball was sent flying toward Liland. But this time, at just the right moment, the prophet held out his hands, creating a barrier before himself which reflected the magic at lightning speed back at the demon. He was too late to have reacted to it, and that same feeling which had come over Rose was soon falling over Will as well.

His horns and wings began to disappear, along with his confident attitude. His face reddened, and they could practically see smoke coming from his nostrils. He looked ready to blow his lid. "What have you done!" he screamed, his fingers locking as his arms shook. "Can't any of you understand that I can't live again without you?" he yelled at them.

The demon looked pathetic as his locked fingers were now gripping handfuls of his hair while he collapsed to the floor.

"Did you expect me to stand there and let you take away my powers?" Liland asked. He had seen this immobilizing magic used by sages before. "It seems that sage magic still works down here...but that's all."

"Yes!" Will yelled back at him. His breaths were taken in heavy huffs and his hands slid across his face as he shed a few hidden tears.

"I think that your motives are absolutely mindless," Liland replied with narrowed eyes. "Don't you see that if they're captured, the world will be destroyed by the gods—and your attempts at gaining your soul will have been in vain?" he asked.

Will's head remained in his hands for a few moments more before he lifted it to look at the prophet. "What are you talking about?" he asked him.

"Oh, so you were unaware? Did it ever occur to you to even wonder why we came here in the first place?" Liland asked.

The weakened demon looked back at the man with a frown on his face. He felt patronized by him. "It did cross my mind briefly when I noticed you here..." he trailed off. "But ever since the hydra escaped, it's been far easier to get to Hell and back to the surface. Though the passage through here is never a delight, I figured maybe it was out of curiosity...or maybe you just couldn't wait to see me again," Will said.

"That's an awfully bold assumption for someone who was crying a second ago," Rose muttered with crossed arms as she kept her eyes away from the man.

"The ones who murdered your parents," Liland said to further the subject.

Disheartened by Rose's comment, the demon's eyes remained narrowed and skeptical and a frown still graced his lips. "And?"

"They're trying to bring down the gods...and possibly the whole world with them," Liland explained.

Will felt a bit stupid and had begun to push himself off the ground. He wouldn't admit this out loud, however. "I guess that makes sense," he said. "So what? You wanna try and stop them? If they've got the power to take down the gods, they're not something to be messed with."

"We're hoping to cross that bridge when we get to it. For now, our only source is Cyero, so we don't have a lot to go off of regarding their location," Rose said.

Will made a clucking sound and said, "Were you expecting to change something by telling me this?"

"Actually, we were hoping it might convince you to join us," Liland answered.

The blond demon looked at the prophet as though he were speaking some sort of foreign tongue. He chuckled and crossed his arms. His cocky attitude was quickly returning. "You need *me*? It seems like your little group has a lot of people as it is," he said.

"It's better than having you meet up with us every few days to try and kidnap us," Rose shot back coldly.

Will placed a hand onto his chest dramatically. "Ouch, Rose. I'm so very wounded," he said, his tone dripping with more sarcasm.

Liland looked at the girl curiously, but also pleaded with his eyes for her to stop her insults toward the demon in order to better convince him to join them. This look was brief, however, and quickly returned to Will so as not to let him catch on. "We may have a lot, but those numbers may amount to nothing once we reach the end of this perilous journey, and if that happens to be the case, then what will we have accomplished? What I mean to say is that we're going to need all the help we can hope to get," he explained.

Will watched them all for a few moments, deep in thought. Was he really going to join those he once was trying to capture? The ones who had wounded him?

The demon looked to the side. "Sorry, but for my own reasons, I'll have to decline."

Liland sighed. "You're stuck in here with us anyway."

Will looked around before coming to the realization that Liland was right. He had blocked off the other exit by splitting up their group.

"Do you think you are being at all hasty about this? We could make a deal," Rose said.

Will hesitated for only a moment before leaning in a bit more. "What kind of deal?"

"I can promise we will get your soul back. But you must promise to help us," Rose said.

"No can do. I don't make promises," Will answered.

"Why not?"

"Well, I can't break a promise if I never make one," he explained.

With a sigh, Rose realized she would not get through to him. "Fine, then," she said, and did not pry any further.

* * *

Step after step, the god and the fiery redhead kept moving further and further into the endlessness of the chasm they had both been shoved into against their will. Though there were plenty of twists and turns, there were no forks in the road since they began walking and the air stayed silent between them ever since their incursion.

But just because it was quiet, didn't mean that the god hadn't been able to read things from the girl, even with her back turned to him. He sensed a lot of frustration within her, but also fear and worry. She seemed to care a lot about these people she had spent much of her time with. Cyero admired that about her, that she could form such strong ties to others so easily and could refrain from severing them even if it placed her life on the line to do so.

Through that determination, faith, and goodwill, he saw something more: pain. *Can pain truly be this powerful?* Cyero thought. *To turn against loved ones just to feel relief from it?*

"Amaya," said the ice god.

She turned her head a bit to look at him. It was the first of any dialogue between them for about half an hour. "What?" she asked.

"Your friends...do tell me about them," he said.

Amaya looked forward once more. "That's quite the request coming from someone who wanted to leave them behind a while ago," she said. "Besides, you're supposed to be a god; shouldn't you already know all about them?"

Cyero sighed at this, which slightly agitated the girl. Her question was completely logical to her.

"There are limitations to my powers, you know. I may be a god, but I'm not an all-powerful being like you might think. And neither are the rest of us," he explained.

"Really? Because from what I've seen of the others, you don't seem to level out compared to them," she said.

"I saved your life, Amaya," he said, referring to both instances at the lake and the tower.

"And I'm saving yours." She looked back at him with a cold stare in her umber eyes, not a hint of amusement within them.

"So you won't be telling me about them then?" he asked.

"I mean, if they're just fodder to you, I don't see any reason why I should."

"You know, you're really quite the hypocrite."

"Excuse me?" She looked even angrier now.

"I seem to recall a few times when *you* were threatening to leave everyone behind too." Cyero had her cornered now.

Amaya heaved a sigh. "Two days ago I felt fine," she said. "But it feels like a sickness is coming over me." She didn't elaborate.

"A sickness?" Cyero tried to coax it out of her, but she didn't reply.

They continued walking, and Cyero was sure she had forgotten his question until she answered him. "You're right, I'm not treating them well. I don't know what is wrong with me."

Just then she noticed something pricking at her neck, causing her to scratch it. Her finger had snagged on something, however. She slid it along the string until she finally came across the object hanging from it. "What is this...?" she asked. "I don't remember wearing a necklace," she said.

"Ah, yes, I forgot to tell you," Cyero replied. "It was a demon that caused you to lose consciousness earlier. After some negotiating, I convinced him to turn to our side, and he gave us the necklace you're wearing in order to call upon him should we require his assistance," he explained. "It's a whistle, I believe."

Her eyes lingered upon the object a while longer before letting it fall against her chest once more. "I see," she said.

At last a fork appeared on the road of their journey through the perplexing chasm. Amaya immediately chose the opening that in theory should have led them back toward where Rose and Liland were.

"Why did you choose this direction?" Cyero asked her.

"I'm hoping it will bring us back through one of the tunnels that led to where they are," she said. "There was another tunnel in that room. There must be a way to get back there."

"Even if there were, don't you think if they had escaped they might be trying to find you as well?" he asked. "And what about that demon? If he's trying to capture Rose, he would be looking for the exit to Hell, right?"

Amaya let out a growl of frustration and turned her head to look back at him. "Look! I just want to find them, okay?"

"I'm trying to help you find them," Cyero said calmly. "I'm saying the best course of action is to try and get out. Because either way, if they escaped or if they were captured, they're going to be trying to get out as well."

Amaya closed her eyes and clenched her teeth. She hated to admit it, but he was right. "Dammit."

"It's all right," Cyero said. "Let's just keep going, okay? We will find them."

Amaya felt slightly reassured by this and let herself breathe a little easier.

* * *

The only sound keeping Rose sane inside the confines of the labyrinth was the scraping of their shoes against the rocky cavern floor. Each step she took was another racing thought, ranging from her feelings about Will eventually joining them, to her fear of the dark and—most prominently—her growing worry for Amaya.

"What's on your mind, Rose? You haven't talked this whole time. The dark scaring you or something?" Will's voice rang out.

"No," she answered quickly. "I'm thinking about Amaya."

Will rolled his eyes. "If I didn't know any better, I'd think you two were married. Calm down, she'll be fine," he said.

Rose narrowed her eyes at him. "That isn't what I meant," she said, "I was talking about the way she's been acting recently." She shifted her attention to Liland.

"I agree...and am also hoping it doesn't become an obsession," he answered.

"I'm trying to prompt her to a more diplomatic approach toward them."

"What are you two talking about?" Will asked.

"Ever since Amaya found out that her parents are the ones infecting the gods with this 'Taint,' she's engrossed herself in thoughts of killing them, and doing so as fast as possible," Liland explained. The demon looked off to the side uncomfortably, which Rose duly noted. "Anyway, I do recall you saying something like that to her in Silkmaw," he said to her

"You really think vicious murderers would willingly turn themselves in?" Will's voice gave out a low tone, aside from his normally upbeat one.

"I was hoping that once they see us again, they would be more open to the possibility of change," Rose answered.

"You're really naive, aren't you? Do you think they give a damn about either of you? They're just a bunch of cold-hearted bastards." Will was beginning to sound a lot like Amaya, and it made Rose's stomach turn.

"Why do you care?" Rose hissed back unintentionally. "You're trying to capture us anyway, so what I do should be of no concern to you."

Liland did find it rather strange that Will was considering their own issues, but on the other hand, they technically had a common enemy, he deduced.

"It's rather curious," he said. "But it makes sense that you're so passionate in your sayings. After all, you hold your own reservations toward them, don't you? It makes me wonder about you."

"It doesn't matter," Will replied.

"Oh? But it seems to be such a touchy subject to you."

"Doesn't matter to *you all*, I meant. Once I get my hands on you and Amaya, none of this will matter anymore. I'll be back to my old life again," he said, his hand gesturing to Rose as he spoke.

"And what makes you think you will?" Rose asked.

"Because I need my soul back—and *I'll* get it."

Rose saw a coldness in his eyes that she had never seen before. She knew how selfish the man's motives were, but at the same time, she was usually always able to see a sense of humor in him. Now, it was completely vacant.

She was on the verge of tuning out her surroundings once more until her ears caught wind of some distant noises which sounded like talking. "Hold on..." Rose said and turned around so that she was facing a passageway they had walked by. "That sounds like Amaya and Cyero!" About to rush toward them, she was yanked back by the hem of her dress.

"Don't, unless you wanna get trapped, let them come to us." When she looked back, it was Will that she saw had stopped her. Though it was rather unpleasant, she was glad he had done so. There was no way to know if Amaya and Cyero hadn't already exhausted any possible exits from the tunnel she had nearly dashed into.

As she suspected, soon their faces emerged from the tunnel and Amaya ran forward. "I'm glad we found you as soon as we did," Cyero said, keeping pace with her so as not to be left behind. "Amaya was worried about all of you."

The girl gave a huff, revolted at hearing Cyero describe what she had done since departing.

"How doubtful, considering her earlier behavior," Liland said.

Is he teasing me? thought the accused girl. But she did feel guilty about their earlier confrontations. "Listen, I apologize for the way I was acting, I suppose I did get a bit out of control...I'll try to keep my feelings at bay from now on."

"Thank you, I appreciate and accept your apology," Liland said calmly. But Rose didn't necessarily believe her statement. After all, she always held strongly onto what she felt and how she dealt with it.

"Hold on a moment. *He's* still with you?" Amaya glared at Will.

"Do you have a problem with that?" he hissed back at her.

"Actually, yes I do. You've tried to kidnap us on multiple occasions; you're the reason we were split up in the first place."

Will stroked his chin with two fingers. "Ah, I suppose I did do that," he said as though he were oblivious to the fact, but the truth was quite the opposite.

"We were stuck with him after splitting up with you two," Liland told her. "And I don't see it being very likely that we could escape from him."

Amaya stepped closer to the demon, and despite her height disadvantage, she still intimidated him. "You had better watch your back when we get out of this labyrinth...because I'm not letting you get in our way again," she sneered before walking past him.

"She's really not too friendly, is she?"

"I don't see any reason she should be—at least not to you," Liland replied before leading the rest of them onward.

When Rose found the opportunity, she moved a bit closer to Liland. "Should we tell the others about the prophecy regarding Will joining us?" she asked quietly.

Liland shook his head. "I don't suppose Amaya would be very fond of the idea. And if Will were to overhear us, I'm sure he would be against it as well," he replied.

"But it's a vision of the future, right? So even if they knew, they wouldn't be able to keep it from happening," Rose pointed out.

"It's a bit more complex than that, unfortunately," he said. "The future isn't set in stone; it's paved by what we do and what we say. The prophecies I receive are merely possibilities based on the 'path' we're on at a given time. The more people who know of a possibility—especially if it has something to do with them specifically—the greater the chance of a change being made. You see, when people know their 'fate,' they try to change it more often than not. I'm sure if we were to tell Will that he's destined to join us, he would be set against it and act more hostile to us than usual, just to prove that he won't. This would cause us to follow a different route than what I had prophesied—and may put us on a more unfavorable path where he wouldn't end up helping us."

The labyrinth splayed for their wandering feet to follow as they aimlessly traversed its dimly lit passages. The pace was slow; dreadfully slow. It seemed no matter how many times they went through a tunnel, it would bring them no closer to reaching its end. It was beginning to frustrate Amaya, and even Liland felt unnerved. He and Cyero had begun a conversation about the maze within which they had been trapped—likely to tear away from the feeling of claustrophobia—but Amaya, Will, and Rose, who had fallen slightly behind the others, were tuned out from them.

Amaya's eyes never left the Will, and it would be untruthful to say he hadn't noticed it. But he chose not to say anything about it. After all, it wasn't as though her reaction to his presence was unwarranted.

"What do you plan on doing once you throw us to the wolves and get your soul back?" she asked him out of nowhere.

He craned his head in her direction. Will hadn't expected the girl to speak a single word to him, so when he heard her voice, he was shocked—startled even. He was curious to know what had interested her.

But now that Will was taking time to consider what she had asked, he hadn't a clue how to answer her. "You know, I don't think I've ever really thought about it. But living again will be a lot better than being stuck in a soulless body," he said.

"Surely you jest, right?" Amaya looked far from satisfied with this answer. "You're willing to sacrifice two lives for your own, and yet you don't even have a reason for it." She huffed and shook her head. "You're no better than our parents...so...selfish."

"Amaya, you shouldn't be so rude to him. Maybe he *does* have a reason and is uncomfortable with sharing it," Rose said.

Her gaze shifted to Rose. "Why does it sound like *you* know the reason?" she asked. "It's not like you haven't hidden things from me before..." she added callously.

"I'm just as in the dark as you are about it," Rose answered, taking to a more defensive tone.

"If we're the lives he's trading for his own, then it's only fair if he tells us."

"No one said I was being fair," Will cut in.

In the midst of their bickering, Rose felt a shudder crawl down the length of her body. A skittering feeling fell over her, almost like bugs with thousands of tiny legs, a millipede perhaps. "What was that...sensation...?" she said under her breath. Neither Amaya nor Will noticed it, so she looked ahead and parted her lips to ask Liland or Cyero if they had. But no sooner had she done this, had she heard rumbling coming from behind her and turned her upper body to see its origin. Mortified, she watched as large rocks came tumbling down in front of her with Liland and Cyero on the other side, looking panicked before they vanished out of sight.

"Dammit!" spat Amaya. "We got split up again!" When Rose turned back toward the other two, she saw her friend's fist collide with Will's cheek. "This is probably your fault! You were trying to get us away from Cyero and Soren this whole time, weren't you?"

Rose decided to ignore her friend's mistake regarding Liland and tangled with her arms to restrain her. "Amaya, please stop!" she said. "You can't blame him for that. We were distracted," she pointed out. But it didn't stop the threatening look from reaching Amaya's face.

"I bet you that's exactly what he wants you to think," she hissed.

"Calm down, it's not like I can do anything while we're in here anyway," Will told her. He was leaning against a wall, hand clutching the bruise blossoming on his face.

"So you don't deny that those were your intentions?"

"Arguing about this isn't going to get us any further in here... let's just keep going, okay?"

If it hadn't been for Rose holding her back, Amaya would have charged after him as he walked past them. Instead, she was released once she stopped flailing in Rose's grip.

They lagged behind Will once Amaya was free to walk again, and she didn't bother pursuing him, left to wonder what the bruise that she had certainly left on his cheek looked like. "What has been going on with you lately...?" Rose asked in a voice Will couldn't hear. "You were never this...compulsive."

Her friend left an answer abandoned in the air between them. She wanted to know why the question made Amaya shift uncomfortably. "I understand finding out our parents are still alive must have come as a shock to you...but it's almost as though you've completely forgotten how to be compassionate," Rose said. "Do you want to talk about it?"

"There is nothing to say," Amaya responded quickly. "It's repulsive to know I'm related to such filth...what about you? You seem to be completely fine with all of this."

Disbelief accompanied the expression Rose returned to her companion. "You really think I'm just—what—complacent with this?" she asked, not expecting an answer. "I'm sick with rage that our own parents would do such things. But I also know that they must have experienced great pain, as we have, in order to reach their current mindset; that they feel they must eradicate

325

the whole world just to feel solace from that pain. That's why their lives deserve to be spared."

Amaya pondered Rose's response for a few moments before opening her mouth to answer again. "I'm afraid we will probably never see eye to eye on this."

Rose shuddered just as she had before. "What is that strange feeling. Did you feel it as well?" she asked, completely straying from the subject.

"What feeling?"

Rose squinted her eyes before scratching the back of her neck, hoping it might quell the unnerving sensation. "It almost feels like bugs crawling all over me...it's very unsettling," she answered. "I felt it just before the passage to the other tunnel closed."

"I couldn't say, I haven't felt any such feeling," Amaya replied.

Rose decided to brush off the impression it left on her and took a deep breath to suppress it, even if breathing in ash from the day before left her lungs heavy. The stuffiness from the cavern's interior didn't help. "Come on, we should catch up to Will." She took a big step forward, breaking into a jog.

Though reluctant, Amaya soon followed after her.

16: Blood of the Centipede

Twelve years ago

Ruki pounded his fist against the wall in front of him. "Dammit. It figures that we would run into such a roadblock at this point," he huffed and looked to the others.

"We need the spell no matter what; we will have to find a way to get that book," Chasaka said.

His wife frowned a little bit. "Can this not wait a little longer until we figure out what to do?" she asked. "Those scoundrels banished our children to Tochfuyu, they were nearly executed. We must go retrieve them before they change their minds."

The four of them were silent—all but Ruki. "Hold on," he said. Tapping his chin a moment in thought, he added, "Maybe we should leave them there."

"What?" Sage practically shouted the question.

"Listen," Ruki put his hand out to calm her down. "Keeping them secluded will allow their hearts to remain pure, and once they're old enough to face our ideals and see them the way we do, then we will find a way to have them safely brought to us," Ruki explained.

Sage held her other hand while she felt everyone's eyes bearing into her. "Whatever we must do."

* * *

Present day

Sage turned as she heard footsteps coming up the stone stairs of their hideaway. "Welcome back," she remarked. "Did everything go well?"

Chasaka didn't look happy, however.

Teira seemed upset also. "While we did strike Aessatia enough for her to know our presence, we hit a snag," she said.

"A snag?"

"Yes. Our children escaped before our little pawn could reach them, and now it seems they know about everything," Chasaka answered.

"Not only that, but they're traveling with the Astrian demigod and Cyero," Teira cut in.

Ruki walked from behind them, and, having heard their conversation, said, "Not to worry, there is still hope for our plan. But first things first, we must eliminate the prophet and the god from the equation. Cyero will be easy. He was a fool to have emerged from his hiding place, and the prophet should be no trouble either."

"And the book?" Teira asked.

"Everything should fall into place once they're out of the picture. Chasaka, why don't you and I head out?"

"Wait!" Sage stopped them. "Would it not be safer if we all went together?"

"Sage," Teira chided her. "We aren't letting our emotions get in the way again...are we?"

Sage closed her mouth and didn't speak again. "Of course not," she said softly. "I only meant it might be easier to eliminate Cyero and the demigod if we were all together."

"You've never doubted us before," Chasaka said accusingly. "You will see her in due time...because she and Rose will willingly come to us."

The two men left after that, leaving their wives behind.

* * *

The walls of the cavern crawled their way beneath Liland's skin, and the longer it stayed silent, the more he thought of the endless twisting and turning that warped each narrow passage into the labyrinth that it was.

"This labyrinth certainly does its job," he said to Cyero, trying to avoid the aversive feelings being slowly etched into his skin.

"It's certainly distasteful to be stuck in such a cramped area... and it almost seems like the passages are getting more narrow," answered the god.

More crossroads were presented to them. "We shall go right," he said so that the three behind him could hear. At that point, choosing which way to go had become a game. He and Cyero had been taking turns deciding which passages to lead the five of them through.

They hadn't taken more than six steps before they heard rumbling coming from the left. They whipped their heads in that direction.

"Will is getting away with them!" Liland yelled and dashed toward the opening. The last thing he saw was Rose's horrified face before the falling rocks blocked their paths. "Damn." The demigod clenched his fist. He had already known he wouldn't make it in time to save either Rose or Amaya, but disappointment still settled within him. "We shouldn't have let them stray behind."

"Don't fret," Cyero quickly warned him. "We're all heading for the same exit, so we will find them no matter what."

"Assuming that we make it out before they do..." Liland trailed off.

Though Liland found the place to be wretchedly silent, he wasn't going to force Cyero to fill the gaps he seemed to so dislike. The ground and walls and ceiling slowly blended together, plunging them deeper into the endless maze. Would sleep soon find them? What about an exit? He didn't know. Soon the minutes faded into hours and fatigue was starting to settle on the man. But the god walking beside him appeared to be as fine as ever.

Just as Liland could no longer stand the quietude, Cyero spoke up, as though he could read his mind. "Do tell me about Amaya and Rose," he said. "I tried asking a similar question to Amaya earlier but I never received an answer."

Liland perked up, almost excited to finally have some communication. But once the question fully registered, he found no words to respond with. He had never considered the two girls in such a way before. He had his own thoughts about them, of course, but was it truly possible to summarize them on the spot?

After a moment he answered, "There is a lot more to the two of them than the surface reveals. I never thought I might have to tell someone my opinion of them...but in honesty, I love them both as though they were my own." He felt no sense of discomfort in saying this. "Even though we haven't been together for all that long, we have been through so much already. It would be hard to imagine life without them."

"I see that you're close with them then," Cyero surmised.

"I see it that way...but I'm not sure Amaya would agree," Liland said, squeezing in the ghost of a laugh.

The god of ice nodded his head. "I can see where that might be true," he said.

"Don't paint her in black just yet though," Liland told him quickly. "Beneath the distrust and abrasiveness, she really does have a kind, caring heart. There has never been a time when she wasn't concerned with Rose's wellbeing, and she's always ready to jump into battle whenever trouble is near, even if it was painfully clear that she's ill-equipped for the situation." A smile creased his weathered lips as he remembered their epic battle with Adione, but it didn't last long. Liland knew the righteous, compassionate Amaya who once walked by his side would likely soon drain away—being filled instead with contempt and indifference. "When first we met, she never much expressed her feelings regarding her parents, but she was always quick to take caution of everything because of how they left her and Rose. I think her reaction to this is a byproduct of her trying to keep everyone safe, even if she's going about it the wrong way."

Cyero lowered his head, eyes remaining on the demigod beside him. "I can see that loneliness is what has driven her...and what is driving her even now." They mindlessly weaved through another passageway. "And what about Rose?"

"Ah, they're like two parts to a whole, they're much like Noctis and Avius from the legends," Liland said. "Where Amaya lacks, Rose excels. Rose is kind and compassionate, always regarding others before herself. She shows hints of her determination when she finds herself holding a strong opinion, but I know she isn't confident in herself. Often I found her following Amaya—hidden in her shadow, quiet and without opinion—and I can tell she may have been like that even before we met. But I know this journey has changed her, as it has changed all of us." The man found himself chuckling again. "I know it's silly, but sometimes I insert myself into a fatherly role where I know I don't belong...I never imagined I might one day marry and have children of my own, but I worry for them as if they really were mine."

A sorrowful look met Cyero's silvery-blue eyes. Being cooped up in his frigid library left him with infinite time to read legends and stories about human love and companionship. It felt trivial to him, but he tried to understand the scrawlings whenever he read them. But hearing Liland talk in such light of girls who had left a bitter taste in his own mouth—as far as their relationships between one another—inspired Cyero.

"Why do you appear so somber, lord Cyero?" he asked.

His ears perked up, having nearly forgotten that the man had even been there beside him. "Sorry, it's regretful to say, but I envy you, Liland."

Liland hesitated his response and scrunched his face. "A god? Envious of me?" He needed to make sure his hearing wasn't failing him.

But sure enough, Cyero nodded his head. "I wish I could have such deep, meaningful bonds as you've established. Being locked away in my sanctum has prevented that for a long time. Of course, the fault is my own, but I always found being a companion to a mortal was difficult in the past," he said. "In fact, if I recall correctly, the last ones I knew so well *were* Noctis and Avius."

Liland stared at the man dressed in white robes adorned with that red velvet scarf, wonder filling his eyes. He may have been staring just a little too long though, because it certainly caught Cyero's attention. "What is it?" he asked.

"My apologies, I just find it simply incredible that you truly met Noctis and Avius when they were alive. What were they like?" Liland wondered.

"Now that you mention it, they were similar to what you said about Amaya and Rose...Noctis with his brooding stare but an innocent heart, and Avius with her kind smile and reserved nature. But in the end, they were as you described: two parts of a whole," Cyero explained. "It was long ago, so my memory is probably stained...but if I had to describe them, that's the way I remember them best."

They walked on in almost blissful silence for a few moments more before the ground beneath them shattered, breaking the tranquility with it. Liland yelled, gasping sharply as he hit the hard ground below, falling on top of the pile of rocks that had given way.

As the dust settled, Liland saw that Cyero was able to use his powers and had used a block of ice to cushion his fall. They had fallen into another atrium, much like the one that the hydra had once been shackled inside of. There were torches posted all around it, providing a feeble light to the massive room. There wasn't much to see, only the grimy bones that lay beneath the pile of rocks that Liland had landed atop. But ahead, there were scribblings of words on the atrium wall which Cyero dismounted his pillar of ice to read.

After finding his own footing, Liland joined him. Part of it was written in Highspeak, the language with which he was familiar, but there were a few characters that he didn't recognize, but held a likeness to the former written language of the gods. "The Burrower," Liland said out loud, squinting to make sure he was reading the bottom three characters correctly.

"Omu," Cyero finished for him. "The Burrower, Omu," he clarified. "In other words...the creature who carved out this labyrinth."

Liland felt a chill go down his spine and shuddered. Whatever had carved out the labyrinth must be enormous to have left such large imprints in the rock. "Does that name strike you as familiar?" he asked, stifling yet another shudder.

Cyero nodded. "Omu was the first creature to enter the rift. It sculpted this labyrinth and still continues to even now. Rotos used it as a defense mechanism to keep demons from leaving the rift, and placed the barrier around it to ensure they couldn't use their own powers to escape. There is no doubt the creature may be lurking down here..." he trailed off.

"And...might I ask what this creature is exactly?" said Liland.

"A centipede."

Upon turning around, they saw a bundle of deep black ligaments that shined in the dim lighting radiating faintly off the torches. Each segment of the myriapod was defined by the orangy luster between each suture. It looked slimy, disgusting— *revolting*. Its deep black, beady eyes were disguised in the darkness, but it was clear from how its antennae waved toward them like an earthworm writhing in the dirt that the creature had noticed them almost as soon as they had fallen into its lair.

Cold, sharp, invisible claws raked down Liland's spine as his eyes locked with its huge tapered jaws. On instinct, he created Fulgur, tightly grasping its shortened form with his trembling hands, disregarding that this previously would have been impossible.

The atrium shivered as Omu's plentiful legs skittered across it, approaching the intruders. It flailed its disgusting feelers all over their bodies, sizing them up, sniffing for their blood; their fear. While Cyero held none, Liland was filled to the brim. The leathery ligament whacking him all over his body was far more interested in him than Cyero, even moving the second away from him to devour more of Liland's scent.

Liland could no longer hold back the emotions caused by this crawling feeling and let Fulgur extend to its full length. His arms moved far faster than such an enormous creature, and thus the head of the ranseur sliced cleanly through its antennae. Its mandibles parted widely shortly after having endured such pain, and its elongated body lunged toward him.

Cyero swooped in front of the centipede before it could reach Liland, then jumped out of its way with the man in his arms—and farther away from their only exit.

* * *

Rose had nearly reached her capacity to withstand the dark halls of the maze. "I'm ready to collapse...I'm so tired," she said softly.

Amaya was beginning to feel the same, her legs aching; her energy exhausted.

"We've been walking for hours now, you realize that, right?" Will asked them. "If you two are so tired, you could rest."

The redhead shot a glare his way. "Like I would ever trust *you* when I close my eyes," she hissed.

Will shrugged his shoulders. "Suit yourself."

Ahead of them was a light that didn't look like that of the torches posted on the walls of the cavern. It brought hope to Amaya and Rose, and their pace picked up.

"That must be the exit, right?" Amaya asked. She started to sprint toward it, only to be stopped by the sound of rumbling and crashing while the tunnel through which she had been running convulsed with those noises. With it, Rose's skin began to crawl again, this time, the sensation growing more uncomfortable.

"What is that?" Rose asked them.

"We may have hit a roadblock," Amaya said.

When Will and Rose caught up to see what she was talking about, they stopped at the edge of a gaping hole separating one side of the tunnel from the other—the one that held their exit.

Shards of rock trickled from the edges of the hole where it had broken as the cavern continued to shake. Will snatched Rose away from the edge, just in time for it to fall away. But before it did, she saw something flash past the opening.

"I think there may be a way to get past the hole to the exit!" Amaya exclaimed as she held onto one of the torch mounts so she wouldn't fall. She pointed to a jagged edge reaching farther out toward the other side of the gap than the rest. "But we have to get to it before it falls away!"

"Wait! I think I saw Liland and Cyero down there! I think they might be in trouble!" Rose shouted back over the rumbling. She squirmed from Will's grasp and approached the hole again.

"Rose, no! You don't know what's down there; you could get killed!" the demon said, his arm shooting out to grab her again.

She dreaded agreeing with him, but Will had been right—and Amaya didn't want her friend throwing caution to the wind. "They can handle themselves down there, we don't have powers in here!"

"I can't leave them alone, I'm going!" Rose replied and broke free from Will again, taking the opportunity to jump down into the hole. The height was rather immense, and a sharp pain shot through her feet when she landed. As she recovered, she looked straight ahead to see Cyero and Liland struggling against the huge burrower. But she noticed that Liland was holding the weapon which had once been reduced to nothing by Cyero. She looked up to the hole. "Come down here!" she shouted at the other two staring down at her.

Amaya sat down on the edge of the crack in the ground and started to slide down before feeling a pair of arms hook around her body. "Look out!" Will's voice shouted from behind her. He slung the young woman up over his shoulder and jumped across the gap just as some rocks collapsed beside the hole in the ground.

"Stop! Put me down this instant!" Amaya flailed her body, trying to escape the man's grasp as he leaped. But her fighting was fruitless; the hole down which Rose had jumped was growing farther away. She felt her heart stop beating—no—she felt nothing at all. Only ringing in her ears as adrenaline rushed through her veins.

Will dashed through another opening, secluding her from her friend once again. She escaped a bit too late and her body rolled onto the ground. "What is wrong with you! How could you just leave her there! You need her too, don't you?" she screamed.

"Wait! I—" Will began to say. Amaya pushed her body off the ground and got up to start throwing punches at him. He flinched back, about to dodge to the side until something halted her. The sound and heat of a rushing flame blew past them. Amaya's fist had been mere inches from Will's face, and even with all her anger, this stopped her.

She turned to look past them, her eyes locking with another being. She was dressed in deep red robes and had scars marking her face. It was almost impossible to tell she had any semblance at all to a woman as she was horribly disfigured.

"The...Light...?"Amaya read the characters embroidered on the creature's robe, being unable to read the one below it. "What does that other one say?"

"Thia! That's Thia!" Will yelled in a panic.

The woman rushed at them, carrying a hilt attached to something neither of them had seen at first. It looked like a shining thread—nothing but a long needle. Amaya moved away from her charge and Will dodged in the opposite direction.

"Who is Thia?"

"She's the one who lights all these torches! She's extremely dangerous!" Will answered. "I never thought I'd encounter her." He said this more to himself than to Amaya.

Thia spun around, her movements fast but graceful.

"What are we supposed to do?" Amaya asked frantically. "We can't use our powers!" Amaya knew they were in trouble. There was a slim crevice they might be able to squeeze through on the other side of the opening, but she had a feeling this creature wouldn't let them pass so easily.

* * *

By the time Rose had joined the action, Liland and Cyero were taking turns keeping Omu at bay. Cyero tried to freeze the centipede's many legs, but they were strong and didn't stay still for very long. When he could, Liland launched himself forward, using the length of his lance's blade to try and cut away its legs or at least damage them. But this didn't hinder the beast's movement as much as he had hoped.

"Rose!" Liland hollered over to her, shocked to see her there. But in his moment of vulnerability, Omu nearly snatched his head from his shoulders, had it not been for Cyero shoving a pike of ice through its body and saving Liland's life.

Rose mustered up all the willpower in her body and tried to create her bow once again. But by then it was too late. Omu had shifted its muscular weight enough to shatter the ice away and resume its attack.

"Rose, get out of the way!" shouted Liland before throwing his body at her to dodge the centipede's mass. Fortunately, due to its colossal length, it recovered from the attacks more slowly.

"Sorry, I was trying to make Diluvium, but it's not working," she said.

Liland pushed himself off of her and picked up Fulgur from the ground. "Stay here and try to draw it again while Cyero and I keep it away from you." With that, he had gone off to help Cyero.

Rose closed her eyes again, trying to focus on conjuring the weapon, but the sounds of battle were distracting her concentration. Each grunt that Liland made caused her to open her eyes, only to see that they were succeeding in fending off the creature. She could still feel that skittering all over her body every time Omu moved.

It lunged forth its jaws at Cyero, only for him to jump back just far enough away so they wouldn't pierce him. "Liland, try to pair the flesh connecting its pincers to its head," he told him.

The demigod nodded and spaced himself away from Omu. It paid no attention to him and lashed out a number of times at Cyero, dripping black blood from the wounds that were being inflicted to the beast. The tangle of actions that unfolded between them were tense—jaws repeatedly snapping shut like a vice, crunching together like the sound of a falling guillotine. Liland could see that the god was struggling to counter any movements that Omu would make, as they were fast and carried weight with them, but neither could find a clear opening to strike.

At last, a pillar of ice shot from the ground, launching Cyero into the air before he changed into his enormous wolf form. His height nearly matched up with the centipede now. He sprung from his hind legs and pounced atop Omu's body, pinning it with his paws while his bared teeth latched onto one of its segments.

For the first time, Omu let out an ear-piercing shriek as it struggled against Cyero's body. Liland pushed off the ground with his lance once again and quickly readied the blade to strike with it.

While Rose focused, she found herself feeling the layout of the labyrinth, as though the entire thing were a map in her mind. She could feel Amaya and Will's presence in another part of it. The sound of metal clashing made her eyes fly open. Fulgur's blade had collided with one of Omu's pincers which snapped the shaft, sending one half flying across the atrium and Liland plummeting to the ground.

"I missed," he spat in frustration. He held tightly onto his right shoulder. Thick red blood oozed from it and stained his hand. When Fulgur had snapped, the head had flown back and sliced through the cuff tendon in his shoulder. He tried to fall back but the pain was almost unbearable.

Just then, the beast reared back its head and closed its pincers around one of Cyero's legs, using its segments to throw him off.

Rose could no longer stand there and watch—something needed to be done. She focused once again and when she did, some rocks flew at her, coming from the pile of rubble caused by the ground that gave way earlier. The rocks formed a linear shape in front of Rose, their rugged edges chipping away until their form revealed a sword. It became black like obsidian and a light blue vine started to grow around its blade as it shaped itself. From the grip grew the crossguard, which was made of a shiny azure alloy. The blade of the sword cast off its deep color and turned a silvery hue, polished and clearly tempered by divine power. When Rose opened her eyes, she examined her new blade and took hold of it.

Omu wriggled to gain better footing and lunged toward Liland just as Rose had begun sprinting toward it. She despised the power she felt coursing through her, enhanced by the rocks surrounding her, but to protect Liland, she would gladly swing that sword. She used the ice that Cyero had created and jumped off of it, making sure to aim the edge right where the centipede's pincer met its flesh, severing it.

"Cyero! You must bind it so we can finish cutting off the legs!" Rose shouted.

Cyero ran toward her. He was limping a bit from his injury but used his ice to keep the writhing entity still. Rose was lacking in physical strength, so swinging the sword was quite the task, given its length, but she was still able to cleanly cut away one of Omu's legs.

"This method will never work if we hope to defeat it," barked Cyero.

Omu recovered from the blow delivered by Rose at an alarming speed, and when it did, it lashed the full upper half of its body at her. The impact hit her like a boulder ten times her own size and sent her flying through the air. Seconds later, she slammed hard against the wall of the atrium.

Rose stiffened as she slid down the wall and crumpled, unable to move from the shock of sudden pain.

"Rose!" she heard Liland yell. His hand was still clutching his shoulder as he stumbled toward her. He let go of his arm to help her up.

"No, no," she said, looking at his blood-drenched hand. "Keep pressure on that wound." She pushed herself up, grunting as she did, and held her stomach where Omu had struck her with its heavy exoskeleton.

Liland heeded her instruction and held onto his shoulder again before slumping back against the wall. Rose gripped tighter onto the sword in her hands and readied it again. She watched for a split second as Cyero battled Omu. Both had such substantial weight to their attacks that the cavern was rumbling even more than it had been before, rock and dust raining from above as a result.

Though her body was on fire with pain, the adrenaline pumping through her, forced her to ignore it and rise to attack again, her legs going as fast as they would take her to reach Cyero. His massive body landed beside her, recovering from another of Omu's attacks.

"I think I have an idea." Purple blood spilled from his jaw, it appeared the centipede must have slashed it with its remaining pincer. "Get on my back," he demanded her and leaned down so she could get on, leaping away just before Omu could snap at him again. His mouth opened and he breathed out a plume of frigid air at it in retaliation, thus slowing down its movements as it thundered toward them.

"What is your idea?" Rose asked him.

"Using my powers, I'm able to propel my body through the air and stay nimble. I'm going to try and run straight past it, and when I do, use your sword to cleave as many legs as you can," Cyero explained.

"Understood."

By that time, Omu had regained its mobility from the stiff cold that once bound its muscles. "Get ready," Cyero growled.

Rose positioned her sword at her right and before she could even take in a breath, the god dashed forward, causing her to grasp the hilt of the weapon tighter. Within mere moments, she felt the blade plunging deep into Omu's ligaments, severing one by one until Cyero's run came to an abrupt halt at the end of its body. When he turned to see the condition in which Rose had left the beast. Its entire left side had small yellow protrusions coming from each segment of its body that were now leaking black blood, no doubt where the legs once held it up. Omu could no longer stand up on that side.

"This is our chance! We must get Liland and get out through the hole in the ceiling," Rose told him.

Without another word, Cyero ran cautiously around the writhing centipede. Even if it could no longer move, he still wanted to be safe. Once he reached Liland, Rose carefully helped him onto Cyero's back and with that, he began making his way toward the hole above them. "Now we need to find Amaya and Will," Rose said.

"What happened to them?" Liland asked.

"Will ran off with Amaya when I came down here."

A screech interrupted her, and Rose turned her head to have just one last look at the creature, only to see that its legs had completely regenerated. Her stomach sank and she hopped off Cyero's back, which caused him to turn his head as well.

"Rose what are you doing?" His question had been answered almost as soon as he saw the creature behind them regaining its composure and readying itself for a charge straight for them. "Oh no," he muttered.

"Get Liland to safety above us. I'll hold it off until you return," Rose told him.

"Are you sure you can do this?" Cyero asked.

While the thought of fending off such a creature by herself was terrifying, the thought of any of her friends getting hurt or even killed was even scarier. "Go quickly!" she demanded, eyes focused on the creature.

In response she heard his footsteps retreat with the backdrop of rumbling caused by Omu charging toward her.

Rose didn't know what to do; her mind panicked. She wouldn't be fast enough to dodge the creature racing toward her on thirty-five pairs of legs. As they did, she could feel that same skittering across her body. At that very moment, a realization came to the girl. *Is this feeling over my body...Omu? Have I been feeling his unrest below the surface of this cavern the whole time?* Her eyes were locked with the blank eyes of the barreling creature. *I know!*

It all happened in a matter of seconds: Rose placed her sword in the ground and held out her hands, focusing on the chilling sensation all over her. The ground shook more, knocking the girl off her feet as a thick wall of rock blocked the centipede's route. Omu's hard body crashed straight through the rock, but not without stunning it first, allowing Rose to escape from its path, sword in hand.

All I need to do is fend it off until Cyero gets back, Rose told herself. She distanced herself a good ways from Omu while it recovered again. Keeping her eyes glued to it, she awaited its next move and prepared to make another wall of rock if the need arose.

Instead, Omu lifted its body onto its rearmost legs and again, the ground shook. This time, it was caused by the burrower itself. She hadn't expected the ground to break apart and for the fragments caused by the invisible impact to float up from it.

345

There was no time for her to react to it either, as the boulders came hurtling toward her, smashing into her body.

Rose collapsed to the ground. The impact had been so great that she her head was bleeding and her ears were ringing so loudly that she could no longer hear. Her vision was useless as everything was blurred into a painting of colors blending together. All she could sense was the feeling of her surroundings thundering, akin to a war hammer, and her skin continued to crawl.

Blood formed around her head, her body in so much pain it was numb. She heard the faint roar of something she couldn't make out as she lay still on the ground. Allowing unconsciousness to consume her was a more favorable option at the moment, and she even closed her eyes to make it more reachable.

But her eyes fluttered open again, an unknown force driving her eyelids apart. But why? Why was her exhausted body forcing her to awaken to nothing? What was the point? Her blurry vision began to merge together into legible shapes. She blinked her glazed over eyes, now fighting to escape unconsciousness. Her hands shook as her fingers dug into the ground, clutching reality.

In a second, her vision returned and she saw Cyero in his mortal form, holding a black scythe in his hands. He was so fast in each movement he performed that she wondered if her vision had truly completely returned. The crest of the scythe dug into the centipede in multiple places and when her hearing tuned back in, she could hear the sound of Omu's skin being torn apart by it. Once immobile again, Cyero appeared in the air, scythe raised over his head before bringing it down upon the beast's first segment, completely severing its head.

Rose tried to drag herself to her feet, but she felt something holding her down. Slowly, she turned her head to see what it was, only to find one of the boulders that had landed on top of her lower half. Fortunately, nothing felt broken, though she couldn't be sure if that was simply her body going into shock from the pain. She tried to see if she could move the rock using her powers, but it was no use—she was completely focused on the pain wracking her body.

Cyero rushed over to her and placed his hands on the rock, forcing his ice inside until it eventually cracked and exploded, relieving the weight from Rose's body. Even though she was no longer trapped by the boulder, she still couldn't bring herself to move.

Cyero leaned down and lifted her from the ground. "Are you all right, Rose?" he asked.

She didn't respond to his question for a moment, then finally looked at him, realizing that he was trying to get her attention. "Yes, I'll be fine," she answered hoarsely.

Cyero carried her to the hole in the ceiling and lifted them both up on a pillar of ice, where she saw Liland slumped against the wall on the side of the labyrinth. "Look at you both, covered in wounds." The god placed Rose down beside Liland and looked at them both collectively.

"We need...to find...Amaya." Rose was conscious, but it was clear she was fighting to stay that way.

"Before any of that, we need to dress your wounds," Cyero replied. He took off the crimson scarf from his neck and used a shard of ice to cut it in two pieces. With one, he tied off the wound around Rose's head, and with the other, he tied up Liland's wound. After that, he began gently pressing against different parts of Rose's legs. "Just making sure nothing is broken," he told her.

Thankfully, her legs weren't broken, however, the same couldn't be said for one of her lowermost ribs which she had already been holding from the pain. Other than that, she escaped unscathed, save for the head wound and, of course, the bruises that had already formed. She lifted herself to her feet once Cyero had finished, wincing as she did. "We have to press on until we find Amaya." They knew it had to be well past the middle of the night in the overworld by now, so both Liland and Rose were exhausted, to say the very least.

"You both should really be resting your wounds. Aren't you tired?" Cyero asked.

Rose and Liland looked at one another, both seeming to understand exactly what the other was thinking. "Yes," said Liland, "very much so, but making sure Amaya is safe is our priority, or we won't be resting easy."

Cyero nodded. "Very well...then we will continue on." He was beginning to understand what drove both of them forward, why some humans held such determination inside.

Could another life truly be so precious as to protect it with one's own?

17: Blood of the Light

The sound of sword meeting flesh hissed throughout the chasm as Will and Amaya danced around Thia's sword. It had only been mere minutes since the battle had begun, yet her thread-like sword was already tearing them both to pieces. The weapon was like nothing either of them had ever encountered before. Because it was so thin it was hard to see, and it could change from being loose and flowing to stiff and powerful.

Thia would shoot a ball of fire toward them, but when they moved aside to dodge, her terrifying speed would meet them wherever they landed and slice them up a few times with her sword.

"This is all your fault," Amaya said bitterly to Will as she moved again to avoid the fire. She sidestepped in order to swerve around her sword but even still, the thin blade still swung around to catch her arm.

Amaya cursed Cyero for having made her sword disappear before they had even entered the place. If not for that, she could have at least counter-attacked. At this rate, Thia would simply continue out-speeding them and keep swinging at them until they had no blood left to bleed.

"There's still a chance," Will replied from across the room. They tried to stay separated from one another so she couldn't attack both of them at once. "I can use spells from my book down here, but I haven't recovered from the hex I put on myself earlier yet. If we can just wait out her attacks until then, I should be able to create an opening for us to escape through."

Amaya dove out of the way of another swipe. "Why would you put a hex on yourself?" she asked in frustration.

"Listen, I wasn't expecting that prophet friend of yours to reflect my magic."

Amaya growled, and in a bout of sheer anger she threw a punch at Thia, but she quickly realized her mistake when her hand was grabbed by Thia's mangled one. Thia swung her arm down to slice off Amaya's hand, but Amaya brought her leg up to meet the blade instead, the steel toe of her grieves clashing with the blade with a loud CLING! In her astonishment, Amaya was able to wrench her arm from her grasp and recover to a safer distance.

* * *

"What was that thing we fought back there?" Rose asked.

After battling against the creature of which she spoke, they had decided to venture back to its lair and begin making their way through the labyrinth using Rose's earth powers from beneath, since she was able to sense their companions' presence.

"Its name is Omu. It helps protect and maintain this place, much like the hydra. The hydra is the only nameless one out of the three that exist here," Cyero replied. "Omu is known as the Burrower, the one who carved out each of these individual tunnels and when it's empty, it collapses them all before carving it out anew. It's really incredible. Thia is a being known as The Light, she's the one who lights all the torches lining the walls. The hydra protects this place while Rotos ensures that no demons make it past the tower."

"What a wonder this place is," Liland said. "But if Omu is dead now, how will the Labyrinth continue to change?" he asked.

"Omu will revive itself in time, so there is no need to worry about that matter."

Meanwhile, Rose had been using her powers—albeit, cautiously—to cut her way through the ground toward where Amaya waited for her. She didn't know what it was, but she could sense something high-strung happening wherever Amaya was. By and by, the feeling became more intense, and Rose figured they must be getting close.

* * *

Kkshing! Amaya's foot clashed with Thia's blade once again. For the moment, it was the only thing she could use to parry her attacks, and it was working. But Thia's swings never let up, never faltered, never waned. Amaya's legs ignited with every kick she threw out to block, sometimes using one straight after the other. The toes of her grieves were getting dinged and nicked each time sword clashed with steel, and sometimes her feet would receive the blow instead—shredding her stockings and splattering her blood onto both the blade and the floor.

351

Both looked annoyed—Amaya with Thia's persistence, and Thia with Amaya's. Thia's hand reached out to burn Amaya, only for the girl to quickly dodge out of the way. But when she did, Thia closed the distance between them once more and swung her sword horizontally. It would have completely severed her head if Amaya hadn't ducked out of the way. The blade caught her hair in the mix, however, and sliced it away, tendrils of her red hair pooling at her feet. Any lady would have panicked at the sight of a massive chunk of her hair falling to her feet, forever cut away from her. But Amaya gave barely any thought to it.

"Will, hurry and do something!" Amaya looked almost as unruly and disgruntled as Thia at that point, her choppy hair pooling messily over her sweating face.

Will kept trying to focus on Thia, remembering his book's teachings, and at last he was able to cast a spell. He used the same one on her as he had used on both Rose and himself. "There, that should at least prevent her from using the fireballs," he said.

Thia stopped in her tracks. Her sword had been in its loose state, but Amaya noticed it turn solid once again and wondered what else Thia had up her sleeve. Amaya prepared to counter— even though her legs stung and ached from the cuts and being overworked—but in a split second, Thia had leaped into the air, sword in hand, as something came springing up from the ground right where she had once been standing.

Amaya saw a flash of white and then deep, thick purple splattering all over the ground. Thia had made a downward dash and cut a nasty gash straight through Cyero's abdomen. Amaya didn't think she had ever changed expressions so fast; from hopeful to absolute terror. The god sputtered and choked on his own blood. Then Rose and Liland came from the hole that Cyero had emerged from.

She was speechless; she didn't know whether to be happy to see the others or mortified about what had just happened.

Rose, quickly adapting to the situation, lifted her sword with her feeble arms and caught Thia by surprise, striking her. As Thia recovered from the recoil of her wound with the sword still lodged in it, Rose shouted, "Everyone, down here!"

Rose quickly ushered Amaya and Will to the hole which Cyero had first emerged from, Amaya helping Cyero to get up and hold his stomach together. Each of them filed underground. Rose left her sword lodged inside the demon, knowing she would just have to make another if she needed one again. She used her powers to seal the hole above them, hoping whatever creature was up there couldn't break through. Thankfully, there were no signs of that happening.

"Is everyone all right?" Rose asked them.

Liland tended to Cyero to the best of his ability using his only functional arm. "I think it's fair to say we're all in bad shape," he said. He looked back to see the conditions of both Amaya and Will who both had gotten some nasty wounds.

"Liland severed a tendon in his shoulder, and I believe one of my ribs is broken. But I managed to use some of my earth powers while fighting something else in here, so once we're all ready to move, I can get us out of here," Rose said, determination lining her tone in spite of how bad of shape everyone was in.

"Are you sure we should really carry on right now? If we're safe down here, why not rest and let us all recuperate for a while until we're feeling more energized?" Amaya asked.

Rose shook her head. "The creature we ran into was the one who carved out these caves. We managed to subdue it long enough for us to escape, but Cyero says it will soon regenerate; and once that happens, I have a feeling it will be coming after us," she explained.

Will nodded his head. "Sounds reasonable enough."

Amaya shot a glare in Will's direction. "I vote we trap him inside here with the creature and be on our way without him," she hissed.

"Wait," rasped Cyero. "He's a demon, isn't he?" He looked at the horns, wings, and tail which had sprouted again from Will's body once the hex wore off.

"What of it?" Her glare traveled to Cyero.

"Well, it might be helpful to have him around, given that we know next to nothing about this place. He might be a useful asset to finding your parents' base of operations," he answered.

Amaya said nothing, her gaze returning to Will. *I suppose he might be of use...considering he doesn't go behind our back,* she thought.

"Hold on, don't I get a say in this? I said that when we get out of here, I'd take you both with me," Will cut in.

"Please, you can't even remember a simple spell," Rose replied.

Will looked suddenly discouraged by that, but still shot back with as much fire as ever. "If you knew half of what it takes to learn a spell, you wouldn't be saying things like that. But at the same time, all of you've been through the wringer since we got here, so taking you shouldn't be any trouble at all."

"Well then, I suppose we shall see once we escape from here," Amaya said to him.

Cyero's wound had already stopped bleeding by then and so he stood, urging the rest of them to follow. "Arguing here won't get us any farther. We have to keep going."

"Are you sure you will be all right?" Rose asked with concern on her face.

"I'll be just fine," he assured her. "Unlike that of the demigods, the gods are able to heal their wounds much faster. That's what makes the Taint so dangerous, it prevents us from healing our bodies and slowly etches its way into our minds until we lose control."

Rose turned to create another walkway for them to travel. From what she knew, the exit wasn't far from their current position.

"So does that mean that you aren't infected yet?" Liland asked as he and the others followed along the path ahead.

"Indeed. I locked myself away inside the Ice Sanctum, and thus they were unable to infect me," Cyero explained.

"Then how were we able to get inside so easily?" Amaya asked.

"The only way to get inside the Sanctum is through the front door. As long as it's locked, it can't be infiltrated from the outside."

"The exit is just above!" Rose exclaimed, interrupting him.

The others looked on with anticipation as she reached up toward the ceiling and focused on breaking it away. When it did, dull red light flitted in from above. Cyero was the last to exit, having helped everyone to the surface.

At last they had all escaped, and their new surroundings were nothing like any of them were expecting. They stood upon dry, eroded ground that stretched for miles in all directions while an empty, arid wind hit their backs. There were lone shrubs here and there and even evidence of trees that once stood, including one they had surfaced beside. It was crooked and warped, branches reaching out for water that didn't exist in the barren wasteland. Above them sat a deep red moon; the only thing lighting up the perpetual darkness around them. It was strange not to see a vibrant array of stars accompanying it, even in a cloudless sky.

Liland looked the most astonished of them all. "I don't understand, Hell was always described in texts as a land of jagged crag and fire, lit by its evil moon and scars of viscous lava flowing in deep crevices that stretched for miles below the surface. But this...is desolate."

"From what I was told, that's what this place used to be like until it eventually cooled into what you see now," Will said.

"You're both only half right," Cyero interjected. "Actually, Hell used to be a paradise before the Great Fire consumed it, where the demons could rest in peace and not be tempted by the overworld to return to it," he explained. "If anything, we should be thankful it's like this. I, for one, wouldn't want to be dodging lava and fire at every turn."

"That aside, I'm glad we all made it out of there alive. We should rest our bodies so our wounds can heal," Rose said. "We can figure out which way we're going when we awaken."

No one disagreed with the suggestion and happily rested on the ground, even if it was horribly uncomfortable. But Amaya had no intention of sleeping just yet. She was still intent on making sure the others were safe while they slept, her eyes laying intensely on Will.

As the hours dragged on, Amaya saw nothing of suspicion and stood up, making sure to be as quiet as possible. Her body still ached and wished she would listen to it and rest, but she didn't, of course.

She continued onward, making sure she was a long distance away from everyone else, but as she carried on, she felt a sinking feeling that she was being watched or followed. *I suppose I shall have to face whatever it is. No point in running away,* she thought. She hadn't yet reforged her sword so she was reluctant to turn; nonetheless she stopped and whipped around, only to find that there was nothing there. "I guess it was nothing," Amaya said, though she was still unsure.

She faced forward again to continue walking, only to jump with a frightful shriek as she came face to face with a figure that couldn't be seen in the dark. "Don't you ever sleep?" Cyero's voice asked, his face marked with disappointment, even in the darkness.

Amaya sighed with relief as she heard the familiar and reassuring voice. It made defining his face much easier for her. "Of course I do, what are you doing awake anyway?" she asked.

"I heard your footsteps as you were walking away and I was curious as to what you could possibly be doing wandering away from everyone, especially with all those wounds."

Amaya sensed distrust in his words and a glare found its way across her face, her eyes narrowing. "Plotting my revenge against you all, clearly," she said sarcastically. "I was looking for my parents to aid me, but I suppose I failed at keeping that a secret."

The ice god's stomach dropped and his stance grew sharper. "What? You were planning to betray us?" he asked, his blood starting to rise.

"Are you truly that dense?" she insulted him. "I was going to train. I haven't had much chance to figure out how to use my wind powers yet and we will be meeting mine and Rose's parents soon, so I wanted to be ready," Amaya explained. She was sure this explanation would simply calm him down and then he would leave her alone. But he kept talking, much to her dismay.

Cyero sighed at her. "I understand that you're worried, but getting sleep will be an important aspect of eventually fighting your parents. You will need your strength," he replied, his arms crossing as he looked down at her.

"Strength won't mean anything if I don't possess my full potential," Amaya said to him. "Rose has already learned to use both of her powers."

"Ah, so that's what this is about. You're envious of her?"

"That has nothing to do with it. Look, I don't know why everyone is so intent on stopping me from becoming stronger so that I can actually put a stop to the issue at hand! Especially you, since you did absolutely nothing when you sat, perched safely in your prison of solitude, and watched as our parents left the tower to infect all your brethren with the Taint that you, yourself, said was lethal! And yet...you say I need to slow down; to rest—"

"I was afraid of them!"

Both stood there wide-eyed, staring at one another. Cyero seemed regretful while Amaya looked absolutely dumbfounded. "You...a god? Afraid of them?"

"Yes, I was afraid," Cyero admitted.

"But—"

"They have a strong drive to put their beliefs into motion, which is what makes them so terrifying. They don't stop until they've achieved their goals—and they care nothing about the consequences of reaching them. Do you understand yet? They nearly killed me once, all to attain the information about how to reach this place. And I, a powerful god, was incapable of stopping them."

Amaya was full of remorse at that. At first, she didn't fully realize the magnitude of what they were up against. For her, it was easier not to imagine it because she hadn't yet borne witness to the true strength they possessed. But now being fully exposed to the reality that a demigod could cause even a god to hide away in fear, she was starting to understand why he sat back and did nothing for so long.

"I'm sorry," she apologized. "I didn't realize at first how strongly you felt about them. I thought that you were simply being selfish, but I now see that that wasn't the case. However, it's all the more reason to hone my strength whenever possible so that you no longer have to live in fear."

"Perhaps then you will accept some help?" Cyero asked her.

Amaya was reluctant to accept this at first, but it was rather important that she learned what to do. "But how are you supposed to help me? You only know how to use ice, and I need to learn how to use the wind."

"That may be so, but even though each element requires a different mindset and focus, they're all one and the same, the only difference is the element the abilities deal with," he answered.

"Then I suppose you can help me," she answered.

"What shall I teach you first?" Cyero asked Amaya.

"I suppose it might be best if we start with the basics and then move on to wind. I haven't used much of my fire powers at all," she replied, to which the man nodded.

"Then that's where we will begin," he said. "Start by creating and maintaining a flame in the palm of your hand, try to keep it the same size."

It was more difficult than he made it sound since she kept losing control of it, causing it to start burning her hand. But Cyero was able to rapidly shoot ice at the flame to extinguish it before it could consume anything.

"I don't understand this! How will this help me at all?" Amaya asked. Admittedly, her weariness was making it hard to concentrate.

"Focus harder. Pyromancy takes patience and an extraordinary amount of control, and maybe even a bit of wit," Cyero replied.

"Wit? Are you calling me stupid?" the redhead asked with a displeased look on her face.

"Of course not." His silvery-blue eyes shifted upward, trying to think of a better way to word his suggestion. "I suppose what I mean is that sometimes it doesn't have to be as hard as you make it seem. There are ways around its complexity," he said.

Amaya sighed and stared down at her hand in disgust.

A thought came to her head while she focused on her hand. She would try to focus on using the wind to maintain control of her fire. Though she had no idea how to use it, she would try.

"Believing in yourself is one of the first steps to learning how to use your power," Cyero said to her.

Ignoring him, the girl created a flame in her hand once more. She thought back to the beginning of her journey when she had used sheer willpower to stop the bear that had been chasing her and Rose. It came naturally back then, even though she had no idea at the time that the wind had been her own doing.

Each time she felt herself losing control of the flame in her hand, she would channel her energy into pushing the flame back into place once more, and it was working most of the time.

"See, I'm doing it!" she yelped in celebration.

"Well, there are your basics. Part of using fire is being able to aim your blows. Without control, you can never hope to hit your target. Now this is a bit more advanced, but see if you can ignite this from where you stand," Cyero said before blowing frost toward the ground ahead of her, solidifying it into a crystal.

Amaya opened her right hand, aiming it at the ice. She used her flames as well as the wind she was able to produce earlier, shooting a blast of fire at the ice crystal. The fire she had ignited was able to maintain its direction with the help of the wind guiding it until that blast of wind grew more powerful and she was able to ultimately melt the ice.

"Wonderful job. Wind can be an amazing offense. Not only that, but its ferocity can be used as a considerable defense," Cyero said.

"Like a shield?" the girl asked. She had no idea what made her think of that sort of weapon.

"Precisely."

Amaya thought about how she had been able to create her sword with fire. She held out her hand and began to focus once more on using the wind, this time trying to create something with it. But when she did, it started to slice her hand. She gasped and lost focus, hissing through her teeth and holding her sliced fingers.

"What happened?" Cyero hadn't seen what happened and when he started walking toward her to see what was wrong, she hid her hand.

"I was trying to create some kind of weapon with the wind," she said.

Cyero shook his head. "It takes mastery of a single element in order to create a holy weapon. You're far from ready for that," he said.

"Then how did I make this?" she asked as she created Sacris Ignem again.

He marveled at the object before him. She had made the object once before—that he knew—but after seeing her poor control of the fire, it was difficult to imagine that she could have done it again. "But...how?"

"I don't know," Amaya answered. "It happened suddenly. One moment it wasn't there, the next it was. That was back when we fought against your sister, Adione. Everyone was in danger, and I was forced to stay back since I had injured my arm, but I jumped in at the last moment and created it. Perhaps that had something to do with it?"

It sounded plausible, but he still had no idea, so he didn't answer. "It might be best if we returned for now," he said.

"What? But I've only just begun to use my secondary powers," Amaya said, disappointed.

"You shouldn't exhaust yourself. It's important to know when to give yourself a break. The night has been long already. In fact, I think dawn may be peeking over the horizon in the overworld by now. You look tired too," Cyero pointed out.

Amaya sighed, letting him be right. "Fine." She put her sword in the sheath that had been created along with it.

They turned to make way for their group again. When they were visible, she was surprised to see that Will was still among them, fast asleep. "Does his presence worry you?" Cyero asked her.

"Very much. I don't trust him at all."

"Put your mind at ease tonight. I don't require as much sleep as you do, so I'll keep watch until you're all well-rested," he assured her.

Amaya looked down at the dry, cracked ground as they walked before gnawing on her lower lip. "Thank you, Cyero," she said softly, finally looking up at him. "For offering your help and everything."

This earned a smile from the man, which she had never seen before. Despite his being the epitome of cold, his smile resembled the radiance of the sun, its tendrils reaching out to wrap her in its warmth. "You're absolutely welcome, my lady." Cyero placed his hand over his chest and bowed his head.

Amaya was shocked to see such respect being sent her way, especially from him, of all people. "'My lady'?" she repeated.

"Well, you've shown me respect, isn't it only fair if I return it?"

Her mouth hung ajar, just staring in awe of this man. By then they had returned to their campsite.

Liland was just waking up, his eyes cracked open to stare at the starless sky. He turned to them as they entered the camp. "Where were the two of you?" he whispered.

"I couldn't sleep so I left to do some training," Amaya whispered back in reply. "He followed me."

Liland looked at Cyero, wondering why he had allowed her to expend even more of her energy, but he didn't answer, only sat in silence.

"You should have been resting," he said to the girl.

"I know; we weren't gone long, so I'll be resting now." She tried to ignore Liland's nagging and laid down after answering him. That was the end of all conversation for the rest of the night; everyone was far too tired for argument. Even Rose slept soundly. All but Cyero, who remained awake, as he had said he would, eyes drifting to Amaya a few times.

Out of them all, she intrigued him the most.

18: WOLF'S BLOOD

When they awoke in the perpetual darkness, Liland was the first to come to the horrible realization that their rations had run dry, leaving their stomachs empty. Their only sustenance from now until they found food would have to be the water that Rose made whenever they were thirsty. By then, Will had agreed to lead them in the right direction. He had pointed out a distant mountain range where the demigods they were looking for had allegedly set up their base. Rose, Liland, and Cyero seemed completely passive with allowing Will to lead the way, but Amaya had no faith in him whatsoever. She knew this had to be a scheme of his, but by now she knew they would write off her worries as distrust, even though he had proclaimed his determination to capture them hours before. But it was something they could put their hope into, and they didn't have any other information to go off of regarding the direction in which they *should* be heading.

Rose was still as afraid as she had been for the entirety of their travels in Hell. Her trembling made her fall behind the rest of them.

Cyero happened to glance back and notice her, slowing his pace to fall in step with Rose. "I couldn't help but notice the smell of fear on you ever since we came to this realm," the god said as he looked her way.

"Catch up, you two," Amaya called back to them.

"I'm going as fast as I can!" Rose yelled back to her, but she didn't change her pace. "Sorry, is it bad?" she said more quietly to Cyero.

"'Bad' seems to be the wrong word for it. Just worrisome," he replied. "Is there a further reason for it?" he asked.

"Well...don't tell anyone up there but...I'm afraid of the dark," Rose said, swallowing hard as the words left her mouth.

"There is no shame in fearing the dark here. It hides demons, of course," Cyero replied assuringly.

"The demons don't scare me as much as the dark itself,"

"Why is it simply the dark you fear? Do you fear the unknown?"

"I don't wish to talk about it; you're making it worse." Rose's chest swelled, memories brought to her mind.

"Sometimes speaking about feelings can help them relinquish," Cyero answered.

"Well...I guess it started when I was younger...I don't remember exactly how old I was," she began. "It's not a memory so much as a dream. It was dark and I was in bed, and on either side of me were two cloaked figures. They reached out to me, and I closed my eyes and started to cry. I tried to call out, but I couldn't speak, and then I heard a voice I didn't recognize calling my name. I finally was able to open my eyes at that point, but I still saw nothing. That's when I woke up," she described.

Cyero looked at the young woman with hooded eyes as he sympathized with her. "I'm truly sorry that this happened to you," Cyero said.

The girl looked down before picking up her pace a bit to catch up with the others. She was just in time to hear Amaya complaining about their lack of food.

"I'm so hungry...are you sure there is no food at all around here?" she asked Cyero.

"Unfortunately, the fires that once burned here have left the land completely barren. As far as meat, you would have to feast on a demon, if you were to come across one at all," he began.

By then, Will had caught up to the rest of them and had heard the man speak. What Cyero had said caused both Amaya and Rose to look back at Will.

"He's talking about underlings—not me!" Will growled back at them, causing them both to laugh quietly. "But...there's an oasis around here...if it hasn't dried up yet."

"Would there be plants there?" Amaya asked.

"Hm...likely not."

Amaya's expression turned sour. "Then what was the point of mentioning that?"

"Well, shouldn't Rose be able to grow some sort of food with her earthy powers or something?"

"He does have a point...I think it would be worth making a detour," Liland replied.

Nestled between the dry and freezing desert of Hell was an oasis which Will had spoken of before. Out of the vast land and the thousands of leagues it stretched across, there sat only that small capsulation of water. Nothing grew around it except a few very small blades of grass.

Rose had crouched her body down beside the water while the others took the opportunity to rest their aching feet. It seemed that no matter how much they rested, their feet would never feel soothed. Amaya had taken off her shoes to stroke them. She looked off toward the distant mountains where Will had been directing them. "How long until we reach that mountain? It still seems so far away," she said.

"It's as though we haven't moved at all," Rose added.

Will turned around to look at the distant mountain range surrounded by black clouds. "The Denizen mountains are huge, so while they appear close, they're still very far away. From our current standpoint, I couldn't say how long it would be before we get there."

Amaya had grown captivated by something in the water. Perhaps not within the water itself, but upon its surface. She saw herself staring back into her eyes. The water was so calm and unmoving that she could see her reflection, even with only the deep red moon above her. "Is that me?" she asked.

Due to the fact that she had been so quiet, Cyero, who was near her, had been the only one to hear what she had said. "Have you never seen your own reflection before?" he asked her.

The girl shook her head. "Tochfuyu was covered with ice which we thawed to use as drinking water. I had only ever seen it distorted, never clearly like this," she explained.

Cyero looked between the water and the girl looking down upon it. "Are you happy with it?" he asked her.

Amaya stared for a long time at it before closing her eyes, her brow scrunching as they did. "No, I hate it," she said. "It reminds me too much of my father," she answered. Her nails dug into the mud below her and she grabbed a handful of it before throwing it into the water, destroying its delicate tranquility.

Cyero pulled back one side of his lips and looked off to the side. "Why do you see your father when you look at yourself?" he asked.

Amaya looked up from the surface of the water at Cyero. "Why would I not? I look and act just like him; I find it hard not to," she admitted.

The ice god shook his head. "You're nothing like your father," he replied.

"You only say that because he made an attempt on your life once. I haven't. What if I had tried to kill you?" she asked.

"I don't think you could," Cyero replied. "You would have to be possessed by something as evil as him to do that." The god lifted his hand as he looked at the water, which caused some to leave the oasis and form into a ball of ice, which fell into the hand he had held out. He took the ball of ice and rolled it in the mud before showing it to her. "You're rough on the outside, for sure. But inside...you possess a kind heart and a beautiful soul." The ball of ice in his hands shattered, turning into sparkling ice crystals which floated gallantly to the ground.

Her pools of umber remained on his pale hands, captivated for a brief moment by the words he had spoken and the demonstration of what he meant. Then she shook it off. "If you think poetic metaphors will make me like you any more, you're quite mistaken," the girl replied, turning her head away before crossing her arms.

Cyero sighed. "Think of it this way, Amaya. Look at all the wonderful people you've compiled as your companions. Look at the cause you're fighting for. A person like Chasaka wouldn't fight for things like this. He's obsessed with power and controlling how much of it humans should have. But the truth is, our ties and collaborations with one another—it's that unity which makes us powerful," he explained.

This caught the girl off guard. By then the ripples in the water had all but stilled and Amaya could look back at her reflection.

"The food is ready, everyone," Rose said.

Amaya said nothing more on the subject and instead got up to join the others in their meal. Once they finished, they were on the move again. Though Rose's quick harvest hadn't yielded many results, it would have to do since they couldn't carry much more.

They hadn't been walking more than a few hours before Amaya had tripped over something, her body slamming into the ground. "Ouch! Really, this place is terrible!" she complained as she looked up.

Cyero and Liland, who were at the front of the group, looked back at them.

"I would assume the rest of the ground may be unstable with its condition," Liland said. "Step lightly," he said.

But just as he and Cyero took a step forward, the ground beneath them rumbled before giving way. Both men fell into a large ravine below, screaming in pain as they landed.

Rose, Amaya, and Will ran to the land's edge, staring in horror as they took in the current situation.

"Cyero, Liland, are you all right?" Rose called down to them, urgency in her tone.

The ice god and prophet coughed as dust and debris settled from the collapse of the ground.

"Don't worry, we're okay!" Cyero called back.

"Dammit," Amaya spat.

"How are we going to get them out of there?" Rose asked, barely able to see either of them with how dark it was.

"Do you see a way out?" Will called down as he examined the dark area.

Cyero looked around down below. "There is a tunnel to our left, the other way is barricaded by rocks!" he called back to them.

"We're coming down there!" Amaya shouted, prepared to jump at the ready.

"No! Don't jump; if we're stuck, then you all shouldn't have to be as well. Stay where you are and we will find our way to you," Liland commanded them.

It was a poor waste of the energy they had tried so hard to build up. "Wait, Rose, could you use your earth powers?" Amaya asked her friend.

"I can try," she responded and reached her hand down to try and lift a pillar with the two of them on top. But she was struggling to hold it up and dropped it.

"It's all right, don't waste your energy, it will be fine, I'll just use my ice," Cyero called up to her.

They watched while he helped Liland to his feet. Their footsteps echoed throughout the porous ravine, which seemed like more of a cave now that the ground above them covered the sky. It was inevitable that at least one of them would have fallen down there, as the landmass stretched for miles down with no hope of a way out. Cyero and Liland were merely the unfortunate victims of its danger.

Once Liland was standing again, Cyero began to raise them up on a pillar of ice. It rumbled as they slowly rode it toward the surface.

Then a loud crash echoed throughout the huge crevice, followed by the two plummeting back down. Cyero's ice had completely shattered like glass. As they fell, the shards of ice twinkled around them, and just past them, a wall of fire ignited.

When they hit the ground, they could see just what—or rather who—it had come from. There stood Chasaka's brooding figure, dead eyes almost completely blackened by corruption, another Sacris Ignem clutched lazily in his right hand. "When I pictured the demigod of thunder, I never would have thought of someone who looked so weak." He laughed. "You both look like helpless prey."

Those maniacal laughs echoed brutally inside Cyero's head, and his senses told him that Chasaka wasn't alone.

Above them, Amaya's heart was racing, her body fighting tirelessly against Will and Rose's grasp. "Stop! Let me go!" she screamed at them. As soon as she saw her father's figure below, she had been prepared to jump down and meet him in battle. She clawed at their skin and kicked her legs, even biting with all her strength, but no matter how much she fought, they wouldn't let her go.

"Amaya! Please, you can't!" Rose cried.

Amaya was almost breathless, sick with rage as she kept struggling. "I'll kill you! I'll kill you, Father! Do you hear me?" She screamed her throat raw, body quaking as she started to cry.

Chasaka grinned, hearing the faint screams of his daughter. "So they really are with you...I did meet Amaya, but I'm sure you knew that," he said. Then his expression turned cold again. "But right now, I'm here for you two."

"Where is the other of you, I know they're hiding in here," Cyero hissed at him.

"You ruined the surprise," Ruki's voice sounded as he, too, emerged from the darkness. Chasaka held a flame in the palm of his hand so they could all see.

Cyero's senses immediately amplified upon seeing Ruki. Each hair on his body stood up and smells, touch, hearing, vision, and even the tastes in his mouth were amped up incredibly. His mind went rampant with it all—the earthy, humid smell of the ravine ripped into his nose, the rugged feel of the ground his arms were implanted to, the radiation of the heat from the fire, the sounds of the fire waving in the air as it moved, the sound of droplets hitting the floor, and the sight of the people in front of him.

"My, I never anticipated we would meet again...not here anyway," the male spoke to him.

"Ruki..." Cyero breathed out.

"Not after we left you sitting in a pool of your own piss and blood," he added.

Cyero's teeth were clenched down to the point of nearly breaking, and they probably would have if he didn't suddenly roar at them. His ears went back as he shifted into a large wolf, leaving Liland to stare in shock as he tried to snap at and scratch both of them. But alas, they were far too agile for an animal so large to catch them and dodged out of his way.

Liland's arm hadn't yet fully recovered and fear ate at his stomach. He was unsure of how exactly he was going to make it through a fight against the two. But he was curious; what exactly did they want with them? He thought that of all people, they might have come to collect their children or at least attempt to kill them. But Chasaka had said himself they had no interest in the girls.

Liland gasped as a thought came to him. "Cyero! Pull back! Don't engage them!" he shouted and got to his feet. "We need to get out of here!"

Cyero retreated beside Liland cautiously and looked over at him. "What is it?" he barked.

"They're here to infect you and get rid of me."

"How clever," Chasaka said. "You deduced that in just those few moments? Well, I suppose that's exactly the reason you must be eliminated." A plume of deep purple flared to life along the blade of his sword, and when Ruki pulled out his trident, Mithys, its forked points also possessed the poison.

"They aren't going to let us escape without a fight," Cyero told him. He returned to his mortal form and pulled out his black and icy blue scythe, holding its shaft with one hand in a reared-back position.

Liland considered his arm, but he knew that for Cyero and the sake of those waiting above, he had to fight; he had to try. Using his left hand, he reached back for his condensed lance and held it forth before enlarging it to its full extent.

"No, you stay back," Cyero ordered him. He knew full well of Liland's injury, but didn't want to announce it to their enemies.

"I'm sorry, but I can't," Liland answered and moved his arm forward to parry an incoming attack from Ruki's trident. The blade of Liland's lance and the fork at the end of Ruki's trident locked together. Like their weapons, their tense gazes clashed with one another. Within moments, Liland began to struggle. Only having one arm to handle a two-handed weapon was proving to be a considerable challenge.

Cyero stepped forward to help him, but the swipe of a white-gold blade stopped him from moving. He looked over and his eyes intertwined with Chasaka's deep red brooding ones. They were filled with intent; a deadly one.

Cyero's arms came forward, the crescent of his scythe reaching out to parry Sacris Ignem, knocking it back and staggering Chasaka. "Impressive," he growled in a mocking tone. "You seem more prepared now that you're not holed up in your little prison of ice." Chasaka dodged another swipe from his blade. "That makes this a bit more bothersome, but definitely entertaining," he said.

The god of ice was far from pleased with his mocking behavior. Chasaka had defeated him once in battle, but he didn't intend to lose again. A dark look came over Cyero's face and he gripped tighter onto his scythe, rasping a growl through gritted teeth. He rushed Chasaka again. There were no chances to take—he needed to strike Chasaka before he could strike him.

The two became entangled in a dance of blades, metal hissing and screaming as one swung and the other blocked. Cyero was huffing after only a few seconds, but wouldn't let his body give way. He swung with ice coating his scythe's crest, and as he went on his muscles cried out in pain. Each time he looked forward though, it didn't even seem as though Chasaka was breaking a sweat.

Chasaka swiped upward to block the god once again, this time exerting a huge burst of energy that caused an explosion. It was enough to bring the scythe back over Cyero's head, but Cyero used it to his advantage and leaned his body into the blow. Once his blade touched the ground, Cyero flipped himself over it to gain distance from Chasaka.

"Getting tired already?" he sneered. A chuckle left his chest. "And I was only beginning to play." He approached Cyero with his sword pointed toward him. Meanwhile, Cyero was lurching as he struggled to take in air to feed his starving muscles.

Without warning, a churning blew through the air until a crash echoed through the ravine like cannon fire. In a split second, Amaya had escaped from Will's grasp and threw herself off the cliff's edge. In the air, she drew her sword and let the weight of it carry her to the ground below, not caring where it struck when she landed. The impact hit so hard that her sword snapped before releasing a shockwave of fire from it, blowing back the four who had been fighting down there. Amaya lay on the ground, trying to recover from the fall. It was only sheer will that pushed her back to her feet, her broken sword tempering once more with her fire.

"Will, we must go after her!" Rose exclaimed once her friend had jumped.

Without a moment's hesitation, Will grabbed Rose into his arms and jumped off the cliff as well, wings bursting through his shirt as he flew down, landing a safe distance away from the enemy.

Rose formed her sword—the Blade of Keshō—and rooted her feet against the ground.

Ruki had been thrown to the ground due to the shock of Amaya's flames and lifted his head before slowly rising to his feet. "Are you mad? Throwing yourself off the cliff like that."

Amaya's eyes held an intensity like the very fire in her veins. Daggers sliced through him as fire enveloped her sword. "What nerve have you to jest?" she screamed and swung her sword. She channeled all that white-hot anger into the palm of her hand and a cutlass of flame flew forth from her blade, flashing white before returning to the normal, destructive orange color.

Ruki dashed to the side, his feet skidding the rocks, but Amaya didn't let up and kept swinging. The more she closed in, the harder it became for him to dodge. She brought her sword up over her head then swung it down, only for it to crash into another metal. When she looked up, she saw it was Rose's hands that were attached to it, keeping Sacris Ignem from piercing Ruki. "You must stop!" she cried.

A wave of anger flooded Amaya's body and she swung her sword in Rose's direction, the flames burning her hands and causing her to drop the sword. "Get out of my way!" she said and shoved her. But by that time, Ruki had regained his bearings and thrust his trident straight toward her. It pierced, skewering both hers and Liland's stomach. She didn't realize until a mere second before that the man had intended to get in the way of the blade to stop it from harming her. In the end, it managed to harm them both.

"Amaya! Liland!" shouted Cyero as he surged forward, holding out his scythe.

Chasaka slashed his flames at him, scorching his overcoat and leaving the white stained black. It staggered the god, but he was able to retreat just before the blade collided with his skin. The impact of the blow caused Cyero to lose his footing.

The feeling of hitting the ground was crushing—not physically, but he knew the very moment his feet failed him that he had lost his fight against not only Chasaka, but the Taint as well. Even as time slowed while he saw his enemy raise his infected blade over his head, Cyero couldn't move out of the way fast enough. He saw his horrified face in its reflection and let out a bellowing cry as the fire-brand stabbed him.

On instinct, his hands reached for the sword's double-edge, even if it cut his fingers. His legs squirmed as he tried to free himself. The infection consumed his blood and he could feel its blight igniting his veins. His breath wheezed, eyes pleading for mercy as they stung with tears. Guilt washed over him with a numbing sensation, knowing that each and every one of his siblings had suffered a similar agony. It began as a vibrating tingling, then turned into an intense warmth that flooded his abdomen. Most of the pain came from the intruding Taint, although his adrenaline wasn't doing him much of a favor in quelling the stab wound.

"You look just like you did twelve years ago," Chasaka muttered before removing his sword from the god's abdomen. When he looked up from the work he had made of Cyero, he saw Will staring astonished at what he had done.

Images of Will's mother and father being murdered by these people flashed through his mind. He felt so sick he couldn't move, and he could tell that Chasaka could read the fear radiating off him.

Chasaka turned his back on the boy, knowing he had no nerve left to try and strike him. He and Ruki met between the chaos and examined what they had done.

"It wound up being a little messier than I intended...but I suppose the ends justify the means," said the water demigod. "Shall we return?"

Chasaka nodded his head and turned toward the right where a faint light shined, signaling an exit.

"Father...Chasaka...wait," rasped Rose's voice. When they turned back to look at her, they saw tears filling her eyes and trailing down her cheeks. There was blood all over her hands since she was attempting to stop the bleeding from her comrades, even if the liquid was excruciating against her fresh burns. "Why are you doing this?" Her gentle voice was the only thing in the empty air aside from the occasional grunt from her wounded friends. More tears escaped when she closed her eyes. "You're hurting so many people..."

The silence weighed heavy on her, waiting for one of them to speak.

"Sometimes, one must do harm before the good can finally come." Those were the only words Ruki offered her before they both disappeared into the blackness of the ravine.

Rose slumped back, feeling overwhelmed. She looked between her three wounded comrades multiple times. "Will, what do we do?" she sobbed.

Amaya, Cyero, and Liland were all bleeding from terrible wounds and she couldn't deduce if Liland's or Cyero's was the worst. Liland had been pierced straight through his back, and the Taint inside of Cyero's injury was eating away at his exposed flesh, albeit, slowly. She could hear him wheezing out slow breaths, even though he was farther away from her than the others.

"You need to apply pressure to the wounds somehow, and use your water too," Will told her. He erased the fear that once was written on his face and kneeled beside Cyero, who was clutching his laceration with both hands. With one, he reached up weakly to shoo the demon away from him. "Go," he croaked. "Help Rose tend to the others..." Talking itself was almost unbearable, yet he kept his screams of agony inside. Even the slightest movement intensified the pain in his stomach.

Will looked over at Rose who was hastily using her water to clean out Liland and Amaya's wounds. "She's all right on her own for now," he said. He removed the remainder of Cyero's cloak and used the sleeves as a tourniquet to stop the bleeding.

Cyero looked into the demon's eyes, which were distracted by his wound. Even as his stomach wrenched from the pain, he found himself wondering why he was so relentless. *Didn't he wish to leave and capture Rose and Amaya?* he thought as his vision blurred.

"Keep your eyes open," Will demanded of him. But Cyero simply couldn't abide and lost consciousness. "Dammit." He tied the sleeves a bit tighter around Cyero. "Rose, he needs water, quick," he said urgently.

"Go to him...we will be all right," Liland told the girl. Though torn between the three of them, Rose got up to tend to Cyero. She splashed water over his wound, hoping to alleviate the bleeding.

"I don't understand," Rose said. "If it took this much to infect him, how did the other gods not realize what had infected them?" she asked, not expecting an answer.

Will looked with somber eyes at the mess that had been made of the god. "This was an act of terrorism…if his intent was only to infect him, I don't think it would have resulted in this," The demon felt sick to his stomach seeing how much of the purple blood had mixed in with the water Rose was applying.

She shook her head. "How can they be so cruel?" Her gaze redirected to her hands which were quaking from anxiety and the burns that stung her. "Will, I don't know what to do anymore, this feels hopeless." Lifting her head, she looked at him, eyes glazed with tears.

"Why are you looking at me as though I would know?" Will asked her. "That's for you to figure out. But I can tell you one thing; if you think sparing your parents is still a good idea after all of this, I don't know how much longer you're going to survive."

Rose's chest was hollow—like everything that was once inside had been stolen away from her. She knew from within that he was right, but there was still a small piece of her that believed she could pull her parents out from their corruption.

"This is a real shame though," Will said. "I had a healing spell in the book I lost that would help these three."

The girl beside him perked her head up and looked at him. Having picked up the book all that time ago, she still had it with her. She quickly pulled it out of her dress and showed it to him. "This book?" she asked him.

"What? You had it all this time?" Will started to sound angry.

"There is no time for that, just help them!"

Will looked down at the god in front of them then back at Amaya and Liland. Snatching the wounded girl and then Rose would be a cinch. They were both vulnerable with no one to protect them, not even themselves. She saw the look in his eyes and knew exactly what he was thinking.

"You must make a decision, Will," Rose said. "You can continue to sit there staring at Amaya and me, wondering if you should make the move that will help you get your soul back and leave the world behind for your selfish desires, or you can take the book from my hands and help us right now." She stared him dead in the eyes when she offered this ultimatum, hoping he would pick the second choice.

Will threw back his head and let out an exasperated sigh, a growl squeezing through his lips as well. He ripped the book from the girl's hands and browsed through the pages, searching through the words that were illegible to her. Once finding the page, he placed the book down and hovered both his hands over Cyero's wound. It glimmered a faint green glow as Will muttered words under his breath, words that Rose couldn't understand no matter how hard she listened.

His eyes were closed as he concentrated on healing him. After a few moments, he opened them, only to see the wound hadn't changed much in appearance at all. "Something is preventing the spell from closing the wound." His head turned to Rose.

"The Taint must be some form of spell then, rather than sickness," she said. "One that leaves wounds unable to heal."

"I don't know how they did it, but they managed to create something that counteracts the cells that heal the body. The spell I was using speeds cell respiration, but the fact that not even *that* worked is a serious problem...I don't know if he will heal from this," Will explained.

Rose looked worried. "And you're certain you were doing it right?" she asked, only to receive a nod in return.

She bowed her head and closed her eyes. "I see." Rose looked back at the rest of her comrades. "Go and heal them first, I'll keep applying water to his wound."

Will got up after nodding and walked over to the others, all the while, Rose's eyes stayed on Cyero; more specifically, the wound in his stomach, which was still steadily spilling his vital fluids. She kept staring at it, thinking about what could have happened if she hadn't tried to stop Amaya, and all at once her worries returned to her. Even so far in their journey, she wondered if it would all be for nothing in the end. Their efforts wasted. Their struggles in vain. The bloodshed unnecessary.

Though it may have been destiny like Liland had told them from the very beginning, she still couldn't resist the urge to blame and castigate herself for deciding to embark on this expedition into darkness. She kept her tears hidden and her sobs silent.

19: A Promise Written in Blood

Cyero awoke to the sounds of conversation in the air. His body no longer lay in the ravine, staring up into the crack where the sky shone down, but on the hard ground with contorted trees around him, not a single leaf in sight. They appeared to be resting in a burned-down shelter, jagged splinters of wood surrounding them with black covering the parts where the fire once ate away at it. When he sat up, he groaned from the pain in his stomach and looked down at his wound which was wrapped with all sorts of makeshift materials and parts stained purple to keep the bleeding at bay.

Dread passed through his body as he remembered the reason the wound was there in the first place: he was infected by the Taint. He knew his body was being invaded by it, but he felt normal, which made the feeling that much more volatile.

When he looked to his left he saw Liland lying with his eyes closed. Beside him, Amaya sat back against a tree. She looked deep in thought.

Upon turning his head to the right he saw Rose and Will talking to one another. They sat side by side with a book in front of them, and though they were a bit away from him, he could still catch their words.

"I just wanted to be sure I can help if things end up getting messy when we make it to the mountains," Rose said. "I just thought the spell might be useful. Plus, I kept the book safe all this time."

Will sighed. "I guess you have a point. There's a translator in the back of the book because I had a hard time figuring out what everything meant, so if you can't read something, you could refer to that."

"I understand you use it for specific spells and all of that, but I was wondering why it was so important to you," she said.

The demon seemed uncomfortable revealing the information she was asking for; something she duly noted. "Well, my parents were mages," he finally answered. "This book is actually the reason your parents murdered mine. I don't know what's so special about it, but they needed it enough to take their lives just to get them to hand it over."

Rose looked down at the book, zoning out on the illegible pages. "I see..." she trailed off.

"I guess I just kept it with me out of spite for them, but after a while...I started to force myself to learn some of the spells. Maybe that was out of spite too. I was never naturally gifted at this stuff like my parents, so I'm still inept at most of it even though I understand it conceptually." Will's eyes trailed to the girl's hands. Her fingers were small and slender, like twigs should he reach down to snap one. But they were covered in burns. It felt wrong to him to see them look so maimed. "We should probably work on healing your hands," he said, brushing aside the subject of his parents.

Rose could tell he wasn't fond of talking about that part of his life, so she didn't return to the subject. "Go on," she told him.

"A lot of spell-casting has to do with your mindset. You might have a better time getting it to work since you're a demigod. Magic's already written in your blood," he began. Will looked down at the book and started to recite the scripture. "*As long as you have a will and an open mind, simply cite the incantation and your hands will heal.*" He looked back at her. "I'll start so I can demonstrate for you, then you can do the other."

Will reached his hands forward and clasped them around one of her hands gently. They completely erased hers from visibility since they were so big in comparison. He started to mutter the incantation that would heal her hand.

But after a while, Rose was starting to lose hope since nothing was happening. "Is something the matter?" she asked.

"Sorry, it's a little hard to focus with you staring at me," Will replied.

Rose's eyes popped wide, having not expected that to be his response. She turned her head away after. "I apologize, I didn't realize. Continue," she said.

Will began again, and after a few moments his hands started to glow the verdant color she had seen before. She could feel a cool relief wash over her skin aside from the uncomfortable burn until it slowly melted away.

When Will removed his hands, she looked at the one he had been holding, only to see that the burns had completely gone away. She marveled at it. "What a truly incredible power..." she trailed off.

"Yes," said Will. "All right; your turn."

Rose placed her healed hand over the damaged one and looked down at the stated incantation. She recognized the mutterings as those Will had spoken when healing her comrades and began to speak them for herself. It was hard to read fluently, but eventually her hands began to emit a gentle green hue. She could feel the burns beginning to diminish just like they had when Will did it.

"Look at that, you're doing it," Will congratulated her.

Cyero heard a sudden shuffling beside himself and ceased his eavesdropping to see what it was. Amaya was getting up with her sword in hand. "Where are you off to?" he asked.

She turned her head with a start. "Don't keep surprising me like that," she hissed.

"Sorry."

"I was going to see if Rose wanted to train with me. We have been sitting here for quite a while, waiting for you to wake up," Amaya explained.

"I see...it may not be a bad idea."

Their talking had stirred Liland awake with a groan. "Oh? Cyero, you've awoken," he said. "How are you doing?"

"I'm all right," he assured him, though the feeling of the Taint being inside was still a daunting one.

Amaya walked away after that. When she approached her friend, anxiety came over her. She certainly carried some guilt for what she had done to her, but she couldn't bring herself to apologize for it.

She agreed to train with Amaya though, and no conversation ensued about the once-present burns upon her hands. Had Rose forgiven her? Or perhaps she was simply ignoring it, knowing their precious sliver of remaining time couldn't be wasted on such a frivolous thing.

This crunch of time meant the two would need to be at their best in order to win a potential fight between them and their parents. Amaya still had yet to create the weapon trademarked by the element of wind, Ventum Praesidium.

The others, lacking entertainment and interested in the matchup, decided to look in on the exchange.

Rose stood across from Amaya, the two looking into each other's eyes with confidence. Even feeling weak and hungry, they still had determination written on their faces. But Rose was hiding fear. Amaya was powerful. Could she truly match up to her strength?

Amaya had her sword drawn while Rose held her own in addition to Diluvium strung across her shoulder should she decide to use it as well, an unfair advantage to Amaya.

"When faced against anyone, you must always be sure to keep your core tight. Fighting with a weapon won't always be an option, so it's important to make yourself familiar with stances," Cyero said to them.

But who would make the first move? Both were stuck in place, unable to construct how they might begin and who might end it. They had never been pitched against one another before. The thought of harming one another traced the better parts of their minds, telling them this was needed.

Amaya drew in a deep breath and clutched the sword resting between her fingers a little tighter. She felt a weight force its way into her aching feet and she charged forward, sword raised. She would start the fight.

Grunting, she swung Sacris Ignem, but Rose was able to parry with the Blade of Keshō, holding it sideways. This exchange went on quite a few times, Amaya attacking while Rose would parry, their metals resounding each time they clashed.

It was like two strangers choosing to dance with one another. Even if they had known one another so long, neither were able to predict the movements of the other. But as the fight went on, each movement flowed into the next, one sometimes taking dominance while the other fought to regain the ground they had lost. Both were formidable adversaries toward one another.

Cyero watched with intent as the two continued on, noticing each movement they made, as did Liland.

"There is much to work with here," Liland said quietly to Cyero who nodded in response to him.

"Amaya lacks control...she wishes to strike whenever she sees opportunity and doesn't calculate her attacks, but when she does land a blow, it's destructive. Rose, on the other hand...she moves with more agility and is better at defending and dodging, but she lacks character within her attacks," Cyero explained.

Liland stroked his chin while he watched the two battle one another. "There was much to learn just watching the beginning of the battle...Amaya took the first strike," he said.

Cyero nodded. "She's hasty."

Liland looked off in the distance toward the mountain. "I worry there won't be enough time to train them properly," he said softly.

Will looked over at Liland as he spoke, remaining silent.

"And their parents...they've had years of training," Cyero said.

The prophet beside him shook his head. "No matter. We will prepare them as much as possible. And it isn't as though they will have to face them alone, we will be with them the whole way," he said.

Cyero looked at Liland with worry in his eyes.

While Liland may have been right, there was still the danger of the Taint. He could already feel symptoms of it beginning, though he hadn't yet mentioned it to the others. He didn't want to cause any of them to panic.

Still, he nodded his head. As long as they made it quickly enough, he would be able to join them in their fight and end this catastrophe once and for all. Their attention returned to Amaya and Rose once they heard a loud grunt.

It was clear to see the grunt had come from Amaya, who was now facedown on the ground with Rose standing over her, sword pointed at the back of her head. Amaya's sword was stuck in the ground beside her.

Both were out of breath, panting desperately for air. Rose had even broken a sweat, which was good. The exercise had been keeping them warm.

"Wow, what did you think of that, Amaya? That was a good fight," Rose said.

Amaya rolled over and looked at her friend. She didn't look very happy. "Yes, it was. You did well," she said.

Rose was reminded of the fear she had been holding onto since the beginning of the fight.

"Again," Liland said to them. "This time, try to use your powers a bit more," he said.

After Amaya stood and dusted herself off, she looked at the prophet with a curious look. "How will we do that without hurting each other?" she asked.

"Part of sparring involves getting hurt a little. If things get too out of hand, I'll stop you," Liland said.

Amaya yanked her sword from the ground and readied herself to fight once more.

"Begin," Cyero said once both were ready again.

Their fight ensued with Amaya using her fire to try and strike Rose, but she cut away the embers with her sword. This time, Rose used Diluvium to attack. It was difficult to hit straight on, so she created some pillars of rock beneath her feet to gain some level on her friend.

The fight was over just as soon as it began, ending once again with Amaya panting on the ground, her sword steaming beside her since the water from Rose's bow had put out its flames.

"This isn't fair, shouldn't she only be able to use one of her powers since I haven't fully mastered mine?" Amaya asked as she stood once more.

Liland shook his head. "This is a training session for both of you, not just you, Amaya. She has to get used to using her powers as well. Think of it as an opportunity for you to practice as well.

You don't have to keep the pressure going the whole time. Take a bit to calculate your moves. Predict and strike," he explained.

"Well, I can't read her mind," the girl answered with a frown. "And how am I supposed to think? It all goes so fast."

"If you go up against your parents, they aren't going to allow you time to think," Liland answered. "Now, again."

With a growl, Amaya faced Rose once more, her eyes narrowing. This time, her attacks were more erratic because of her growing frustration. She lost once more, this time with liquid burns from the water arrows skimming her.

Cyero looked over at Liland who returned the knowing look. "Once more, Amaya. Think, this time. Try to calculate," he said.

Amaya inhaled a deep breath as she looked at her friend. Though Rose's attacks may have had the intent to win, they never held the intent to harm. She was holding back.

This time you won't prevail.

Once more, she was knocked onto her bottom toward the end of the battle.

They trained until the moon was fully dim. Amaya was the one who pushed to continue each time the battle had ended.

Both girls ended the training with marks and scrapes all over themselves. Amaya was beyond frustrated by now and swung her sword out of her hand where it clanged to the ground. "Enough!" she yelled through her ragged breathing.

"Yes, I was just about to suggest we call it quits too. We must have been at it for hours," Rose replied. She was growing nervous that her friend had become increasingly irritated with each battle she lost.

Amaya glared at Rose and shook her head. There must be something wrong with her. How could she not beat Rose when she didn't even want to fight in the first place?

"You did well, Amaya. We will call it a night," Cyero said to her from the side.

Her bronze gaze caught the god's and she stared at him for a few uncomfortable seconds. "Don't patronize me. You know she completely destroyed me," she said and sat on the ground.

"I wasn't patronizing, I was being honest with you," he answered but was ignored by her.

She felt hopeless, lost beyond anything. If she couldn't beat Rose, her skill would absolutely pale in comparison to her parents.

Rose went over to her troubled friend and kneeled down next to her. "Amaya, are you angry with me?" she asked quietly.

"No," Amaya replied. "But I'm leaving to go train more."

Rose felt her heart drop into her stomach. "What? Why? Are you not tired?" she asked.

"Why do you think? If I can't at least beat you, I would be killed within moments when I fight our parents," Amaya replied.

The blonde shook her head quickly. "Amaya, that isn't true, we have made it this far together, we can do this," she said reassuringly.

But Amaya was dead set against it. "Just get out of my face, Rose!" she snapped.

"Amaya..." Rose trailed off as she felt pain swell in her chest.

"I'm going!" she yelled at her.

"Sorry," the other girl said. But she knew her friend needed space when she was upset and stood to walk toward the others looking at Amaya while she headed in the opposite direction.

"What happened?" Cyero asked. None of them had really heard the conversation.

"Amaya is going to train more...she thinks she's too weak," Rose replied as she walked past him.

The ice god's eyes lingered on the blonde girl who lay secluded now from the rest.

With her gone, that left Cyero, Will, and Liland to linger.

The demon's golden eyes shifted over toward Liland. He had been feeling something crushing his chest for the duration of the day. "Liland...do they fight often?" asked Will quietly.

Liland looked up, thinking through all their days they had spent together. "They never really used to. The first time was shocking," he said. "It was only before this entire journey began... Amaya was having doubts back then. I wish she would have more confidence in herself. She's powerful. I know deep down she's scared that she isn't."

Will nodded his head in response. "I don't think it's worth killing herself over...I'm sure you'd find a way through this. You always seem to pull through in the end," the man said.

"That's true," Liland said. "I'm sure she will turn around. She's hungry and tired. I think that's what's driving most of her frustration."

Will nodded again. Worry filled in the spaces where words of enthusiasm would be. "Do your prophet powers tell you the future? Do you know if you'll win?" he asked.

This caused Liland to laugh a little bit. "That isn't quite how it works," he said, amusement lacing his tone. "I can only see glimpses of the future. I would have all the answers if I could see everything."

Sighing, Will traced his finger into some of the loose dirt on the ground, some of it getting caught under his nail. "So you don't know at all?" he stated more than asked.

"No. All I can hope to do is put my faith in them and make up for what they lack. They haven't disappointed me so far. They're so strong, and I can't blame Amaya for faltering. Many would have given up far before this point. But if anything can pull humanity through this crisis, it's spirits like theirs. Part of being able to win is accepting the consequences if you don't... no matter what, it's as fate intended, and I'm okay with that," Liland explained.

Will rubbed his cold arm, his eyes watching the ground. "So it's faith, then? That keeps you going, I mean?" he asked.

The prophet nodded.

"I don't know how you do it...the future's so uncertain. And you accept death with open arms," the demon replied.

"You shouldn't let your anxieties fester. Whatever happens, will happen; and if you don't put your all into the cause, well, that's what will bring about the downfall of the world's sovereignty. We need all that we can get. Let's not continue on this. We will need our sleep, and dwelling on it will only prevent rest," Liland said.

They all fell silent after that.

The others were asleep while Will lay awake. He was too uncomfortable, too worried about what was to come. Amaya and Rose were at odds with one another, the defiant redhead still vacant. Then there was Liland, whose only hope was in the ruthless hands of fate that cared not of the pawns it used to weave its story.

He felt abandoned—like he was the only one with a shred of rationality.

* * *

Amaya stared at a wilted tree while her feet stood upon the eroded ground, her sword in one hand. She glared at the crooked stature of the object, her mind finding it hard to picture that it had once been anything other than what was there before her now. She was too closed-minded to ever imagine leaves, vast and plenty upon its dead, twisted and tangled branches; to see warm bark upon its cold, dry trunk; a husk of what it once was. It was begging to be struck down, clinging to the parched, cracked dirt by its dead roots—and looking at it made her *want* to do it.

The tree would clearly be no match for her edge, so how could she deem it worthy enough to hone the sword in her grasp? Her face scrunched in anger, her hands holding tighter to Sacris Ignem's hilt until she could no longer bring herself to lift it and cut down the sad, languished snag.

Amaya looked down at the brilliant steel clasped within her fingers. *Am I truly worthy of wielding you?* she thought. *If I can't bring myself to bring your edge against a dead tree, how am I meant to cut down my parents?*

When the sound of footsteps came behind her, she turned her head and looked at their owner. To her surprise, it wasn't Cyero or Liland coming to tell her to go to sleep, but Will, standing there with a blank expression.

The two held gazes with one another for a long moment. "What do you want?" Her voice was quiet, but her tone was cold like the night, blending in with its harshness.

"I just wanted to talk to you. I couldn't sleep and there are some things I was thinking about," Will replied.

Amaya lowered her head a little, her eyes still on him, waiting for him to speak.

"Rose is really worried about you, you know that?" he began.

"And?"

Will paused for a moment, trying to gather his words. "I was like you once upon a time."

Amaya held her stare at him, her eyebrows furrowing for a moment, wondering where exactly he was going with this, and what exactly he meant by *like you*.

"When your parents took mine away from me, I was livid, sick with rage. At the time, I'd have done anything to gain the power to put an end to their lives. That's what injustice does to you…when you feel weak and powerless and are taken advantage of by the strong, obviously you're gonna wanna try to get justice for what happened to you. But…revenge? It took away more than I gained from it, Hell, I gave up before I could get it…because I lost so much trying to get my justice. I lost my life, my soul—literally—and now I'm scrambling to get it back."

Amaya bit her tongue. There were many things she wanted to say to Will; she was offended that he assumed revenge was what she wanted. This wasn't some selfish ploy.

"What I'm trying to say is...you should stop while you can. You're making everyone who cares about you worried and...even scared of you. Vengeance is a dangerous thing. I barely know you and I'm watching it consume your life—"

"You're so wrong," Amaya cut him off. "This isn't about me. This is about getting justice for the weak, whose lives have been destroyed by those monsters—including yours. You and I are nothing alike," she spat.

"But you're throwing away your humanity to do it!" Will finally snapped. It was obvious that the girl was in denial about her behavior. Was she ashamed of it? Was she unaware of it? Regardless of the reasons, Will wasn't tolerating it.

She reared back her fist and punched the lone tree with all the force in her body. It hurt so bad that she wanted to scream but she held it inside, her mangled hand bleeding at the knuckles. "Unfortunately, sacrifices have to be made if you want to save the world," Amaya answered. Then she picked up her sword and brushed past Will to return to their campsite.

He looked back, watching her go before sighing and shaking his head. "Women are so complicated..." he mumbled to himself.

When Amaya returned to their campsite, she lay down against the hard floor of the scorched home. The remnants of the civilization served as a cover from the freezing air. The mortals whose bones weren't used to such extreme temperatures were growing intolerant of this place. Even the two girls who had spent most of their lives in the cold weren't prepared for the chill it offered.

They lay scattered about the porous remains of the most structurally-sound building they had found. Exhaustion carried most of them to sleep, even Rose, but Amaya lay awake still, eyes watching subtly as Will found a place to lie. She had chosen a spot in the corner of the ruined home. She stared at her pale, shaky hands while cold tears streamed softly down her cheeks. Each breath she took clouded in the air. She had been sobbing quietly there, eyes closed as she tried to rest her debilitated body.

She heard some creaking and opened her eyes, which stung now with sadness. She brought her hands up with utmost elusiveness and wiped away the tears that had stained her cheeks. Then she felt a presence fall over her and rolled over a little to look at what it was.

What she saw were stormy yellow eyes looking down at her. "Liland," her lips uttered.

"I knew I heard crying," the man replied.

She watched him for only a few moments more before rolling back over. "Your ears must be deceiving you then...I haven't been crying," she lied.

Liland didn't look convinced and sat down next to her. "Really? Then why do your eyes look red and puffy?" he asked in a whisper.

Heat rushed to Amaya's cheeks quickly after that. "Well, I..." she trailed off, unsure of how to respond. "You wouldn't understand," she whispered back.

"That's a bit unfair to assume. You haven't even told me what is the matter," Liland replied.

Amaya pressed her lips together, trying to resist the urge, but she couldn't. "We have been down here walking for days and it doesn't feel like we're getting anywhere," she explained. "I miss the surface, but even there I have nowhere to return to. Down here there is no food...no light," She began to tear up once more.

"No warmth...nobody, just yourself. I think I know why this place is called Hell...it isn't just the place where demons live...but it's solitude. And I believe that's the only kind of Hell there is." Silence befell them once more. "Why did you save me yesterday?" she asked.

"What kind of question is that? Why would I not save you?"

"Because I've just been a burden to you all since the very beginning."

"That isn't true...your recent actions may have gotten us all into trouble, but you're a valuable asset to us—"

"So you only did it because without me there would be nobody to save the world?" Amaya cut in. "We all know Rose is too afraid to raise her weapons against them."

"You didn't let me finish," Liland said. "Can you not see your companionship matters to us as well?"

"But why..." Amaya trailed off. "If saving the world weren't an aspect, I would be replaceable."

Amaya heard him sigh from behind her, a sure sign he was getting frustrated. "Despite the way we disagree at times, I still care for you," he admitted.

"Then you care for nothing," she said. "When this all ends—*if* it ends—we will all go our separate ways and you will no longer be forced to put up with me."

"Do you truly hate yourself that much?"

Amaya's eyes snapped wide open and she rolled over to look at Liland. "Excuse me?"

"Are you telling me you love yourself then? If you did, I don't believe you would be questioning my actions, can't you be grateful?" His eyes were filled with many emotions. "I saved you so that you could see this journey through and finally attain your peace, that way you could finally stop being so angry at the world. So, please...care for yourself more." He stood abruptly and walked back to where he had once lain, leaving Amaya to ponder his words.

* * *

The empty night crawled on at an excruciatingly slow pace, and as it did, Cyero awoke. He lifted his head to the sky to see that the red moon hadn't yet brightened, signifying daytime in the overworld. He still felt sleepy. But it was something which had awoken him in particular. It sounded like walking against the worn flooring.

His head craned around to see the bodies of everyone still there and intact. He breathed a sigh of relief. This place was unpredictable, and it had been quiet for a while so, in truth, he had been on his toes, waiting for something to happen.

He laid his head against the wood once more, closing his eyes to return to sleep. But almost as soon as he did, they fluttered open once more while his ears picked up the sound of creaking. Cyero looked to his right to try and catch whatever might be making this noise, but again, he could see nothing.

Then a terrorizing scream was heard to his left, causing him to whip his head in that direction. It had been Rose who emitted the sound. She had jolted from her sleep with her hand clamped over her side. "What happened?" he asked urgently and stood to aid her.

The scream had awoken everyone else and they all lifted their heads groggily to see what was the matter.

"S—Something scratched me!" cried Rose.

Cyero removed her hand upon arriving at her side and examined what she was clutching. Sure enough, there were three gashes aligned atop her skin.

Will, who had been beside her peered over her shoulder to see what Cyero was looking at. His stomach dropped.

"I don't understand, there is nothing here," Cyero said.

"No," replied Will. "Those are three scratches. Something is here," he said.

The others crowded around Rose to see what it was she had screamed about, and when he heard this daunting response to Cyero, Liland knew just what he was talking about.

"A poltergeist," said the man.

Rose placed her hands back on the wound and started to heal herself. "A poltergeist? What is a poltergeist?" she asked.

"They're a type of demon...one that's lost its physical form and tends to attach itself to places that hold significant emotional synergy," Will replied.

"So what do we do then? Should we leave?" Amaya asked.

The thought of leaving was unfavorable to all of them since they were still tired, but they didn't see another way around the ordeal.

"I think that would be the best option. If we want to avoid conflict, it may be best to just leave. We wouldn't want to risk upsetting them more by staying," Liland replied.

The others nodded and stood, trying to shake away their tiredness at least for the moment until they could get somewhere safer.

The whole way, Cyero was clutching his former wound, trying to keep his expressions of pain discreet.

Their feet carried them to the edge of the scorched village where they stopped once more. Rose had collapsed, pain lancing through her ankle as she clenched it. She released yet another yelp as she tried to stop the pain.

Will stepped forward. "They must be drawn to her," said the demon as his eyes looked around. Not even he could see whatever kept attacking her.

Cyero narrowed his eyes at Rose and created a large icicle which he hurled toward her. But when it struck, it had pierced not her, but something which had been hunching over her. The sight was horrific and made Liland and even Will flinch away.

Rose screamed and tried to scramble from beneath the creature, which let out a hollow wail before fading into nothingness. "Was that it?" she shouted.

Cyero's eyes stayed slanted as they scanned around, they alighted to a silvery glow as they darted about. "There are more than just one," he replied. "Come on, we have to run." Cyero shifted into his wolf form and urged the others to get on. The Taint felt much less prominent in this form, but it was clear to the others that it was very much there, making them hesitant to board him.

"Cyero, the Taint," Liland muttered.

"You won't be infected, please get on." Cyero felt humiliated, knowing that his body looked all out of sorts and the gash on his belly was likely leaking vital fluids again.

But to prevent any more injury, the remaining four of them got on the wolf's furry back and allowed him to carry them away from their resting place. His paws occasionally snagged on hollow roots and other such while his passengers felt the lash of dead branches against their skin as Cyero blew past them.

They ended in a deeper part of the dead forest, far from the scorched village. Cyero had grown tired by only exerting himself a little, which he knew was a bad sign that the infection was beginning to suck away his life energy. Will, Liland, Rose, and Amaya dismounted the wolf and sat down while Liland stood beside him still, trying to be sure he wouldn't collapse any second.

"How many different types of demons are there? Seems like we have come across so many different ones," Rose asked.

"Allow me to explain," Cyero huffed. "There are four main types. The first is underlings, soulless monsters created by Waru, which seem to have no real intelligence. They attack and kill simply out of bloodthirstiness and act as dogs for Waru. He sends them to the overworld to retrieve meals," he began.

"Like the type you and I ran into, Rose," Liland said to her.

It made sense to her since the demon which had attacked them from atop the mountain didn't seem capable of speech.

"Next is the animal class, like Athelstan, the demon we met inside the Tower of Twilight. Next, there are humanoid demons, like Will. Both of which were created through making deals with Waru who keeps their souls untouched so long as they uphold their end of the deal with him: to serve him without hesitance.

The animals are said to be the worst class of demon, as they're said to have given up their humanity in their thirst for power and will serve Waru without question. Although, some were created in Hell, not born human at all. And lastly, of course, there are poltergeists, like we just saw," Cyero explained. "They live in spirit and possess no physical form, nor are they capable of doing so. A poltergeist is created when the soul of a human or animal is devoured by Waru."

Will shifted uncomfortably, his rigid movements something Rose had taken note of.

"One thing is for certain. We will need to watch our backs from here on out," Liland said. The group went silent thereafter and were back to trying to fall asleep.

But Will lay awake, his thoughts running rampant about the recent realization of his predicament. He sat there, watching the dark, cloudy sky which would never spout rain from its gloomy fixture. He wasn't going to try to sleep and would rather use this energy to keep watch in order to alert the others if there happened to be trouble.

But Will hadn't been the only one to stay awake. Rose was too. She couldn't shake the feeling given by Will's reaction. She got up, trekking across the distance between them and sat next to him.

She felt out of place there. It was still difficult for her to trust him even after she saw the decision he made to help them when they were buried deep within the crevice the day before.

"I noticed you didn't seem very comfortable when Cyero talked about the poltergeists," she said.

Will leaned his weight back onto his arms and put his head on his shoulder, humming in response to what she had said. He didn't want to say anything regarding it.

There was no other conversation between them until Rose spoke once more. "You know, you never did fully explain your motives for wanting to capture us. I mean...I suppose you did, but you never said why."

"I don't see why it's relevant at this point. We're going to save the world and all that, and then I'm going to get my soul back, right?"

"Does it have something to do with those poltergeists?" she pressed.

A sigh left Will and his hand ran through his hair. "A bit..." he trailed off. "I made a deal with Waru a long time ago that I would get my parents back in exchange for my soul. But he tricked me. He brought them back as undead shells of their former selves. Before he offered me a chance to regain my soul, I had spent so long grieving over them that I nearly lost myself. I was on the edge of ending it all. But I decided to try and kill your parents myself, I knew it would take my despair from me...or so I thought," he began. "After tearing myself apart to try and kill them, I came to the conclusion that I needed to get my soul back so I could live again and set things right. But when I approached Waru, he said I would need to bring you both to him alive in order to get it back. At first I refused. I didn't want more people to die, I was scared of what he might do to you. But then I found out that it was *your* parents who had killed mine. And my heart was set upon getting you both no matter what," he explained. "But now the existence of everything hangs in the balance. And so does my life...it's like Cyero said...if a soul is consumed by Waru...they become a poltergeist. I'll be a ghost clinging to one last bit of my existence, with no escape if I don't bring you to him."

Rose stared down at her hands while Will poured out the story of his life to her. She understood his reasons—not that it excused his actions. He had been wronged and wished to live again.

"I told you before, Will. We're going to get your soul back. But you must not betray us."

Will looked down toward the ground, pursing his lips before answering. "I won't leave, I promise."

Rose looked over to him with widened eyes. "I thought you said you don't make promises," she pointed out.

"I can make an exception," Will replied with a smirk.

Rose gave him a smile and got up. "I'm glad to see you changed your mind...I'm going to get some rest, you should as well," she said before turning to go back to where she had once rested.

Will watched her go but turned his head away from her once she lay down to settle in, and again, he was left in a silence that wouldn't soon last.

"You want your soul returned to you, do you not? It would be a shame if something happened to it," a guttural voice spoke into his mind.

Will's heart sank low in his chest, knowing exactly who was speaking to him. The king of Hell, none other than Waru himself. He remained silent, trying to ignore his mocking threats.

"If you don't return to me immediately, I'll devour your soul. Is that understood?" Waru snarled at him.

Will's eyes scanned over the people around him, who had finally begun to accept and trust him, more or less. His gaze stopped on Rose and stayed there for a moment as the words of his promise weighed heavily on his shoulders. Will closed his eyes tightly, as if trying to quell the pain that had arisen from this before turning his head in the opposite direction of the group.

"Yes," he responded quietly.

"Good. And I'll know if you plan to go against me. So don't expect to get away with any scheming." With that, Waru's voice faded away and Will was at last left with a deafening silence.

20: Blood of the Promise

When she awoke, Rose had gone off deeper into the snaggy woods. All night, thoughts of her friend plagued her mind, even wormed their way into her dreams. Amaya's strong will was beginning to break her own: her will to carry on. She feared what might become of them when this nightmare was over. *Would things go back to the way they were? Or...*

Her thoughts trailed off as she hugged the trunk of the tree she had climbed. She was looking out across the flat plains of Hell. What she was looking for, she didn't know. But perched on the highest, most stable branch of the tree is where she felt safest. Even if darkness surrounded her from all directions, she felt safe being so high up. It was almost impossible to see more than twenty feet ahead of her, even though the blood moon's glow had returned. Such a dim light made seeing what was far before her almost impossible.

She had hoped that perhaps climbing higher might help clarify what lies ahead, aside from the mountain which was silhouetted by the orange glow of torches lining its paths.

Was she trying to scout danger to keep it from her friends? Deep down, she knew that must not be it—but if not, then what? What was she searching for?

Rose started when she heard tree branches rustle and looked down to see where the noise had come from. When she did, she saw Cyero below, climbing toward her.

"Cyero? What are you doing here?" she asked.

He sat on a branch across and slightly below hers. "I was searching for you and Will. I didn't mean to startle you if I did," he said. Cyero leaned back against the tree trunk, head rotated and tilted upward to keep his eyes upon her. Her pale form was hard to see in the darkness, even at such a short distance. In fact, it was perhaps her complexion which allowed him to see her in the first place, since her clothes were so dark.

Rose scrunched her eyebrows. Last she knew, Will had been with the others and she didn't recall seeing him follow her. "Are you sure he isn't with you? He isn't here," she said.

She saw him nod his head, his silvery hair reflecting as much of the moon as it could. "I'm afraid not," he said.

"Then we should go; he might be in trouble," Rose said.

"Hold on just a moment. There was something I wanted to discuss with you," he said.

She paused as she had been about to downscale the tree. She supposed Will was quite capable of handling himself—for the time being, of course—should he have truly found himself in danger. "Okay...what is it?" She returned to a relaxed position.

She heard his soft sigh penetrate the absolute silence around them, neglecting to look his way now because of how she was sitting. "You're a kind, young girl, and I've noticed time and time again that you're always in favor of life and seeing the good in others."

Rose lowered her head, eyes falling to her lap. She knew where he was going with this. "Yes..." she trailed off.

"Well, I'm not sure Amaya is very far from the manner in which we should approach this...issue."

There it was. She had been trying to avoid the thought ever since Will had talked to her about it. Regrettably, she had been second-guessing her perspective of it. "Even if that were the case, I'm unsure if I could raise my weapons against them," Rose answered.

Cyero could no longer see the girl and, like her, was staring off into the perpetual darkness in the opposite direction. "What is it that holds you back?"

"I've never found killing a living creature to be an easy task," she began. "Even when I was living on my own with Amaya, I still felt a bit of guilt when we needed food. I always made her do the hunting." She exhaled softly. "And these are the people who gave life to me. Amaya, and now you, too, are expecting me to raise a weapon against them."

"Perhaps they did give you life...but are you truly okay with allowing them to take yours—and the lives of the whole world—so that they may turn it anew?"

"That won't happen."

"It will if you approach this with mercy on your mind," Cyero cut in. "Think of the lives they've already taken in cold blood."

The god of ice heard a soft sniffle, shattering the silence that took place after he spoke. He turned his body, allowing a minimal vision of Rose. She was doubled over, shoulders shaking. "Rose?"

"I don't know what to do," she sobbed. "I wish there was a way to do this without ending anyone's life."

"But there isn't," Cyero replied. "As a god, no matter who it is or what they've done, I'll always wish diplomacy over violence. But there is no other way."

"Hold on," she said, getting her emotions under control. "What about Will? He was able to use a spell that could temporarily bind powers." She lifted her head. "I'm going to go and find him." Rose began climbing her way down the tree, Cyero lifting his head as he watched her.

"Wait, Rose, that isn't—"

"I'm sorry, I'll be back with him!" she shouted back as she began sprinting through the dead forest.

Heaving a sigh, the god, too, began making his way down the dead root.

Happiness was surging like the fountain of life through Rose. She could hardly believe she had come up with a sound plan to take care of this mess without having to harm her parents. She didn't know where Will had gone off to, but she was determined to find him.

Soon her legs carried her to the edge of the ancient stark forest, and though she hadn't found the man yet, she was still determined. Rose was going to turn around until she heard the air above her blowing like a gentle whistle. She lifted her head, only to see Will flying away from the forest. "Will, stop!" she shouted. Alarmed, he fluttered his wings to halt himself before landing. "You're leaving?" Rose asked quietly.

"Rose, I ca—" Will started before being cut off by the girl, who was standing a few feet away from him.

"After everything...after I trusted you, even after all the things you did...You know we can help you get your soul back; do you really have so little faith in us that you're willing to betray us all?" Rose let out a small sigh before continuing. "You promised just last night, I even thought we might have started to become friends, but I guess not. First my parents, then Amaya, and now you...am I that easy to abandon?" the blonde girl finished with tears in her eyes.

Suddenly Will was right in front of Rose, his hands holding her face gently, their lips only inches apart.

"Stop," Rose said quietly. "Not if you're just going to leave." They stayed like that for a moment, one thinking of what to do, and the other awaiting his decision.

Finally, Will let go of her face, taking a step back. "I'm sorry," he said before turning around and taking off into the sky, leaving Rose alone.

The girl stayed where she was, glistening eyes watching the demon fly away. She looked down at the cracks in the ground which branched out in all directions. She was beginning to lose hope. If Will was gone, she thought, perhaps it was meant to be that she would have to face the fear that blighted her. But she didn't understand why he had gone away. Rose assumed that Will was en route to whoever had sent him out on his quest in the first place in order to alert him of their location.

Her feet scratched against the dry dirt as she turned to head back to the others, but she stopped herself, watching Will fade out of sight. She turned once more and raced off in his direction, hoping her legs wouldn't betray her. She tried to keep him in her sights.

He soon reached the Great Snag, a huge decaying tree larger than any other in the forest, none so surprised to see Waru perched atop one of its hollow branches. The tangle served as a landmark before the mountain, and it was a miracle the thing could even support his weight, given his immensity. He was a large dragon-like beast with enormous wings, six legs, six eyes, and six horns.

"I was beginning to think you wouldn't show," the brooding demon bellowed.

Will chuckled nervously. "Well...here I am," he said.

The creature leaped from the branches of the Great Snag, his six spider-like eyes—all framed by his horns—focused on Will and his huge wings tucked behind his back once more. That was when Rose arrived, taking cover in the dead foliage around the dead root. She cowered at the sight of the beast and tried to condense her body to keep herself well-hidden. She listened in on the conversation and peeked out through some of the branches surrounding her. Rose tried not to move, not to even breathe, fearing the creature might harm her if she was found out. She could hardly believe the scheming nature of the man she once thought of as a friend.

"Take me to them then," Waru said. "We haven't much time to waste."

"See...about that...I came to meet you here because I had some questions to ask you first. You're fine with that, right?" Will asked.

"Yes," answered the demon. "So long as there aren't many."

"What do you plan to do with them?" he asked after a few moment's hesitation.

"Why does it concern you?" Waru asked.

"Well...you know what I'm doing with my end of the deal... it's only fair I know your motives too," Will said.

"I don't have time for childish games, Will. Take me to them now," Waru growled at him.

"But why do you need them so badly?"

"I need them for something important. Whether they live or die, that's up to them," Waru replied.

This made Will's chest swell uncomfortably. He didn't like the thought, even though deep down, he knew that killing them had likely been Waru's plans for them all along.

The demon beside him could read it all; every single emotion going through the soulless man's head in that very moment.

"Why did you come here?" Waru asked him.

Will could still give no answer.

"Why do you hold reservations? How can you expect me to do business with such a naive boy?" the demon asked. "Where do you hide the—"

That was all Will could take. He felt like he couldn't breathe. That voice was suffocating him, snuffing out his life. "I'm going back...I have a duty to uphold."

Rose didn't know why, but she felt relief fall over her. She supposed after believing for a while that he had betrayed them, it was nice to hear that perhaps Will hadn't completely lost his faith in her—in all of them.

"And what duty is that, Will?" Waru asked as his eyes narrowed upon the back of his head which he had turned to him.

"To defeat the four demigods waiting for us somewhere around here," the demon replied. "And we have a lot of ground to cover now that I've deceived them by leading them here."

"This is your last chance, foolish boy. If you don't lead me to them now, I'll devour your soul right before your eyes," Waru growled as he began to pace toward him.

Rose widened her eyes. Had Will truly led them astray? Wasted their time? She wished she could emerge and yell at him for sucking dry the little time they had to get to hers and Amaya's parents.

Waru bellowed a deep fit of laughter as he saw the terrified look in Will's eyes when he turned around. "After that, it won't be long before your physical form is in danger of fading away," he growled.

"If I do, at least I can say I put up a good fight until the very end," Will replied. "Also...I have a good hunch as to where those four are hiding," he said.

"Unfortunately, you no longer have a choice in the matter. As it seems your mind's been made and you will soon die, you should know what is going to happen to them. Chasaka, Ruki, Teira, and Sage need them to fulfill their plan. Soon, demon-kind will reign supreme over the surface with the eradication of gods and demigods. Though, you've done well in leading them in this direction. Now that they're closer to the mountains, I'll have no problem fetching them."

"That's what I thought. You knew I was going to die with or without my soul...so you didn't care about giving it up for Amaya and Rose," Will explained. "This was never about my soul in the first place. It was about you playing fetch with those four hounds so that you could prove your usefulness...so that they would spare you. But they're lying to you, you know. You're going to die too. Just like the rest of us. You think they care about you? You're nothing but a pawn in their game."

A deep growl gurgled in Waru's throat. "Those are bold words for a dead man," he sneered. His large tail swept forward and wrapped around Will, pulling him off the ground and into the air. After that, he slammed his body against the spot where he once stood. The impact left a dent in the cracked ground and was enough to injure Will quite badly. He landed with a grunt.

Will glared at the creature who reverted to his mortal state. The king of demons in his full state of glory approached the ailing demon. He held that menacing stare, glaring past his eyes and into his soulless chasm.

Rose clutched her sword in her hand and readied herself to fight back to save Will. But she froze. Suddenly, her body wouldn't allow her to move at all. *How could fear stop me now? Especially after I've made it this far?* Rose thought.

Waru picked up Will by the neck, his fingers donned rings covered with gems of all different colors. Will knew one of those rings belonged to him; the one containing his soul. His heart thumped wildly in his chest, realizing he was powerless against this mighty being. But still his glare persisted. "Look at you, the ruler of all demons...bested by some mortals...again," he sputtered as he choked.

Rose covered her eyes, she couldn't watch if Waru had decided to take him out. She felt absolutely pathetic here, but also wished she could force Will to stop talking.

"Why do you still speak?" Waru growled at him. "You should have gone quietly." The demon's grip grew tighter around Will's throat. Will's hands shot up to wrap around the larger one's wrist in a pathetic attempt to pry it away.

Rose shifted her weight, and as she was about to stand, a voice rang out.

"Waru, that's enough."

Will's eyes flicked over in the direction he heard this noise. What he saw was a man standing there who was far smaller than Waru and even himself. It was almost amusing to hear this man giving Waru orders.

He dropped to the ground after that, coughing to regain his breath. "If he won't show us where his little friends are, I suppose we will just have to retrieve them ourselves," the other man said.

"Go ahead and try it," Will spat. "Unlike me, they won't fall into your hands so easily."

The man with blue hair chuckled lowly. "No need to worry about that." His body loomed over Will's, his hand extending toward him. When he did this, Will's head was encased in a bubble of water.

The demon held his breath under the water. He wouldn't give himself up. But seconds passed by like agonizing minutes and soon he could no longer hold his breath. He could feel his lungs giving way to the pain inside of them.

He passed out from the lack of oxygen, and when he did, the demigod released him. He picked up the demon and slung his body over his shoulders. "We will return to the mountains now," Ruki said to Waru, who turned to follow him toward the mountain.

"Are you saying we should stop trying to find them?" Waru asked.

"They will be coming for us anyway," Ruki replied. "I believe you were missing the point of why we needed him. He still has the book we need to keep the infection from receding. When that happens, we will lose our control over the gods." He looked at his henchman. "If he brought our daughters to us it would have been a plus, but it doesn't matter as much now."

Understanding, Waru questioned no further and allowed their return to the mountain to ensue in peace.

Rose's feet hammered against the cracked ground, shedding dust behind her as she raced back into the forest to find her friends. Her heart was racing, tears flying past her cheeks while she ran, hoping the breeze from her momentum would clear them away before anyone saw them. When she came to the little clearing in the dead forest, Rose skidded to a halt and huffed, haunched over while Amaya and Liland stared at her, wondering what was wrong. Cyero was there too, wondering if her panic had been caused by some new development regarding Will.

"Is something the matter, Rose?" Liland asked her.

Rose gave him a rapid head nod before she could speak then stood up straight. "Will is in danger."

Cyero's ears perked up. "What? What happened?" he asked.

The girl didn't know what else to say. Will had tried to betray them, however, he had changed his mind. But would anyone believe her if she told them—namely Amaya? She had no other choice. If they were to save him, she had to tell the truth.

"Will tried to betray us."

Shocked faces stared back at her, all but one: Amaya's who looked at the others. "Please, why are you all acting like this is a surprise? I knew he was bound to do it at some point," she said.

"Please, wait, before you—"

"No, let me guess, you're about to tell us that this whole time, he's been leading us in the complete wrong direction and now we need to first save the traitor from whatever mess he got himself into, and then start from square one again, trying to find where to go next? What mook," Amaya said. "I knew right from the start that we shouldn't have trusted him. But all of you simply assumed that he was good, that he could change, but nobody ever really changes, do they?"

Rose approached her friend after that and threw her fist at her face, her tears returning to her eyes, both her emotions and pain flowing through her from the punch. Amaya's upper half swung back from the impact, but she regained her form before she could fall, not daring to strike back.

"If you would just be quiet for one moment, maybe we could stop wasting time with trivial things like this and actually get somewhere!" Rose gasped for air after that, watching while blood trickled down the bow of her friend's lips. Liland tugged Rose back from Amaya to calm her down. "I can take this no longer," Rose said. "Will was leading us to the mountain to deceive us, yes. He left so he could meet Waru. But Waru is working for our parents, he's being swindled by them. Waru tricked Will. Our parents needed the book he had, and now he's been captured! He's in danger!"

Amaya wiped the blood from her lips. "So what...you expect us to go the extra mile to help him after he did that? Who cares if Will ended up leading us in the right direction anyway, he was still going to tell Waru where we were so he could kill us!" she yelled.

"You're wrong! Once he figured out that Waru was working for our parents, he went against him. Do you not see that he still has faith in us?" Rose shot back.

"At the last minute! What if it had been too late by the time he realized he was being foolish?" Amaya insisted.

"Stop! No more yelling!" Cyero interjected. "Arguing like this is getting us nowhere—"

"I think it's taking us miles from where we were," Amaya said. "Showing us where our loyalties lie." She shot a glare Rose's way. "It seems to me that Rose is more concerned with the demon than with any of us. Who is to say it wouldn't put us in more danger to try and rescue him?"

Liland felt Rose's body shift in his grasp like she was about to go back for more, but he held her firmly in place. "Don't. We're all tired and hungry and have been walking on for days now. We have faced many hardships and run into roadblocks along the way. I get that we're all frustrated but we can't risk falling apart now." He looked at the others, making sure their mouths kept quiet.

Rose spoke up after a moment. "I'm trying to be compassionate, Liland. Can we not agree that if it weren't for Will, we wouldn't know where to go or have even made it out of that crevice? What if your wounds had been too serious for your bodies to heal on their own? You and Amaya would both be dead," Rose explained.

Liland took a deep breath and looked at Amaya; her face was dark with anger. "Amaya, I think it would be smart to help him, we

need all the hands we can get in order to win against your parents."
He knew saying this was bound to draw out a negative reaction.

"Does my opinion carry no weight to any of you? What if he
betrays us again?" She raised her voice. "We don't need his help,
once things go back to normal, we can go our separate ways."

"If only that were true," said Rose. "There may not be enough
time left for him to live. He told me he made a deal with Waru.
He said that once Waru consumed his soul, he would fade away.
When I saw them there, Waru threatened to eat his soul! Once our
parents realize he doesn't have the book, they will likely dispose
of him! We have to help him get his soul back. I promised him
we would!"

"We? You can count me out of that! Why would you ever
volunteer me for something like that?" Amaya screamed.

Rose tried to bite her tongue, tried to hold back from saying
anything cruel to her, but she could do so no longer. "You're right.
It was mindless of me to volunteer the help of someone as shrewd
as you...Sometimes I wonder why it is you agreed to help me save
the gods in the first place, all you think about is yourself."

Amaya opened her mouth to growl something back at her,
probably something that might bring her to tears, but the dead
bushes behind her rustled less than subtly, and she and the others
turned their attention in that direction.

When the figure which had indeed been hiding within
emerged, Amaya, Rose, and especially Liland widened their eyes
at who they saw.

It was Daniël.

21: Old Blood

When Will opened his eyes he was met with more blackness, save for the occasional dot of light presented by some torches across from him. He was in a cage made of wood and quickly found himself wondering why someone would keep him inside such an unstable binding.

He tried to steady his blurry double vision, eyes squinting and scrunching. Just as he was finally regaining his vision, he felt a crushing impact sent straight into his jaw. Will doubled off to the side, head down, sweaty blond hair sticking to his face. He felt the clinking of heavy shackles, just now realizing that he was bound.

He felt his muscles scream and hunger nagged at his belly. Blood was smeared on the stone floor from when he had been struck; its rough surface had scraped his knees when he jerked to the side. Not even a grunt had the strength to worm its way through his lips.

"Where is the book?" demanded a female voice which Will recognized.

He slowly lifted his head, peering through the curtain of hair over his eyes. Though being hit had caused his vision to blur once more, he still recognized the face dancing across his line of sight even though the details were harder to see in the darkness. She had brown hair and a twisted root growing from her right eye, a small bloom budding on one end. Her neck was only attached by branches, much like the one growing from her eye socket.

"Teira..." he muttered. He recalled when the woman had visited him in his old village where he met Rose in the graveyard. It seemed so long ago when things were right with the world—if even a little.

"Silence, beast!" she screamed back at him.

In a single moment, Will felt something hot across his left eye. Instantly he realized that the searing hot pain was followed by the warm trickle of blood running down it. He jerked back again, unable to move much else than that. His good eye looked up at the woman, this time glaring at her. "Unless your words are of the location of the book, you may not speak," she said. Agony ingrained itself into the top of Will's head as he was slowly lifted by his hair so she could look him in the eye. "I warned you, did I not?" She expected no answer from the demon but hoped he would so she could take pleasure in striking him again. When she received no reply, she continued, "that if you didn't hand over the book, you would regret it."

"Yeah...I remember."

Teira grinned and let go of his hair. Within a moment, Will saw her leg swing up, only for his head to be wrenched backward while an explosion of pain radiated through his jaw once more, blood flying from his lips. This time, he let himself whimper, and when he slunk back into the position he was bound to, he dared not look at her.

"Well...? Do you regret it?"

Will closed his other eye, wishing he had some way to tell Rose to abandon the book in her possession. But, of course, he couldn't.

"Yes," he muttered.

Teira looked at the washed-up whelp, all sorts of mercy drained from her remaining eye. "You can end your suffering here and now if you tell me where you've hidden it," she said. "If not..." she trailed off.

Will could hear the woman shuffling and he braced himself to be stricken once more. This time her foot came barreling into his stomach and he doubled over, his body so shocked that it couldn't even produce a scream. But he felt a warm, earthy substance come up his throat and spill onto the ground. He saw his blood again.

Will no longer had the strength to hold himself upright— even on his knees—and collapsed, his face smashing into the ground. The pain it caused was nothing compared to that of his stomach, which was excruciating. Perhaps she had broken something—at least that was what it felt like.

Teira gave him a moment's rest, watching his pitiful position while his blood seeped around him. "So? What is your decision?" she asked, listening to his gasps for air.

He went on panting, but Teira was growing impatient and lifted the sword in her hands to strike him again. "I'll die, then..." Will muttered.

Her salmon-colored eye stared at the demon, internalizing his answer, and then a grin weaved its way onto her lips. "Die? Who said anything about dying?" she asked. "No, no...you won't get the pleasure of taking your last breath, of having your agony relinquished from your body. No, I'll beat you until your flesh rips apart—until your nerves grow tired of feeling pain. Normally I couldn't bring myself to do this, but since the situation is rather dire, I'll give you one final chance. Where. Is. The book?" she insisted.

"All right. I'll tell you," Will hissed through his teeth.

Teira stood silently, waiting for his answer, arms crossed. Then, she heard him mutter softly and leaned closer. "Speak up. I know you can be louder," she growled.

Will lifted his head, their eyes meeting.

Then he spat at her, a mixture of blood and spit landing directly on her cheek. He knew this would seal his fate, but he couldn't help but feel victorious that he hadn't missed.

Teira shut her eye and brought her hand to her cheek to wipe away the spit. "You insolent..." In a fit of white-hot rage, she slammed her foot down into his left arm, completely shattering the bone in mere seconds. A crunch sounded throughout the room they were in, followed by loud, horrific screaming.

* * *

A masculine, yet distorted voice filled the area between the trees. "Get them, now." Again, the bare brambles rustled and through them walked the five dogs which were once sealed away, all growling at the four beings in front of them.

426

"I don't understand...we...we buried Daniël, and his dogs were put into the barriers," Rose murmured, her voice trembling as the dogs approached.

Liland couldn't bring himself to speak. The sight of his former friend risen from the dead was something his eyes couldn't bear to see, and he had to look away. From one glance, he saw his once-hazel eyes turned red surrounded by deep black and his skin melting away from his bones while purple sludge infected them. Needless to say, it was a nauseating sight; not even Cyero's wound bothered him as much as Daniël in his current state.

"Wait! If they're here, then that means they escaped the barrier...and so have the gods," Rose realized.

"So then what do we do?" Cyero asked. He kept a watchful eye on the dogs. He was hardly in any condition to be fighting, but readied himself to do so anyway.

"We put them back in their graves where they belong," muttered Amaya as she drew her sword.

"What!" Rose exclaimed over the sound of the barking and growling from the five dogs.

"No, she's right," Liland said. He slowly opened his eyes, fixating them on his friend. "That isn't the Daniël we knew— that one is long dead—but this..." he trailed off. "This sickens me." Liland narrowed his eyes and Rose saw the growing fury within them. "This is something I can't forgive." The deep gurgle of thunder roared in the sky as Liland removed Fulgur from its dormant state, electricity flowing around its shaft. "Don't allow them to escape with their lives. The corpses of our friends will never be used as puppets again."

The dogs charged forward, lips drawn back with froth brimming on the edge of their teeth. Amaya shoved Cyero back, warning him not to engage with the enemy, knowing how weak he was. He could barely stand.

Ao was the first pup she encountered, though one could hardly call him a pup. On his hind legs, the great dane stood well over her height, but his jaws were easy to parry with her blade, which lit ablaze on contact. The fire burned away more of the dog's decaying fur and skin, exposing more of the Taint infecting beneath. The sight of it made her stomach churn.

"Try not to make them suffer! End this quickly," Cyero said from behind her, keeping on his toes.

"So what if I don't? It isn't as though they could feel this anyway, they're nothing but husks used to do Chasaka and the others' bidding," Amaya argued, grunting as she parried another blow.

"You're wrong! They can feel the pain of the Taint inside their bodies and every blow you deliver."

Amaya's head spun around to him. "Just stay out of this! I'm losing my—" She yelped as Ao's inciscors latched onto her forearm, causing her to drop her sword. When she did, Chio ran up from behind him and picked it up by the hilt, charging at Amaya after doing so.

Rage boiled in Amaya. She was far too tired, far too hungry to have any further patience in putting up with such things. From her palm, she launched a ball of fire at the dog, scorching her body. But she leaped through the flames and slashed the weapon at Amaya, fur on fire and all.

It wasn't the first time she had felt the blade of Sacris Ignem against her skin, but it was the first it had been caused by her own. She scrunched her brow, having doubled back from the blow which had slashed her chest. Amaya thought of how she had previously used the wind to fuel her flames. But in that moment, fire was absent from her mind. She called upon a violent gust of wind and blew back both Ao and Chio, not caring that the wind had sliced her hand as it had done before. Ao and Chio flew backward, Chio letting go of her sword, which flew airborne, flipping until it struck down one of the dogs Rose had been fighting. Sacris Ignem had pierced Milo's skull, killing him instantly and taking the girl aback.

She knew she couldn't stare for long as Rex was quick to pick up the slack. Being a pitbull, the dog was rough and burly. He was slow, but his bite packed heavy force. Rex lunged forward, jaws unhinged, only to be stopped suddenly by the blade of Liland's lance. Fulgur was lodged between the dog's teeth, keeping his jaw from closing, but he kept trying. It sliced the inside of his cheeks and cut away at his gums, freeing some of his teeth from them, but Rex's mind was so far gone that he simply continued trying to free himself from the lance. It was a sobering scene to both Rose and Liland. Liland wanted to remove the weapon from Rex's mouth, but knew Rose would be in danger if he did.

Rose climbed into the branches of a tree and pulled out her bow and arrows, stringing in one after the other, firing them at Rex to put an end to his suffering. She was still quite inept with the weapon and missed many of her shots, and the ones that did strike landed in insignificant places. She simply hoped she wouldn't strike Liland with it.

While in the tree, another of the dogs, Hiro, barked ravenously at the girl, raking his claws into the trunk of the tree in an attempt to reach her.

A yell of agony suddenly echoed across the small clearing in which the fight had ensued, causing Liland, Rose, and Amaya to look over from where it had originated.

Fury overtook Amaya's body when she laid her eyes upon the origin of the screaming. In the few moments she had taken to retrieve her sword from the body of Milo, Daniël had strode across the chaos and taken out his crossbow. He had strung a few quarrels into the weapon and shot Cyero with all of them. The god lay helplessly on the ground whilst the puppet of their former comrade strung up another quarrel.

"No! Stop!" Amaya screamed, her face red with anger. She continued trying to yank Sacris Ignem from its bloody pedestal, but it wouldn't budge. She could no longer bring herself to care if she charged forward with her sword in hand and left it the dog's carcass. Amaya sprinted toward Cyero, who flinched back from being shot once more. "Wind, be my weapon!" The sky echoed with her plea and the branches of the dead trees clashed together, shivering.

The clouds above lit up from Liland's thunder while Amaya's wind rustled the trees. It all went dead silent, the element collecting in her hands and glowing until it took physical shape. A silver shield with sharp edges appeared in her right hand and, coming upon Daniël, she swung it out in front of her. She heard a loud slash as the blade of her shield sliced his arm in two, dismembering him immediately. The arm that was once attached to his body fell to the ground followed by a thud as the crossbow he had been holding hit the ground too. Daniël's eyes flicked over to where she had cut off his arm. He released no screams, but Cyero could feel how much pain Daniël was in radiating from every fiber of his being.

From the quarrels that had budged their way through his flesh, Cyero could feel aching coming from deep within. His muscles were on fire and his body felt faint. There wasn't a doubt in his mind that the quarrels were meant to infect his body with more of the Taint. He was in danger.

Impulsively, Amaya created her sword once more from the flames of her blood and thrust it through Daniël's back. His skin bubbled and melted away while more of his vital fluids spilled onto the ground.

Liland glanced over, his eyes widening in shock at what she had done. He just barely had a chance to open his mouth to yell at her before being tackled to the ground by Rex. The blow of the beast's thick skull against Liland's chest knocked the wind straight from his lungs.

Rose had jumped down from the tree she was in and drove Rex back before helping Liland. Her eyes caught occasional glimpses of Amaya's struggle against Daniël, holding a deep desire to help her. Then she noticed that Hiro was stalking behind her.

Through Daniël's struggle for life, he managed to speak. "You don't want to hurt those you're supposed to protect, do you?" His voice was distorted but his words came without fault—as though the person saying them wasn't the man in front of Amaya, but another being altogether.

Her brown eyes stared into the corrupted man's, sensing deep down that this must be the work of her parents. She wrenched the sword further into Daniël's body, saying around his shoulder,

"Just wait until we find you, you will regret everything." With that, she drove her sword through the man's body.

He screamed like the control over him was gone, mortified, the sound deafening.

Each dog backed off from its opponent and rushed to the aid of their master. They trampled over Amaya, jaws unhinged and claws outstretched for ambush.

All at once, the girl was attacked as blood splattered and ran from opened flesh.

Liland and Rose rushed to her aid, but the brute force of the creatures was overwhelming for the girl, helpless beneath them. She howled in pain, shield flailing and legs flying to fend them off since her sword was lodged inside of Daniël.

Cyero brought himself to his feet, using his scythe to stabilize his footing. Finally, he swung it at the dogs that were attacking Amaya, backing them all away. To his surprise, the Taint receded from the five dogs and Daniël, leaving them lifeless corpses. All but one. Hiro was still managing to breathe without being under the influence of the Taint, but his body was littered with wounds. It was likely his life would soon end too.

Rose rushed to his aid. She wanted to save him if she could and placed her hands on his poor battered body. Tears came to her eyes, realizing the true devastation of this disease. "I don't understand...how did he come out of it?" she asked.

Amaya crawled to her friend and sat up slowly, holding various wounds littered across her body. She ached badly from cuts, scrapes, and bite wounds in her flesh, and her muscles felt as though they were on fire.

Cyero's chest swelled with sadness, his own eyes beginning to water as he mourned the inevitable loss of the poor pup. "Rose...s—stop..." he pleaded with her, his voice slightly distorted as he walked slowly beside the dog. "Look at his condition, he's suffering..." he trailed off.

"That's why I'm trying to save him!" she sobbed as she continued to try. Her heart slowly broke as she knew her efforts would be in vain. She slowly raised her eyes to look at Cyero's, which were welled up with their own tears.

Amaya kneeled down beside her friend and grabbed her hands, gently pulling them away. "Rose...it isn't going to work," she said with a melancholy tone. She noticed that no matter how many times the girl muttered the incantation, the dog wouldn't heal.

Cyero closed his eyes and mustered up his last bit of strength to pick up the bleeding dog, regardless of the fact that the red liquid dripped onto his clothing. "My friend...you will soon be at peace..." he trailed off as his tears finally began to slip from his eyes.

Amaya didn't understand why the god was so emotional over the loss of this dog. But Rose understood perfectly. She knew how much all the creatures of the world must have meant to him; not only that, but he understood how much he suffered from his own affliction.

"I—I...I shall freeze his body and lower his temperature," Cyero said. His eyes began to twitch, his pupils changing dilation every few seconds. "N—No..." he muttered.

"Cyero...?" Amaya said skeptically as she watched the strange behavior.

Fangs grew inside the ice god's mouth and his ears began to fade into black. He growled animalistically at Hiro and clasped his hands around his neck, starting to squeeze it. He held the animal in the air with one hand and stared at his closed eyes, almost as if he was waiting to see what little life was left in him slowly drain out.

"Cyero, what are you doing?" Rose shouted at him as each of them stared at the scene in shock.

Rose got up and ran at the ice god, grabbing his arm to try and pry it back down to make him let go. But with his other hand, Cyero slashed her across the cheek with his nails, which had sharpened to points. She gasped and was taken aback by this, holding her cheek as it bled. He started to growl before putting his hand on his head as his growling turned to sobs. His changed features returned to normal as he dropped the canine body from his hand. "You all need to leave," he said as he held his head.

"But, Cyero—" Liland tried to reason with him, but was quickly cut off.

"Go now! All of you, leave!" he snapped.

The male demigod hesitated for a moment, only to realize what was really going on. "He's right, his condition is nearing its peak, we must leave now," Liland said.

"Don't worry, Cyero! We will help you!" Rose was devastated by this, but Amaya stared with indifferent eyes.

"I know it's sudden, but if you want us to make it to your parents alive, it has to be done," the prophet said and proceeded to guide them out of the forest. The trek was quiet but fast-moving. Once they were a safe distance from the forest, Rose turned her head to Liland.

"None of that made any sense at all...how did Daniël become infected?"

"I've no idea," replied Liland. "All I know is that we need to get to the mountains as soon as possible. It's likely Thosus and Adione have already escaped and have begun wreaking havoc on Folkvangr...and if that's true, then that means Buhus and Vadu have as well," he said.

"We have to go then," Amaya said with urgency as she turned and began walking away from the place they had stopped. Her mind continued to rage. She thought back to when she had moved so impulsively to protect Cyero when he was being hurt. She acted like she did when Rose got hurt...or at least how she used to.

* * *

The moon dimmed upon their long day of travel, its dying rays painting the sky an even deeper black, yet their journey was far from over. They stood before the towering landmass of mountains, staring into the bowels of its entrance. Fear of the unknown haunted them, fatigue weighing on their battered beings. Wind bellowed through its core as the three of them began trekking the makeshift stairs which began at the entrance.

Thankfully, there was only one possible direction—other than backward—to go, that being forward. But deeper in, a light began to filter in throughout the dark, indicating something at its end. They soon discovered a dimly-lit room with stairs that continued on the other side.

Oddly enough, it was empty, or so they thought, as the majority of the room's darkness hid its deeper corners. The travelers were about halfway through the room before hearing the clanking of metal echo through the chasm. They each paused to examine the origin of the noise. The metallic clanging rumbled the area a second time and a growl bellowed from a mysterious creature.

Before they knew it, a triplet of crimson eyes were staring at them from the other end of the room. It stopped them in their tracks and didn't seem to be moving toward them, or at all for that matter.

"It's just as Ruki said...you all would make your way here eventually," a low voice sneered.

Rose shuddered when she heard the name of her father uttered through the lips of the shaded beast. Her father was so close now.

"My father is here," Rose said. "Take us to him and the other three that are working with him." She placed her hand on the hilt of her sword subtly, so as not to cause any sort of alarm to the beast.

But he still noticed her movements and bellowed a chuckle from deep in the pit of his stomach. "You amuse me, child. What is your name?"

"Rose," answered the girl.

"Rose...and the other?" His eyes shifted over to where her friend was standing.

"Amaya," she said.

They saw the eyes disappear into nothingness before reappearing shortly after. "You must be dying to see your parents after so long..." the voice trailed off.

"Quit toying with us...tell us where they are!" Amaya lashed out with her sword, setting the room alight for a few moments.

"You will see them in due time...but they may be closer than you think," the beast replied.

Amaya had been getting ready to ask just what this creature cloaked in a dark enigma had been trying to say, but something dealt her a blunt blow to the head and she collapsed.

Like her, the others standing at her side had fallen to the floor.

* * *

Rose peeled open her eyes, only to be greeted by a stabbing pain all over her head. The air in the room she had found herself in was stale and dry; hot and unpleasant. A groan left her throat as she tried to shake away the grogginess from being unconscious.

Her eyes flicked around in a few different directions so that she could examine her surroundings. There were wooden bars around her. Beside her, Amaya was staring into her lap with furrowed eyebrows.

"A—Amaya? Where are we?" she asked feebly. She felt incredibly weak, even breathing felt like an almost impossible task.

"We were imprisoned," Amaya answered her.

Looking to her other side, she could see that there were a multitude of cages surrounding them, from what she could see in the dim lighting of the room. They were filled with demons; underlings and animals alike. But first and foremost, she saw Liland...and Will.

They were in a cage separate from hers and Amaya's. "Will? Is that you?" she asked.

The demon looked to be in terrible shape, even worse than the girls. His body was dappled with deep bruises, some having even split open with dried blood staining them. One of his arms was broken and his left eye was swollen nearly shut from a deep gash going down it.

When he heard her voice, he looked over at her and the ghost of a smile grew onto his lips. "Rose..." he murmured, his voice hoarse.

"What did they do to you?" she asked, scrambling to one side of the cage.

Will shook his head slowly, closing his eyes as he did so before looking back at her. "Never mind that...you all need to get out of here. Chasaka, Ruki, Sage, Teira...they're all too powerful. It's too late...you have to get out of here while you still have a shred of life left," he explained.

Seeing Will in this state broke Rose's heart and tears stung her eyes. "We aren't dead yet. It isn't too late," she said. "Do you know a way to get out of this?" she asked.

"No," he answered. "These cages were made by Teira...they nullify the use of your powers, so trying to break them is useless."

"There must be a way...we have come this far, we can't stop now," Rose said.

Everyone was silent, like they had all lost every shred of hope. Even Liland was speechless.

Rose lifted herself to her feet, her knees shaking. They felt like jelly and she had to lean her hand against the wall to keep steady. She looked around until she spotted a huge sleeping beast across from them. Could it be the same one that had imprisoned them?

438

"Hey!" she called out to it.

When she saw the two triplets of red eyes flash open, she knew it was the same creature. The beast stood and craned its head to look at Rose. "Quiet your squeaking, rat," he sneered.

"No," she said defiantly. "I have a deal I want to make with you."

"You're in no position to be trying to make a deal," Waru said. But it intrigued him, so he didn't silence her.

"Let us all out...four against one. If we lose, you can do whatever you want with us. If we win, we go to our parents, and you have to return Will's soul to him," Rose said.

Liland, Amaya, and Will all looked at the girl with astonishment on their faces. Had she completely lost her mind?

Waru chuckled in a low tone once more. He knew there was no chance that these washed-up dogs would last even five minutes against him. Hell had starved, battered, and deprived them of sleep—there were too many odds against them.

"I agree." This surprised all of them, especially Rose; she hadn't expected the demon to so readily agree to this.

"Rose, are you mad? Will is in no condition to be fighting," Amaya said.

Will shook his head. "If I'm needed one more time...I'll give it all I have," he said.

The wood bars around them fell away, releasing them all. Almost immediately, Amaya, Rose, and Liland were feeling at least a little stronger now that those traps were gone.

Waru bared his discolored and blood-stained teeth at them. Normally he didn't fancy the time to be messing with prisoners, but the opportunity had been too rich—and it had been so long since he dug his claws into anything.

Growling rumbled in the throat of the dragon-like creature, anticipation rising in his bones as he waited for his now-free prisoners to make the next move. But his six eyes scanned each of them with a look that was indecipherable at first—it almost came across as pitiful. However uncharacteristic of the demon it may have been, it made sense that this was in his eyes. Looking at the four of them all lined up like slaves worked down to the very bones their starved skin was plastered to, was almost more pitiful than the fate they would all soon share.

Amaya was the first to bolt forward into action, having completely underestimated their adversary. They had dealt with huge opponents before, but none like Waru.

It was as though the demon had anticipated her movements and, despite his immense size, was able to knock the girl directly to her side, body scraping the rough floor.

The demon assumed his mortal form and ripped a sword from a sheath which hung at his thigh. In this form, he would be far more agile. He charged the others, sword grasped beside his face as he thrust it forward, his target being Liland.

Liland weaved around the black steel, dipping afterward to plunge forward his lance.

Waru's sword was in front of his lance within moments, emitting a high-pitched shriek from this clash.

The two began a dance of death, exchanging arm swings and grunts with one another; and though it appeared to be a dance, no movement was graceful. It led them dangerously close to the edge of the battle ground, leaving Liland nearly backed into a wall, the blade of that demon a mere hair's breadth from his neck.

"And then there were three..." the demon whispered, the breath from his words hitting Liland's face.

Before his blade had a chance to draw a drop of blood from the demigod, Waru adjusted his grip on its hilt, spun it so it faced downward, blade toward himself before thrusting it backward—right into Will's body.

Will stifled his screams of pain as he stared at the back of the demon's head who had stabbed him while blood drizzled down his chin, falling down to the cold steel below it.

Liland's eyes widened. He had expected to die there, but it was Will who had been hurt instead.

After several stunned moments, the blade was removed from Will's chest, leaving his body with no support with which he could use to stay standing.

Liland moved from the tight space the demon had created to encapsulate him. He held out his hands to help Will, but was quickly yanked back by his shirt and tossed away. Waru abandoned Will to return to his trifles with Liland, who was then aided by Amaya.

But the demon hadn't accounted for Rose, who rushed toward Will to help him.

Will sat limply against the wall, clutching the gushing wound in his chest as he fought for consciousness. With urgency, Rose brought water to Will's wound to clean it and use the spell he had taught her to heal it, but the demon slowly grabbed her hands and gently moved them away, causing the water to splash uselessly beside him. "You have to go and help the others," he said weakly. Rose shook her head, pulling her hands from his grasp as she formed more water in her palms.

"But you will die," she said shakily as she attempted to press the water to his wound a second time.

"There's not enough time. It's too late." Will shook his head slowly as he grasped her hands and moved them aside yet again, this time using both hands and holding on a little tighter to keep her from trying to heal him again.

"I can still heal you if you would just let me." Rose tried to pull her hands away, but his grip was too firm to get out of.

"The others need you," the man said.

"We need you too! I'm not letting you die," Rose argued, still struggling to pull her hands from his hold.

"Rose... please," Will said softly, causing her to stop and look up at him.

"I can't leave you," Rose said as a tear slipped down her cheek.

"But you need to," the demon insisted.

The girl shook her head again as she finally wrenched her hands from him and began to heal him once more, muttering the spell quickly before speaking to him again. "I can still save you— we will win this, and we will get your soul back, and then you can be human again. You don't have to die!" Rose exclaimed as her eyes focused hard on the wound, willing it to heal. Will smiled a bit despite the pain in his chest.

"You've already done so much for me—you reminded me what it was like to trust, to have friends...to love." Rose was caught off guard and looked back up at him as he said this. "But you and I both know that there's no time for this. So go.

Please," Will finished. "But before you do..." There wasn't much time left for him to continue talking, he knew. "There is a spell in the book that can help you defeat your parents, if you find yourselves unable to beat them with your strength alone. It will enhance your powers. It's near the end of the book, but don't try to use any of the other spells there. They're too dangerous." His eyes were directly on hers. "And whatever you do, don't let your parents get their hands on it."

Rose nodded, staring at him for a moment before finally moving her hands from his wound. "I'll come back for you," she promised, to which Will smiled.

With the last of his strength, the demon leaned forward, his lips inches from hers before stopping abruptly. His glistening eyes looked into hers for a moment. "Thank you," Will whispered finally before leaning back against the wall, his eyes barely open.

"Please at least try to heal yourself," Rose said.

"I will, I promise," Will replied. He weakly cupped some of the water beside him and placed it on his chest as he began to recite the spell.

Rose lingered there for a moment, wiping at the tears that streamed down her face before standing and running toward the others, forcing herself not to look back as she did.

Will stopped reciting the spell and watched her retreating form with a pained smile before closing his teary eyes.

The others were already trying to drive back the pursuing force; he was strong and agile, making it almost impossible to land even a single blow on him. But there wasn't much he could do when faced with Rose's weapon.

Anger scrunching her face, Rose had nocked an arrow between the string and arrow rest. After letting it fly, it was fast to strike Waru in the nape of his neck. The pure water flowing around the steel of the arrow burned the demon and steam wafted away from the wound that slowly ate away at his skin, peeling away the flawless purities of his mortal form, and uncovering the beast hiding beneath it.

She pulled another arrow from the quiver at her side and let that one fly as well, this time striking the large beast in his impure form. With him stunned and in pain, Liland was able to lash him with his lance and a bolt of lightning.

Footsteps dashing forward sounded through the room while Amaya chased her victim, leaping up to his head and raising her arms above her head to deliver the final blow. And at last it was dealt; the steel of Sacris Ignem plunged straight into the bone making up the beast's skull.

Distorted screams rumbled in the air around them until silence covered them within the next moment, the demon dissolving away into ash, leaving Amaya to plummet to the ground.

Rose and Amaya looked at one another, one sending the other a weary smile. But Amaya could feel nothing but pain and a desire for more justice than had been given to her.

There was a flash of soft light behind them, and upon noticing it, Rose turned immediately to run toward Will and knelt down beside him. He looked at her with a weak smile, his newly-reverted brown eyes half-closed but trained on her for a moment before slowly closing them. His demonic features had gone away.

Rose tried once more to heal him now that he was unconscious and could say no words to tell her to stop. She tried while the others paced behind her, watching her try to make the man live.

Liland kneeled beside her and placed a finger to Will's nose. Cautiously, he brought his gaze to meet Rose's which was busy focusing on the deep red below them.

"Rose," Amaya said.

The girl knew what her friend was going to say, she knew it down to the tone in her voice with which she would deliver it. But she wouldn't allow it.

"Stop," she said, "I need to focus."

Liland and Amaya shared the same melancholy look with one another, both knowing exactly what Rose needed to hear to get her to stop trying to pick up the pieces of a heart which had shattered into smithereens.

"He—"

Rose burst into tears at hearing just the simple pronoun to describe the one she was trying to save. "Don't say it, please." She dropped her head between the arms which were firmly placed upon his unmoving chest and closed her watering eyes.

Liland shifted on his knees and firmly removed the girl from the puddle of blood she was kneeling in. There was no time to be doing useless things. "He's dead, Rose."

Rose felt her chest set on fire, creating an obstruction to her breathing which she needed so that she could have room for the sobs that left her throat. Her hand was clamped over her chest as though it matched that of Will's. It may as well have.

445

"He finally got his soul back, after all that time, a—and he died before he could..." Rose choked up, unable to continue speaking.

Amaya looked at Liland after having set her sympathetic eyes upon Rose while she cried. It was best to let her mourn. After all, what use was there in continuing forward if Rose couldn't even stand on her shaking legs?

But when her crying didn't cease, Liland forced her to stand, her hyperventilations doing nothing to blow away the hair sticking to her face. "Rose, it's time to continue," he said.

She knew she needed to keep going, to push forward, to not give up—but her heart was gluing her in place.

"I knew I heard something. You see, Chasaka?" a voice from behind made them turn.

22: MATERNAL BLOOD

Amaya, my dear, what happened to your lovely long hair?"
Chasaka's voice echoed in the chasm.

Amaya's chest tightened as she witnessed her father and mother emerge from the shadows along with Rose's too. At last, they were all in front of her, a sword's length away. If she moved swiftly, she could behead them in one fell swoop and, clutching the hilt of her blade, she swung forward. Ruki thrust forth the trident in his hands and caught it between two of the three prongs.

"Is that any way to greet your parents after twelve long years?" he asked, shoving her sword away.

Amaya huffed a breath of air through her nose, her teeth clenched absentmindedly.

"Don't be rash," Liland said softly to her.

Her eyes flicked toward her father. "I was promised death if I raised my blade against him again. I don't see why I shouldn't continue."

Rose could hardly contain herself. Seeing the faces of her parents, which she could only remember with smiles upon them, made her warm inside. For a moment, she forgot their wrongdoings; the lives they took in cold blood with their own hands and the ones their pawns took. The one she had come to love, the sanity of her best friend, and many others she would yet discover. She could have willed her legs forward to embrace them if only she hadn't remembered all of those things at once. Her feet were glued in place.

"Come now...you wouldn't wish to end up like your uncle, would you?" Teira said to Amaya.

Amaya widened her eyes, her sword lowering, the blade clanking on the floor. "My uncle..." she murmured. For whatever reason, the image of her meeting her father in the village that had burned to the ground came to mind and a paralyzing realization struck her. "You." She pointed the tip of her sword at her father. "WHAT DID YOU DO TO MY UNCLE?" she screamed. Like an angry cat, she bristled. With her core tight, she felt the world around her begin to decay. She suspected exactly what Chasaka might say to that.

Both Liland and Rose dropped their jaws.

"I murdered him...and then the toxic monarchy of Lucus fell," Chasaka stated flatly.

Amaya's steel-toed greaves thundered against the ground of the mountain as she stormed toward her father, her shield and sword raised, one to protect, the other to kill. The pure rage in her eyes was like wildfire to the calm forest that was Chasaka's eyes. In the split second it took to reach him, Amaya wondered how he could keep such a stagnant expression after admitting to killing her uncle; his own flesh and blood.

This time she wasn't stopped by anyone—just some unknown force behind her. Within moments, her hands were restrained behind her back, weapons disappearing into nothing. These hands she felt on her wrists were freezing compared to her own. She turned back, only to see a pair of red eyes staring back at her. She gasped inadvertently upon seeing that it was Cyero who was holding her back. The soul that once dwelled behind those eyes appeared to be swallowed by a sea of sin and corruption. The god—no—the man she had come to know as a companion was no longer broadcasting through his irises of blue, but instead trapped in a void of crimson.

Her gaze upon his only lasted a split moment, within which she internalized the loss set before her, and then she turned back to the man controlling him. She was right in her father's face and could go no farther no matter how much she tried to struggle and fight against the grip that bound her hands together. A smirk had grown onto his lips. "I see so much of myself in you... it makes me so proud," he said. "You have something I want," he said to all three of them.

"We're willing to make a deal with you," Teira said. "Hand over the book in your possession, and we will relinquish the curse on the gods...If you do so willingly, we will spare your lives and theirs...if not, we will have no choice but to take it by force."

"You bastards," Amaya growled. "Why would we do that?"

"Hold on," Rose interjected. "What will you do with the book once it's in your possession?"

"Come now, Rose...Don't you want to see the world restored to peace? Will it matter what we do with the book in the end?" Ruki asked her.

Amaya had turned her head back, staring at her friend. "Can you give us time to consider?" Rose asked suddenly.

Liland gasped. "What?"

"You can't be serious!" yelled Amaya.

Rose's eyes flicked toward her friend first, trying to convey silently that it would be better to weigh their options rather than blindly decline the offer. But Amaya was blind to the possibility. All she could see was the danger and deception being presented, knowing that handing the book to them could be the jewel in the crown of their plan. Though she wasn't sure how they discovered that the book was in their possession, she had an idea.

"Very well," said Ruki. "You will have no more than an hour to give us your decision...but choose wisely." His eyes flicked toward the others and urged them to follow along.

Cyero's hands fell away from Amaya after that, and he began to depart toward the stairs with them. But as they walked, Sage glanced back at the group of three behind her.

She stopped. "Hold on," she said, causing the others to stop and turn toward her. "I'll stay with them to ensure they don't conspire against us."

Chasaka's eyes flicked toward both Teira and Ruki, who then nodded their heads in agreement. "Fine then," he said and leaned closer to her. "Alert us as soon as you know anything."

Sage listened as their footsteps faded from her earshot and kept her eyes upon the others. Slowly, she approached them and took note that Rose had been watching her carefully.

"What are you still doing here? Can't you leave us to make our decision in peace?" the blonde asked. Her eyes were narrowed at the woman. She may have felt differently about Sage and those she worked with before, but now she wished for nothing more than to end the suffering they had brought upon the world.

"Rose, please," Sage said softly. "I want to help you."

The air around them fell silent, like an empty field lying between two distant forests on a calm day. But the atmosphere felt far from calm, especially with how Amaya's eyes bore into those of her mother's, brown like her own.

"Leave now," Amaya hissed. "If anything, you will wait for our guard to drop and strike when we least expect it."

Sage shook her head. Amaya's hostility drove knives into her chest that made her lower her head, as if in shame of herself. "I'm so sorry for everything we have put you through," she began. "For leaving you in solitude for so long. If I could take it all back, I would; I swear it, I would."

A loud clap broke the tense air. Amaya's hand had slammed into her mother's face, causing her head to jerk away. But she didn't retaliate. Her only response was a whimper of pain and sadness.

"Don't speak such swindling words, vile woman. If you had any interest in stopping this, you had all the means to do so," Amaya said. "And at the end of it all, you still choose to tease me with that which I desire most. If only you were capable of sincerity."

Sage stayed silent and dared not to meet the eyes of the daughter she had let down. She knew that betrayal was where Amaya's rage had stemmed from, and she couldn't bring herself to be angry over any of it. "You're right, Amaya..." she said in a tone that contrasted her daughter's. "It was my negligence and foolishness which perpetuated all of this...it could have been avoided, somehow or another, I could have helped...but I was afraid." She lifted her gaze to meet Amaya's, like a tiny drop of water to a blazing flame. "It was too late by the time I opened my eyes to the cruelty. I was afraid if I spoke against them, I might be killed."

With a furrowed brow, Amaya reached forward and grabbed her mother by the throat, squeezing with all her might. Sage's hands flew up to hers in reaction, trying to pry them away, but she still refused to use force to do so.

"You're nothing to me," Amaya growled, though her words lacked the venom she once pumped them full of. It had been stifled by a hitch in her breath, the quivering of her lower lip. "You revoked your own title of 'mother.' And I—" A tear had been about to slip from her eyes until her arm had been wrenched away from Sage's neck.

With anger in her eyes, she turned to see it had been Rose who did this.

"Amaya, stop," Rose insisted. "Can't you that see she's genuinely shameful for what she's done?" she asked. The two locked gazes for a moment before Amaya ripped her hand from her friend's grasp.

"You wanted to consider giving them a book of spells that could allow them to do just what we have been trying to stop them from doing," she hissed back.

"That isn't it at all," Rose quickly shot back. She glanced at Sage who was rubbing her neck to ease the pain her daughter had caused. Something inside of her begged her not to trust the woman, yet her mind still brought her back to the welcoming smile Sage always wore across her lips; the laughs they shared. She knew Amaya couldn't be so blind to not picture it as well. And perhaps that was why she was so angry; she was conflicted by the forces of past and present battling inside of her, tearing at her insides. She wanted desperately to soothe that pain.

Rose closed her eyes, knowing what she needed to do. "I wanted to make time for us to figure out a plan...if we go in blindly, we risk doing something careless," she said.

"So you announce it right in front of her," Amaya growled, eyes glaring back at Sage.

"Please," begged the woman. "I want to help—"

"Then prove yourself," said Rose. "What can you offer? Anything would be helpful."

"Hold on," Liland cut in. "I have to side with Amaya here. Are you sure we can really trust her?" he asked.

Rose looked at her companion with uncertainty, which was rather worrisome to both Liland and Amaya. "In honesty...I'm not," she replied. "But I don't see any other option for how we can come out of this without more death."

"I can prove myself," Sage said. "I can tell you what the plan was, through and through," she added.

Amaya crossed her arms, looking at her expectantly. "How can we be sure you aren't lying?" she asked.

"You can't," Sage quickly answered. "But I'm saying with all my heart that I want to preserve and help fix what is left of this broken world and forge a path to mending it. If that means my final moments are here helping you put an end to this madness, then so be it."

Amaya still seemed unconvinced, but Liland and Rose were more satisfied with her answer. "Go on," her daughter pressed.

Sage thought for a moment, trying to gather all that had happened up until that point. "I would like to say it began when all four of us faced the unfairness this world had to offer. Chasaka was alienated in his own home, with only Kye to remind him of the boundaries that separated him from a normal human. He murdered his own father to free himself from the binds that kept him tied to a life of hurt and torment...all of us had similar stories, really. I was taken away and tortured for years by a cult that wanted to erase our kind from existence. Ruki's stepmother shamed and abused him, and Teira had the rights of her own body stripped away from her.

The world turned its back on us because of things we couldn't change...and I'm sorry that you both were dragged into the world already bearing immense weight," she explained.

Their stories were hard to hear, but they sounded familiar, at least to Rose and Amaya, and even Liland could identify with some parts of it. "That's truly awful," he said. "I can't fully blame you for turning your back on the world when it turned its back on you. But all of this...what does it prove in the end?" he asked.

"I don't understand," Amaya said. "If your plan was to do this from the very beginning, then why did you have us? Why did you bring us into the world knowing you would just destroy it in the end?" Sadness diluted by rage filled the chambers of her heart. She felt the spindles of her being reaching out for a connection that would never come.

"It began as part of our plan...It sounds cruel, but that was where the idea originated from. You see, the two of you are the direct descendants of Noctis and Avius, something we discovered reading a book of prophecies. That means that you both have the ability to end the cycle of reincarnation, a vital step to our plan. But...from it, we actually grew to love each other," Sage replied as a tear slipped from her eyes. "In the moments your father and I spent together, we felt our pain slowly melt into something warmer than that...and I can only envision that Ruki and Teira felt the same. Somewhere along the way, their vision grew clouded by that pain and still, they wished to destroy the unjust world and create a balanced one in the end—which is surprising, considering everything your parents went through to have you." She looked at Rose as she spoke.

The blonde girl stopped, an uneasy feeling coming over her body. "What does that mean?" she asked.

Sage looked down at her hands and fiddled with her fingers. "Ruki and Teira aren't your real mother and father," she said.

Rose's heart skipped an entire beat. In fact, she could swear she died at that moment. She felt like her body had just been plunged into a sea of winter, her face going pale. Her stomach felt nauseous and she swallowed hard to keep herself from throwing up everywhere. Amaya stared at her friend's face, watching her life collapse right before her eyes but holding the catastrophic pain within. It was clear she became numb on the outside—while inside she was being torn apart.

While Rose fought this inner war, Sage continued. "Teira found out that she was unable to have children herself, more than a few times, which she and Ruki were devastated about. But an offer they couldn't refuse came upon them. A giant metal creature flew down from the clouds, different than what the Astral Clan used to use, and they offered them a child from the heavens. That child was you, Rose," she said.

"But then, how does she still possess the powers of a demigod?" Amaya asked her.

"Of that, I'm not sure," Sage answered. "That's everything I know."

Liland had his eyes on Rose the whole time Sage spoke, noticing how torn she was over the subject, and it shocked him when she completely avoided it. "What did they want the book for?" she asked.

Rose breathed in deeply, trying to force herself away from the pain it caused her. But she couldn't stop thinking of the dreams which haunted her in the night, of the dark figures looming over her and stealing her away from familiarity. Still, she forced them out of her mind, or at least to the back of it. They needed to focus on the task at hand. She couldn't worry about her personal woes now.

Even Sage was surprised by her reluctance to continue on the subject, and Amaya had been about to pry, but stopped as her mother continued. "There is a spell inside that has the ability to increase their hold on the gods with the Taint. The Taint itself is like a mind control which we can manipulate. For now, the Taint is temporary and will soon recede if they don't get the book to complete the spell," she explained.

"Then we burn the book," Amaya said and crossed her arms. "Part of me still doesn't trust you...but it's all we have to go off of. Thank you for helping us," she said.

Sage smiled, a warmness filling her as her daughter dropped her hostility for just a moment. "Of course," she said. "I don't mean to go all soft at a critical moment but...I truly did miss you, after all these years. I'm happy that I was able to see your face once more."

A knot balled up in Amaya's throat and tears stung her eyes. Despite all the anguish and wrath that vibrated within her veins, in the end, she really did miss her mother. "I missed you too, mother," she said, surprising even herself.

Sage leaned forward after that and embraced her child in a hug. Amaya couldn't bring herself to think of all the trifle and hardship that would have forced herself away. It felt like Heaven to finally experience love where she once thought it dead, never to return.

As this took place, Rose looked down, pursing her lips as tears came to her own eyes. She sobbed once before feeling a pair of arms fall around her. "Are you all right?" Liland's voice whispered softly to her, not wishing to alert the others of her crying.

Shocked by this, Rose shook him away from herself and then squeezed out a quiet, "No."

Liland looked the young woman in the eyes, his eyebrows pulling together, waiting for something more.

"All this time I've been chasing after something I once had. I was so close to having it again before it was stolen from beneath me...only to now realize I was chasing after nothing in the end," she explained.

Liland offered her a sympathetic look and grabbed one of her hands gently. "It will be okay," he said.

"I'm truly sorry, Rose," Sage said, causing them both to look over. She and Amaya had broken away from one another as well. "I wish I could have told you much sooner than now. But I'm glad that now you know the truth."

Rose hesitated for a moment, shaking off Liland's hold on her once more, then asked, "Where did I come from, then? If they aren't my real parents, then who is?"

"I don't know a lot in that regard. Ruki and Teira kept a lot to themselves...but they said the people who offered you to them were called—" She was cut off by a whimper of agony. The blade of Sacris Ignem had been thrust violently through her midsection, blood taking the place of words Rose longed to hear. The vital fluid streamed down her lips as it filled her mouth and the sword was removed. Her limp body fell to the floor right in front of Amaya, revealing Chasaka standing behind it. "Amaya, I love you..." she whispered over a pool of blood.

Chasaka looked displeased at the very least as he watched his wife's body collapse. "What a shame...but I guess there really is no need for all four of us to complete this." Beside him stood Cyero, glaring at all of them. "She was a fool...thinking she could defy us beneath our own noses."

Amaya screamed as loud as her lungs could carry her voice, her legs racing toward him. But before she could reach him, his fist collided with her jaw, sending her to the ground. Behind her, Liland charged forward, removing his lance from its dormant state and thrusting it forth. Chasaka watched him with emotionless eyes. The spike of his lance was a mere hair's breadth from cutting through his clothing before Cyero charged forward, taking him by the wrists, and within moments the weapon clanged onto the rock floor as Liland's hands were secured behind his back.

Chasaka walked past them, sheathing his sword with his sights set upon Rose as she stood frozen in fear of the chaos that had just unfolded in front of her. He reached forward and grabbed her by the hem of her dress. "Give me the book or your friend will die right now." He gestured to the two of them, Liland held back with one of Cyero's hands while the other held a huge icicle to his head.

Rose didn't know what else to do. She felt helpless and, with shaky hands, reached into the satchel bag at her side, handing him the book.

Chasaka took the object from her and briefly inspected it before shoving her to the ground. "Cyero, you will imprison them once again to be dealt with later," he said. He turned away after that, and as he did, ice formed around Liland's hands, encasing them within while Chasaka approached him, taking him by a fistful of hair on the top of his head. "And you will be coming with me...you can help me read this text, prophet."

Rose and Amaya stood to their feet, recovering from their fall. They watched as Cyero's scythe formed between his hands. "What are we going to do? There are only two of us now; we can't possibly take him down ourselves!" Rose exclaimed.

Amaya chanced a look toward her fallen mother before forcing herself to avert her gaze. "Oh, we will," she murmured softly as Sacris Ignem formed within one hand while her shield, Ventum Praesidium, formed in the other. "I'm not dying until I drive my blade so deeply in their chests that they feel the agony of each and every life they took."

"But we shouldn't be rash. Remember, this body is the real Cyero. He can only take so many hits until he's killed." Rose pursed her lips and looked toward her angered friend. "Wait, I have an idea!" she said. But by then, it was too late. Cyero had come barreling forward, swinging his scythe at them to drive them apart.

"You had better say it quickly!" Amaya shouted back.

"The whistle on your neck, you can use it to summon that demon from before," Rose answered as she dodged another swipe from Cyero. He clenched his teeth and reacted to her statement, spinning around to Amaya before taking another swipe at her which she deflected with her sword.

Despite knowing what dangers might come from summoning a demon, Amaya quickly took the small orifice hanging around her neck between her lips and blew into it. The sound that resulted was high-pitched and ear-splitting. Amaya had to cover her ears as she blew hard into it.

Within seconds, the creature appeared out of a bog of shadows in front of her. But they quickly realized that he was badly injured. Blood and wounds painted his fur and one of his ears was missing. Amaya only had the time to take a quick glance at his condition before being forced to parry another attack.

"Oh, the lot of you again," growled Athelstan before distancing himself a bit.

"Cyero told me you would help us if we used that whistle you gave him," Amaya replied while closing the distance between them and herself.

Athelstan returned to her a brief growl before extending the claws he was equipped with. "Well, you couldn't have called at a better time," he said before bolting forward then disappearing into thin air. "It's a minefield up there." Cyero gasped and fell to the ground with a grunt after that, both girls noticing blood coming from the backs of his ankles.

Athelstan crawled out from within another shadow and looked at the two with his yellowish eyes which had only a sliver of black slicing through the middle of them.

"Then the other gods *have* escaped?" Rose asked him.

"Every single one of them," answered the demon before looking back at Cyero. "So what's your plan for taking care of this one?"

"We only need to subdue him for a while," she replied.

Cyero started growling as though he were no longer human, fingers grabbing handfuls of his own hair as he pulled at it, his scythe crashing to the ground. Then at last his body changed shape into his much larger wolf form where he then let out a more animalistic growl. "Then it's taken care of," Athelstan replied.

As his massive wolf body charged at them, Athelstan, too, shifted his shape into that of a humanoid one. His body was still bloodied from the plentiful wounds that dappled his skin with two horns protruding from his forehead. He held out his hands toward Cyero, Amaya and Rose still readying their weapons to hold him back. But before he could reach them, the shadows in the room changed with him and Cyero was stopped mid-run. Something black and oozing had latched onto both his hind legs, restraining him from moving any farther. He fought and growled as he writhed in the grasp of the shadows.

"I can't hold him here for very long, so if you don't want him dead, I suggest you both come up with a solution," Athelstan told them.

Amaya and Rose looked at one another, silently trying to figure out a way to keep him restrained. "Use your earth powers," Amaya told her. "Like your mother did to keep us held prisoner. I bet you could do the same to him," she said.

Rose nodded her head and held out her hand toward Cyero. When she did, the sound of splintering wood echoed throughout the chasm of the mountain as a cage wrapped around Cyero. Upon doing so, Athelstan's shadows had fallen away from the beast, who tried desperately to claw and bite his way through his binds.

Amaya breathed a sigh of relief, her gaze lingering for a moment on Cyero before returning it to Rose. "So...what is our plan of attack now?" she asked. "Chasaka stole the book."

Rose nodded her head then reached into the sleeve of her dress to pull out a wrinkled piece of parchment paper. "While you and Liland were trying to deal with him, I ripped out the page...at least I hope this is it," she said while scanning it over.

Athelstan looked over the young woman's shoulder at the piece of paper in her hands. "You can read this jumble of lines on paper?" he asked, pulling a frustrated face.

Rose gripped the paper a bit tighter. "Before he died, Will and I studied this book for a while, so I picked up a few of the symbols...I just hope I can read it without the translator...there was one written in the back of the book. I forgot about it in the moment," she explained.

"What's it for?" asked the demon.

Rose flipped over the paper upon finishing reading the other page. "They are spells. Will told me there would be dangerous spells in the back of the book. Like, look here at this one," she said and showed both of them the paper. It depicted a man who appeared to be sucking the life from a tree. Then in the next, it showed him growing flowers and different plantlife with his hands. "This one says it's possible to steal away the life force from another creature and use it for yourself. Even without these spells, who knows what other ones they might have access to." She looked toward Amaya, who appeared to be deep in thought.

"Then we should try to use these two ourselves. We can take a few moments to remember the incantations and then use them against them," she said.

Rose turned her attention toward Athelstan. "What will you do?" she asked.

"You're the ones who called me here, you tell me," answered the lynx-turned-human. He crossed his arms. "I could always come with both of you for support."

"We don't need any more casualties." Amaya's expression was tense. "You can stay here and ensure Cyero doesn't escape while we're fighting, is that clear?"

It was obvious in Athelstan's own features that he wasn't pleased to be taking orders from a human girl. But he nodded anyway. "Fine then, I didn't want to be risking my neck for a couple of meat sacks anyway," he growled then turned from them and assumed his animal form once more. "I'll stay."

With that, Amaya and Rose began examining the paper once more, reading as much as they could within the course of about fifteen minutes. It didn't seem like enough time with the way their minds were racing, flipping through thoughts of their next task. They still needed to find Liland, so they couldn't afford any more time to be wasted on memorizing the two spells. Amaya took the paper into her hand once they were finished and allowed her fire to burn it to ash.

Rose slung Diluvium across her back while she readied her sword in the other. "We have to hurry and find Liland...I hope they haven't killed him," she said.

Amaya took one last glance toward Cyero as her friend began walking toward the stairwell that their parents had left through.

"Hold on," she said and parted in the other direction, toward the cage that the god had been held captive inside. She kept her distance, seeing as he was eyeing her with blood-thirsty eyes.

Her heart thundered in her chest and ears, knowing what was upon Rose and herself. She had full understanding that she may not live to see the light of day again. That she may not live to see Rose again, or Liland...or Cyero. "Thank you for everything, Cyero," she said, hoping her words would reach him. "I was never the kindest to you and I'm sorry for that...but if we somehow pull this off, I hope we can see each other again," she added then looked toward the floor. "And if not, my memories with you shall be counted among the ranks of those I cherish that I'll take with me to my bitter end." She wished to reach her hand forward to touch the god's snout, but withheld from doing so, knowing she may lose her hand if she tried.

"All right then, get on with it...the world isn't going to stay intact forever, you know," sneered Athelstan.

Amaya looked back at him before taking a deep, albeit shaky, breath. She clenched her fists, a sudden rush of determination filling her. And with that, she turned and began walking back toward her friend.

"Rose...before we go, there is something I wish to say to you as well," she said, stopping her friend from going forward.

"What is it?" she asked her, noting the dreadful look on her face.

"I wanted to apologize for the awful things I've said and done to you. For burning your hands, for disregarding you and everyone else...it was all uncalled for and I wish I had treated you better...even though I thought my actions were right," she said. "The way I treated you was wrong...and if we make it through this alive, I promise I won't ever let my selfishness cloud our friendship again."

Tears began to fill Rose's eyes and she reached forward to wrap Amaya in a hug. "I accept your apology...and I'm sorry too for the things that I said to you," she murmured softly through a sob.

The two girls stayed that way for a moment before realizing that they must part and face their parents. "Let's go," Amaya muttered, drawing her sword and shield as they tread forth toward their final ascent.

23: Corrupt Blood

An arid wind collided with Chasaka, Ruki, and Teira's skin as they stood atop the mountain outstretched toward the moon that painted the dark sky a deep red and was shrouded by bundles of clouds. On their makeshift platform, they sat, tearing through each page of the book in search of the spell they needed.

Tears ran down Teira's face, glistening in the faint glow of the moon. "At last...we will be able to create the world anew...to walk forward from this era of darkness and corruption," she said. "We must find that spell."

Happiness swelled in each of their hearts as they stood around Chasaka, devouring each page of the book.

"I feel like I can empathize with the gods who created this world...seeing it start over and become anew...clear with a fresh slate..." Ruki trailed off and breathed a sigh of relief. "And after our lives are taken, that will truly be the end of all gods," he said.

* * *

Rose and Amaya ascended the main staircase of the mountain, their footsteps kicking up dust as they climbed. It wasn't long before they heard weeping.

Looking at one another for a brief moment, the two decided to investigate the noises they heard. The staircase trailed off to both left and right slightly below the steps they had halted atop, heading backward from the trail. They chose the left path which led to a smaller chasm, similar in layout to the one they had departed from, and found Liland inside a cage. He lay against the ground, the sobbing they had heard was coming from his pained voice.

"Liland?" asked Rose timidly.

The prophet looked up, strands of his hair plastered to his face while his reddened eyes—or rather, reddened *eye*—searched to see who had been speaking. His sight was too blurred by tears to make out a distinct shape and blood ran down from where his right eye should have been. "R—Rose...? Is that you?" he asked. He wasn't sure if he was hallucinating or if it really was Rose who spoke to him.

"It's me, what happened to you?" she asked and kneeled before the cage.

His visible hand shook as he tried to ball it into a fist, the other was clamped beneath his body. "Y—Your parents, they... they tried to get me to decipher the pages...i—in the book...but the page they needed, it was missing and I..." he trailed off, trying to lift his body to show what he was clutching. It was a gaping hole within his body; the hand over it shook violently. Tears rolled down both Rose and Amaya's faces as soon as they saw this. Neither could contain their emotions.

"L—Liland," Rose said, a sob shaking her voice.

467

"It's all right...I've accepted my fate," he said before letting his body fall to the floor once more, he had no strength to hold it up even a little.

Rose shook her head quickly and grabbed onto the bars of his cage. "Amaya and I...we're putting a stop to this now," she said.

The prophet's remaining eye shifted up to the girl, his free hand reaching toward the bars of the cage, trailing up one of the ones upon which Rose's hands had been clasped. He touched one of his bloody fingers to hers. "Thank you," was all he could manage. His eye wanted to close. He was too tired to remain cognitive.

"LILAND!" Rose yelled as she slammed her body against the cage. Her shouting scared the prophet's eye opened once more. "Keep your eye open," she said with anger across her face. "No matter what. I know it's dark and I know you're bleeding a lot, but just..." she trailed off. "Focus...focus on anything, stay awake...You will live to see tomorrow no matter what."

Liland's eye got teary again and he cried as he had been before. "I will. I'll stay awake," he said to her.

Amaya wiped away her tears and kept her eyes on Liland while Rose got to her feet again. "Come on," said the redhead, her gaze returning to her friend. "We need to find them."

"They went higher up after they left me here...I believe all that's left is the peak...be careful," Liland offered them feebly.

Rose nodded her head, and with one last glance at the man who had helped them through their many hardships, the two made way for the stairs once more. The blonde girl could hardly contain the rage boiling within her. Ruki, Teira, and Chasaka had taken and damaged everything she cared about. The man she loved, her companions; even her own name had been tainted in the blood of their betrayal. She now understood what it was like to hold onto just one thread of patience, to feel how Amaya had felt since the very beginning.

They emerged at the top from the stairwell, the moon projecting a harsh beam of red piercing through the darkness and illuminating the platform, revealing the remaining three at the top: Chasaka, Ruki, and Teira—the wrath, the evil, the destruction. Amaya and Rose watched the backs of their heads. They were oblivious to their presence until the sound of Sacris Ignem scraping against her sheath as it was drawn alerted them to it. All three of them turned to find their daughters, anger and irritation clashing between their eyes.

"This is your final chance for surrender," Ruki howled against the silence. He showed them the insides of the book, a page torn from a non-existent gradient. "Maybe you thought we wouldn't notice...foolish of you to interfere."

"The page was burned," Rose replied. "There is no longer a reason to plead innocence, to run, to hide. Here we stand atop the peak of everything, and still you plead your cause will be just. You will claim the lives you took weren't for naught and you say we would regret our decision when death is inevitable either way. Only yours will be certain."

"The world will mend once the fail stitch is removed," Amaya added.

Chasaka glared at them then ripped the book from Ruki's hands by the pages, tearing some away while others remained partially intact. He discarded it like it meant nothing, the pages left in his hands burning away into ash. "You've ruined everything..." the man trailed off. "Ruki. Teira. We will need to find another way to end the cycle. I can't bear to look at their faces alive any longer." He drew his own sword from its sheath and charged toward them. In turn, Teira and Ruki slid their own weapons out, following after him.

With his free hand, flames burst through to strike the two of them, driving the two girls apart to escape the blast. Chasaka swung his sword left where Rose had jumped out of the way. She prepared to make her own move but was knocked off her feet by the shaft of Ruki's trident.

At the same moment, Teira and Amaya shared their own exchange. The sound of their swords clashing together reverberated off the air, like white noise in their ears which were filled with blood carrying adrenaline to their veins.

Teira's skill with her sword was quickly made evident as Sacris Ignem was torn from Amaya's grasp by a swipe of the other woman's blade. It crashed to the ground and as she thrust forth to stab, Amaya brought her shield in front of herself to block it, staggering both of them for a moment.

Teira dove back toward the girl immediately, taking a couple more swipes at her in places where she looked unstable. But Amaya held her ground, keeping steady as she blocked each blow. She grunted every time the blade of Teira's sword clashed with her shield, knowing she wouldn't be able to defend for very long.

Teira sneered at Amaya as she put some space between the two of them, only to go in for an overhand slice. But Amaya parried her once again, and again when Teira threw out a sideswipe. Amaya tried to push back, which led to her failure. Putting space between Teira and her shield only served to allow her to knock the steel from Amaya's hands, cracking her blade.

While Teira recovered from it, Amaya burst forward, closing in around her sword, even knowing it left herself vulnerable. Amaya grabbed her shoulders then drove her knee up into Teira's stomach. But Teira twisted just in time, taking the blow to her side.

Dropping her sword, Teira grabbed Amaya's wrists and spun her, slamming her down against the ground, letting her body weight cushion her own fall. Both hit the ground with a grunt, only for Teira to grab a fistful of Amaya's hair and start slamming her head back against the ground. Every time her head smashed against the rockface, it exploded with pain, her ears ringing while she cried out, trying to free herself. But it was hard to focus on finding the strength to do so with how badly it hurt.

Once Teira was satisfied, she stopped and let Amaya's head rest on the ground, only to grab her own sword from beside them and raise it up and to plunge it into her heart. But her hands were unstable and she failed to do so, striking her shoulder instead.

Pain flooded Amaya like a frozen lake rushing through her body before filling with the warmth of her blood. She writhed beneath the blade that impaled her then lifted a shaking hand to blast Teira with a wall of fire, driving her back with Sacris Ignem in hand. In the chaos, Amaya failed to notice Rose calling out to her as she rushed toward her.

Rose had somehow managed to fend off Ruki and Chasaka, but only for a moment as they were charging headstrong toward her. Ruki reached out with a vine of water and yanked back on his daughter's ankle. She skidded against the rough mountain surface, her shoulder scraping as the sleeve of her dress tore apart. Rose chanced a glance back at her father, who was nearly upon her, then focused her attention back to her friend. Her mother stood back with her hand on her face, trying to heal the burn Amaya had left behind.

Rose shut her eyes and braced herself. Then the ground beneath their feet began to rumble, it cracked and crumbled away, leaving them all to crash down to a lower level of the mountain. The explosion of rock left a cloud of dust in its wake. Even dizzy and in pain, Amaya managed to break her fall with her wind then staggered her way to take cover behind a pile of rubble that had fallen from the ceiling. Rose found her way toward her own set of rocks and readied herself behind them, trying to allow herself a moment to recover from both the fall and a few of her earlier wounds.

When she came up with the idea, Rose hadn't pictured the aftermath to leave behind the blinding dust cloud that now blanketed the room they were in and tried to keep her ears alerted to any sounds.

Fear collided in Rose's chest, ears picking up the pattering of feet drawing nearer to her. The dust petered apart for just a moment, allowing her to see Amaya clutching her left shoulder behind a pile of rocks. Rose scrambled over toward her, trying not to make a sound while doing so. When Rose appeared in front of her, Amaya jostled, frightened for a moment and then relieved when she recognized her friend.

"Are you all right?" Rose asked Amaya before her eyes flicked toward the wound she was grabbing, blood oozing through her fingers, painting them red.

"The bitch stabbed me good," Amaya spat, trying not to look at her shoulder.

Rose brought water into her hands then let it spill into the wound. The girl winced and hissed through her teeth as it stung her. Both perked their heads when they heard the sound of shoes scraping against the debris once again.

"You're both cowards...hiding from us," Ruki spat. He sounded distant.

"Come out, brats!" Chasaka growled. They heard fire sear from behind them then blast a hole in the side of the mountain, allowing in some of the red glow from outside. His voice sounded farther away than Ruki's.

Rose looked back at her friend. "I need you to buy me some time. If you use the spell, you should be able to distract them long enough," she said before making her way toward one of the walls, hiding behind the debris as she went to avoid being seen.

"Come out of hiding, cowards!" Teira yelled as she opened a hole in the ground, causing a boulder that was in her way to plummet into its depths before closing it back up.

Having witnessed this from where she stood, Rose shuddered at the thought of meeting the same fate and quickly turned back toward her destination. But as she did so her foot hit a small rock, causing it to bounce loudly across the ground. Instantly the three demigods turned in her direction.

"There you are," Chasaka said with a malicious grin, fire forming in his hands. But before he and the others could walk toward Rose's location Amaya jumped up from her hiding place, holding a newly-formed sword and shield in her hands.

"Hey!" she yelled, getting their attention. She closed her eyes and began reciting the incantation she read on the page, hoping she was saying it correctly. As she did so, the three demigods collectively attempted to stop her.

Teira raised her hand, a thick vine slithering around her while Chasaka ignited it. Ruki lifted his weapon to throw at her.

However, Amaya's shield had morphed into a new shape, forming a transparent wind covering around her as she continued to speak. It repelled the elements the three of them were trying to hurl at her.

Rose had successfully made her way to the wall and placed her hand upon it, closing her eyes as she focused on reaching out toward the creatures lurking in the mountain. Her plan was to mix the reprocessing spell that she had seen on the torn page with the healing spell, though she wasn't sure if it would work. If it went as she hoped, however, the spell would remove the dark power from the monsters within the mountain and heal them simultaneously, and then she could use the extracted powers against their parents. She began to recite her spliced version of the incantation she had read. Though she couldn't see it, she could feel the energy from within her body beginning to branch out like veins, traveling out from her hand and spreading throughout the mountain, toward the creatures.

The beasts were drawn to the spell's power like magnets, latching onto it as they were enveloped by it. Rose placed her other hand on the wall, growing slightly fatigued from the spell. It was hard to continue. The creatures writhed as they became trapped in the holy energy bursting from her being, their corruption being pulled forcefully from their bodies and traveling back to Rose.

* * *

Athelstan walked back and forth in front of the wooden cage containing Cyero, who circled inside his confines, growling. The demon was growing restless and wondered what was happening at the top of the mountain, wishing he could be a part of the fight. He thought about what he would do once the battle was over. If they lost, he would likely be killed. If they won, then what? There was nothing left for him in Hell now that Waru wasn't there to give him orders, but he had nowhere else to go and no one to go to. His thoughts were cut short when his ears pricked, causing him to stop his pacing. Something was headed his way.

"Finally, some action," the lynx growled as the two intruders came into view. They were animalistic demons that resided in the mountains, ones who had come from the overworld, unlike Athelstan, who had been created in Hell. The job that was given to him by Waru, aside from killing poltergeists, was to kill demons when they escaped like the ones racing toward him. He flexed his claws, prepared to attack, but just as they came close to him they slowed to a stop. Then Athelstan felt something pulling at his form, making him feel lighter. He shook his fur, trying to force it away, clawing at the air around him.

The two demons before him started glowing and their forms began to change, wisps of light flowing up above each of them while dark smoke flowed from them as well, traveling up through the ceiling. The creatures were beginning to lose their solid forms as they began to regain the purity they had had when they were alive.

* * *

Rose could feel the dark power of the demons entering her skin, and she pushed further despite the pain and the overwhelming feeling it brought. However, that power was becoming too much for her to take in all at once—not even a demigod could take in that much darkness without succumbing to it. Her body felt heavy, and a grievous sensation wormed its way through her being.

Rose felt a hollowness within, begging her to take more than she already had to fill the void. She stole more from the once-corrupted beings, causing them to collectively scream out in pain before they went dead silent, their lights vanishing as they turned to nothing.

The lynx was beginning to yield to the magic flowing into him until it suddenly changed, latching onto him with force. Athelstan turned to shadow, attempting to sever the ties the magic had to him to no avail. It did the same to the other two, who shrieked in pain before their lights faded out and they were gone. Abruptly, the magic's connection to him snapped, leaving as quickly as it had come. He turned back to his solid form and slid to the ground, breathing heavily.

Then Rose stopped, for there was nothing left to take.

* * *

Amaya had finished the incantation and a mixture of fire and wind had burst from her body, shooting at the demigods who had surrounded and continued to attack her shield. It hit them forcibly, causing them to lose their footing and slam into the walls. It had also served to clear away the dust.

Two of them had been knocked unconscious from the blow, but Chasaka had managed to remain awake, though wounded. The man stood, glaring at his daughter. He knew that she was almost untouchable with the power of that spell, but he also knew that there was no chance the girl knew fully how to use its temporary power.

"Amaya—" he began, planning on distracting her until it wore off, but the girl stopped him with a blast of fire.

"Shut up," she ordered him as her shield fell away. "I'm sick of listening to your voice. You do nothing but hurt me and everyone around you." Amaya pointed Sacris Ignem toward him, which was enveloped in blue, red, and orange embers and had almost doubled in size. "It ends now."

Her father took his weapon out as well and they charged at each other with fire in their eyes.

Ruki slowly regained consciousness as this happened, leaning against the wall to help him to stand as he watched the one-on-one battle that had ensued. He looked around, seeing Teira lying on the ground on the opposite side of the room. But before he could make his way to her, something caught his attention out of the corner of his eye. Ruki turned to see Rose kneeling in the corner adjacent to the one he was standing at. She was hiding, cowering in fear.

He began limping toward her, drawing his trident as he did so. The man figured that he might as well kill her now before she regained her confidence.

Amaya sent yet another row of wind and fire at Chasaka, throwing him into the wall where Ruki had been making his way toward Rose.

At this point the spell's power was beginning to fade, growing weaker by the second. Chasaka didn't have the strength to stand, but he was still capable of blasting her yet again. Amaya slid her foot along the smooth stone below her and avoided the flames, forming her own ball of fire in her palm.

Before she could release it, she caught sight of Ruki, who was standing several feet from Rose, the prongs of his trident trained on her. "Rose!" she yelled.

Ruki glanced back at them before turning back to Rose. "Stop! Don't kill her, even if she isn't your daughter!" Amaya yelled at him. "You received her from the heavens because you wanted a child, didn't you? You can't say that you didn't care for her, even in the few years that you had her!"

Ruki paused for a moment, keeping his eyes on Rose. "We didn't want her, we *needed* her. She's just a pawn. We never loved her." The man threw his trident toward Rose.

"No!" Amaya screamed. But Rose's hand shot out, catching the trident before it could pierce her skull, freezing the weapon before crushing it to pieces. The three stared at the girl in astonishment as she stood, back facing them. "Rose?" Amaya asked quietly. She could sense something was off about her friend, negative energy radiating from her.

Ruki approached Rose warily, forming another trident in his hands. "Turn around!" he demanded. Rose whipped around as instructed, grabbing his weapon and destroying it with one hand and seizing him by the collar with the other.

The girl's eyes were black, her expression empty. Rocks began to rise from the ground, covering Ruki up to his chest as water pulsed from Rose's hands, enveloping his face.

The girl emitted a beastly snarl as she froze the water surrounding him. Finally Rose pressed her hands together and the man was crushed by the rocks and ice, killing him instantly and leaving an explosion of blood to remain in his wake.

The remaining two could do nothing but stare in surprise, frozen in shock of the monster that stood before them. Rose looked around before catching sight of Teira, who remained unconscious, and began walking toward her.

Chasaka had recovered his composure and fire flared to life once more in his hands. He, too, attempted to make Rose falter, but she flung her head to the side, letting the ball of fire he sent toward her flash past while she continued in the direction of the woman. She snarled, forming murky water laced with rock in her hands.

Before he could try to stop her again, Amaya pushed her father back with a blast of wind which sliced up her hand as she used it, her control of the element still unsteady.

She knew her friend had been changed as a result of the spell, but it was helping them. So she needed to protect her. "We aren't finished yet," she said, pointing Sacris Ignem at him. But as she did, her weapon began to morph back to its normal state and she felt the last of the spell's power leave her body.

"I don't have time to deal with you," Chasaka growled, lifting his own sword.

His ruby eyes narrowed to slits and, holding out his hand, he summoned another ball of fire which was first red and then turned to violet. He whipped it toward her and it slammed into her body before she could lift her sword to block it, searing away the clothing which once covered her midsection and scorching her stomach.

She screamed and writhed in pain as she was blown back from the fire. Her skin was raw from the terrible burns and now all she could feel from every movement was unwavering agony. It took an immense amount of energy to have sent out that power, leaving Chasaka just barely able to carry his blade.

Rose approached Teira, drawing her sword from its scabbard. As she did, the brunette woman slowly lifted her head. She raised her arms above her head, hilt of her sword in hand. But just as Rose began to bring her sword down upon her, Teira's fingers reached out, growing into deep oak branches and piercing the girl through the stomach.

Her mouth hung agape as cold blood slid down her body. Rose's hands loosened on her sword and it fell from her grip, stabbing Teira through her shoulder and pinning her to the ground as it dropped.

"Rose!" Amaya yelled from across the room, tears stinging her eyes as she stood up, clenching her teeth so hard she felt her jaw might break.

She shoved back her father with a blast of wind before rushing to her friend's side. But Teira refused to allow this and struggled to her feet, even with the sword stuck through her body. Branches started to form across the wound, holding the sword in place. This time her arm extended toward Amaya, another tree-like limb sprouting from it in an attempt to penetrate the other girl as well. Amaya swung her body around and deflected the branch with her sword, incinerating the ones that reached out to her. The flames that came from her sword traveled up Teira's arm. The rest of the swing ended with the end of her sword just grazing Teira's neck which, too, was made of those branches.

"Foolish child," she spat. Her burning arm extinguished the flames that otherwise enveloped it and formed into her own sword, she swiped it downward and knocked away Amaya's sword, going for her own swipe. She managed to slice open the corner of the girl's lip, sending blood streaming down it. When she staggered, the woman swung at Amaya once more and slashed a wound into her burned stomach before going for a stab that went through the girl's side, just barely missing her spleen.

Amaya doubled over in agony, trying to reach for her sword as she did so. But she knew this would leave her completely vulnerable, and could almost feel Teira's sword rising above her head.

When she looked up, she saw that her suspicions were true. But the image of her didn't last long as she was then slammed into the wall beside them where she had once been recovering. Amaya looked off to the side to see that Rose had freed herself from her mother's oak branches and was treading toward her.

She paled as she watched her friend walk by, a menacing feeling radiating off of her. For a moment, she felt scared of what she might do to her own mother. Her hand wrapped around Teira's throat and lifted her while Amaya watched, frozen in horror. Her other hand was used to rip her sword from her mother's shoulder, spilling blood onto the two of them while the hole tried to mend itself.

While Teira choked and sputtered, she reached out her hand in desperation to stop the attack. Teira lifted a pile of rubble behind the girl, forcing it toward her. A large rock came hurtling toward the back of Rose's head and smashed to pieces against it. She bled from the back of her head, staining her blonde locks the crimson color, but she didn't flinch from it at all. Instead, she put space between the two of them, only to dive back in a short second to cut with her sword, drawing a straight horizontal line which had been about to strike Teira but she ducked out of the way just in time, leaving her on the ground against the wall once more.

Teira scrambled desperately away from her, and Amaya could hear the panic in her voice, unable to move from her spot. "No! Rose, please!" she cried while her daughter came close behind her.

But Rose didn't respond and formed a small pillar of rock on her side, which Teira dodged clumsily, stumbling on her hands and knees as she sobbed in fear. When she dodged to the side, another rock pillar caught her and shoved her onto her back, shattering the bones in the middle of it, orchestrating a brutal crunch as she landed and screamed while her body registered the pain.

Thick tears coated the woman's face while Rose stepped toward her, each step instilling more fear inside of her.

Amaya thought it inhumane. Rose could have ended her life by now, from what she saw when she killed Ruki. But now she was toying with the fear her mother was giving off.

Finally, Rose was upon Teira, who had curled up into a pathetic ball of nothingness while rock and oak tried to shield her from danger. But Rose sliced it away, and once her mother was vulnerable, she thrust down her blade, impaling Teira's chest once again, this time being sure to remove it. Still, those annoying branches kept trying to mend her, which Rose sneered at.

Rose swung her blade across the floor and cut Teira's body clean in half while the woman screamed out in pain. Blood swarmed through her lips, drowning her in it while whatever was left flooded through her severed torso.

Amaya listened while her friend breathed heavily, leaning the weight of her body on her sword. "Rose, are you all right?" her friend begged, no longer receiving an answer.

Rose felt her consciousness return for a brief moment, but her head almost immediately grew heavy and she collapsed to the side.

The exchange had taken so little time that Chasaka had been unable to prevent it and was still recovering from the blow dealt to him by the wind. Amaya's eyes stayed on Rose. Teira was no longer alive as far as she could tell.

With Rose unconscious, Amaya would have to face the man across the room by herself, and her wounds would cause movement to prove difficult.

But now was no time to be giving in, she knew. Amaya stabilized her body as she noticed her father coming at her, sword readied. She, too, lifted the heavy weapon, her muscles crying out for her to stop this torture—but she refused to listen until she was dead.

They clashed, tired bodies moving desperately to wound the other. There was no longer tactic involved—just sheer will to survive. They exchanged blow for blow, carving up their skin until they crossed swords, both staring at one another in the eyes, breathless, sweat and blood dripping from every part of their bodies.

Chasaka flicked his arm upward, breaking the clash between the two before reaching forth his left fist and punching the girl across the face. It was enough to make her stagger without knocking her down. However, he reached forward after this, swiping his sword and slashing her chest with it, leaving behind a painful, burning gash. This made her fall and, at long last, Chasaka stood above her, blade pointed at Amaya's face.

Her body screamed in agony and tears stung as they streamed down her cut-up face.

"You shouldn't have defied us. Your death could have been quick and peaceful; you could have helped to save this unfixable world. But instead, you've chosen to die this way. You were given so many chances, daughter," he muttered.

He placed the point of his blade against the ground, edge right above her arm as his dark eyes glared at her. She no longer recognized this man as a father. What was this that stood above her?

A most blood-curdling scream left the girl, one so loud the mountain shook at its release. Beside her lay her right arm, which Chasaka had taken the liberty of removing with his blade. Shaking, she gripped tightly onto her sword with her other hand, and with every ounce left of her strength, she swung her sword, cleaving her father's leg. His screams weren't nearly as horrifying as hers, but it left him tumbling on top of her. Both lay in a slowly-forming pool of blood beneath their bodies, the liquid oozing from their wounds.

"Your mother and I..." Chasaka sputtered as his cheek rested against the ground. "We always loved you..." he trailed off.

Amaya lay there for a long moment, trying to see if that statement sounded even remotely correct in her head. Perhaps it was the fault of her body slowly losing the vital fluid of life. Or perhaps her father truly had said this.

"What a load of shit," she muttered. A deep growl erupted in her throat. "I think your idea of love has been profoundly distorted!"

She kept her hold on Sacris Ignem.

"You're right...I couldn't love a fool; a pawn. But your mother...she did. But now that's gone...maybe if I couldn't mend this world...at least I'll be free from my own suffering...and soon you will too," Chasaka replied, gripping his sword as tightly as possible as he propped himself up onto his remaining knee.

He raised his sword up above his head, bringing it down toward the head of the girl's form. But Amaya held her sword as steady as she could, her father's blade nearly piercing her.

"You're the only fool," she spat.

Her sword clashed with his on the way down and landed into her father's chest while Chasaka's slipped and pressed into her own.

She stared into her father's eyes as he wheezed, blood from his mouth dripping onto her cheeks and neck. She kept her tired gaze trained on him, watching the life drain from his eyes.

Heavy breaths left the girl as blood filled her lungs and her eyes slid around the destroyed area. White-hot pain and warmth filled her wounds. Blood painted the stone floor, and four bodies lay still around her like the debris scattered about. Amaya used her hand to remove the small length of the sword that was inside her, not caring that it nicked her hand. She didn't care anymore. The pain she felt everywhere else was too great to mind more bloodshed.

She left her sword and ran to Rose, blood falling from her body as she tried desperately to make it far enough to maybe die at her friend's side. A small puddle of blood had formed around where she had placed her. Amaya quickly began checking her vital signs. She breathed but it was shallow, barely able to be felt.

She didn't know what to do, her mind raced as she felt her consciousness gravitating toward nothingness. "Rose? Can you hear me?" she said softly. Worry grew inside of her like cancer. "I'm so sorry for everything that I've said and done to you...I know it would have soon come to this...but I wish I hadn't been so callous along the way," she said. She let her body fall beside Rose as her head began to feel warm and fuzzy, but uncomfortably so. She felt like she was suffocating. "I don't want to die..." she trailed off.

With her missing arm, there was no way she could carry Rose anywhere, they would surely die where they lay. "I...lo..." she trailed off, feeling ten feet above the ground. In a moment, she felt herself go into shock, greeted by an overwhelming feeling of immense pain. But it didn't last long as she was soon surrounded by an empty blackness.

* * *

Pain exploded inside of Amaya as she opened her eyes. It was like being gored by a bull, taking the blunt force of a bear upon her body, having a sword shoved through her all at once. Indescribable. Yet she couldn't scream out.

Not even questions raced her mind as she peeled open her eyes. She had done everything she had set out to do, unsure of why she even came to in the first place. She almost wished she could have died...and yet she was alive.

"You're awake," a voice said.

Amaya's eyes slowly trailed across the ground she was level with, landing on a pair of feet before going up as much as possible. She didn't have to see their face to know who spoke and allowed her eyes to rest. "Liland..." she murmured softly. Over the pain carving her up, she felt tiredness, she felt her hunger and thirst. How much had she truly endured for all of this? "Did we do it...?" she asked.

"You did." She could hear the smile in his voice.

The girl shut her eyes and drew in a painful breath before letting it go. "The gods...are they saved then?" she asked.

Liland looked at the breathtaking view of the sky above which was punched out by a single dot of red surrounded by black. There was a smile on his lips still. "I haven't felt this much at peace in a very long time, Amaya," he said. "I think we have reached the end at last..." he trailed off.

"And Rose? She's all right as well?"

Liland looked over to the girl that lay on the opposite side of him, fabric wrapped tightly around her torso. "She's lost a lot of blood...but with some time to heal, I don't doubt she will recover."

"Good," Amaya said with a small smile. "How did you get out of the cell?" she asked next.

"The cage had fallen away, and I knew it meant that you two had won. I kept my eye open and stayed awake, then I came to you. You were both unconscious," Liland explained, pausing a moment before continuing. "How did it feel when you finally killed them?" He bit his bottom lip. "Did it feel as good as you imagined?"

Amaya scrunched her brow which stung to do so. "No..." she trailed off. "I wish we could have done things Rose's way... my mind was numb in the moment it was all happening...but thinking back on it...it's a terrifying feeling to steal someone's life from them...even despite the countless ones they stole from others..." She paused. "And after it all...there is nothing to be taken from it...Rose and I...if we make it back to the surface... there is nothing waiting for us. We will be alone. Again."

Liland took his gaze from the sky and turned it toward the girl lying on the ground in front of him. "I will," he said. "I'll wait for you...I...love both of you."

Amaya opened her eyes again and slowly lifted her head so she could see Liland's face, meeting his eyes.

"We shouldn't be hasty...we're still here...not yet there."

Liland nodded at this, turning to face the sky again. Amaya followed suit, though she seemed more distant than before. "I just hope everyone on the surface is doing okay," she said after a moment of silence. The two remained quiet after this.

24: Sovereign Blood

When Amaya found the strength to stand again, she and Liland agreed that it was finally time to depart from the wasteland they had spent so long inside. Rose hadn't yet awakened from her unconsciousness, so they began descending the inside of the mountain with Rose handled gently in Liland's arms.

Soon they reached one of the middle floors of the former hideout and found Athelstan curled up beside the cage that Rose had created for Cyero. It was hard to see in the darkness as most of the flames that once provided a small amount of light had gone out, but upon peeking around Liland's shoulder, Amaya saw the god lying in his mortal form surrounded by what she had assumed to be the debris from his cage.

The other cages that once held imprisoned demons within them had fallen away too, leaving their unmoving corpses in the wake of the power that had been stolen from them.

Amaya made her way toward the two amongst the cages, causing Athelstan's head to perk up. "Looks like you made it, hm? Well...most of you," he said, his eyes falling upon her missing arm that had been wrapped in pieces of Liland's cloak.

But Amaya ignored him, timidly walking past before stopping where the cage used to be. "Is he...alive?" she asked.

"He passed out a little bit ago and turned back to this form," Athelstan replied.

"I promised him he would make it...so we can't leave without him," Amaya said, turning her head briefly toward Liland before stepping past the debris carefully. She then knelt beside the unmoving body of the god and placed her hand on his shoulder which was exposed by his torn clothing. But she noticed something from the corner of it and pulled it aside.

She gasped at what she saw. "T—Taint. He's still tainted," she said as panic fell upon her all at once. "I don't understand, we killed them; they're all dead."

"Calm down," Liland said from behind her. "His body probably just needs time to heal from the infection. But now that there is nothing perpetuating it, I'm sure he will recover in no time,"

Amaya took a deep breath, alleviating her fears before turning Cyero onto his side, though it was hard to do so with only one arm. She could hardly believe her eyes as she saw his chest rising and falling. Her chest swelled, her heart pounded.

"Cyero?" she called out softly.

His nose wrinkled a bit, his face stirring as the girl's eyes trailed to the Taint eating away at his neck. She tried to tell herself it would be fine, that it would soon vanish, but she still worried about what she may see when he opened his eyes.

Nothing could describe the solace that she felt when at last his eyelids fluttered open, revealing his icy pools of blue, no longer reddened from corruption. She felt a tear fall down her cheek as she took in a deep breath. "You're okay," she said in assurance to herself. She wiped her face before her tear could fall onto him.

"I'm glad you are as well," he rasped softly before slowly willing himself to stand up. His eyes fell upon the Taint wrapped around his fingers then looked toward her, only to gasp when he discovered her stump wrapped in bits of Liland's cloak and the blood that stained more of it around her chest. "Your arm," he said worriedly.

"I'm all right," she assured him.

"What about Rose? Where is she?" he asked and looked past the girl toward Liland who was carrying her seemingly lifeless body. "Oh no..." he trailed off. His stomach sank as he pushed himself to his feet.

He had been about to approach, but Liland turned his side toward him to keep him away. "She's alive, no need to worry," he said as the god scanned his face, biting his lip as he took in his and her wounds. He looked back to Amaya, examining the wounds she had endured as she stood.

"You all sacrificed so much...for my siblings and me," he said. "Was it worth it? An eye? An arm? So many lives?"

"If it means preserving this world, I would say yes," Liland replied.

Cyero kept his eyes on Amaya, wondering what her answer would be. "I agree," she said. "We should go back. We need to see what is left of it."

"If you're all going back up, then I'll join you," Athelstan said.

Suddenly everyone's faces fell. "It will be another long road ahead before we can reach it," Cyero trailed off.

"I can take you all back to the top of the tower, but it will take a lot of energy...I'll have to rest once I do this," the demon said.

"Thank you, Athelstan," Amaya replied.

The lynx nodded then closed his eyes. A dark circle formed around the five of them, and slowly they felt the energy in their bodies being suppressed until at last they were enveloped by darkness. When it melted away, they stood atop the tower they had come from. The hydra's body lay across from them where they had left it, and Rotos was nowhere to be seen.

Athelstan had collapsed on the ground from the exertion before his body was absorbed into the necklace still hanging around Amaya's neck.

Returning to the surface world revealed devastation—on the edge of complete annihilation. From the top of the Tower of Twilight, the three travelers looked out upon the wasteland. It reminded them of Hell, the place from which they had at last returned. The evening sky blended into a world covered in desolate flames eating away at the trees in the forest that surrounded the tower. Below them stretched brackish water for miles, its depth unknown; and the trees, if not scorched where they stood, were blown over and scattered like fallen dominos.

This was the current state of the Aessatia—decimated.

This was the world they had worked so hard to save. But Amaya and Liland could only smile upon seeing it.

"It's hard to believe this tower is still standing," Cyero said.

"We should return to Barness," Liland said as he searched for the capital's direction, just barely being able to make out a shape from the distance.

No one objected, and thus they began the tower's descent. When they reached the ground, they were waist-deep in the water, which stung their wounds. They didn't make it very far past the tower before Liland had to stop. "Sorry...it's getting harder to carry her" he said, letting one half of Rose's body slip into the water so he could rest his muscles.

Cyero shifted into his wolf form beside him, allowing them all to see just how badly the Taint had consumed him. It overtook his entire abdomen and was doing its best to reach his back, some spreading to his legs and up his chest toward his jaw. "All of you, get on. We will reach the capital as quickly as possible," he said, though, the others were hesitant due to his condition.

"Are you sure? You must be just as tired as the rest of us," Amaya said.

Cyero considered her for a moment before shaking his head. "I'll be fine, don't worry yourselves over me. You've done enough. Come on then..." he trailed off before leaning himself down.

Sighing, Amaya hoisted herself up onto Cyero's back, doing her best to accommodate with only one arm and tried to help Liland as he dragged both himself and Rose upon the large wolf's back. When they were secure, Cyero stood up straight and set off in the direction of the capital.

Silence enveloped the group for the long hours they spent trekking to Barness. Among all else, it remained mostly intact. A few districts had large boulders engraved within craters, leaving houses destroyed, some flooded by water; rubble was scattered about overall.

The four of them headed through Barness to reach the castle, each step aching Cyero terribly, but he had to press on. When they reached the front gate, Cyero allowed his passengers to dismount and returned to his mortal form. It was late at night by then, and the capital appeared empty as they continued on.

As they walked, they could see where most of the citizens had gone. There were two gods standing in front of the remains of a fountain that once adorned the central square of the first district, providing clothing and food for those who had lost their homes. The first was Adione, whose physical form Amaya had never seen before, leaving her unrecognizable. The second was Thosus.

They both looked weak and tired, but they still continued helping every person who came to them. Amaya, Liland, and Cyero made their way over to them, moving carefully past those who were in line, who stared at them as they passed, gazing at their war wounds.

Adione saw them first, her eyes transfixed on them, which drew Thosus' attention toward them as well. "Well, would you look at that..." he murmured and allowed them to approach. It was the first he had seen of Cyero in quite some time. Not only that, but it brought a smile to his face to see everyone was still alive.

"Thosus," said Amaya and approached him. "I'm glad to see you're back to normal."

"Mostly, yes," Thosus replied. "When I awoke, the world around me was flooded and in flames, the ground split apart in some places while thunder and lightning stormed the skies above. It's an utter catastrophe...but when I realized that I was no longer watching the destruction from within my mind, I knew that something had changed for the better. I knew you had to have figured something out, because I was alive and I didn't feel ill any longer. So...thank you," he explained.

"Brother, are these the three?" Adione asked from beside him. She was a beautiful woman in her physical form with long grey hair tied back loosely to keep it at bay.

Thosus nodded in response to her question, and the woman's eyes shifted to them. "I apologize for the hardship I gave to you all...I would like to properly introduce myself. I'm Adione," she said.

"Save your apologies, it was nothing you could control," Amaya said. "It was our parents in the end who were controlling your minds from within Hell. They were the ones who infected you with that terrible disease," she told her.

"Lord Thosus, Lady Adione, who are these people?" asked one of the commoners.

Cyero turned to the man, but he addressed all the people around him. "People of Barness!" he yelled to silence their chatter. "This is Amaya, Rose, and Liland! They're the ones who saved all of you along with my brothers and sisters. I know that I've been negligent of you for a very long time, but I'm here now, and it's my firm promise not to abandon you again," he explained.

Murmur ensued among the people once again. Most had never seen their god in the flesh before, as he had locked himself away from them for so long, and Cyero could tell from the dialogue he picked up that they were talking about him. But something he heard, in particular, caught both him and Amaya off guard. "So is he the new king now?"

A sudden realization dawned upon Amaya as she heard him speak and sadness overwhelmed her. "That's right...Zyair and my uncle..." she trailed off.

Cyero looked to her with a somber expression. He had been conscious when Chasaka had revealed his actions of murdering the former king and Amaya's uncle. The god's eyes shifted toward Liland, who appeared worried as well. "Without a king to lead the people, Lucus would likely fall apart," he said.

"May I please have all of your attention once more!" Cyero shouted. "Lucus has seen much hardship in the past regarding demigods and all others that wish to oppose her. With the loss of our king, the structure of our kingdom will quickly fall apart. We require a strong leader with the will of a bull and the gentleness of a stag. That's why, within my divine right, I crown thee, Liland, as the next rightful heir to the proud Lucian throne; and henceforth from this day shall he rule and be long-lived. While it may be true that he doesn't contain a drop of Lucian blood within his veins, he's the last known survivor of the massacre that happened twenty-two years ago, an Astrian; a demigod, and he—along with Rose and Amaya—has preserved Aessatia from meeting her doom as we know it. It's for these collective reasons that I deem him worthy of the role as Lucian king." This was about as close to a coronation speech as he would get at such a time as this. "Are there any objections?" All were silent.

One by one, each remaining citizen bowed to Liland, who had a look of utter shock upon his face. He looked at all of his new subjects. Even Amaya bowed down to the man.

"What is your first order as king?" Cyero asked.

Liland thought hard for a long moment before clenching his fists. "The punishment placed upon the demigods Rose and

Amaya is to be lifted from this moment on, and they're to be treated as heroes for their efforts to the preservation of Aessatia."

The Lucian citizens cheered along with one another, crying tears of joy. "And lastly, we're all going to play a role in the rehabilitation of this land. After its destruction, who better to help it prosper once more than those who love and rely on it so much?" Liland said.

* * *

The night's remaining hours were spent divvying out the rest of the rations to everyone who required it while Rose and Amaya, at last, were able to rest within the comfort of the infirmary. Thankfully, it still stood and contained supplies for properly dressing their wounds. By the time the sun was beginning to caress the sky with its brilliant red light, Liland had decided to return to check on them. When he entered, only Rose was awake and sitting up while Amaya slept on one of the beds beside her.

"Oh, you're awake...it's good to see you," he said as he approached, and wrapped the young woman in a hug before sitting down in one of the chairs beside her bed. "How are you feeling?" he asked.

"I'm in a lot of pain...but I think I'm managing well," she answered. "But...it isn't exactly the first thing on my mind. The last thing I remember is being taken ahold of by that horrible feeling." She paused before continuing, "I'm shocked to be back in Barness now. How are things? Is everything all right?"

"I'm sure you have a lot of questions, but you don't need to worry yourself right now; the kingdom is in my hands. Cyero, Adione, Thosus, and I have been tending to the survivors.

Aessatia was torn apart while we were gone, but we will work on rehabilitating it. For now, we must focus on what matters," Liland explained.

Rose stared at him, her mouth agape. "Hold on...what do you mean when you say 'the kingdom is in your hands'?" she asked.

Liland managed a small smile as he looked at her. "I mean that I'm its new king...Cyero made me Lucus' king. Since...Zyair was killed." His tone dropped as he finished.

Their attention was drawn across from them as Amaya began to stir in her sleep, and she groaned as her eyes fluttered open. "I can't get any sleep with you two talking," she said.

Liland chuckled at her childishness. "Actually, I'm glad you're awake...there was something I wanted to discuss with you both," he said. "I thought about it a few times before now, but was never sure if I should bring it up because I was scared of how you might react, but now I think I'm certain..." he trailed off. "I would like to take both of you in...as my own. I'm unsure if that sounds strange to you or not, but...to me, it sounds meant to be. I want to be there for you both the way your real parents never could, I want to take care of you and continue to grow and learn alongside you."

Both Amaya and Rose stared at the man, wonderment filling their eyes.

Their parents had truly wronged them in ways none could ever imagine. Rose was no longer even sure if her real parents were still out there or not. But could it really be that simple? To just accept Liland as a father figure?

"This is a lot to consider..." Amaya trailed off.

"Absolutely," Rose put in immediately. "I would love for you to take us in," she said, a smile adorning her lips.

Amaya's eyes flicked toward her friend, lingering there for a long moment before returning to Liland. She wasn't sure how to feel about the whole thing. On one hand, her real parents were dead and were never much of parents anyway. But on the other... could she really bring herself to allow this? To open herself up to him?

"I..." she trailed off. "I think...I would be okay with that as well," she said.

A huge smile came across Liland's lips and tears came to his eyes. His heart swelled. It felt complete for the first time in his life. "Thank you," he said, at a loss for any other words than this.

He got up and leaned forward to wrap his arms around Rose, keeping her in a long hug while Amaya watched them, pondering her decision as she did. Rose, on the other hand, began to cry too, tears drenching her face as she sobbed away the sadness that had weighed on her heart for so long, allowing Liland to lift it. The soothing hand he brought against her back helped her cry, and soon he pulled away, wiping away each tear that remained on her face.

Then, he made his way around to Amaya's bed and wrapped her in a hug of her own. But her body was rigid as he did so, and he could feel it. She tried not to feel anything while he kept his arms around her, waiting for him to pull away. But he never did. Instead, he spoke. "Amaya, it's okay..." he said. It seemed hearing these words was all it took because she then let out a heart-wrenching sob and allowed the tears of her own strife to leave her eyes. She wept with her new father and hugged him back with her only remaining arm.

"I'm so sorry for everything I said to you both...For everything I did, I'm sorry for all of it. Please forgive me," she said through a barrage of sobbing and crying.

Rose stood from her bed, feeling unstable for a moment before letting herself relax as she leaned down to put her arms around both Liland and Amaya. "I already told you I forgive you, Amaya, it's all right," she said.

"Yes, as do I," Liland replied.

After a long moment, the three of them broke apart, each going back to sit in their original places to wipe away their tears. "Sorry," Amaya said. "I didn't mean to get hysterical."

"It's all right, I think it was very much needed after all we have been through," Liland said.

Amaya lay back down after that. "I think I'm going to try and sleep again...before the morning gets too bright," she said before closing her eyes.

Liland sat back in his chair and let out a sigh, keeping quiet so she could fall asleep. Rose didn't feel like going back to sleep though, her mind was too active to allow it, even though her body craved rest.

After a half-hour had passed, a clicking sound pulled their attention toward Cyero as he entered the room. A smile pulled at Rose's lips to see him alive and well. "Cyero, it's good to see you," she said as he walked toward them.

"Ah, I see you're awake. It's good to see you as well. I'm glad you're okay," he said. He went over and wrapped her in a hug before crossing to find himself in a chair beside Liland. "I think we did well today."

"I agree...I'm still having trouble grasping that I'm king now," Liland replied.

"I think it's wonderful," Rose said. "The role fits you well; you will be a great leader."

Liland bowed his head, placing his hand upon his chest. "Thank you, Rose. I truly appreciate that," he said. "Would you like to find one of the castle rooms? I'm sure it would be much more favorable," he offered.

"That's all right," replied Rose. "I would rather be with Amaya here...I don't want to force her to wake up again."

"You can go," Cyero said. "I can keep her company. Get some rest, you need it."

Rose looked at Liland, both understanding what he truly meant. After the shared glance, Rose got out of bed and left the room in Liland's tow, leaving Cyero and Amaya alone.

The ice god's soft eyes stayed upon the sleeping form of the girl and he released a sigh of relief. He moved himself and his chair over beside her bed and simply sat there, watching her chest rise and fall. He knew that the girl felt at peace, and it brought him happiness knowing she no longer felt the weight of the world upon her shoulders. Soon, watching her was no longer enough, he needed to touch the woman. He reached his hand forward and began to stroke her cheek softly with his thumb then ran the back of his hand along her forehead.

This woke the girl, her eyes fluttering open before fixing themselves upon Cyero. But he didn't take his hand from her. Seeing his face brought a smile to hers. "I'm happy you're alive...I was scared, you know," she muttered softly in the quiet morning.

"Me too," Cyero replied. His hand rested itself in her hair. "How is your arm? I can only imagine the ferocity of the final battle," he said with a small smile.

"In a lot of pain, but I'm coping with it," Amaya said.

The two held each other's gaze for a long while. They could easily spend eternity doing this and had to physically drag their eyes away from each other's.

"Amaya...about what happened when you summoned Athelstan..." he trailed off. Amaya's cheeks grew slightly reddened hearing the god speak of this, but she didn't deny that it had happened. She knew it had and so did he, and she didn't find shame in it. "Did you truly mean that?" he asked. "That you would cherish every memory you spent with me?"

"Wholeheartedly," she answered quickly. "I...don't want to withhold my feelings behind anger and distrust any longer. I wanted to say that I really appreciate that you were there for me even when I pushed you away. When I pushed everyone away, they were all still there for me. I never understood why *you* did, because we had only just met."

"I can't explain it myself," Cyero replied. "But when we spoke...I envied you." He looked down before returning his gaze to her eyes. "I longed for the type of bond that you and Rose and Liland shared with one another. The kind that wouldn't break no matter how hard you tried to sever it. I've always wanted that. But, like you, I found it hard to trust in others," he said. "But I want to trust you."

Amaya pulled a smile. "I want to trust you as well, Cyero. I'm glad you won't be locking yourself away again once this is all over," she said.

"Me too," he answered, a smile meeting his own lips. He didn't know what it was, but Cyero felt a warmth inside his chest which he hadn't before, and keeping his eyes on Amaya made it uncomfortable, so he averted his gaze. "I won't keep you awake, I'm sure you're still exhausted," he said to her. "Would you like me to take you to one of the castle's sleeping quarters? That's where Liland took Rose."

The girl nodded her head and began slowly trying to sit up.

"Don't strain yourself, let me help," the god said, reaching forward to help her.

"I got it, I got it," she said, shooing his hands away. She eased herself to her feet at last and turned to the god. He stood also, towering over her. He pulled the girl against his side and began leading her out of the room.

They crossed from the military barracks where the infirmary had been stationed to the castle interior where Cyero led her up a flight of stairs before stopping at a room with double doors. "I assume this must be where Liland led Rose. It's the two-guest bedroom," he said.

Amaya nodded her head in response. "Thank you, Cyero," she said.

"Good night, Amaya," he answered and placed his hand on her head, ruffling her hair a bit. "May your rest bring you comfort and good dreams, while awakening leaves you rested." With that, he turned and headed back the way the two came.

When Amaya entered the bedroom, she found two beds sitting beside each other on one side of the room. Rose lay fast asleep in one of them, so she chose the bed opposite her friend and settled herself in as comfortably as possible.

"Amaya, is that you?" Rose asked, scaring her a bit.

"Yes," she answered. "I thought you might be asleep. Is everything okay?"

"I can't sleep, my mind is racing...and I'm in a lot of pain," she said.

Amaya sat up after that, encouraging her friend to do the same so they faced one another. "We can talk if you want to," she said.

Rose's eyes flicked toward the main source of light in the otherwise dark room; a double door covered by sheer curtains leading out to a balcony. "Are you fine with going outside?" she asked with a nod of her head toward the doors.

Amaya nodded so they got up from their beds and walked out to the balcony. They saw the world again from their perch in the upper level of the castle. It was Rose's first time seeing the world as the gods had left it. Her eyes lingered on the boulders resting in craters scattered across the capital, to the water outside the walls, and the fire that burned the distant forests. "It's so terrifying to think how close they came to actually achieving their goals," Rose said.

"I know..." Amaya trailed off. "Before we came back, Liland asked me how it felt to finally attain my vengeance. I feel sick calling it that...I...didn't like taking my father's life, no matter how much I always said I wanted to. What about you? That spell... you seemed far different when you used it. Do you remember anything?"

Rose looked down at her fingers resting on the stone railing and scraped her nails against the grain. "I..." she trailed off. The young woman began to think back to the battle and how she used her powers to put an end to her mother and father's lives.

Even now, she still felt the evil inside of her, flowing beneath a layer of sanity. "I don't remember anything after using the spell," she said. She felt awful for lying, but recollecting the event was something too painful to withstand.

"I think it might be best to leave the world without our powers for awhile...at least for me. I couldn't bring myself to use mine again," Amaya replied. "Perhaps we should find a way to end the cycle of reincarnation. My mother mentioned that we had the power to do so."

"It would have been what they wanted to do, but I can't help but agree. For years until now, demigods have abused the power at their disposal." She paused before continuing, "I think it would be safest to leave it out of mortal hands. For good," Rose said. She turned her head toward her friend, noticing the necklace wrapped around her neck. "What happened to Athelstan?" she asked.

Amaya followed her gaze toward her chest where the whistle rested. "He got us to the top of the tower using some kind of magic. He's been resting away somewhere ever since," she said.

"I would like to thank him for helping us, would you call him?"

Amaya picked up the summon and placed it to her lips before blowing into it, creating that quiet whistling noise. Beside her, a bog of shadows appeared, soon revealing the still-wounded body of Athelstan. He wore a scowl on his feline face, his ears back.

"Honestly, did you truly run into something else you couldn't handle on your own?" he growled before taking in his surroundings fully. "Hmm...the castle?" He looked up at Amaya. "Why am I here? I told you I needed to rest. I'm still very weak."

"Don't blame her, I told her to bring you here," Rose interjected. "I wanted to thank you for helping us." She knelt down to the animal's level and gently stroked his fur with the back of her hand.

Athelstan shook his head and swiped at the girl's hand. "Don't mention it...I only came because you called with that damned whistle." He turned his back and sat down, his remaining ear plastered against the back of his head.

Amaya took the whistle from her neck and looked at it as it rested in her hand. "If this thing causes you so much trouble, why haven't you destroyed it?" she asked.

"I can't," Athelstan told her. "Not by my hand."

Amaya threw the whistle to the ground after that and stomped her foot against it, shattering the artifact.

Athelstan flicked his ear when he heard the crunch and turned around. "You...you broke it," he said.

"Well, I guess that means you're free," Amaya told him, a small smile on her lips while the lynx looked at her in wonderment.

But he said nothing in response, and Rose gave him a curious look. "Is something wrong?" she asked.

"It's nothing," Athelstan told her. "But now that I'm free...I don't know what my purpose is...where I'm meant to go," he said.

"You will always be welcome here, Athelstan," Rose told him.

"That's a strange sentiment coming from one of your kind," he retorted.

"Are you incapable of being grateful?" Amaya asked him. "Just because you're a demon, does that mean your heart is purely evil?"

"You showed us that isn't true," Rose said. "So...you're welcome here whenever you please—as an equal. I think the past couple of decades have proven that putting others below us never ends well."

"Perhaps gods may not be so bad in the end," Athelstan said.

Amaya rubbed her eyes a bit and parted her lips in a yawn. "Well... I'm going to head inside, I need to rest," she said.

"I shall join you," replied the lynx, then turned to follow her.

As Amaya had been about to depart, she turned to find that Rose wasn't with her. "Rose? Are you coming?" she asked.

Without looking at her, Rose said, "I'll be there in just a moment. I just want to stay out here a little longer."

Amaya's gaze stayed on her for a moment before she shrugged and went back inside, leaving Rose on her own.

She blew out a soft sigh and looked up at the sky, the only thing left intact through all the destruction. The dawn barely greeted the night at the horizon, the stars hardly visible. She closed her eyes as she listened to the voice of Sage echo in her mind. *They offered them a child from the heavens,* her gentle voice rang out.

When she opened her orbs of cyan, she found the sky dappled with stars once again, only a soft slice of white to disturb its otherwise tranquil beauty; a star racing across it before disappearing in the red of dawn.

About the Author

Hannah Whittaker is a first-time fiction author and artist, and has been writing for eight years. She graduated from high school in 2020 and is excited to let her writing career take off. At twelve years old she began writing the first drafts of *Sovereign Blood* and has worked tirelessly at it to ensure that it's the best it could possibly be. Hannah prides herself on elaborate character arcs and hidden meanings within her carefully-crafted writing, and is very pedantic on finer details, making sure no question is left unanswered and nothing is without explanation. Hannah has always used her imagination in her writing leading to her greater interest in fiction.

Hannah lives in Central New York with her family and her cat, Gemini. She hopes to find a career in writing and make a name for herself in the community

Hannah can be contacted at hwart.writing@gmail.com and @hannah.writing on Instagram.